As Time Goes By
Love and Revenge

Pat McDonald

Copyright © 2024 Pat McDonald. All rights reserved.

No part of this book may be reproduced or transmitted in any form or by any means, graphic, electronic, or mechanical, including photocopying, recording, taping, or by any information storage retrieval system, without the permission, in writing, of the publisher. For more information, send an email to support@sbpra.net, Attention: Subsidiary Rights.

Strategic Book Publishing
www.sbpra.net

For information about special discounts for bulk purchases, please contact Strategic Book Publishing, Special Sales, at bookorder@sbpra.net.

ISBN: 978-1-63410-235-3

Dedicated to

The welcoming people of Scotland
May your doors always be left open

Acknowledgements:

Some of the places in this book whilst they are real places the author has spent time in, they are borrowed images for the setting of this work of pure fiction. None of the characters described within these pages are people either living or dead and none of the more gruesome happenings actually happened. Neither did the author imagine them happening whilst surrounded by some of the most beautiful scenery and places on earth. That came later.

My thanks, as always, to JD for our many happy jaunts to Scotland without which my imagination would never have found fertile soil to settle and grow.

PROLOGUE:

The overhead tube lighting on B wing came fully on, intermittently, depending on their respective need to be replaced, whilst at the same time the blare of a claxon began its monotonous drone. Those prisoners not outside in the exercise yard or fully employed elsewhere, heard the running feet before they saw the additional prison officers enter the block. The older, more established lags, lay down on the floor, their hands behind their head, they knew from experience what to expect. Newer inmates stood bewildered or were elbowed out of the way by the running prison officers, whilst a few others emulated the older ones.

The more violent, or just plain crazy prisoners, jumped into fights, settling old scores given the opportunity of the distraction; they didn't seem to mind when the teargas arrived. The direction of the panic centred on one cell where guards found the most hated prisoner on the wing, an ex-police officer, lying in a pool of blood, his eyes open staring in surprise, he was no longer breathing.

Later Bart Bridges took it upon himself to tell Lily and Nessa as sympathetically as he was able, Lily's ex-husband, Martin Frances, was reported to have taken his own life in prison. He watched for any tell-tale sign of lingering loyalty she might still have for a brutal husband who beat and raped her partner Nessa within an inch of her life. He recognised stark shock appear on Nessa's face as she sat down heavily on a nearby couch, her mouth forming the 'w' of 'what', though not quite making the sound.

At first, Lily stood impassive, frozen to the spot, her face a blank mask; no shock, no emotion, nothing. She turned to walk over to the sideboard, where she pulled open a draw, picked out a small rectangular business card to bring back to where Bart sat. In a stoic unemotional voice she said, "Martin would never kill himself, not whilst I am alive for him to torment." She handed Bart the business card, "Grigoriy Novikov found Martin in prison whilst looking for the car his daughter Anna was seen in with her husband Warren. Martin told him the car was mine and the address where I was living at the cottage. He found me because he thought I knew his daughter. I assured him I didn't. I told Mr. Novikov Martin sent him to me because it was the only way he could continue his reign of violence by using other people to hurt me." She turned to face Nessa. "I told him about what he did to us both. Novikov said he knew many men like Martin during his life. He gave me his card with contact details, said if I ever had any more trouble from him he would make sure he didn't bother me again."

Bart looked down at Grigoriy Novikov's real name (not Novak the one he has used since he came to the UK) with a mobile telephone number embossed on the little white card. He wondered if the man heard about the bomb at castle Daingneach where Lily works, perhaps thought it was meant for her. He handed the card back to Lily not asking the question whether she ever phoned it.

He didn't want to know.

CHAPTER 1

Emily Hobbs had been sitting for nearly thirty minutes in her new black mini in one of the parking spaces in front of the emporium at Aboyne, intermittently flicking her windscreen wipers to clear the fine spray of rain. She was pleased there were many other cars parked otherwise she might have looked conspicuous sitting there with many of the shops closed half day on a Thursday. She flicked the wipers again noticing the few people still out shopping walking past huddled under colourful umbrellas, were burdened by heavy shopping bags or boxes of groceries. Every once in a while she wiped the condensation from the inside screen to enable her to see, hoping she didn't draw too much attention.

The person she was watching entered the emporium nearly half an hour ago. The time Emily recorded in a small note book on the seat beside her. She would use her notes later to produce a report for the client who engaged the Bartholomew and Hobbs Detective Agency to collect evidence of his wife's infidelity he assured Bart she was engaged in. After several similar observations Emily anticipated the attractive young woman she was following, would drive back home in the family Range Rover to Tarland, there to remain until she fetched her two children, a boy and a girl, on foot from a nearby school. Such was her general routine.

Since she began the job, Emily acquired a measure of sympathy for Jenny Williamson. She appeared to be a pleasant, quite innocent sort of young mother who was clearly devoted to her children. She could tell as much from the way she interacted with them. On the one occasion she observed Harvey Williamson, the client, with his family, he seemed altogether quite different. He appeared stern faced, in keeping with her impression when she met him at their initial meeting when they agreed to take the assignment. She didn't take to him at all. She gave him the nickname 'Ernest' because he was altogether too earnest in his overall manner especially when he expressed the belief his wife was cheating on him, although he offered no real evidence why, other than 'he knew'.

Jenny Williamson was much younger than Harvey, who Emily learnt after searching the internet for background information, was the CEO of a well-established Advertising Agency. She discovered, whilst chatting to one of his employees, a chance meeting in a local café near to the Advertising Agency's offices, he already had one failed marriage to his name.

During her impromptu chat with the member of 'Ernest's' staff Emily implied she wanted to work in advertising, asking the girl what working at the agency was like. The rather talkative girl was far from complimentary. She suggested if Emily waited long enough there would be a vacancy for her job. She was given more information than she would have believed possible about Ernest's liking for younger women and his hands on approach to management practices.

Emily began to believe his failed marriages were possibly due to his unfortunate personality, notably he was boring in the extreme, as well as having a roving eye for his secretaries. Apparently, so far he has married two of them. The fact, confirmed by the girl, surprised Emily greatly, given his not very attractive physical features; very protruding watery eyes with rather large lips, they always seemed to be wet, making Emily shiver with revulsion.

However, the occasion she saw 'Ernest' out with his family, she could perceive no similar distaste in Jenny Williamson, who by her behaviour clearly doted on her husband as well as her children. Emily, a little critical for one so young (she just turned eighteen) entertained the passing thought perhaps his bank balance was a little more attractive, after all Jenny Williamson lived in a very nice family house out in the posher part of Tarland and was obviously no longer expected to work. The thought made Emily feel guilty, she silently chastised herself for becoming too cynical at such a young age.

Emily tried not to dwell on the passing of her eighteenth birthday she once (before Robbie Cowan, her boyfriend, left her) held high hopes of celebrating in style. Robbie promised her he would wine and dine her after a disappointing trip over to Grantown-on-Spey to positively identify the con-man Edward Petersen, newly released on parole from prison, where he met Lily John's ex-husband, Martin Frances. They discovered Martin sent him to claim the cottage Emily was living in at the time with Lily.

In Grantown, Robbie wanted to treat Emily to a nice meal in the restaurant of the hotel where Petersen arranged to meet her or rather to meet the fictional Marianne Peace's granddaughter, Chloe. Emily was pretending to be an elderly business woman, under the pseudonym of Marianne Peace on a fake Social Media account she set up to entice Edward Petersen to make contact. He was claiming to be the nephew of the deceased owner of Lily's cottage and therefore sole heir of the property.

The evening turned out differently, Emily only managing a cup of coffee with Robbie before her enthusiasm overtook her. Pretending to be Chloe, she decided to actually meet with Petersen. He tried to drug her to get her up to his room, as Robbie watched them from a nearby table in the hotel bar. The evening, like her eighteenth birthday celebrations, was a huge disappointment, something she wouldn't have told her mother about if they hadn't become estranged from each other when Emily moved to Scotland.

Putting herself in danger would have confirmed to Thelma Hobbs her daughter wasn't equipped to live on her own. Emily always felt she was a disappointment to her mother, especially after refusing to move to Grimsby with her to work in yet another of her 'greasy spoon cafés'.

After posting cryptic messages in some leading national newspapers, Emily managed to make contact with Bart Bridges who invited her to work with him in his second clock shop in the Highlands of Scotland where they both live as clockmakers and private investigators. Emily sighed at the thought of how lucky she was finding him, even if she was only doing a mundane observation of 'Ernest's' unsuspecting wife.

Disturbing her reminising, Emily's mobile buzzed with an incoming text message from her P.I partner, the Bartholomew part of the agency, asking 'where was she'? She responded by calling him back as she didn't want to lose sight of the shop doorway in case Jenny Williamson came out whilst she was typing a message back to him.

"Hi," she greeted him with the deliberate false cheeriness she adopted of late when he answered. "I'm outside the emporium in Aboyne waiting for Mrs 'Ernest' to come back out." She flicked the windscreen wipers again to clear her view. She caught sight of the tartan umbrella being put up as Jenny Williamson re-emerged from the shop with a coil of garden hose and an additional shopping bag to the ones she already carried when she entered the place. Emily couldn't help thinking you wouldn't need a hose to water the garden with the current weather conditions. "I've got to go, she's just come back out and will probably be driving back home as she usually does."

"Okay, lass, see you later," Emily could hear the subtle concern in Bart's voice, present for several months, *ever since Robbie left.*

She didn't want to think about Robbie Cowan, certainly not while she was engaged on an assignment for the agency. She needed to stay focussed. She had done far too much thinking about him already, *time to let him go.* A difficult thing to do knowing she would be following Jenny Williamson back to Tarland. In fact, quite natural to think about Robbie given he owned a bungalow there, one he inherited from his mother when she died a few years back. Emily only visited the bungalow a couple of times because Robbie was ashamed of how shabby his home was, usually he didn't invite people back there.

He confessed to her he had done nothing to it since he moved from his own place in Aberdeen to look after his alcoholic mother, dying from Liver disease. He always intended to sell the bungalow to buy another flat back in the city. Time moved on with most of his finances being spent on learning to fly microlights, after which he bought one of his own.

Flying was his abiding passion, something he began to teach Emily to do after he helped her through her driving test. That was all before he was suspended from his police job because of a complaint lodged against him by Gina Taylor, a strange young girl Emily knew was fixated on Robbie. Emily had been subjected to many conversations with her whilst shopping at the Co-op store in the village where Gina worked.

Even now the accusation of gross sexual misconduct riled Emily, not only because the claim was false, getting him suspended pending a disciplinary investigation, it also ruined his exemplary police career, possibly forever. Undoubtedly, the charge was the beginning of their 'troubles' and subsequently put an end to their relationship when he went away. In addition Emily survived an attempt to force her off the road whilst taking Robbie's car back to Tarland and where he reported the incident to his colleagues in the police.

As she was being interviewed in his front room by a traffic police officer, he received an anonymous threatening telephone call from someone telling him the complaint would 'go away' if he complied with whatever he was asked to do, otherwise much worse things would happen than a mere near miss.

Eventually, the police withdrew the disciplinary against Robbie. They obtained evidence from Operation Graffiti as well as the aerodrome CCTV recordings proving the complaint to be false. The complaint was a ploy by a locally organised criminal syndicate Operation Graffiti were investigating, and their way of recruiting serving police officers into their corrupt organisation. Despite evidence getting the sexual misconduct investigation closed, Robbie was required to remain 'suspended' otherwise Operation Graffiti's lengthy investigations would be compromised.

Over the past few months, Emily tried to work out at what point she lost Robbie. Whether because of Gina Taylor's accusation or the subsequent bomb at the wedding of Laird Mungo MacLeod to Mary Macaulay; whichever determined Robbie's decision to join Operation Graffiti when the offer came, she neither knew nor understood. Most of all she didn't accept he couldn't clear his name or to resume his role as a local beat officer. He tried to explain, the last time she saw him, but she was too devastated to take anything in. Certainly after hearing some of his words, '*I have to go away indefinitely*', made their way into her mind. Everything else after became a blur.

What she did know was their plans to refurbish his bungalow whilst he was suspended on 'garden leave' would no longer happen and a great wrench, having looked forward to doing the work with him. The loss of their closeness was unbearable being the only time in her life she felt like that.

At least ever since she lost contact with her cousin Peter when his parents were convicted of the murder of Bart's next door neighbour at The Art Gallery in Wainthorpe-on-sea. These events shattered Emily's life completely. Her parents split up, her father left altogether, Aunty Elsie and Uncle Mark were imprisoned for murder and her cousin Peter Draper disappeared, she believed changing his name to disguise who he was.

Emily sighed at all the images her thoughts conjured up. She started the mini's engine to follow Jenny Williamson back to Tarland. Whilst she knew going back to Tarland would open up her parting conversation with Robbie again, she would avoid driving anywhere near his bungalow because seeing the place only emphasised her loss.

CHAPTER 2

Bart closed down the call from Emily already regretting his text checking up on her. He tried so often these past few months not to fret about her. He started when she began to show signs of brooding after Robbie left to join Operation Graffiti. He knew from his last conversation with Robbie he would be working undercover, wherever they saw fit to send him based on their intelligence leads. Bart knew very little more, there wasn't much Robbie dare tell him. What he did pick up, although only a hint, there would be a danger to his life or consequences to anyone connected to him and the reason he needed to make a clean break with his past.

If the local criminal organisation ever suspected he was still working for the police and not as his 'legend' suggested, he was a disgraced copper, sacked for gross sexual misconduct from the complaint by Gina Taylor on their behalf, he needed to protect everyone he knew. There had already been an attempt on Emily's life. Bart could see, in the short term, a clean break was the only way Robbie could continue working as a police officer. To stay around the area would attract criminal attention putting anyone who knew him in danger.

Of course, Bart had no idea how much of what Robbie confided to him he also told Emily when he came to say goodbye. He wasn't privy to their conversation in the back room of his clock shop, The March of Time. In the days following Robbie's departure, he guessed, by her reaction, he told her very little because she seemed bewildered, becoming withdrawn. Bart hoped as time passed by she would become less so. He desperately wanted her to return to the enthusiastic young woman he saw emerge after she came to live in Scotland.

As her eighteenth birthday approached, then passed, if anything she grew even more absorbed, despite his attempts to make her birthday a pleasant occasion. With a meal surrounded by all their friends bringing presents, he could see for her the gathering was ruined by the absence of Robbie. He saw the same shadow cloud her face, fearing it would become a permanent feature. Robbie's departure changed her outlook on life entirely. Bart was at a loss how to address the damage.

He did, of course, try. Firstly by doing what initially he was reluctant to do, formalising the Bartholomew and Hobbs Detective Agency. He placed an advertisement in the local newspaper to demonstrate to her his commitment. He hadn't considered the enterprise much beyond their initial search for Emily's father Tom Hobbs. It proved quite an easy task. Emily discovered, during a conversation with a man called Taffy at the hostel where her father stayed temporarily, he moved to live in Nottingham where he got a job with an insurance company. Taffy received a postcard from Tom informing him he lived in a bedsit in the Forest Fields area.

Emily drew up a list of Insurance Companies in Nottingham, telephoning them individually only to discover none would give out information about employees. Except in one case, she remembered because her father once told her the company was his biggest rival when he worked in Wainthorpe-on-Sea. The lady she spoke to seemed to be about to say something before she paused, then told Emily all their calls were recorded for training purposes. Bart explained was a way of saying she couldn't tell her anything about Tom Hobbs because it would be picked up by her bosses.

Bart's intuition led him to telephone the company Emily indicated. She listen as he told the person who answered he was in the process of setting up an insurance policy with them, needed to obtain more information then to ring back to ask for Tom Hobbs to complete his application. Even Bart was surprised at how easy it was to put Emily back in touch with her father.

The second mission of the Bartholomew and Hobbs Detective Agency was to find Emily's cousin, Peter Draper. Unknown to Bart, Emily searched Facebook from time to time to find him albeit without luck. She periodically updated her own account with a random post, in case Peter wanted to contact her.

Bart Bridges knew nothing about social media or any of the packages in general. To him the internet was a mystery. He couldn't understand why anyone would want to submit personal information for the world to see. He remembered some of his mother's oft quoted sayings he thought irritating at the time, though he found himself using the older he got. As he aged he came to think they were quite reasonable. 'Never wash your dirty linen in public' was one such saying. As a young boy, when he took everything literally, he couldn't understand why you would want to do such a thing.

The few times he caught glimpses of Emily's Facebook page, he saw the absolutely incredible things people posted about themselves. They were often accompanied by photographic images and shocked Bart, making him wonder what his mother would have said about posting such things.

The evening Robbie Cowan called round to tell them he was going away was when Emily showed them both a direct message on her page from someone called PD James. Emily said there was a cryptic message, "Saw the photo in the papers of the castle bomb. Looks like you next to the clock man. Are you okay, M?" from her cousin Peter. She explained Peter loved the Dalgliesh TV crime series. They once argued when she told him the author PD James was a woman. Peter wouldn't accept a woman could write such a thing, which was always a joke between them. Bart saw the PD might stand for Peter Draper confirming for him he changed his identity when he left Wainthorpe after his parents were charged with murder.

Since finding the message coincided with Robbie's departure, Bart hadn't asked her whether she replied. He thought it best to leave things alone. He knew how much Peter meant to Emily when they were younger. When Peter went away she lost her only friend. Bart thought with Robbie leaving her also, the two things were too similar in nature to bring up for discussion.

Instead, as a means of diversion, he placed the advertisement about the Detective Agency's services, being surprised to be contacted by Harvey Williamson the first week he ran it. When he met Mr 'Ernest', as Emily started to call him, he took the case against his better judgement, having taken an instant dislike to the man. He agreed to take the case for two reasons. Firstly, he knew from his own experience the job would be one of those predominantly boring tedious 'follows'. Secondly, following a young woman with two small children living in a good area would be safer than following a man, his intention being to give Emily experience of surveillance as a means of distracting her from her grief over Robbie.

Since then the subject of Peter Draper's message hadn't come up, nor did she offer anything further about it. At the time, he left Emily and Robbie to go into the back room because he hoped she would explain to Robbie who Peter was. Whether she did or not she never told him.

What he did know is Robbie certainly imparted his news about leaving to her during his last conversation because he saw Emily was shocked when she emerged from the back room after he left. The following days saw such a change in her Bart worried endlessly about her wellbeing. As a consequence 'The Bartholomew and Hobbs Detective Agency' was formalised in order to distract her from her grief.

CHAPTER 3

Emily followed Jenny Williamson back to Tarland, parking in her usual spot at the top of the hill overlooking the four bedroomed house 'Ernest' owned. One of the nicest plots, the house began the next phase of the newest estate in Tarland. Where Emily was parked she was surrounded by older long established bungalows, *like the one Robbie owns a few streets away*, on a corner beside an overgrown privet hedge. She parked here a few times before to observe what she considered was Jenny Williamson's usual routine.

She knew in fifteen minutes she would go out to fetch the children from school. The miserable drizzle having thankfully stopped, Emily no longer needed to keep flicking the windscreen wipers, a giveaway the car was occupied and likely to draw attention.

Emily heard the engine before she saw the battered jeep creep past her, the left indicator flashing to pull into the free space in front of her mini to inevitably obscure her view of the 'Ernest' house. *Bugger!*

She contemplated starting up the mini to move before the driver got out of the jeep. She dithered a bit too long, saw the driver's door open and the petite figure of its occupant jump out. She recognised Nessa McKinley immediately by the swish of her long auburn ponytail even before Nessa looked directly at her.

Today Nessa abandoned her greasy car mechanic's overalls in favour of jeans with a hooded jacket. She recognised Emily or rather the Mini Cooper she recently helped her to buy and smiling walked directly over to the car. Emily beckoned her towards the passenger door, leaning over to unlock the door for her to climb inside.

She could see Nessa's surprise at her being there by her, "Hi?" Emily heard the barely disguised question in her voice. "How's the mini doing?" Clearly her initial thought was Emily must have broken down to be parked where she was.

"It's great, I love it," Emily enthused trying to think quickly how she might explain being there, "I didn't expect to see you here."

"Och, that's ma Da's place," she pointed towards the driveway entrance beyond the hedge where Emily was parked.

"Oh, I see," she forgot Nessa came from Tarland. She knew Robbie from their school days. Of course, Emily was aware they lived close to each other in those days, having no idea exactly where her parent's bungalow was.

She needed to explain why she was there. "I'm on a job," Emily confided, nodding down the hill in the direction of the Williamson's house. "Do you know any of the people on the new estate?" She didn't want to say anything about the job or who she was following.

Nessa glanced down the hill as far as she was able to see with her jeep blocking the view, shook her head, "Och, that's the posh end....I donnae know anyone down there. None are ma customers." Nessa knew people with a lot of money would go further afield than a small place like McKinley's Autos to have their cars fixed. A lot of them would be company cars so they were likely to take them to Aberdeen, McDougal's having most of the bigger company contracts around the area. After a pause she added, "Would you like me to pull on Da's drive so you can see better?"

Emily caught a glimpse of Jenny Williamson's Range Rover backing onto the road down the hill then drive off in the direction of her children's school. "No, I've got to go, thanks for the thought."

Nessa took the hint something was happening when Emily urgently turned the key in the ignition to start the mini. She opened the door to get out, "Catch yer soon, yeah?" Nessa wanted to talk to Emily about Robbie ever since he left without a word. She hadn't dared broach the subject because she was warned by Bart she was struggling with the whole thing.

Nessa stood watching her drive off. With her mechanics eye and ear for motors she observed with approval the mini moving down the hill, take a right turn before she went into the house to face up to Jock McKinley's acid tongue.

He always began every conversation with the same thing, moaning at last she bothered to come to see him, before he laid into her about *that young scally* she set on to help her cope. Hamish McGregor was a young qualified mechanic she employed when Jock stayed at home to look after her mother before she died. He resented the action bitterly at the time. Nessa wasn't sure whether it was because her mother's needs were too demanding of him or he would rather be at the garage. She also suspected her father realised someone as young as Hamish would do the job better than he now could. Nessa emphasised how Hamish worked extremely hard though no amount of telling him would convince her father.

* * * * * *

Emily drove carefully following the Range Rover, keeping to the speed limit as she made her way towards the Primary School a few streets away. It was unusual for Jenny Williamson to drive the short journey to fetch her children, made more surprising since the rain had stopped. When she settled some distance away she watched her get out to wait at the school gates with the other parents. She made notes in her book recording Jenny appeared to be carrying two small colourful bags, the sort you would use to put a birthday gift in. Both were decorated with a blue bow trailing matching ribbon from the handles.

She could hear the bell announce the end of the school day before the doors burst open discharging an assortment of children in disarray, some with one long sock down, dragging coats and bags behind them, all looking for their respective parents who, along with

Jenny Williamson, stood together outside the school boundary. One or two of them were accompanied by a dog on a lead, whilst others were standing with a pram or pushchair with younger siblings.

Emily could recognise the Williamson children as they left the school building. Their ages she could only guess at though the boy looked slightly older being physically bigger than his sister. Both were extremely sweet, obviously favouring their mother's good looks Emily was pleased to note. *Lord help anyone who resembled Harvey Williamson!*

The Williamson children appeared to be excited, bouncing on the spot when they reached their mother, their hands grabbing at the gift bags she was holding. Emily could see the little girl was wearing a party dress under her unbuttoned coat.

Jenny Williamson took their school bags from them swopping them each for one of the gift bags. The boy began to poke about inside his bag and was reprimanded by his mother who looked worriedly around her at the parents assembled until she spotted a man surrounded by a collection of small children. She walked hers over to join the group, spoke to the man who seemed to be counting the children, then took them over to a large people carrier where he load them one by one inside. Jenny stood watching, until the car pulled away, to wave goodbye to her children.

Emily surmised they were being taken to an after school birthday party. She made notes in her book beside her, one eye watching Jenny Williamson return to her Range Rover she assumed to travel back home. She started her mini, slowly drew out into the traffic flow two cars behind the Range Rover expecting her to turn right towards her house. The left indicator light came on. She sighed deeply, disappointed she couldn't finish her stint to return home like on all the other occasions when Jenny Williamson picked her children up from school. Emily assumed she would then prepare the evening meal for 'Ernest' returning from work.

Tempted though she was not to continue to follow her, she put on her left indicator with a sigh. Jenny Williamson appeared to be cutting through the older part of the estate mostly made up of bungalows.

When Emily began to recognise the sequence of roads, then even some of the features of the bungalows, she knew they were close to Robbie's street. She was horrified when Jenny turned into his road. She immediately slowed the car, her heart beginning to beat a little faster knowing Jenny would lead her past the familiar bungalow. She spotted the For Sale sign in Robbie's front garden even at that distance. The shock made her legs turn to jelly and she juddered to a halt unable to move any further.

She cut the engine, lowered her window to take in air, fearing she might pass out. *Robbie put his bungalow on the market?* The action was such a final end to his life there she could barely breathe. Hadn't she convinced herself his moving away was only temporary? Emily watched in disbelief as Jenny Williamson slowed down almost to a stop before turning onto the bungalow's drive. She gasped with disbelief when Mrs 'Ernest' got out of her car, scanned the road both ways checking to see if anyone was watching her, then walked over to the front door digging deep into the shoulder bag she was carrying, she pulled out a key to let herself inside.

* * * * *

Bart heard the shop bell tinkle from the back room of The March of Time having closed up as usual at five o'clock. He anticipated Emily was returning from her surveillance of Mrs 'Ernest', the name he also came to think of Jenny Williamson as, after hearing Emily call Harvey Williamson 'Ernest'. He listened for her usual, "Helloo," he always got whenever she came back from anywhere. He strained hard, the greeting didn't come. He suspected for some time his hearing was deteriorating. He could hear the door to the shop close, followed by Emily's footsteps running up the stairs without coming through. This alone was enough to indicate to him all was not well.

He moved into the passageway, stood at the bottom of the stairs next to the internal door to the garage, silently listened for movement above. He thought he caught a faint sob drift downwards from Emily's bedroom and began to worry, his first thought being she had bumped the mini. The car he knew was her pride and joy, having a prang would upset her greatly.

He crept into the shop, now cloaked in gloom as the light of the day began to fade outside. The ticking clocks whirred before they jumped into the quarter past five routine he was so used to he hardly ever noticed. He walked over to the shop door to peer into the street at Emily's car parked at the kerb. There was sufficient light to show there was no damage to the driver's side. He left it, went into the back room to sit in his arm chair to wait for her to come downstairs. She didn't come down at all leaving him to spend a fitful night worrying about her.

CHAPTER 4

Next morning the smell of sizzling bacon filled the back room of The March of Time as Bart stood tending his frying pan, his mind reflecting on the possible reasons to take his young partner straight to her room the evening before. He heard the creek of the door behind him indicate Emily silently entering the room. Without turning he enquired, as he usually did, if she wanted a bacon sandwich. The game they played allowed her to refuse on the basis she didn't believe his preoccupation with pork products was in anyway healthy. Her morning muesli he referred to as 'rabbit food' completed the exchange.

Today he was shocked when she replied, "Yes…….please."

At first he thought he misheard, so asked, "Brown bread or white?" knowing Emily only ever ate brown bread.

"White, toast, with brown sauce," her voice was flatly monotone.

Intrigued, Bart could resist no longer, he turned to find Emily still in her dressing gown looking pale. Her red-rimmed eyes affirmed the sob he heard the previous evening.

"I know," she said defensively. "Not my usual healthy breakfast. I need comfort food. You seem to thrive on it." She managed the barest of smiles which did nothing to lift the sadness in her eyes.

"What's wrong, lass?" Bart's voice, a mere whisper to its usual resonance, showed all the worry he was feeling.

She moved silently to sit in her fireside chair pulled the fluffy dressing gown around her for comfort. Bart busied himself putting more rashers in the frying pan and two more thick slices of soft white bread in the toaster. Emily remained immovable, staring into the flames as they danced around the logs on the open fire, her face the picture of torment. The flames reflected in her eyes. If anything Bart thought she looked even more troubled than during the days after Robbie Cowan disappeared from their lives.

She remained trancelike until she sensed him place a plate on the table beside her, with a cup of tea in her usual bone china Crown Derby cup and saucer. The one, hand painted with pink and yellow flowers displayed a few noticeable chips, but Bart was unwilling to throw it out. Similarly his Willow Pattern cup and saucer, was her car boot find she presented him with when she was a fifteen year old school girl working a Saturday job in his first clock shop, Time and Tide, in Wainthorpe-on-sea.

Unusual for such a young girl, she told him tea should always be drunk from china tea cups and made in a proper teapot using leaves, not tea bags. At the time he thought she sounded like an elderly spinster, although since, realised was a rebellious notion directed against her mother's methods in the café she owned with the pretentious name of The Silver Teapot. The café was where Emily helped to wait on customers using small depressing stainless steel pots with teabags on strings dangling inside held in place by the lid.

She looked up at him, "Robbie's bungalow is up for sale," she said simply.

The statement shocked him. Even Bart harboured hopes Robbie's move away to work undercover for Operation Graffiti was a temporary one. His last conversation with him hadn't exactly implied as much, but neither did it refute the idea. What he definitely understood from Robbie's parting words, he was to remain 'suspended' from his police role indefinitely. It wasn't an option for him because he would lose all the police skills he acquired since he joined the force straight from school. His career was long enough for him to know policing was the *only* thing he ever wanted to do.

Bart's primary worry at the time was Robbie might be forced to go into the Witness Protection Programme, like he had, been required to change his identity and disappear into a new life entirely, leaving everyone he knew behind. A worse fear still, Emily might go with him and Bart would lose her completely.

The idea made him realise for the first time he considered her as much a daughter as if she were his very own child. To Bart's relief, Robbie confided he would be joining Operation Graffiti. At the time, Bart thought the situation a much less final option, one he could come back from after the operation delivered retribution to its criminal targets.

After a long thoughtful pause, Bart asked, "How do you know?"

Emily hadn't yet touched her bacon sandwich, merely sipped the tea with shaking hands before admitting, "I followed Mrs 'Ernest' after she left her children with another parent to be taken to a party straight from school....." She looked up at Bart who could see distress flick across her face. "She led me to Robbie's street where I saw the For Sale sign in his front garden ...and..... she parked on *his* drive then let herself into the bungalow."

Bart stopped himself from reacting with surprise. He tried to keep a neutral expression because he didn't want to show her any of the alarm he felt. He kept his question *'are you sure?'* unasked. Emily wouldn't misinterpret something like that.

"I don't understand...." she said shakily, a quake in her voice.

Similarly, Bart wasn't about to admit he was also perplexed. Instead, the part of Bart Bridges, the professional private investigator, automatically came into play, "Did you notice the name of the Estate Agent on the For Sale board?" he asked calmly.

Emily frowned remembering only the numbness from the shock of seeing Jenny Williamson enter Robbie's bungalow as if she lived there.....whilst registering the furtiveness as she scanned around her to see if she was being observed.

Emily shook her head slowly trying to picture the scene, "I stopped at the top of his road," she said as if to explain. She could picture the board in the garden, made from new wood, fixed into the ground. *Why could she remember that?* The sign was a symbol of the finality of their relationship.

"So you couldn't read the details on the sign?" he prompted.

She shook her head again before she realised why, "No.... no because the board was facing outwards. I only got the side view. I couldn't see what was written on it."

"Ah," Bart said. He understood she hadn't actually driven past the bungalow, guessing she also didn't stay around to see how long Jenny Williamson spent inside the place.

Apologetically she added, "I should have looked.....but....."

"It's okay, lass," he said placing a hand lightly on her shoulder. He already decided he would go out to Tarland to have a look for himself; the whole thing intrigued him. He said, "Eat your bacon sandwich before it goes cold."

* * * * *

Bart lowered the driver's door window of his old Peugeot 208, raised his mobile phone to click off a couple of pictures of the Estate Agent's For Sale sign outside Robbie's bungalow. The agent's name, Nelsens, meant nothing to him. They weren't one he remembered seeing when he was looking for a place to settle in the Highlands. He thought he registered with all of them to receive their 'properties for sale' listings. Perhaps the Agents were new. The length of the grass on the tiny square piece of front lawn showed no one had been living there for some time.

Robbie Cowan left his bungalow several months ago after receiving a telephone threat and resorted to hiding out in a room at the hotel in the village. The call came after Emily had been forced off the road whilst driving Robbie's car, by a motorbike with Gina Taylor riding pillion. The caller warned him not to report the incident to the police, an order coming too late as one of his police colleagues was already interviewing Emily in his front room whilst the unknown caller was on the line.

Afterwards, the spate of car accidents increased. The next one put Mary Macaulay from Castle Daingneach in hospital with head injuries needing her to be put into an induced coma. Afterwards Bart arranged with Laird Mungo MacLeod for Robbie to move to the castle, as much for his own safety as to protect the MacLeod's. He pretended to be the Laird's new secretary, under the name of 'Daniel Roberts', to undertake a security role throughout the lead up to Mungo and Mary's wedding.

Mary was convinced her 'accident' was a serious attempt on her life by rival estate owner Rupert Quinnell. She worked for him years previously. At the time she believed he suspected her of accidentally discovering what he was doing at his farm estate. The experience of working for him left her traumatised because of his apparent delight in tormenting her with threats to destroy any chance of her getting future employment if she were to leave his farm shop.

After the hospital doctor woke Mary from her coma she conveyed her fears about the accident to CID's Detective Inspector Morris who didn't seem to take the accusation seriously. To make matters worse Morris went to the castle to attempt to persuade Mungo and Mary to postpone their wedding and delay their plans to open the castle to the public. Mary's dream was to create a viable 'fairy tale' wedding venue and to use their own, highly publicised, wedding nuptials in the photographic launch for the venture.

On their wedding day, as the couple were pronounced man and wife in the Grand Salon where the ceremony was taking place, a bomb, hidden in their wedding cake figurines, blew up the marquee where the reception was to be held, shattering the castle windows. The blast destroyed a number of the guests vehicles parked nearby. Thankfully no one was seriously hurt by the blast. Afterwards everyone expected the police to take their claims someone was trying to kill Mary, more seriously.

Much to Bart and Robbie's anger the investigation into the bombing, together with the previous attempt on Mary's life, Emily's car accident and Gina Taylor's involvement in these as well as her false complaint against Robbie Cowan for gross sexual misconduct, were all handed over to Operation Graffiti because they were considered to be linked to their ongoing investigations.

Robbie was so angry he made threats to his superiors he would bring a civil case of libel against Gina Taylor for defamation of character and damage to his police career. The threat forced the hand of the powers within the police to decide a better solution was to invite Robbie Cowan to work with them on Operation Graffiti rather than leave him outside, a loose cannon.

Robbie's acceptance agreement was accompanied by the terms he was to operate as an undercover police officer. He felt the arrangement gave him a chance to be part of the investigation to ultimately officially clear his name and allow him to work once again as a rural beat officer. His only regret being, he was required to leave his life behind him, including Emily much the same as if he had gone into the Witness Protection Programme. He was warned there was no way he could keep in touch with anyone he knew whilst he operated undercover.

Bart sat outside Robbie's bungalow, his thoughts drifted through the past happenings making him sigh deeply as he looked at the For Sale sign he just took pictures of. How could he have been so wrong about Robbie being able to come back? He tried once again to remember if he actually said he would be able to return. Any such words eluded him. Bart started his car, driving away hoping he looked like anyone else who might be interested in purchasing the bungalow.

CHAPTER 5

After leaving Tarland Bart drove on to Castle Daingneach. The castle appeared every bit the stronghold it was named after, Bart thought, as he stopped the car at the turn of the drive when the twin-towered battlements of 'the fortress' came into view. He hadn't been back since the bomb exploded on the day of the MacLeod's wedding. The only external sign of the aftermath refurbishment was a solid, elaborately carved new front door that looked as fortified as the castle itself. His clock mending contract had lapsed whilst the devastation caused by the blast was assessed by a forensic team and bomb disposal experts, who took their time picking over the debris.

Once clear, with most of rubble taken away for closer examination, rectifying the damage on the castle itself began. Fortunately only superficial damage was sustained. The glass in the windows took most of the blast with structurally only the front door needing to be replaced. Of course, Mungo and Mary's wedding reception didn't take place and regrettably neither did the anticipated photographs with the esteemed Scottish families who attended the event. Needless to say everyone was thankful the bomb was inexplicably detonated between the bride and groom being declared 'man and wife' and before the guests made their way outside to the marquee for the reception, otherwise there would have been more than the slight injuries sustained when the windows of the Grand Salon imploded.

Bart heard the catering staff were all in the kitchen where the castle housekeeper, Maggie Wallace, assembled them to distribute cups of tea whilst disseminating instructions before the wedding breakfast was served. Similarly, Bart was grateful they already completed setting up the tables in the marquee. Particularly the wedding cake, where the highly explosive Semtex shaped into the distinctive bride and groom figures dressed in MacLeod tartan, sat on top of the cake. The uneaten food from the cancelled reception made headlines in the local Aberdeen news outlets who reported a large number of homeless people ate royally the week following the blast.

Ever since the fateful day Bart suffered much guilt, blaming himself for attracting a second attempt on Mary MacLeod's life. He was responsible for suggesting they bring their wedding forward after Mary recovered from her injuries from being forced off the road. Bart's preoccupation with Robbie Cowan's suspension from duty, pending Operation Graffiti's completion of their enquiries, gave him the idea. He thought with a lot of publicity before the event, Mary's aggressor could be enticed out into the open to try again, thereby speeding up the investigations. In hindsight he regretted it.

On a visit to The March of Time, Mary confided to Bart she once worked at the Quinnell farm where one day she innocently incurred the wrath of Rupert Quinnell. Subsequently, she suffered continued bullying from him. She believed he was manipulating the figures for the farm's daily takings by recording them higher than they actually were. She didn't understand why. However, Rupert Quinnell, in the belief she discovered the fact, subjected her to a prolonged campaign of intimidation by occasionally tampering with her wages, affecting her ability to pay her household bills. She desperately wanted to leave but he threatened he would make sure she couldn't get another job anywhere else. He would tell everyone she was caught stealing from him.

Although desperate for money, she did manage to leave by securing a job at castle Daingneach under her maiden name of Macaulay, thereby dropping under Quinnell's radar. She hadn't seen him since until more recently she spotted him in the castle gift shop, whilst covering for one of her absent staff, where he recognised her.

For some unknown reason he convinced himself she was responsible for a decline in his takings at his farm shop and threatened to tell her employers about her past. At that point he was unaware she was about to become Lady MacLeod of Daingneach. When he discovered she was marrying the new Laird, Mungo MacLeod and they planned to open the castle to the public, he became utterly enraged.

Neither Bart, nor Mungo and Mary, ever think a second attempt on her life would be quite as dramatic as a bomb or so stealthily contrived. Bart heard, via Jayson Vingoe, his friend, the Crime Scene Investigator involved in the forensic examination of the castle crime scene, the police were unable to trace the maker of the bride and groom figurines. In fact no one seemed to know who informed the baker their usual wedding cake accessory supplier went out of business. Neither could they identify who provided the substitute items, '*they seemed to appear to the exact specification required*' the harassed baker told the police.

Bart's guilt in the matter remained with him ever since. Today was his first opportunity to return to Castle Daingneach since the fateful day. He was in no hurry, even though he knew he would have to face Mungo and Mary eventually. As a diversion he threw himself into formally setting up the Bartholomew and Hobbs Detective Agency, as much to help Emily cope with Robbie Cowan leaving, as to pacify his own feelings. Now, arriving at the castle he knew he would have to face up to the part he played in bringing about the disastrous wedding day.

Bart's tyres barely came to rest on the rough gravel surface of the car park in front of the castle before the new door opened and a smiling Mary MacLeod emerged to meet him. Contrary to his fears she appeared delighted to see him again, "How are you, Bart?" she asked immediately. "I trust you have no lasting injuries. Everyone, thank goodness, seems to have avoided anything major." The declaration went part way to easing Bart's discomfort.

They both made small talk as they proceeded up to the library with Bart noting the inside of the castle looked much the same as he remembered before the blast caused havoc.

"You've done a good job cleaning up Mary," Bart said as they settled down with coffee. "I noticed the splendid new front door."

"Yes, the old one was too damaged, taking a lot of the blast and probably helped to protect much of the interior from destruction.....only one or two of the artefacts were lost. I think perhaps a lot more of the clocks now need attention. I hope you have capacity to do the work? I hear you have a new venture?" Bart was surprised to see Mary with a sparkle in her eyes as she enquired.

"Yes, indeed, although we are proceeding slowly only attracting the more mundane kind of work I remember from my previous P.I life," he noticed Mary was listening with interest. "You know the marital infidelity kind." He sounded almost bored at the idea.

"I'll remember, if I ever need you," she said quite seriously before she gave a giggle when she saw Bart's shocked face.

"I expect there won't be too many cases to stop us attending to the clocks. They are my biggest love. I must say Emily has a natural flare, with the same passion as me."

"As long as covering your shop, mending clocks and running the agency will allow you to," Mary said quite seriously.

"Yes, we have been talking about getting someone in to help with the shop when it's open," he said leaving aside their conversations about the possibility of taking on some casual investigators should the need arise. The idea came about after a conversation one day with Jay who wondered if ex or retired police officers might be a good source for extra help as investigators.

Changing the subject Bart asked, "Were any of the clocks damaged in the blast?"

"Not structurally, I don't think. One or two stopped.....understandably really given the pressure of the blast....most of those are in the rooms where the windows blew in," she said.

"Ah, that would do it.....there may be fragments of glass in their mechanisms," he said nodding his head thoughtfully. Mary looked serious for a moment. "What is it?" Bart asked.

"I can't get out of my head how lucky we were," she said to Bart's surprise.

"How can you say lucky?"

"Well, I don't know whether you know, the week before the wedding we changed our plans where to hold the reception," she could see his puzzlement. "It was my intention to hold the reception in the banquet hall. You know the largest room we have here?"

"No, I didn't know, why did you change your mind?"

Mary laughed, "We didn't expect everyone we invited to accept." She looked to Bart to see if he understood the significance. "You know because Mungo used to be Laird Munro's ghillie whilst I was only a shop assistant," she laughed again. "We invited people from some well-established Scottish families, not really expecting them to come. To be honest they were invited more for publicity for our proposed wedding venue business. Sceptically, Mungo thought they wouldn't come because they would regard him as a fake or pretender, rather than entitled.....that sort of thing."

"But *they* didn't?" Bart queried.

"Or they were curious to see us for themselves," she laughed. "Anyway, when they all accepted we found we needed extra seating, *so* we got the Marquee fortunately available at the last minute. This was why the cake got left outside and not........" Mary's voice faded. They stared at each other thinking what could have happened in those circumstances, both considering whether the detonator wouldn't have triggered as early or perhaps when everyone was seated inside the banquet hall.

"Heavens!" Bart breathed.

On his way out Bart noticed the portrait of Seumus Grant, the first Laird of Daingneach, had been moved from the library into the entrance hall down stairs. He stood marvelling at the portrait, at the likeness between Seumus Grant and Mungo MacLeod. Who could ever doubt Mungo was a descendent of the first Laird? They could be the same person with their rugged looks, wild ginger hair and beards with the same sternness of countenance, he thought.

"Was Seumus Grant's portrait here on your wedding day, I can't say I remember?" he asked.

Mary nodded, "Well we always intended to move him for when we open the castle to the public," she said mischievously. "It's not exactly a DNA match but what used to pass as the same in those days." *Clever* Bart thought.

CHAPTER 6

The news Robbie Cowan's bungalow was for sale deeply upset Bart. The whole idea challenged his belief after Operation Graffiti, Robbie would once again resume his old life. He spent the time driving back to the village going over their last conversation word for word, in case he missed a vital clue, a hint to the contrary. Bart was proud of his ability to read people. His intuition was razor sharp, he could always detect a subtle attempt to mislead or at least he thought so.

Attention to detail was the source of much of his success as a Scene's of Crime officer. He possessed an intense forensic eye honed on every case he undertook. There was a time, after the surgery to remove his brain tumour, he worried his surgeon might have somehow removed this ability along with the meningioma. After the operation he felt absolutely woolly headed, something the long slow recovery process seemed eventually to cure.

Bart's instincts nudged him. The 'For Sale' sign at Robbie's bungalow wasn't in keeping with their last conversation. There was something not quite right about it. The echo of a memory, Robbie saying, 'Look after Emily while I'm away,' was faint, but he was sure was real. There was a hint of a promise to return in the way he spoke.

He made a note of the telephone number on the sign. Later, after arriving at the hotel where he stopped for a bite to eat on his way home, he called the number, whilst he waited in the bar for his lunch to arrive. The call went straight to answer phone message, a young female voice informed him the bungalow at Tarland was under offer subject to contract. He closed the call down staring curiously at his mobile.

Two things occurred to him. Firstly, if a property was still under offer, an estate agent would want to know of any other interested parties in case the pending contract fell through or they could attract a higher price. Everything was possible until the actual contract was signed. Gazumping was a common practice in most property transactions these days, based on Bart's experience at any rate. It was all a question of maximising profits.

The second, perhaps more relevant consideration to occur to him was most estate agents had more than one property for sale on their books at any given time. Allocating their telephone number to only one property was bizarre to say the least. He decided to do a search for Nelsens when he got back to the shop, after lunch.

Today, his primary reason for having lunch at the hotel was to catch up with his friend Helen for a chat. He was prompted by going over Robbie's last conversation, ending with a request for Bart to keep an eye on Helen, *as well as Emily?* Something he hadn't done since Robbie left.

Chuck, the hotel chef, brought his soup, ham salad sandwich with a side portion of chips into the bar interrupting his thoughts with a cheery, "Hello, we haven't seen you here for a while."

"True....things have livened up in my world," Bart replied non-specifically. "How are you? My.....those chips look good!" his praise sounded loud across the empty bar.

As he spoke he spotted Helen through the bar door walking past in the corridor. She looked preoccupied, burdened by a heavy frown on her face. She turned her head to look in, spotted Bart giving him a weak smile as she moved on her way. He noticed she wore a uniform business suit, like the one the manager, Muriel Cameron wore when he last saw her. He was used to seeing Helen in her Domestic Service overall. Bart assumed perhaps she finished her training for the Assistant Manager role she told him about and been granted the position.

Bart was again reminded to seek out Muriel for the chat he meant to have with her some time ago when she confided in him money appeared to be going missing from the hotel tills. That was the day she sent for the police suspecting the barman Finlay Ferguson of taking the twenty pound note Bart gave him as part payment for a whisky, the rest to be put towards his lunch.

The story thereafter was tragic. He believed Finn was so disturbed by the accusation he resigned from his hotel job, leaving the village, because he was wrongly accused of theft. Later Muriel found the twenty pound note at the side of the till where Finn put it. Tragically, on the day he left, he was killed when a car ran him down in the street as he hitch-hiked back to Glasgow where he came from.

The incident, was initially thought by police to be an accident due to the appalling weather conditions, but later confirmed to be deliberate. Since then Bart hadn't been able to catch Muriel Cameron on duty. After several enquiries he was dissuaded by Helen from actively seeking her out. He never understood why.

He was half way through his lunch when Helen appeared in the bar to politely ask after him and Emily. Bart thought she seemed different, less friendly, more officious, as if they were merely acquaintances who barely knew each other. Yet Helen was genuinely distressed by Finn's death having tried to stop him from leaving by offering him somewhere to stay. She felt she should have tried harder; even by delaying his departure she might have prevented his death.

She joined in much of Bart's enquiries into his 'accident', later to be re-classified as murder by the Police. Helen was also responsible for helping Finn's ex-girlfriend, Charlotte Reynolds, to escape from the Quinnell farm, particularly from Rory Quinnell and his mother Delores. Today Helen spoke to him as if they were passing strangers.

Today the most striking thing about her, he noticed, shocked him. The last time he saw her she wore a name badge showing 'Helen, Domestic Services' being her job when he first met her whilst staying at the hotel looking for somewhere to live in the Highlands. After being away from the hotel for two years, she returned and he was surprised to hear her old job was still open to her.

Now she wore a new badge declaring her to be 'Helen Daniels, Manager'. Without a backward glance Helen left him to eat his lunch. By the expression on his face Bart was exceedingly puzzled.

*   *   *   *   *

After lunch Bart arrived back at The March of Time to find Emily sitting on the stool behind the counter having served a customer he passed on his way in. She tapped her wrist after she saw his enquiring look to indicate she only sold a watch strap or a battery for one, the briskest trade they ever did. A time piece purchase was rare.

"I ate lunch at the hotel," Bart said without much enthusiasm, still ruminating on the drastic change he found in Helen. The realisation, her last name was Daniels, was something he hadn't known before. "I saw Helen," he added whilst passing through to the back room taking his coat off.

"Is she okay?" Emily followed him picking up he was far from okay himself. She stood in the doorway trying to assess his mood.

He shrugged, "I'm not sure, lass." Emily waited for the rest, watched him sit down in front of the fire, then get up again to place another log into the flames. By the way he grabbed the poker from the fire companion set on the hearth, gave the logs a few hard jabs, Emily could tell he was upset.

She came into the room to sit in the chair next to him, "What's wrong?"

For a moment he stared at her as if trying to decide what to say, "That's just it……everything is wrong." Emily sighed, patiently waiting. She knew better than to force Bart to explain himself. "Helen or rather Helen 'Daniels' is now the Manager of the hotel. The once friendly, and I will add rather timid lass we once knew, has been replaced by a very aloof, but ultimate polite professional substitute."

"Manager?" Emily picked up, ignoring the rest, "Are you sure."

"Yes, indeed!" He suddenly had the most bizarre thought concerning a film he once saw about a small town in America where women were being replaced by substitutes of their former selves becoming model wives or mothers, the title he couldn't remember. There was a sinister plot within an old fashioned men's club to provide the members with a 'better', more obliging replacement wife, with all their less attractive faults removed. Emily stared at Bart waiting patiently for him to explain. "Stepford Wives!" he yelled suddenly remembering the film title.

Emily laughed heartily, "You think Helen has been cloned?"

"No lass," he said suddenly seeing the funny side of his weird thought. "Yet she does appear very different. Possibly taken over by aliens would be a more realistic answer?" he suggested grinning.

Bart's telephone beeped an incoming message making them both jump. Emily got up to put the kettle on leaving Bart to retrieve his phone from his pocket and she heard him leave the room. After finding his glasses on the work table in the shop he read:

Can we talk? At Linn of Dee, 5 o'clock, tell no one. H

CHAPTER 7

Although surprised at the text, Bart was also intrigued as to how Helen Daniels knew his mobile number. He'd never given it to her or used the number in any of his advertisements, for The March of Time clock repairing service or the one advert he placed in the local paper launching the 'Bartholomew and Hobbs Detective Agency'. Years previously whenever he stayed at the hotel, before he moved up to the Highlands from Wainthorpe-on-sea, he was always cautious to hide his whereabouts. Certainly the main reason he discarded all his previous telephone numbers when he left his Witness Protection life behind.

He survived for a long time without having a mobile at all, remaining incognito without any means of communication and why, when Emily was looking for him, she resorted to placing cryptic messages in the classified ads of national newspapers. She needed to warn him his ex-witness protection handler Steve was asking questions about him in Wainthorpe. She always remembered his habit of buying Sunday newspapers to take to her mother's café when she helped her there on a Sunday. Helen having his mobile number was inexplicable.

He was also surprised she would still be living in the cottage along the Linn-of-Dee road given she was now the manager of the hotel. The job came with accommodation. He expected she would have moved into the manager's bungalow at the back of the hotel. Recollecting the place made Bart feel queasy, he certainly wouldn't want to live there. The bungalow was where his friend Philip Miller, the previous manager, lived and where he was brutally murdered.

Bart visited him at the bungalow a couple of times and knew from speaking to Robbie Cowan the police found the place in a terrible state the morning they were called by the unfortunate member of hotel staff who found Phil's body, beaten bloody beyond recognition. They were only able to identify him by his DNA.

Robbie didn't go into much detail about the scene, whilst interviewing Bart at the time, because he was visibly shaken by what he found. Bart heard a lot of details from the rumours circulating amongst the foreign staff, started by the first one at the scene. Bart heard Phil Miller's killer, Martin Frances, was particularly brutal in trying to extract information from him. For some reason Frances believed Phil knew where his wife Lily was living. His temper, the forensic report confirmed, got progressively worse, as did the injuries inflicted, because the unfortunate manager could only deny knowing anything.

Helen's message left Bart wondering if perhaps the hotel chain no longer used the bungalow as the Manager's living quarters. What interested Bart the most about the message especially after receiving her public show of detachment earlier in the bar, was why the subterfuge around meeting with him? Thinking about their previous contacts Bart realised he only ever spoke to Helen when there was no one around to see them together, the fact only registering with him after receiving her message. She must have been extremely careful. Why?

Mostly their meetings occurred when she came alone to the clock shop. There was one particular night when a few of his friends met to discuss Finn's death. On other occasions when he saw her at the hotel, they were quite alone, with only a couple of times, when he ate in the restaurant, he noticed she always appeared to be taking an order for drinks. On those occasions he recalled how nervous she was, looking around to see if there was anyone watching her. *Such odd behaviour,* only just registered any significance

The one occasion he went to her cottage along the Linn-of-Dee road was with Robbie when Helen appeared distressed at them finding where she lived. He remembered her saying, *'If you could find me this easily anyone could'*! Bart and Robbie were surprised to find Charlotte Reynolds with her there. Helen admitted helping her to escape from the Quinnells, firstly by hiding her at the cottage before she disappeared altogether shortly afterwards. Later Helen told him 'Charlie', as she was known when she lived with Rory Quinnell, went back to England, something Bart readily accepted without question.

Dwelling on the matter wasn't going to give him answers. Only Helen could when he met her later. Remembering that day with Robbie prompted him to look at the pictures of the 'For Sale' sign at his bungalow. He pulled them up on his mobile to check the estate agent's name – *Nelsens*. He wanted to see if they had any other telephone numbers on their website. Emily's laptop was conveniently sitting right in front of him on the work table in the shop. He sat down, raised the lid, saw she was viewing the graffiti photographs Jay took of the wall in the old Tour Bus building behind the hotel when he processed it for forensic evidence of local drug dealing.

The abandoned Tour Bus Building was where, when out walking, Bart last saw Finlay Ferguson, going through the overgrown rear garden to enter through the back door. Bart guessed he was sleeping rough there, before he left the village. He supposed Finn gave up the flat over the Co-op store he once shared with Charlotte, after she moved out to live with Rory Quinnell.

The graffiti itself, produced over many years by local school children who met in the abandoned building where drugs were sold to them, were extremely disturbing to say the least. He looked once again at the frightening images of sharp toothed monsters, faces of horror film murderers interspersed with delicate flowers and love hearts. There was one he saw declaring 'GT loves FF'. He knew Emily believed was Gina Taylor's schoolgirl crush on Finlay Ferguson when he was living with Charlotte planning their marriage.

That was one broken relationship Gina was connected to, the other he knew about, of course, being Emily and Robbie. He wondered how many more she had ties with. As far as he knew, Gina wasn't directly responsible for Charlotte leaving Finn. That was the result of Rory Quinnell's pursuit of her. Bart subsequently learnt from her it had been his mother Delores' idea to get her away from the village to run their new bakery at the Quinnell farm. She wanted Charlotte to bring her cake recipes with her to the bakery to market them as Quinnell produce.

Bart remembered Charlotte (he could never think of her as 'Charlie', that was always a boy's name to Bart) telling him about the day she first met Rory Quinnell sitting together with his mother Delores. They came into the café on Main Street where she worked, tasted all of the cakes she baked for the owner. Bart asked her if they made her an offer she couldn't refuse to run their bakery for them.

Her sad reply had been, *'He chased me, he charmed me, then he offered me the thing I always wanted, so yes, I suppose you could say I got an offer I didn't refuse'*, one she admitted to Bart she came to regret very quickly. The bakery was never hers, like Rory implied. They sold her cakes under the Quinnell label, with all the profits going into the business.

Charlotte became an unpaid member of the family, she was told with *all the benefits of being family*. She lived in a cottage with Rory on the estate, under strict control by Rory's father Rupert whose taste for young girls everyone seemed to be aware of but was largely ignored by all concerned in order to maintain a lucrative business. Bart heard how she wasn't even allowed to drive any of the estate's cars, or have one of her own. She was chaperoned wherever she went, she told him, like a prisoner being taken out for trips to the dentist under escort.

Bart looked at the graffiti on the screen again. The word 'bogeyman' jumped out at him. He guessed written by Finn before he left, possibly even the night before. When Jay took Bart to see the graffiti days later, Finn's name had been expunged using some kind of acetone after Jay took his preliminary pictures of the wall. Even so, Bart thought the bogeyman might be the person Finn was so scared of he decided to leave the area altogether, indicating to Bart perhaps being wrongly accused of stealing from the hotel bar was the least of Finn's worries.

Later, Bart found out Charlotte met Finn purely by chance one day in Aboyne when she was 'taken out' shopping by Delores Quinnell. During their brief meeting on Finn's birthday she told Bart she felt a glimmer of hope they might get back together again. She gained Finn's agreement to meet the following week but he didn't show up. Charlotte learnt later from Bart and Emily after they found her at the Quinnell farm café he was killed hitchhiking back to Glasgow.

Bart sighed deeply, having a sudden surge of sadness for the two young people he thought probably rightly belonged together, only they were parted by death. In Finn's case *the bogeyman* looked to be a reality, not only Emily told him, a name they used in movies for an assassin, like John Wick. Bart's mind filled with the graffiti images of monsters, only their victims were Finlay Ferguson and Charlotte Reynolds.

He heard Emily shout from the back room she had made some tea. He quickly closed her computer in case she saw him looking at the screen she left open. He didn't want her to think he was checking up on her. He tried not to show he was alarmed she was still looking at them. Yes, he did ask for her opinion when they were investigating Finn's hit and run, but the criminal investigation went to CID when the police evidence showed he was run down deliberately. Afterwards the case got sucked into the ever expanding remit of Operation Graffiti.

"Now there's a thing!" Bart said under his breath. He didn't voice his second thought *I wonder if the operation was named because of these graffiti images?*

Once in the backroom Bart accepted the cup of tea, fetched his own laptop from the sideboard, he sat down in his chair by the fire. He logged on. Emily heard the tinkle of the bell and disappeared into the shop whilst Bart was left alone to search for Nelsens Estate Agents only to be asked if he meant *Nelson's*. He couldn't imagine someone producing a 'For Sale' sign with the wrong spelling. Any professional reference he found to 'Nelsens' was related to planning, design or architecture. *How strange* he thought, his curiosity aroused even more after Emily's sighting of Mrs 'Ernest' with keys to Robbie's bungalow. He opted not to mention anything to Emily being unsure what it all meant.

Meanwhile he needed to find an excuse to meet with Helen Daniels at five o'clock, in itself tricky to think how he might 'tell no one.'

CHAPTER 8

"I've been asked to babysit Daisy at Pitlochry tonight," Emily said returning from the shop, "they want me to stay over because they might be late. They don't want me driving back in the dark." She sighed like the idea was a criticism of her driving skills.

Bart's reaction was to sit up attentively, "Jay was here?" he asked surprised he didn't come through to say hello. He wanted to speak to him about Robbie to see if he knew his bungalow was for sale.

At first Emily looked puzzled, deduced Bart thought the visitor to the shop must have been Jay. She pointed towards the door, "No, that was someone asking for directions to The Moor Hen," Emily laughed. "I got a text from Agatha. I called her back. They have some work thing on they weren't going to go to, then thought she might try me to see if I could babysit. Actually, she didn't sound very keen on going and apologised for it being last minute in case I had something planned." Emily laughed again, cynically this time. "Huh! Imagine me having something planned, eh?" she added her head shook in mock jest. Bart could hear the regret in her voice, he knew being abandoned by Robbie was still very raw. "It will be nice to see Daisy Amelia again, I expect she's grown since I last saw her."

She was delighted when Agatha and Jay named their daughter after her real name, Amelia, the name Bart used on the new shop sign when he took her as his partner in The March of Time. The mention of Amelia made her think about her father who Bart discovered was working for a large insurance company in Nottingham. Tom Hobbs once told her 'Amelia' was a name she would one day grow into. Thinking about him made the feeling of loss return. She made up her mind to go down to Nottingham to visit him.

Bart felt relieved she was going out to babysit, "I'm sure you will see changes in Daisy, they grow really fast," he tried to sound convincing although he knew absolutely nothing about children generally and babies in particular. "We might as well close up early today if people only want to come here in our capacity as a Tourist Information Centre," Bart said sarcastically. "I never did understand why they tucked that one away in The Mews; those sorts of places ought to be situated centrally where people can find them easily, rather than have to ask us." He sounded grumpy although inwardly pleased not to have to think up an excuse to go out to meet Helen Daniels.

Later when Emily left for Pitlochry Bart shut the shop at four o'clock as he often did in the winter. Even with the nights' drawing out the incessant rain created the same effect, making it seem much later. The village sat in a basin, surrounded by protective hills covered in fir tree often keeping the severest of gusty weather at bay. Conversely, during the snowy season they acted like a trap for the heaviest falls, taking longer to thaw. Bart was only too pleased the roads were clear of snow.

The last visit he made to Helen's cottage he was grateful having Robbie to drive because the journey was extremely precarious with the first snow of winter. At the time they had no idea where Helen lived. They were drawn by the light showing in the window behind closed curtains, whilst most of the other cottages looked deserted. Helen's cottage was confirmed when he recognised his own car she borrowed the previous day, partially tucked under a tarpaulin at the back, showing some of his number plate.

They were there because Helen used his car to drive over to the Quinnell estate to meet with Charlotte Reynolds. They wanted to find out if she knew why Finn was so afraid before he left the village, then were concerned when Helen didn't turn into work the next day, fearing she might have been seen out there by of one of the Quinnells, Rupert in particular.

In those days Helen collaborated in Bart's enquiries about Finn. The fact made her sudden aloofness seem all the more strange, she had been barely friendly. They left her out there, at the Linn-of-Dee cottage with Charlotte, to get back before being cut off by the snow. Today, of course, he knew exactly where the cottage was. He was driving his old Peugeot, the car he meant to upgrade with something more suited to bad weather conditions. Luckily the snow was keeping off.

When he reached the cottage he found it in complete darkness. Thinking Helen hadn't yet arrived home from work, he drove slowly past the entrance to the drive at the side of the cottage. He could see there was a car at the back covered completely, he assumed, in the same tarpaulin she used before. He reversed the Peugeot down the side away from the road to avoid being seen by anyone driving past. As he backed further in he became aware of a low glow of light through the half-frosted glass in the back door. There wasn't much of a show, enough to tell him the cottage must be inhabited. He got out, walked over to tap on the door.

The car ignition key sounded loud against the glass and echoed through the empty premises. Bart turned to get back in his car, surprised when he heard the key turn in the lock behind him. He looked back to see Helen, wearing jeans and a hooded winter fleece lined jacket, peering nervously through the gap. She beckoned him back opening the door wide enough for him to slip inside. The first thing Bart noticed was how cold it was inside making him shiver. The place smelt of a musty dampness showing him the place was unoccupied.

As far as he could see from the one downlight underneath a kitchen cupboard there was nothing to suggest anyone lived there; no enticing smell of cooking, not even a hint of the aroma of coffee. The last time he was here he only saw the living room with a blazing log fire, lit by cosy subdued lighting from a series of lamps dotted about the room.

He turned to Helen, "What is this place?" It was obvious no one lived here.

She pointed to the small Formica topped table with two chairs inviting him to sit, "This is a safe house," she said simply. "They only use the place temporarily, when necessary."

The words echoed those of Charlotte Reynolds when he found her there, '*Helen promised me this was a safe house where no one could find me*'. At the time he assumed she meant 'safe' from Rory Quinnell because she recently left him at the Quinnell estate and desperately hoped no one would find her. He now knew that wasn't what she meant.

This was a police 'safe house' where they hide witnesses who might be in danger or someone entering Witness Protection, like he once did. The one they took him to years ago, before they set him up with a new identity in the clock shop at Wainthorpe-on-sea, was as basic as the kitchen he was standing in. Looking around the room he could see the place contained the barest of things necessary for a temporary stay.

Bart said, "You brought Charlotte Reynolds here….."

Helen nodded, "She is a key witness for Operation Graffiti," she said simply.

"You work for Operation Graffiti?" he asked sounding shocked.

She was already shaking her head, "Not exactly."

They fell silent again with Bart trying hard to rationalise everything he ever knew about Helen who always seemed what she was meant to be, the supervisor of the domestic staff at the hotel, who went back home to her family in England for two years then returned to the same job he remembered thinking was surprisingly still open to her. "I don't suppose your name is really Helen Daniels, is it?" He realised she was operating under cover for the police. There was barely a shake of the head.

"I needed you to know why I appeared.....well perhaps a little aloof....."

"It's okay, I understand. Only, Robbie told me to keep an eye out for you," he explained. "Before he......" Bart wasn't about to admit Robbie divulged he was joining Operation Graffiti to go undercover, ".......before he left."

"I could tell you were shocked when you saw I am the manager."

"Indeed, it struck me as a little odd," Bart said. "Am I allowed to ask what happened to Muriel Cameron?" He feared perhaps something unpleasant might have occurred, given all the attempts on the lives of the people around him.

Helen thought for a moment before she admitted, "A routine move somewhere else in the chain of hotels, they do it all the time. She only got the role of acting Manager after Mr Miller died, this move was to a permanent post. They like to give their managers a wide experience in different settings, it's company policy." She spoke like she was reading an official statement from the Company's higher echelons before she added in a more caring way, "She *was* also showing signs of stress."

It was a simple explanation, probably in keeping with Muriel's experience there with the death of Philip Miller when she was Assistant Manager. Whatever else was happening there, was something to do with her nervously confessing to Bart money was going missing, although she never actually said she believed the money was being taken by Finlay Ferguson.

"Is that the reason she called the police in when she wrongly accused Finn of stealing the money I gave him?" Bart couldn't help asking. He still felt the action was extreme given the pettiness of the charge. Yes, perhaps a dismissible offence, though surprising to involve the police, when the manager could have easily dealt with the matter.

Helen shook her head, "It wasn't her who telephoned the police…..let's say no more." Helen said quietly. Bart nodded in acceptance. She obviously couldn't tell him why she was undercover at the hotel.

The only other thing Bart learnt before he left her was she was living at the hotel in what she once referred to as the Manager's room. They didn't discuss Phil Miller's bungalow or whether the hotel chain still used it after his murder. They also agreed they couldn't be seen to be as close as they were when Finn left the village; neither did they discuss anything about Robbie.

Bart was left feeling frustrated about the vacant bungalow at Tarland and why the first surveillance subject of the Bartholomew and Hobbs Detective Agency, Mrs. 'Ernest' seemed to have free run of the place. Then there was no saying Helen would know anyway.

CHAPTER 9

The hunched shape of a scruffy man huddled inside his thin hoody, slipped out of the concrete jungle of ramps leading down from the sprawling flats. Now considered an eyesore, they were years past their intended experimental creation, meant to encourage 'community' living. In the 80s they were the remedy to the segregation of people living in boxes on top of each other in high rise flats. The arrangement of walkways deliberately designed so people couldn't avoid meeting, either coming or going, enabling them to mix and talk to each other. Many years later, the consensus was they should be demolished; hence a gradual evacuation, leaving empty flats to encourage squatting and much vandalism by the bored adolescents still living there.

The man, now leaving, being one of the few remaining tenants of the occupied flats, walked briskly down the road towards the shops. The heaviest of the traffic criss-crossed where the Boulevard met the busy intersecting road; the flow only halted one way intermittently by the red stop light at the interchange. He hurried quickly across as the traffic lights changed to green entering the supermarket on the corner where he was met by a surge of heat from the automatic doors opening. In the sudden light of the shop, the man's greasy shoulder-length hair and growth of beard made him look dirtier than he actually was. It was all designed to create an image of the person he was meant to be. Daniel Roberts, out of work and down on his luck.

He didn't linger, moved swiftly gathering items placing them in the hand basket he picked up as he entered the shop – sliced bread, milk, tea bags and a six pack of cheap lager he checked out at the self-check till. Outside once again in the cold lashing rain he stopped off briefly to get himself a kebab from one of the numerous take-outs on his route back to his flat. He was a regular in many of them since he took up his new life; one he hoped he wouldn't have to endure for long.

The place was barely fit for human habitation. The seeping damp caused thick black mould on the walls above the windows creating a damp musty stench he could barely stomach. He felt living here was fitting punishment for ever thinking his bungalow in Scotland, the one he inherited from his mother on her death, was shabby. Compared to this, the bungalow was a palace, resembling a 50s home frozen in time, at least he kept it clean. Even situated in a nice area with little crime, he failed to appreciate how lucky he was to own it at such a young age.

Daniel Roberts who had only been living here a short while was still getting used to his cover 'legend'. He chose to call himself 'Robbie' a derivation of Roberts, in keeping with his real first name because it gave him something familiar to react to if someone were to call him out. Even though his given real middle name was Daniel (after his father who long ago deserted him and his mother) he never used it, because in his mother's drunken rages against 'that bastard Danny' he steered clear of ever reminding her they gave it him. Now Daniel Roberts slipped off his tongue as if he actually owned the name, essential for keeping the masquerade, whilst the nickname 'Robbie' reminded him of who he used to be.

He opened the outer door to the flat and even though he expected it, was instantly hit by the damp musty smell which always made his heart sink. An involuntary sigh escaped his mouth. He couldn't quite shake off the depression he felt since he got here. Although he was aware of his increased use of alcohol, a habit he didn't have until now, he knew about the pitfalls, given the length of time he spent watching his mother's decline. He lived with her up until the end when she died from liver disease, out of her head with the pain.

Even so, one or two beers lifted him from the starkness of his new reality and aided him in making contact with the targets he was sent to get close to, being a teetotaller wouldn't work as they operated primarily from one or two pubs in the area. He chose to emulate his *mother's alcohol dependency to serve the purpose of making him seem vulnerable, in need of work, to attract their attention. The rest was down to his appearance and his perceived desperation for money. There was nothing more appealing to the criminal mind set as the desperate.*

CHAPTER 10

Emily set off home early next day to avoid the traffic, being Saturday people were out for a weekend of sightseeing, shopping or merely collecting DIY materials for home maintenance. So she told herself as an excuse not to leave Bart in the shop on his own too long. She didn't expect the clock shop to suddenly be doing a brisk trade; it was as quiet at a weekend as it was during the week. Even so she felt an urgency to return, politely declining the invitation to spend the day with Agatha, Jay and Daisy when they offered her a guided tour of Pitlochry.

The truth was, the day before whilst she was going over the pictures of the graffiti wall in the tour bus building, she was unable to get seeing Gina Taylor's initials with Finlay Ferguson's inside the love heart out of her mind. Once again the image provoked acute anger in her. Resentment welled up fiercely like bile to her throat making her gasp for breath. She blamed the girl for losing Robbie, the only person she ever really cared about in a romantic sense. *Romance? Was it really romance between us?*

Doubt connected with resentment producing confusion, mingled with the hate she already felt for the strange girl who appeared one moment as a child, the next as an adult, alternating between the two within the blink of an eye. *Romance?* Now she would never know what there had been between her and Robbie. Emily spent the lonely babysitting night analysing, questioning and nurturing her growing hatred.

Yet she had felt close to Robbie before he left. They were beginning to spend a lot more time together especially after his suspension from police duty, the result of Gina placing her false claim of 'gross sexual misconduct' against him. Not for the first time Emily wondered if the girl used the word 'rape' in her letter. The idea Robbie would ever do such a thing went against everything she knew about him.

They became friends first because they liked each other. She was barely seventeen and he was twenty four or twenty five? She was naïve, inexperienced in everything to do with boys. He was shy and understanding with her. He confessed to Bart and Jay when the accusation against him came in, it was ridiculous, he hadn't even had physical relations with Emily beyond a kiss and a cuddle. At the time she was embarrassed hearing him tell them in front of her.

The drive back from Pitlochry was spent painfully resurrecting her resentment for Gina all over again, it began to taste acrid in her mouth. Maybe some of these thoughts were prompted by close proximity to the innocent baby, Daisy. Emily felt she might never be a mother with a beautiful child like her. She stroked the baby's delicate fingers telling herself she didn't want to be a mother anyway, too much responsibility for something as vulnerable as this.

Then another kind of bitterness came crashing in, about her mother, who thought having a child gave her the right to use them for her own selfish ends. Thelma Hobbs made her leave school when she was a promising student who might have gone on to university, wanting her to be her unpaid skivvy in her café, The Silver Teapot. Then after her father left, her mother insisted they move away to Grimsby where she was born. She still had extended family there and could open a new café venture.

Emily refused to go, deciding instead to run away from home to London where she thought Cyrus Bartholomew (*the name Bart was using then*), the clock man, might have moved to, until she finally found him living in Scotland. Now Emily was estranged from her mother who wouldn't talk to her because she hadn't visited her sister, Aunty Elsie, serving a prison sentence for murder!

By the time Emily got back to the shop all her lingering resentments combined, gained force like a geyser about to burst forth into a maelstrom of suppressed rage directed towards the person she knew ruined any chance of her ever having a normal life. *Gina Taylor.*

She sat in the mini outside The March of Time a full five minutes trying to gain back some control, to suppress the latent hate beginning to surface towards the girl who one minute appeared docile, almost sub-normal in her behaviour, then turned into an older, over-confident seductress capable of trying to kill people whilst perched on the back of a motorbike.

Gina was trouble, her mother, Anabel Taylor told her and Robbie when they went round to her house in the village to find out where Gina lived? Anabel told them, Rupert Quinnell raped her when she was still at school, with a Saturday job at his farm. The result was she gave birth to her bizarre daughter, Gina. 'Always trouble' was how she described her.

After too many fortified glasses of 'orange squash' Anabel Taylor, if she was to be believed, told them she left school early, married an older man with a son of his own. Dougie Taylor took money from Rupert Quinnell to keep his mouth shut, marry Anabel and pretend the baby she was carrying was his. In exchange he would make her withdraw the rape charges she brought against him. From police records Robbie confirmed Anabel was given a caution for 'wasting police time' and the matter became one of old record.

Emily recollected how excited she felt working closely with Robbie when they asked questions about Gina Taylor and tried to identify who the rider of the motorbike was who forced Emily off the road whilst driving Robbie's car back to Tarland. Later, Emily and Bart set a trap using Robbie's car to lure the same biker to trail them. They pulled into the Esso garage outside the village, where Emily took two videos of the biker, one with Gina after he picked her up from her job at the Co-op. In neither could they identify the rider because he wore a helmet with a tinted visor.

They already knew about Gina's step-brother, David, from Anabel. By talking to Hamish the mechanic at McKinley's Autos, Emily discovered he lived and worked as a garden centre employee out at the Quinnell Farm. It was Hamish who first revealed the rumour Gina's father was really Rupert Quinnell, a 'perv' he called him, who liked to touch young girls.

Emily treasured the time spent working together with Robbie, knew she would probably be still, if Gina hadn't brought the complaint. Robbie discovered, from receiving an anonymous phone call, Gina's false claim was a ploy by a criminal gang, to recruit his skills in flying his microlight, for their organisation. He thought probably to distribute drugs, around the country. He didn't know who called him, only guessed at Rupert, Rory or maybe even Gina's brother David.

She sighed deeply sounding much like a sob, one of many since Robbie left. She got out of her car trying to shut her mind down from the minutiae of how she lost him, took out her door key to let herself into the shop. She picked up the mail from the floor inside the door, flicked through the pile briefly to see if there was anything for her, shouting, "Helloo!" as she always did when she returned to The March of Time. She left the door unlocked turning the closed sign to open before she went through to the back where the usual smell of bacon lingered in the air. Bart was up at least.

Bart said, "Morning lass how are the Vingoe clan?"

"Very well," she said putting the mail down on Bart's table at the side of him. "Although, I think Jay didn't drive to their evening out last night. He's feeling a little bit rough this morning."

Bart laughed knowing Jay wasn't much of a drinker, briefly wondering what caused him to over-indulge, he knew there must be a reason. Emily flicked a couple of circulars away from the top of the pile of mail exposing a postcard of a kangaroo with a baby in its pouch.

"Looks like you know someone holidaying in Oz," she said walking over to the kettle. "Tea?" she asked turning to wait for an answer she could see Bart's face set in a frown, he looked troubled. She turned back to make the tea to give him some privacy. When she walked back holding two cups, she could see Bart had thrown the circulars onto the log fire and was staring as the flames devoured the paper. She observed the postcard was no longer with the other letters. He must have committed it to the flames.

"Have you got any plans for today?" Bart asked.

"I thought I might do some shopping, unless you have plans to go out or need me to stay in the shop," she said curbing her curiosity. Clearly Bart didn't want to talk about whoever sent the postcard.

"I have no plans other than my usual stroll up the road," she assumed he intended to lunch at The Moor Hen. He often did except on Sunday mornings when he went down to The Griddle Iron café on the corner after fetching a pile of Sunday newspapers from the village newsagent.

Bart stood, picked up the poker gave the logs a jab or two before he added another to the fire. Emily thought the gesture was to ensure the papers he put in the fire were nicely burnt.

CHAPTER 11

The postcard Bart received troubled and delighted him in equal measures. There was nothing written on the card except his name, address on one half and a smiley face on the other, drawn by hand in biro with no explanation, as if the sender wanted him to know they were happy. Of course, he deduced two things from it. Warren and Anna Doyle, whom he financed to leave the country to escape her father, were still living in Australia. They wanted him to know they were happy because either they were about to be or already became parents, hence the joey in the Kangaroo's pouch.

Bart immediately threw the card onto the fire not because he didn't want to be reminded of the newly married young couple he paid handsomely to take away Lily John's car, rather because later he received several unwanted visits from Anna's father, Grigoriy Novikov, a rather sinister looking wealthy Russian who was searching for her. Bart was convinced the man's sole purpose in finding her was to destroy her marriage to Warren Doyle. He learnt from Robbie Cowan Novikov registered her as a MISPER who may have been abducted. Bart, having met them, knew otherwise.

The Russian oligarch personally came calling on Bart because of his rather unpleasant private investigator, Dennis Levin (of Perun Private Investigations), the man he hired to find the couple whom he was sure reported back someone saw them with Bart. Since Bart went to great lengths to avoid being seen with them, he knew the devious private investigator was stringing his client along. He realised he needed to be careful not to reveal what he knew about the Doyles, especially where they went.

That was before Anna's father traced Lily's car back to her in Wales where she once lived as the registered owner, Lily Frances, with her husband Martin whom the Russian discovered was in prison. Novikov visited a delighted Frances who was more than happy to disrupt his wife's life in any way he could. Martin Frances refused to call Lily his 'ex-wife' or to use her maiden name Lily Johns because he still regarded her as his possession. He sent Novak (as Novikov was known in the UK) to the cottage where Lily was then living. Bart was there house sitting alone the night he called. He recognised the man's stretch limo pull up outside in the lane and was greatly perturbed he managed to trace his daughter through the car, back to Lily.

Bart didn't answer the door to him. He realised he needed to be careful not to be linked to either Lily or the Doyles, he felt sure if Novikov/Novak found the young couple somewhere in the world his intention was to take his daughter back and harm her husband, Warren. These were Bart's ruminations whilst left in the shop on his own, until he closed up at noon, to take himself off to The Moor Hen for one of Alistair's splendid Saturday lunches.

* * * * *

Emily's Saturday shopping trip took her off to Banchory for a look around the clothes shops, all of them she found rather dated. During the sleepless night before at the Vingoe's, she turned her rising hatred of Gina Taylor on herself. Her appearance, she considered to be one of the reasons for Robbie rejecting her. She recently turned eighteen, knew she looked older, blaming herself for trying to compensate for the gap in their ages. She had been much too keen to appear mature thinking she might appeal to him more.

This self-loathing she knew began when she was called by Detective Chief Inspector Stanley, the Head of Professional Standards, to answer questions about the day she met Robbie at the aerodrome to go flying. The day he was supposed to have sexually assaulted Gina Taylor. DCI Stanley appeared to be totally fixated on the issue of Emily's age, being seventeen at the time. She knew he was comparing her to Gina, the supposed 'victim', who was a year younger, implying Robbie, must have a preference for young girls. For the interview Emily tried to dress older to compensate for her age, in the hope she would be taken seriously, something she never was whilst living at home with her parents.

After the DCI and the female Sergeant accompanying him left her in the interview room Emily went to find a toilet where she sat thinking over the evidence she gave. Before she got back to the interview room she saw Gina Taylor leaving another room along the corridor. Emily was stunned seeing her there, dressed like the juvenile she often pretended to be. She was wearing a child's dress and cardigan appearing nothing like the 'tart' with red lipstick who turned up at the airport to set Robbie Cowan up for her sexual assault claim.

In Banchory whilst window shopping, images of the child/seductress passed through Emily's mind prompting her to focus on her own appearance. Her self-criticism mingled with the rage she felt for the girl, twisting in her gut until Emily no longer knew who she was or who she was meant to be.

Walking along Banchory's main row of shops she felt so overwhelmed, she wanted to scream, to let out some of the pain now consuming her. She stopped suddenly outside a hairdresser's shop, felt she was losing perspective, her vision blurred, the high street lost focus and people appeared like ghostly moving shapes. She felt so giddy her knees began to buckle. She put out her hand towards the glass window in front of her to stop herself from falling over, bending her head to rest on her outstretched arm.

She heard a faint voice asking, "Miss? Are you okay?" then felt an arm around her holding her as her legs lost feeling. "Come inside and sit down," the voice said as she was helped through the door to a seat.

An older woman's voice instructed her to, "Breathe deeply," before giving her some water to drink.

When her vision cleared, the room grew bright. She could see she was inside the hairdresser's salon, saw the sinks, mirrors and smelt the pungent aroma of ammonia. Like smelling salts, bad though they were, the smell began to clear her head.

The two females staring worriedly at her were dressed the same in black cut off chinos and T-shirts with the shop's name 'A Cut Above' embroidered across the front. Both the older woman and the young girl had dramatic wispy hairstyles, one coloured pink, and the other violet. Emily's first thought was *they must do each other's hair!*

"How are you feeling, dear?" the older one asked. Feeling embarrassed Emily tried to stand up. "No, stay still until you feel better," said the one with 'Madge' on a badge on her chest. When Emily thought of *Madge on a badge* she resisted giggling insanely

"I don't know what happened to me," she said. "I felt faint."

"Suki, get the lassie a coffee," Madge said to the junior girl who Emily thought looked barely old enough to have a job.

Suki?

Emily grinned, trying to hide her mirth with, "Thank you, you're really kind." She was left to sit, to take in her surroundings whilst 'Suki' went to make a coffee. Madge resumed attending an elderly woman with foil papers in her hair, finishing by applying something smelly with a brush to the last two strands of hair before wrapping them up with more foil papers. She kept looking over to check Emily was okay whilst she whispered to the woman as she stood behind her wrapping her hair in a cap.

'Suki' brought Emily a coffee with a wafer thin biscuit in the saucer. She sipped the hot liquid slowly, found herself looking around the salon until her gaze fixed on one of the posters on the wall, from the many hairstyles dotted about the room. The one she stared at reminded her of Lily's short white blonde pixie cut.

When Madge came back, Emily pointed at the poster, "I have a friend who looks like that."

Madge followed her gaze, "Aye, the style *is* popular. One of ma customers came in here a couple of years ago…..she got me to cut her hair the same, she looks like that…..a very pretty girl called Lily."

Emily gasped, "That's my friend's name!" Then she remembered Lily telling her about how she changed her appearance as a disguise when she ran away from her husband. Lily told her proudly she knew he would hate this change in her. Emily remembered she got her new dramatic hairstyle in Banchory.

"She had hair much like yours," Madge reminisced nodding towards the model's picture, "Took years off her," she said rather proudly.

"That's what I need!" Emily exclaimed.

"You want to look like your friend?" Madge scowled a little critically.

"Well, no," then realised she misunderstood. "Not *like* her, she looks really good though. I want to look my age because I feel like a middle-aged woman. I've just turned eighteen." *And probably look like my mother.* "Can I make an appointment? I'll need to see some hair styles because I have no idea what would suit me."

Madge wasn't one to turn away customers. Whilst Emily drank her free coffee and a second cup made by the young trainee 'Suki', she was given hairstyle magazines to look through with a lot of advice about what might suit her age and bone structure. Madge told her someone cancelled their appointment for the afternoon. If she wanted she could fit her in straight away.

Emily's afternoon of shopping for clothes changed completely because the hairstyle she chose to turn her long auburn curls into, took some time to complete. First, the natural curls were cut into the new style, a short bob on one side, with a side parting, her hair combed over to the other side to be cut into a point finishing at her collar bone. Madge introduced light blonde streaks all the way down to the point. The new cut was tamed into a straight style with heated tongues. On completion Emily looked into the mirror barely recognising herself.

Her first thought, *Robbie loved my long auburn curls,* was swiftly followed by, *tough, it's not who I am anymore!*

CHAPTER 12

The first tinge of doubt about the drastic change to her hair hit Emily as she returned to her mini in the car park behind Main Street. She recollected Bart thought her long auburn curls were something special. He told her many times, even back in the days when she was a spotty fifteen year old who hid behind her hair because she hated the way she looked. The bullying by her class mates at school only endorsed her ugliness.

Bart was the first person who made her feel normal until she eventually began to like herself. He always treated her as an equal. He encouraged her enthusiasm for clocks by giving her a Saturday job in his clock shop where he taught her how to dismantle a time piece to its basic components then to restore it to working order.

Once inside her car, she felt like she betrayed him by letting a stranger cut off her hair. She daren't look at herself in the rear view mirror above the dashboard. The guilt made her want to cry. She held onto it, allowing herself to be distracted by the loud music coming from across the car park where a small funfair was set out in the corner, consisting mostly of very young children's roundabouts.

She watched a small brightly coloured car, a bus and a fire engine moving round slowly in a circle with very small toddlers captive inside. They were grinning, shouting, or honking the rides horns. One was fretful, crying to be let out, their arms held high each time the distressed infant went past its parent standing urging them to enjoy themselves.

To one side of the moving features was a limited row of side stalls. A small coconut shy next to a ten foot high striker you hit with a mallet to ring the bell at the top to win a prize from a line of hanging stuffed toys at the side. There were older children and adults clustered around showing much enthusiasm for the throwing/hitting stalls. They all looked eager and competitive. Emily froze when she spotted the girl standing next to a tall man. She was wearing jeans, whilst he wore tight leather pants. Both wore black leather biker jackets, only his was with contrasting blue with white flashes she saw in those flashbacks she got of her near miss with death when he rode the bike at her car forcing her off the road. Each of them was holding a biker's helmet with a black tinted visor.

She knew immediately who they were, knew her name before she turned around to show her face. Even at this distance the red lipstick was visible. Gina Taylor was taunting her companion to get him to hit the base harder with the mallet. To Emily she looked to be having a good time goading him. Any self-hate Emily felt left her to be replaced by outright rage for the girl she blamed for making Robbie leave.

The man turned sideways, pushed Gina Taylor's shoulder hard enough to make her take a step backwards. His face looked familiar, yet she couldn't place him, until the memory came of the day with Bart at the Quinnell farm. He was the garden centre man being reprimanded by Rory Quinnell who Bart called 'The Country Gent' because of the green oilskin jacket he wore with a flat cap. Quinnell furiously yelled into his same face making him drop a potted plant he was transferring from his wheelbarrow to a walkway display outside the café where they were sitting watching the scene through the window.

Today his was the same stoic face as the other time when Rory's words didn't seem to bother him, except Emily could see the girl was beginning to annoy him. This time he was quick to react. The other time he showed no reaction to Rory Quinnell's violent temper. When Bart asked him about what he'd seen, he wrote the whole thing off, as looking worse than it really was. They both saw Rory punch him on the arm, which he denied, saying it was '*his way to emphasise a point*'.

Emily sat transfixed as Gina looked sheepishly away from him across the car park, brooding on his reprimand. She seemed to stare directly towards Emily, yet showed no sign of recognition. The man took a mighty swing at the plate with the mallet and Emily could hear the bell being hit by the puck as it shot upwards with force.

Emily watched the childlike girl turn, jumping with glee on the spot as the striker's attendant handed the man the largest teddy bear from the prizes. He taunted her with the bear, by moving it out of the reach of her outstretched arms. He smiled, relenting he handed the bear over to her, putting his arms around her, she nuzzled into him. The action was the same gesture Emily captured in the video she took of Gina at the Esso garage when she climbed onto the back of his bike, her arms circling him she hugged into his back. If this was Gina's 'brother' David as she believed, she could see Gina's face, no longer hidden by the biker helmet visor and knew this was not a sisterly reaction.

Gina turned her face up to him and he kissed her bright red lips as if to prove it. They walked away from the High Striker directly across the car park towards where Emily was sitting watching them in her mini. Fear rose in Emily, she really didn't want Gina to see her or worse, to try to speak to her, because she wasn't sure how she might react.

She felt choked by the mixed emotions she knew she would be unable to control especially if Gina were to either ask after Robbie or even put on her baby sub-normal voice. That would be too weird coming out of the mouth with bright red lipstick. Emily reminded herself these were the people who tried to injure (if not kill) her. Instinct told her to slip down in the driver's seat to hide.

Emily's mobile began to ring inside her handbag on the passenger seat beside her. She turned to retrieve it, the back of her head showing as she heard Gina and her brother David pass by her car laughing together. Emily answered the call from an unknown number, heard the familiar voice of Nessa McKinley say, "Hello," and then enquire how she was. "Bart says you're out shopping in Banchory today."

Surprised by the call from Nessa, Emily could only confirm it. She was distracted by looking in her rear view mirror at the Taylors a row behind her car. They climbed onto the motor bike she had become familiar with, felt her blood boil once again recalling how she hit the grass verge stopping barely short of a ditch.

Intrigued in watching them she barely registered Nessa's request for her to pop into McKinley's garage on her way home through Dinnet. Before she could think about the request, she agreed. The call finished abruptly with Nessa saying, "See you soon."

She watched the Taylors put their helmets on, before they rode away, only there was a large teddy bear trapped between the girl and the biker's back with only the bear hugging him. When she moved out of the car park up the inclined road to Main Street she caught sight of the bike turning right at the junction ahead. Emily indicated left to drive back home, relieved Gina hadn't recognised her or see she owned a car, *another target for them.*

Emily hadn't spoken to her since the day at the police station when she was there to give evidence, clearly playing the innocent 'young' half-wit child she liked to pretend to be. Once again Emily wondered if during *her* interview she accused Robbie of raping her.

Even though Robbie was cleared of the accusation by evidence from the CCTV Jay obtained from the aerodrome, together with evidence from Operation Graffiti's surveillance, both showing her accusations were lies, the police hadn't made the fact publicly known. Neither did they bring any charges against Gina for her false accusation. Instead, they passed the matter over to Operation Graffiti keeping Robbie permanently suspended from duty so as not to jeopardise their investigations.

Initially Robbie had been angry although later he told her they had their 'reasons'. He gave no explanation. After which he left her completely. Many times Emily tried to recall their last conversation, the details evaded her no matter how often or how hard she concentrated, the whole thing remained a blur. Now she discovered he put his bungalow up for sale leaving her shocked and with even more questions. The whole business was complicated by seeing Jenny Williamson let herself into the place with her own key!

Emily stopped abruptly at a red traffic light along Main Street, heard the screech of tyres behind her as she caused someone to nearly drive into the back of her car. She was so preoccupied she knew she wasn't concentrating on her driving. She held up a hand to the person behind her to apologise. *No more,* she thought, *enough is enough!*

CHAPTER 13

The Mutton Leg public house sat on a corner of a back street, one of the old dingy pubs that had seen better days. In here Daniel 'Robbie' Roberts didn't feel he stood out because the clientele appeared as down at heel as him. This was somewhere he could sit without having to spend too much money or sup too much beer, although he could pretend he was already well oiled before he got there. He had plenty of experience, set by his role model mother, to base it on.

He thought the staff serving behind the bar, as well as the landlady, looked like proper bar maids, left over from the old days, with backcombed bouffant hair styles and too much heavy mascara to highlight the blue eye shadow. Similar to those he came across in the poorer parts of Glasgow when he was new to the police in his training days. They were as hard as nails and not to be crossed; women who could hold their own in a bar fight, more likely to cut others than get gashed on a deliberately broken beer glass. He once witnessed it himself.

He sat in the corner of the public 'bar', not much different to the 'lounge', except the bar contained a regular collection of disparate losers who made their pints last as long as they could, no one was watching or cared. The moribund clientele gave the landlady a chance to slip out from behind the bar once in a while. Robbie suspected she might be supplementing her income. There was always some bloke who followed her coming back at the same time as she did. You would need to be desperate, he thought.

The landlady didn't hire young attractive females or students, she wouldn't want the competition. Robbie couldn't imagine any respectable young lass in their right mind would work in a pub like this.

He knew it was where another kind of business took place. Where underage kids of both sexes came to 'pick up' drugs or bring back the takings. Most illicit business was transacted outside in the corridor near to or inside the lavatories.

Daniel Roberts sat gloomily staring into the remains of his warm flat pint, intermittently sniffing to give the impression he was in the habit of snorting when he was more flushed with cash or rubbing his arm to indicate perhaps he had some irritation there. The whole thing was made to appear like he needed to find work to feed his habits.

He didn't move when the door swung open to admit someone new, he merely lifted his eyes to assess the newcomer. He heard much of the street dealing in the area operated from this backstreet pub, his interest lay with the dealers, not the street runners, one he hoped to become. Intermittently, he went out to the men's toilets where some of the activity took place.

When he first came to the Mutton he was approached by one of the runners who asked a lot of questions, having picked up his Scottish accent, wanted to be matey by calling him 'jock'. He grabbed the youth by his shirt collar, breathed ale fumes into his face and drunkenly assured him 'no one calls me jock' to establish he wasn't to be trifled with.

It was a gamble. Robbie was tall enough to pull it off even if the fierceness was alien to him. He thought someone tough would stand a better chance of being taken on when the time was right. Occasionally, he dropped a few more hints about his made up backstory, devised for his undercover identity. Up till now he had only been observed from afar.

CHAPTER 14

Emily pulled onto McKinley's forecourt at Dinnet puzzled by Nessa's request to call in. Nessa's last words to Emily about 'catching up' spoken outside Jock McKinley's bungalow when she was watching Jenny Williamson's house, she thought was only her being friendly. She could have done without it the way she was feeling after having her hair cut, then seeing Gina Taylor; it was certainly not a day to be sociable.

The clank of the metal door rang loudly over the music playing on Radio Northsound when Emily walked into the garage. Nessa stood with the young mechanic, Hamish in front of a car with the bonnet up, discussing the engine. Both of them in greasy overalls, with ingrained oily hands and one or two smudges to their faces where they inadvertently wiped away perspiration with dirty hands.

Nessa looked over grinning at Emily, having taken a moment to realise who she was. Hamish stood gormlessly with his mouth open, astonished by her appearance and embarrassed by his own. He felt much like the 'grease monkey' he knew he was. Emily temporarily forgot about the drastic change the new hairstyle made to her appearance, everything except Gina Taylor driven from her mind after seeing her again in Banchory. She now showed her embarrassment. A heated flush appeared across her face as she recalled the last time she saw Hamish when she deliberately played on his obvious attraction for her to extract information from him about Gina.

Emily had acted deliberately bashful, to get him to open up about the time he worked at McDougall's Garage in Aberdeen where he first saw the girl. He shocked Emily by revealing the rumour Gina was

Rupert Quinnell's daughter, the result of him raping her mother, Anabel. Hamish seemed to be trying to impress her, making it clear he fancied her. This was something she told no one especially Robbie, her boyfriend at the time.

"Wow!" Nessa said, "Incredible…..it really suits you!"

Hamish didn't or couldn't speak, his mouth remaining open. Nessa handed him a pair of plyers before she led Emily into the small office saying as she went, "Bart didnae tell me you were havin' your hair done." She closed the office door behind them offering Emily some of the filter coffee sitting on the machine as she helped herself.

Emily shook her head, caught the flick of the corner of the longest point of her hair, realising for the first time how different the new style felt. She brushed the strand of hair behind her ear self-consciously, "He doesn't know," she said with a trace of guilt.

"Oh?"

"Neither did I," Emily admitted. "Spur of the moment……and…."

Nessa sat down with her coffee. She could sense Emily was troubled, she didn't know what to say. She sipped her coffee waiting for her to finish what she started. Years of helping at an abused women's refuge taught her not to pressure anyone, allowing them to open up in their own time. Quiet reassurance gave a feeling of safety, was the most conducive requirement to encourage their recovery.

Emily fought her awkwardness for words before she said, "You've spoken to Bart?"

"Yes, I think I caught him napping after his lunch," Nessa laughed. "I might have woken him up."

"Sounds like him. He intended to go to The Moor Hen where he usually manages at least one whisky," Emily smiled wryly.

The ensuing silence became embarrassing after they both ran out of polite conversation. Nessa didn't know how to explain why she telephoned Bart when she actually rang to speak to Emily. She wanted to talk to her about Robbie even though she knew her longstanding friendship with him was always a bit of an issue for Emily. She knew Emily was bothered by her history with Robbie going back to when they were school friends, both struggling with their home lives. Robbie because he came from a dysfunctional family, deserted by his father and living with an alcoholic mother, whilst she was gay pretending he was her boyfriend to cover for not wanting her parents, especially her father Jock, to know. In more recent times, Nessa picked up the impression their past concerned Emily and Robbie hadn't denied it.

"Is he okay?" Emily asked.

Nessa having withdrawn into old memories looked puzzled. "Who?" she asked momentarily confused.

"Bart," Emily frowned.

"Oh, aye, I see," Nessa said. "To be honest I was phoning you...to see if you were okay," she added hoping she wasn't making matters worse between them.

Emily said nothing. She didn't know how to reply because she wasn't sure what she was feeling. After her resent shock about Robbie's bungalow, and the events of her day in Banchory, she felt far from *okay*. She was beginning to believe the act of having her hair cut was an indication she was far from *okay*.

Emily suddenly found herself blurting, "The day I saw you outside your Dad's bungalow, I was following someone for the Agency......" Nessa looked a little surprised if not intrigued. "She....is a woman..... led me to Robbie's bungalow, which has a For Sale sign in the front garden. The woman drove onto his drive and let herself in with a key."

The shock on Nessa's face was clear enough even before she asked, "Robbie is selling his bungalow?"

She stared at Nessa, "You didn't know?"

Nessa shook her head, "No, why would I?"

Emily stopped herself from saying, *because you are so close*, something she always believed. She expected her to know everything, "He hasn't told you?"

Nessa walked over to the coffee machine again, poured a little more into her mug, turned to ask, "Do yer want one?" This time Emily nodded.

When she brought the coffees back Nessa decided to be open with Emily, "The reason I phoned Bart, or rather you, to ask you here, was to find out about Robbie. To be honest, Emily, the last coupla times I've seen him I didnae pay him any heed. I could see he was troubled, but I was full of ma own issues wi'Lily and that damned cottage she was living in." The hold the cottage seemed to have on Lily was well known to her friends. Emily ignored being drawn into a conversation about the cottage, wanting to know more about Robbie.

"Did he tell you about Gina Taylor and being suspended from duty?" Emily asked.

"Yes, I thought it must 'ave been a mistake….Robbie wouldnae do any such thing!" Nessa's anger cheered Emily a little, hearing someone else feel the same way she did. Nessa looked anxiously at Emily, "He did tell me somebody tried to kill you!"

"Yes, they thought I was Robbie. I was driving his car and…..well that was also Gina on the bike….. I did try to warn him about her sometime before. He……." Emily's thoughts strayed to how he called her a 'silly wee girl' because he thought she was being jealous of another female she thought fancied him. Emily sighed deeply. "I think it's why he's gone away." Emily tried hard not to sound vindictive.

She spent the next few minutes updating Nessa on what she remembered Robbie telling her the last time she saw him, before he went away. The detail was flimsy, especially after he uttered the words 'I have to go away indefinitely', everything after faded because her mind shut down. Nessa sat quietly listening before she said, "You must be feelin' so abandoned." Emily burst into tears.

CHAPTER 15

Bart, having been woken up with a start from his post luncheon sleep following his visit to The Moor Hen, only partly took in the telephone call from Nessa. He felt groggy falling asleep whilst ruminating on many of the matters troubling him. The post card from Australia revived unwelcomed memories of the scary Grigoriy Novikov with his rather severe private investigator, Dennis Levin, made him feel uneasy.

His mind played leap frog from the Russian's recent visit to The March of Time, to his meeting with 'Helen Daniels' from the hotel he first stayed at in the Highlands. Bart couldn't work out why she would be installed as manager or for what purpose. He was beginning to regret missing the opportunity to speak with Muriel Cameron before she was whisked off to some other hotel managerial role. He felt sure she would have disclosed more, she did sound worried.

All these images mingled together with thoughts of Robbie's empty bungalow being for sale having such an effect on Emily, until he became quite exhausted. He let his mind shut down completely drifting off to sleep. The surprise telephone call from Nessa woke him, initially making him apprehensive, because he couldn't ever remember her phoning him directly before. His panic reaction was to think something terrible must have happened to Lily.

He was relieved when all Nessa wanted was to speak to Emily, told her she was shopping in Banchory and gave her Emily's mobile number without even asking after Lily before she hung up.

Bart couldn't settle. It was unlike him not to want to spend the day in the shop working on one of his many fob watches, purchased to restore at his leisure. He felt fractious because there was also the matter of what he ought to tell the Agency's first client, the odious Harvey Williamson, about his wife's visit to Robbie Cowan's bungalow. He felt strongly they should never have taken him on. Should he even mention it?

He was contractually obliged to report something back, his gut instinct telling him not to release that piece of information. Added to this, he was disinclined to have Emily continue following Jenny Williamson if she had some link to Robbie they couldn't explain. He decided he needed to keep this piece of information away from Harvey Williamson at least until he found out what her connection was to him.

He deliberately didn't mention to Emily he believed Robbie's new situation put him in personal danger. By informing Mr 'Ernest' his wife visited his bungalow, it might very well compromise his new undercover position. The only choice he could see was to take Emily off the case altogether, then follow Jenny Williamson himself. A previous idea of taking on some help with the agency work reoccurred to him.

After the call from Nessa he went into the shop to open up. He even got as far as the work table behind the counter, sitting in front of the many parts of the stripped down fob watch laid out there, his mind once again returned to those things puzzling him. The ticking of the clocks lulled him into a trancelike state. He barely registered when the half hour chimes began. He didn't hear the tinkle of the bell on the shop door, nor look up until the last chime stopped, saw a woman standing quite still listening to the clocks, only then did he rise to his feet to assist her.

He hadn't heard the usual, "Helloo!" because there hadn't been one. Emily did what she always did if in the shop when the chimes began. She stood perfectly still listening for any slight defect in sound amongst the clocks' mechanisms. She hadn't noticed Bart behind the counter until she turned his way, saw the absolute shock on his face when he recognised who she was. She instantly took the look as criticism of her new appearance.

"Oh, my!" Bart managed when he finally recognised Emily.

Emily's eyes were already red rimmed from crying whilst sitting with Nessa McKinley earlier. She looked about to burst into tears again.

"You hate it!" she cried in distress.

Bart grinned, "Of course not, lass. I didn't recognise you, I thought you were a customer," he said. "Is it real or are you in disguise? You were talking about getting some wigs to change your appearance only the other day."

Emily gave a pitiful half laugh, "No, my own hair. If you didn't recognise me then it wasn't surprising…." She stopped herself saying *Gina Taylor didn't earlier* because she already decided not to tell Bart she saw her with her brother David in Banchory. "Nessa McKinley didn't earlier when I called in," she lied. "Maybe I should change my hair style regularly to fool people we are watching." Her last words came out as ones of defiance. For the first time since leaving the hairdresser's salon she began to feel a little better.

"You look much younger," Bart commented before having time to wonder if he might upset her by saying it.

"Ah, good! That was the idea….it's time I looked like an eighteen year old. I was beginning to think I looked like my mother!" Bart picked up the acid tone. He said nothing. "Which reminds me…..I'm hoping to take a couple of days to go see my Dad in Nottingham soon," she said, "if you can manage without me?"

Bart felt relieved to get off the subject of her hair because he really didn't have any idea what he ought to say to her. He could see she had been crying and wondered if perhaps she was regretting doing it. He on the other hand always loved her hair preferring it to the new style he couldn't fathom with one side longer than the other, he thought was odd.

"What a splendid idea!" he boomed with relief. "Of course you must go to see Tom, I'm sure he will be delighted."

Emily frowned a little, "What about Mr 'Ernest', perhaps now isn't the right time for me to go."

Bart saw an opportunity open up in releasing Emily from the case. "Actually, not a problem," he said. "Jay was telling me last week about someone who is looking for a bit of casual work, ex-police, could be useful as an associate investigator." Emily looked instantly relieved. He would need to quickly find someone willing to work for him.

Emily took herself off into the back room. Bart heard the kettle being filled for her tea making ritual. He sat back down wondering if he dare ask her why she had been crying as well as why Nessa McKinley wanted to talk to her.

CHAPTER 16

Robbie found 'Hunters' a bit of a pretentious place. By combining a steak bar with a public house in an otherwise outdated decor that neither managed either very well, the intention was to attract a better class of customer because eating pubs were becoming all the rage. There was no doubt the place was popular, mostly attracting students from the nearby Further Education College to the bar, being packed out on a Saturday night. He doubted any of them spent money in the steak bar, which was used mainly by families wanting a cheap meal out or by business men away from home.

Robbie cleaned himself up a bit to be able to sit in the place. He washed his long hair, tidied up his growth of beard and put on clean jeans and a t-shirt. He didn't look too dissimilar to the way the students dressed although he felt old in comparison. He heard, whilst sitting nursing his pint in The Mutton, there was something significant about 'Hunters'. The name he knew from his pre-op briefing particularly in relation to the organised side of drugs locally. He knew nothing more.

Someone suggested one of the big crime families, the Bailey's, known for their extortion business, were connected to it. Up until now Robbie had failed to make any headway in getting a foot in their door. He was rapidly becoming genuinely as depressed as he was meant to be acting. Soon there would be no need to pretend at all. In fact, he was sure he was depressed already.

Now, sitting there, he thought maybe a Saturday night wasn't the right time to check the place out. It was so busy he could barely see or hear anything, the music playing far too loud to allow intimate chat. The smell of the char-grilled steaks in the restaurant along the corridor was making his hunger pangs audible, even over the current noise level.

He watched the crowd, six deep at the bar, where three very young barmaids looked hassled trying to cope with the demand.

A, good looking Indian youth with wide coal-black eyes in an innocent face, was forcing his way through the hoards trying to collect dirty glasses from tables where the lucky punters, like Robbie, managed to get seats. He heard someone complain they were served a rum and coke in a pint beer glass. The Indian youth squeezed his way through the waiting students, conveying glasses to the end of the bar where they were piling up. None of the bar staff had time to wash any.

Robbie toyed with abandoning his vigil being tempted to treat himself to a steak meal he knew would mean slipping out of character of his penniless charade. The smell of cooked meat was overwhelming his senses making him feel giddy with hunger.

He got up, leaving the pint glass, sticky with his finger prints from holding for the past two hours, with its inch of flat warm bitter. Immediately a young couple of students pushed their way into his seat to begin heavy petting. 'So much for me sitting watching' he thought as he made his way out of the bar, along the corridor to the men's toilets. Here the enticing cooking smell grew stronger the closer he got to the steak bar entrance facing him.

He pushed his way into the men's room. The smell of stale urine with an underlying hint of bleach overpowered any other aromas wafting through the door. The room was crowded with male students waiting for a chance at the urinals, all of them taken. There were three occupied cubicles with a lot of thumping on the doors by those waiting. All of the youths were worse for drink or some other kind of Saturday night indulgence.

"Get a move on!" one drunken youth yelled. "Or we'll knock the fuckin' door in!"

Robbie was beginning to regret having come in. None of the men either flushed the urinal or washed their hands, the more timid ones ignoring hygiene to get out of the place before anything kicked off.

One of the toilet doors opened revealing a red faced youth, sniffing as he wiped his nose with his fingers, his eyes bright with post coke inhalation. Robbie cynically thought he's either got really bad dandruff or spilt some down his Joy Division t-shirt. The loud drunken youth jumped the queue, forced his way past him to take the cubicle before anyone else could. A second cubicle door opened. A young student with a girl emerged. They too were red faced although not from drink or drugs. The girl took one look at the number of men waiting to use the urinals and bolted for the door before her boyfriend could say a word. He followed her out.

Robbie waited his turn, head lowered making no eye contact with anyone. He managed to relieve himself at a urinal, ran his hands under a running tap at a vacant sink as he passed, before he squeezed by many more youths coming through the door.

Once out in the corridor, the smell of cooking meat hit him again, luring him towards the restaurant door, the heady mix of char-grill with the smell of fried onions too much to fight. He pushed open the door of the restaurant, being met by the warmth, the smells and the cheery smile of an attractive girl standing with the menus made it impossible for him to turn around to leave.

"D'yer have a table somewhere for one person?" he asked her.

"Name sir?" she stood in front of the table bookings glancing down the page.

"I've nae booked," he said with a trace of a Scottish accent. "I followed ma nose wi the wonderful smells, you can call me, Billy Nomates," he grinned making the dimple in his cheek stand out. He got 'the look' he recognised in lots of women he came into contact with – she was attracted to him.

"Well, Mr Nomates we are very busy, but I think I can find you a table tucked away somewhere......you do look hungry," she said cheekily.

"Aye, I'm that alright," he said.

She led him through the noisy crowded restaurant to the farthest end of the room next to one of the doors into the kitchen. She seated him at a small table he thought they only used for leaving trays with dirty dishes on. She cleared the table before she gave him a menu, "I'll be back to set your table if you would like to see what we have on offer." She grinned.

Robbie registered the innuendo was meant to convey what they offered might also include her. Just for a moment, after his amusement faded, he felt a sharp pang of guilt at the idea pleasing him, when he thought about Emily back in Scotland.

The girl returned with a place setting to make the table up. "Would you like something to drink?"

Robbie was tempted to order himself some more beer or even wine. He knew he needed to stay alert, as near to character as he could although he didn't know what he was looking for by coming into the place; at least not then. Robbie went straight for a medium rare rump steak, chips, onion rings with peas, garnished with the token small salad you always got which he thought would, nine times out of ten, be scraped off the plates after the customers left. He was so hungry he could have eaten the plate!

CHAPTER 17

Bart placed the ad for a shop assistant on a card in the Pharmacy's external advertising cabinet because he wanted to get someone who lived locally. The shop was predominantly a pharmacy selling toiletry items, a combination of newspapers with a strange mix of greetings cards, gifts, toys and random household cleaning products. Located centrally, the Pharmacy was used by the majority of village residents and visitors alike. He deliberately kept the ad simple: '*The March of Time requires a part time shop assistant, apply at the shop or telephone*', giving only the shop's telephone number.

He made no specified requirements for age or experience. He knew working in a clock shop wouldn't suit everyone. Most people would be unable to spend any length of time surrounded by the sound of a large number of ticking clocks. He observed many potential customers run out of the shop when the chimes began on the hour, quarter past, the half hour or quarter to the hour. The test for him was to observe the applicant's reaction when they did. Once he placed the advertisement he promptly forgot about it.

Bart returned around half past four the following Monday having spent the day observing Mrs. 'Ernest' out at Tarland. Emily, having gone off for the weekend to visit her father in Nottingham, telephoned to say she was going to stay an extra day. She didn't explain why and Bart didn't ask, after all they hadn't seen each other for a couple of years. He presumed they would have a lot to talk about. He expressed no disappointment with her absence. He felt it would be unfair even though he would have to take over watching Jenny Williamson on Monday. As he expected, the surveillance turned out to be very tedious like in his previous agency when he worked alone.

At least he experienced no surprises or another visit to Robbie's bungalow. She remained at home apart from taking and fetching her children from school. If she hadn't made the one diversion to Robbie's bungalow, Bart would have terminated Harvey Williamson's contract, telling him there was nothing to substantiate his suspicion of infidelity. Bart always felt a scrupulous need to be honest. Unlike the sullen Dennis Levin who he suspected used Bart as an excuse to deliberately extend his visit to Scotland on the pretext of looking for the Doyles, thereby milking his contract with Grigoriy Novikov for financial reasons. To Levin a wealthy client meant rich pickings.

Bart on the other hand would not want to take Harvey Williamson's money unnecessarily. However, he decided not to finish with the job yet because he needed to find out why Jenny Williamson was in possession of a key to the bungalow and what connection she may have with Robbie Cowan, not one of infidelity he was certain.

Bart arrived home feeling weary, a little stiff from sitting all day in his car. All he wanted was a cup of tea with something to eat because he had been ill prepared, unlike the old days, he took nothing to eat or drink with him. He wouldn't let it happen again. He closed the shop leaving the lights off before going through to the back room where he immediately flicked the kettle on.

Bart's land line sat on the sideboard where he could see the message light flashing when he glanced over to check. He deliberately didn't install the land line in the shop because of the background noise from the clocks, especially when in full chorus, would make it impossible for him to hold a conversation should anyone telephone. Of course he wouldn't have been able to hear the ringing if he was in the back room, if the phone was in the shop.

Part of his deliberations around its siting raised the issue of whether he ought to have one at all. At the time he was 'on the run', didn't even have a mobile. He didn't trust even a pay-as-you-go (what Emily dramatically called 'a burner phone') to enable people to track him down.

He eventually got one after meeting Lily Johns, Beth Grant as she went by then, when he discovered her husband was looking for her. Yet another Private Investigator called at his shop asking Bart if he knew her. He realised she was in some kind of trouble buying them both a mobile to keep in touch with her when she lived in the middle of nowhere, at Balmoral Cottage near Crathie, cut off for days during heavy snows.

He walked over to the side board, pressed the play button before he set about lighting the log fire he laid in the grate before he left for his day's surveillance. The tinny voice of the answer machine announced there were three messages. The first message was a female voice with a pleasantly deep Scottish accent explaining she saw his advertisement at the Pharmacy and was interested in part time employment as she lived locally.

At first he was surprised having forgotten about placing the ad. He felt deeply tired after his surveillance and wondered if he was getting too old for the work. Maybe he needed to sub-contract out the surveillance. However, on first hearing her voice he assessed she sounded mature enough for the kind of person he was looking for. He would contact her later.

The second call was one of the many nuisance calls he got, another reason he considered not having a land line. Typically this one was someone trying to update an insurance policy he didn't have. He deleted it.

The third call, a young female voice, began to leave a message about wanting a shop job in the village. She was interrupted abruptly after he heard a stern male voice yell "No!" followed by noises suggestive of someone snatching the phone away. The call terminated, which Bart found extremely odd.

He left the phone when he heard the kettle click off because he desperately needed food. He set about making a bacon sandwich, his second of the day, being all he could manage to make. He ate quickly, sitting for a while contemplating how he might find out Jenny Williamson's involvement with Robbie Cowan.

He hadn't made much progress with the conundrum before his mobile phone began to ring, saw Jay was returning his message to the call he made earlier whilst in his car out at Tarland, to enquire if he or Agatha knew of anyone who might be suitable as an additional investigator for the Agency.

Jay said, "Are you able to talk?"

Bart smiled because earlier he spoke quietly to Jay in case any passers-by were attracted to his presence. He saw Jock McKinley leave his bungalow where he was parked dreading he might recognise him. Bart thought him a totally disagreeable man.

"Yes, my friend, I'm back at the shop," Bart said. "I'm sorry about before, I was trying not to draw attention to myself!" He guffawed at how strange he must have sounded.

"I see," Jay said. "I did wonder. Anyway, about what you asked me...I've spoken to Agatha, she believes there maybe someone suitable who recently left the force on medical grounds," Jay lowered his voice. Bart could hear people talking in the background and assumed he was still at work. He heard footsteps as Jay moved through a door before he spoke again. "Sorry," it was his turn to laugh. "I didn't want anyone to hear our conversation." *Touché* Bart thought. "We wanted to know if you have a preference for a man or woman?"

The question threw Bart momentarily. He hadn't given any thought to gender. He suddenly felt lost for words, "Well...I hadn't really considered. The job I'm on at the moment was one Emily was doing anyway. I suppose.....I haven't got a preference ..... why?"

"Agatha says the police officer she has in mind is female, was a really good cop until she suffered a terrible accident whilst on duty attending a multi-pileup. She was parked on the motorway....well her police car was hit by a speeding articulated lorry.....she was badly injured....." Jay was suddenly aware he wasn't selling the person very well. "I know it sounds bad, but she would be able to perform certain police duties although not all the heavy physical stuff, which is why she's taking early retirement."

"I see," Bart said thinking about how inactive he was all day watching Mrs 'Ernest' picking her children up from school. "There's a great deal of inactivity in our work, surveillance is about producing reports after watching people. I'm afraid it's the boring end of being a private investigator."

"Perhaps Agatha could speak with her on your behalf....she hasn't yet for obvious reasons. If you think the idea is worth thinking about," Jay said.

"Yes, I'd like to meet her if Agatha could arrange something and she might be interested in our kind of work," Bart wondered how badly injured she was and what it might mean to the agency. The thought also made him think about insurance if he was going to take on extra people. The idea of insurance reminded him about Emily who was away in Nottingham visiting with her father, the Insurance man. *Now there's a good contact to have.*

CHAPTER 18

The young woman, whose name on her badge was Kirstie, brought his meal. The plate was huge. Robbie wondered if his shrinking stomach would be able to cope. She told him she thought he looked like he needed a good feed, winked, hinting he might have been given 'extras', what McDonalds called 'supersizing', although he'd never tried it. He hadn't ever eaten as much rubbish as he did now. Junk food was cheap and he needed to keep in character as someone down on their luck; he was taking a risk just coming into the steak bar.

"Thank you," he said. "I'll try to do ma best."

He was tempted to dive in at speed to quell his hunger, which might draw attention. He took his time applying condiments whilst he looked around at the other tables.

Where he sat he was partitioned off from a large table behind him in the corner. As he walked over he noticed the group of men eating together. The tables in his view were a mixture of families or couples. He looked to be the only person eating alone.

He spotted a middle aged man sitting with a young woman. By the fashionable style of her hair she could be a girl, he couldn't see her face to able to tell. By the way the man smiled at her he was showing great affection. Robbie tried not to think uncharitable thoughts about their relationship or stare too much their way.

An angry voice from behind him drew back his attention. He could hear strong admonishments as someone viciously laid into one of the others sitting there. The voice was old, shrill and lacking control. He could tell by the occasional word he picked up one of the men failed to do something for which he was being given an ultimatum. The voice sharply insisted, "You do it!" the 'or else' was an implied threat.

This was followed by a second voice Robbie judged to be the person being reprimanded, pleading to be given another chance to rectify his mistake. He kept saying, "I will, I'll do it, boss!"

Kirstie appeared moving under the weight of a large tray of meals. She walked past Robbie to the table behind him and he couldn't help thinking if he wasn't sitting where he was she would have placed the tray down on his table to take the plates individually to the men behind him.

He heard the admonisher's voice again a little softer say, "Ah, Kirstie my dear! What a star!" The voice sounded broken as if it belonged to someone who was a lifelong smoker, dry and damaged.

Robbie decided he didn't much care for whoever the voice belonged to. He wanted to take a peak to see if his impression of the person as an elderly man was correct, but daren't risk prying. He slowly began to eat his meal.

He heard the same voice lecherously say, "You are lovely, girlie," he made Robbie squirm. He heard the other men laugh knowingly. Turning sideways across the restaurant he caught a reflection of the people behind him in a glass partition. He could see Kirstie handing out the plates, caught sight of the hand of a small wizened looking man in a camel coat slide across Kirstie's rear to squeeze her bottom.

He watched Kirstie rotate her hips to shake off his hand to get away. She walked around the other side of the table with the last plate of food, placed it in front of a man wearing a shiny blue suit, black shirt and sunglasses. His dark hair combed back from his forehead gave him the finishing touches for an Italian Mafia gangster. Robbie was transfixed by the gathering.

The small man in the camel coat held up a glass to make a toast. He could hear his husky cracked voice, "To an otherwise successful week!" The rest of the men each held up a glass to join him giving Kirstie the opportunity to slip away. She hurried past him with the empty tray, didn't speak or look Robbie's way. He could see she was clearly distressed.

Robbie went back to eating his food whilst the table behind him grew quiet as their reflection indicated, their attention was fixed on their meals. Kirstie came back out of the kitchen, walked over to the man with the young woman to place a small tray with a receipt down on their table. When Kirstie turned to walk back towards him Robbie could tell she had been crying by the redness of her eyes.

When she got close he whispered, "Are you okay?" She shook her head and he asked, "Who is he?" he nodded behind him.

Kirstie whispered, "His name is Bailey….he's…" She suddenly looked scared, thought better of continuing. She looked like she was about to bolt back into the kitchen.

Robbie reached out his hand taking hers to stop her and as he looked up he caught sight of the man with the young woman stand up to leave. When the girl turned round she looked directly over at Robbie who caught a glimpse of her face which made him gasp. She looked exactly like Emily, yet somehow younger because her hair was different, a more modern cut. The girl's mouth opened on seeing him. Robbie was aware he was holding Kirstie's hand, looked at them before he pulled his own back.

Kirstie whispered, "Do you know him?" She could see shock on Robbie's face and assumed the name meant something to him. When he looked back across the restaurant the man with the girl, who looked like Emily, was moving towards the door where he held it open for her. As she passed through she turned again to stare at Robbie who was still looking at her. The next moment the door swung closed.

Robbie was aware Kirstie was waiting for an answer. "No, who is he?"

Before she could say any more they both heard the man called Bailey yell, "Kirstie!" Nervously she moved off to his table in response to his summons.

Bailey ordered more drinks and a couple of the others ordered desserts. Robbie found he couldn't eat any more of his meal having lost his appetite. He sat quietly thinking over what just happened.

Firstly, he realised he finally found the man he was there to make contact with and infiltrate his organised gang. He could tell by Kirstie's reaction she was frightened of him. He needed to get out of there as quickly as he could in case the man saw him eating a large meal he wasn't supposed to be able to afford. Robbie took money out of his pocket to cover the bill, putting it down on the table whilst Kirstie was occupied. He left as swiftly as he could.

The other thing which alarmed him more was seeing the girl who looked like Emily eating in a place miles away from Scotland where he left her. Was it a coincidence she seemed to recognise him, or was the look one any girl might give a man who was staring at her?

He hurried outside feeling the need for fresh air to clear his head. The one pint of beer he drank in the bar shouldn't have made him feel lightheaded. He consumed more alcohol every day without any side effects. He put it down to the lack of food inside him.

Walking briskly down the street to the corner, Robbie crossed over the intersecting roads, turning onto the Boulevard leading back to his depressing flat. He held his head down against the slanting rain lashing against him. He hated this town. He wanted desperately to be back up north again because he regretted his decision to join Operation Graffiti, More recently he began thinking they sent him here out of the way because of his threat to bring civil action against Gina Taylor.

In the distance he could see two people huddled under an umbrella walking briskly to get out of the rain. As he got nearer he recognised the couple from the steak bar. He slowed his pace following them along the Boulevard, watched them turn the corner into a road ahead of him.

He stopped on the corner leaning against the wall of a large building set back in its own grounds, saw them stop at the second house up on the right. The young girl turned to close the gate behind her. Robbie saw by the street light this wasn't an illusion brought on by his increasing feeling of homesickness. The girl held an uncanny resemblance to Emily even with the short hair flecked with blonde highlights on one side. He also thought she looked troubled.

CHAPTER 19

Bart was too tired the night before to do anything about his calls other than make a note of Isla Strachan's details from the answer machine. He took himself off to bed knowing he would have to be out early to cover Mrs 'Ernest' again. The second day turned out much the same as the previous one. Bart couldn't help thinking Harvey Williamson was lucky to have such a dedicated wife. He began to question why 'Ernest' was so sure she was cheating on him.

Later when he telephoned Isla Strachan she sounded very keen and was prepared to come into The March of Time whenever suited him. His initial impression of her speaking on the phone was she seemed like the sort of mature person he was looking for, her pleasingly soft cultured Scottish accent appealed to him. He had been wrong before about making an assessment from a telephone conversation, the deciding factor would be her reaction to his clocks. He told her he was tied up the next few days because his partner was away and they would both like to meet her.

Bart was relieved when his second day watching Jenny Williamson went without a hitch. He finished early again, grateful schools closed when they did. In keeping with his bad habits, he decided he would go up to the Hungry Traveller later to get himself a chippy supper to compensate for being unable to go to the Moor Hen for lunch two days running. Alistair he thought would be missing him.

He was logging onto his lap top to enter his two days surveillance on the 'Ernest' file when he heard the bell in the shop, annoyed with himself for forgetting to lock the door when he came back. Clearly, the closed sign was ignored. He walked through prepared for the sale of some trifling item. He stopped abruptly when he saw the girl who made his hackles rise.

He only knew Gina Taylor from her serving him at the Co-op store on Main Street. The only other time he chanced to observe her was one time when Emily met her to find out what she knew about Finlay Ferguson sleeping rough in the Tour Bus Building. He watched her talking with Emily outside from his vantage point through The Tea Room window where he was sitting waiting for Emily to join him. He remembered being disturbed by Gina wearing bright red lipstick, it didn't look right for someone who appeared to be a little girl. Here she was again wearing the same shade of lipstick, this time dressed in older clothes. He thought the lipstick looked contrived.

As he watched her, she moved around the shop, peering at the clocks, occasionally poking one of the cuckoo clock's doors at the apex above the face where the bird would shoot out when the time was right. He was immediately reminded of someone else. A young Detective Constable did the same thing to his clocks back in his days in Wainthorpe-on-sea. He too provoked Bart's irritation as the girl was doing here. If there was one thing guaranteed to rile Bart Bridges, it was someone casually touching his clocks.

"Can I help you?" Bart's voice boomed across the shop. He hoped he didn't sound too angry.

The girl spun round at the sound of his voice, a false beaming smile springing readily to her face as if switch on mechanically. "They are sooo cool!" she gushed. Her voice held a hint of the one he heard many times in the Co-op when she put on her innocent child persona. Right now the voice clashed with the way she was dressed, being made up to look older.

The voice prompted him to recall the third message left on the answer phone the night before. This was the young girl who was abruptly cut off by someone she was with, when she telephoned to enquire about the job advertisement.

He ignored her comment asking again, "How can I help you?"

"I saw your card at the chemists, you want an assistant?" She smiled, swayed a bit where she stood and for the first time Bart did wonder if she might, like Emily confessed to thinking, be a little emotionally immature.

"Haven't I seen you working at the Co-op?" Bart asked to try to mute the shock at the brazen way she felt able to come into his shop, surely she must know Emily lived here after all her name was written for anyone to see above the door – **Proprietors: Bart Bridges and Amelia Hobbs**. When his shop sign flashed in his mind he thought *maybe she doesn't associate Emily with Amelia!*

He saw the juvenile guise drain from the girl's face to be immediately replaced by the other persona Emily and Robbie spoke about, on the day she appeared at the aerodrome to try to frame Robbie for sexually assaulting her - older, confident, with total disregard for Emily's feelings. Bart reminded himself she also rode pillion on the motorbike that forced Emily off the road resulting in nearly crashing Robbie's car.

He closed his eyes momentarily to keep control of his temper and as if his beloved clocks were trying to come to his rescue, they all clicked over in unison to the five o'clock chimes. Predictably, the routine prohibited any further conversation until the sequence completed its cycle.

Gina Taylor responded to the commotion by spinning around to face the wall where the cuckoo clocks hung side by side showing a measure of eager excitement on her face. Anticipation at what they both knew was about to happen when the sequence reached its climax and all the birds appeared for the count of five o'clock. She seemed enraptured, her hands grasped together like a small child might at the expectation of seeing Santa Clause or a flying snowman. The birds shot out, as near as possible together. Gina danced on the spot with glee.

This girl is crazy! echoed in Bart's head.

Bart waited until the last one finished. He observed her behaviour, wondering how someone so childlike could also be capable of all those other things he knew about her and then dare to come into his shop asking for a job.

She spun back to face him, "That...was...awesome!" she cried breathlessly. "I could really work here!"

"Wouldn't they miss you at the Co-op?" Bart asked to prompt some response to the question he already asked her.

As if on cue, the question made her face change again, quickly turning full of anger, "I don't work there anymore," she hissed.

"Oh, didn't you like it?" he asked gently trying to ease her back with a more friendly approach as much to curb his own anger at the girl as to elicit an answer.

"Yes, of course I did!" she snapped irritably. "Everybody uses the Co-op, it's a good place to get to know people. I like doing that."

Strange answer Bart thought.

She began with a frown before turning away as if she was making some attempt to control the fury she clearly felt inside. She continued her inspection of the clocks by walking over to stand in front of the line of grandfather clocks. She looked up at the first, stepped sideways to the next, then the next until she completed viewing the row like she was inspecting a line of soldiers standing to attention on parade.

She spun round again towards Bart. He could see she was more composed, "Are these clocks valuable?" she asked flipping back into her immature identity.

"Well, reasonably," Bart said currently fascinated by the girl. He realised a psychologist would have a real challenge with her.

"What about the job?" she asked.

"Ah, I already have someone in mind.....sorry," he said. "Apart from which, I'm afraid we get very few people in here, unlike the Co-op, I imagine is very busy."

She stopped, pursed her lips, whilst narrowing her eyes before she asked, "If you don't get many people in here, why do you need an assistant?" She looked at him searchingly as if she didn't believe what he was saying and was trying to catch him out. The stare disturbed Bart immensely. He was instantly reminded of a man he once knew. Damien Nance, who called himself an 'Arrangement Consultant', hired by Toni Maola from time to time to 'retire' people he needed out of the way. A hired killer.

The memory was not about the 'service' he offered, more the fact Damien Nance was a pure psychopath. Bart knew a lot about their characteristics. Nance could appear very charming, as psychopaths often do. Bart was aware of the whole spectrum of psychopathic traits, a lot of them Gina also exhibited. He could reel them off against the few things he already knew about her.

He knew she was deceitful and already assessed she was fearless being bold enough to come into the shop to ask for a job. She clearly lacked any remorse or empathy, for what she did to Emily on the road to Tarland. However, the one trait he applied the most to Gina Taylor was 'shallow affect' because she showed little emotion about the situations other people would naturally do.

When Emily told Bart how the girl at the Co-op always asked after Robbie or talked about him enthusiastically with total disregard for Emily's feelings as his girlfriend, all his senses were sent jangling. Close up he could see for himself how she changed from one character to another. He knew she was much more than a psychopathic. She had a split personality disorder. Who knew how many distinct identities she possessed?

He warned himself to be careful how he spoke to her, "However, I can see you have a love of clocks, which I admire greatly. I would like to keep you in mind should I need someone in the future. There is no saying the person I've given the job to will be suited to working here," Bart looked around at his ticking treasures. "It is not always a comfortable place for everyone. Perhaps you could leave your name with your contact details?"

He watched for a reaction wondering which of her identities would respond to the invitation. He braced himself for her reaction.

"O...kay," she said after a pause, drawing the word out. She moved over to the shop counter, picked up a pen lying there, took the pad of paper at the side to write her name and mobile number. Bart watched adding, "I take it you live in the village, so your address would be helpful."

There was another longer pause before she again committed pen to paper, this time she exaggeratedly wrote an address all the while staring at him, not at what she was writing. "I live with my mother," she lied as if she believed it. Bart knew Emily and Robbie went to see Anabel Taylor establishing Gina did not live with her. "You can always leave a message with her if I'm not there." She threw the pen lightly against the counter, turned abruptly leaving the shop.

Bart moved to lock the door behind her. He watched, from the window in the door, her skipping like a small child down The Brae, across the turning circle up towards Main Street, her arms moving together in perfect rhythmic circles as if she held a skipping rope in her hands. *Good Heavens!* Bart thought.

CHAPTER 20

After watching the girl disappear with the man into the large two storey house, Robbie turned back, retracing his steps along the Boulevard. He suddenly felt guilty for abandoning Kirstie to Sid Bailey, the man he knew to be the biggest criminal in the area. Before he went undercover he was primed about the Bailey family, so knew Sidney Bailey headed the extortion side of the family business whilst Charlie Bailey led the drugs empire. He was warned both brothers were violent and to specifically watch out for Sid, who of the two brothers was the most unstable, or 'bat shit crazy' as someone called him. By the rant he heard from behind him earlier, he determined the little weasel in the 'Arthur Daley' camel coat must be Sid as confirmed by Kirstie.

Only part of his decision to hurry back was his concern for Kirstie's wellbeing. She clearly knew things about the Baileys and with a little bit of encouragement might part with some useful information to help speed up his undercover mission to establish how they connected with the people Operation Graffiti were targeting. As far as Robbie was concerned, the sooner it was over the better, then he could return up north. He desperately missed his old life.

Robbie approached Hunters with caution. He didn't want Kirstie to draw attention to him because from what he saw, Sid Bailey had designs on her. The last thing he needed was for Sid to see him as a rival which would defeat his objective of getting into the Bailey Empire. Consequently, when he reached Hunters he didn't go back inside. Instead, he loitered around outside in the car park, semi-hidden behind a smart 4x4, to wait either for Bailey et al to leave, or Kirstie to finish her shift. He hoped she wouldn't give in to him. He dreaded having to see her leave with them.

He was cold and wet by the time the place began to close. The steak restaurant was the first to close. He saw the neon sign advertising the restaurant go off. The bar he could hear by the noise was still serving. He spotted Kirstie leaving by a side door close to where he was hiding. She walked through the few vehicles left parked or abandoned for the night by the drink/drive conscious people who had one too many. He waited a few minutes to see if anyone followed her out before he moved off to catch her up. She too walked in the direction of the Boulevard having got out an umbrella from her shoulder bag to shelter under.

When he got close he spoke quietly from behind, "Psst, Kirstie!" *he whispered. She swivelled round looking afraid until she recognised him, stopping to let him catch up.*

"Ah, the disappearing Mr. Nomates?" *she said,* "Or can I call you Billy?"

Robbie laughed. He was rather taken by her, particularly enjoying the girl's sense of humour. "Billy is fine," *he said. Then he turned a little serious,* "Sorry I left like that, I got a phone call I needed ta deal with," *he lied.* "I was a wee bit concerned about leaving you with the dude on the next table, what did you say his name was?"

They continued walking along the Boulevard, getting closer to where he'd been minutes before. Robbie began to wonder where Kirstie might be heading.

"Sid Bailey," *she said her eyes went wide with contempt.*

"Thought he looked a bit overly friendly wi'yer," *Robbie didn't want to imply she in any way encouraged him. He could tell even by viewing the reflection in the glass her actions were to avoid his roaming hands. He watched Kirstie shiver with disgust.*

"The reason I left by the back way, he's still inside. Him and his cronies hang out in the little room off the bar, they'll be staying behind for lock-in drinks with the Manager," *she said, then coughed as if there was much more she could say on the subject.*

"Was he trying it on wi'yer?"

Kirstie nodded, "Not for the first time! Those young barmaids won't escape either. He once pulled out a fat roll of bank notes with an elastic band round from his pocket, flicked his thumb nail over the edge whilst asking me if I wanted to go for a curry after work."

Robbie looked shocked, "Isnae old enough to be yer father?" he said sounding disgusted.

"Probably grandfather," Kirstie gave a weak smile.

"What did you say to him?" Robbie thought perhaps if what he heard about Sid Bailey was true, he wouldn't take too kindly to anyone refusing him. He remembered at his briefing on the Baileys they were a family who used 'motorway construction' cement to rid themselves of anyone who got in their way or displeased them.

"I told him my boyfriend was picking me up after my shift," she said.

"Is Bailey a regular in the steak bar."

"Yes. He expects the same table to be available for them whenever they come in. I've had to reseat people to allow him to sit there more than once. Wouldn't be so bad if he actually paid....." she could see Robbie was shocked, prompting her to shut up before she said too much. Robbie wanted to ask how he got away with it but stored the question to ask later.

"Do you live round here?" he suddenly asked because he thought he might continue the conversation somewhere warm out of the rain which was coming down heavily as they walked along.

Robbie could see they were approaching the side street where the man with the 'Emily' lookalike entered the second house up. Kirstie pointed to the same road as they approached, "Yes, up off here, do you fancy a coffee, you left before you could have one?"

Robbie nodded, "Aye," hooked his arm through hers to get close enough to shelter under the umbrella even though he was already totally drenched.

They began to walk up the hill, grateful they were moving past the second house, even though he couldn't resist looking upwards to where there was a light showing on the second floor. A thought of Emily drifted through his mind. He pushed her image away. Perhaps he was missing her so much he wanted the girl to be her because of the resemblance. He thought he saw a movement briefly in the darkened window to the left of the lit one, turned away to carry on up the hill with Kirstie.

CHAPTER 21

By the time Emily returned from Nottingham, Bart had a lot to update her on so he failed to notice she appeared unusually quiet. His priorities were to get someone to work in the shop and for them to meet with the ex-police officer Agatha Vingoe recommended as a suitable part-time investigator. To Bart, Emily didn't seem very enthusiastic about either of the ideas, even though she assured him otherwise by congratulating him on moving things along while she was away. Apart from Bart's initial enquiry after her father's health, Emily didn't mention anything about her visit. He felt reluctant to pry although he did wonder if she had a difficult visit with her father.

Isla Strachan, to Bart's delight, was entirely what he hoped for. She was a middle aged woman with a personality he found very pleasant. He was rather taken with her. As to his fears about her potentially working in a noisy clock shop they were soon quelled when they met her.

Isla revealed she liked the sound of a ticking clock because she found them soothing. The other thing she mentioned was her hearing loss, being able to actually hear one was a bonus. She laughed as if she made a joke. Bart, whose own hearing was a problem could only sympathise.

Isla Strachan looked delightedly around her at the array of time pieces on display. Bart was conducting her 'interview' in the shop to test her response to the noise. As an actual test, he deliberately arranged their meeting for eleven forty five to observe her reaction to the noon day chimes, being the longest chorus of the day.

Isla remained smiling during the interval. She seemed to welcome the noise although Bart knew there was a difference between hearing them once to spending the entire day with their incessant repetition.

When all went quiet he confided, "Of course, that is always a good moment to go into the back to make yourself a drink, unless there is a customer in the shop." He felt obliged to point out there were often times during the chiming when customers literally bolted for the door. Years ago he saw a man run off with a rather nice fob watch he was considering buying. He never came back, he told her, so there was a need to be attentive.

Isla Strachan welcomed everything Bart told her, didn't seem at all fazed when he raised the issue of the Bartholomew and Hobbs Detective Agency, which he explained, was also run from The March of Time premises. When he asked how she felt about taking the occasional telephone message for the Agency she assured him she had no problem or with the need for maintaining confidentiality around client information which he emphasised. She even looked excited about the double role or anything else the Agency needed she was only too willing to oblige. After a discreet nod of approval from Emily, Isla was offered the job and went away looking happy at the prospect.

The issue of confidentiality reminded Bart about the visit from Gina Taylor he hadn't mentioned to Emily since her return, mainly because he couldn't predict what her reaction would be. Nevertheless, he knew he must tell her.

"A good time to close for lunch," Bart said walking over to put the 'closed' sign up. As he was locking the door he caught sight of Isla Strachan walking briskly up Main Street and found himself admiring their choice. He thought she was a fine figure of a woman.

When he turned round Emily was smiling. "I can tell you like her?" she teased.

Bart felt himself blush, becoming slightly flustered, "She is what our shop needs!" he said rather sternly, surprised by his own reaction to Emily teasing him. Normally she would make him laugh robustly if she implied any kind of a romance on his part. Emily coughed moving off into the back room having hit a particularly raw nerve.

Bart found her making tea. He hoped his sharpness hadn't upset her because he knew what he was about to tell her about Gina Taylor would. They sat in front of the fire drinking tea with the 'parkin' ginger cake Emily brought back from Nottingham while Bart described his visit from Gina wanting the shop assistant job. He could see immediately Emily was angry.

Bart asked, "Am I right in thinking during the conversations you've had with her at no time did you tell her you lived or worked here, otherwise her visit would be even more bizarre than I actually found it?"

Emily searched her memory of their encounters before shaking her head slowly, "No, I told her very little about myself. She isn't the sort of person who is interested in anyone else – apart from her fixations on older men…." Bart could hear how bitter Emily sounded.

"Or I expect unless a person is of use to her or the people who influence her," Bart added. Emily nodded agreement. He deliberately used 'influence' instead of 'control', because he felt the strange telephone call when the receiver was snatched by someone, could be a significant factor.

After some thought Emily responded, "I may have mentioned living at Crathie with a friend. I certainly didn't say who. I think she did once ask me if I lived with Robbie or as she put it, 'that dishy copper'!" There seemed to Bart to be a slight sneer to her words. After a short silence she added, "My name is up over the door, surely she must know."

"Presumably she only knows you as Emily, not Amelia, possibly not even your last name?"

"Ah, yes. She's not very bright, I think she's probably even forgotten the Emily," Emily said. "I wonder why she stopped working at the Co-op? Can't say I'm not delighted because I can go back in there without fear of meeting her. I'll see what I can find out tomorrow."

They spoke no more about Gina, discussing briefly the upcoming meeting with Michelle McElrae, the ex-police officer recommended by Agatha.

*   *   *   *   *

Next day Emily drove to Tarland to continue watching Mrs 'Ernest', whilst a relieved Bart was left alone in the shop. She told him she would pick up some shopping on her way home from the Co-op to make discreet enquiries about why Gina Taylor no long worked there. Together they decided to continue with the Harvey Williamson contract, being a good case to try out Michelle McElrae if they decided to take her on as an associate investigator. Bart was making himself a mid-morning cup of coffee when he heard the shop bell; going through he found Nessa McKinley waiting.

"Ah, in time for coffee," he greeted her warmly, surprised to see her there. "How is Lily?" he asked quickly to give her the chance to put his mind at rest she wasn't there with bad news. They walked through to the back room. Nessa assured him she was very well, deliberately not adding *now she doesn't live in Balmoral cottage*. They sat down in front of the fire with their coffee. He was unable to assess her mood, Nessa was always serious and hard to fathom.

"I take it this isn't a social call in passing?" Bart asked. Unless she closed McKinley's Autos she must have left the young lad Hamish in charge.

"I came 'cos I didnae want Hamish to overhear what we would be talkin' about," Nessa explained. "I need yer opinion on something that happened the other night."

Nessa explained she went back to the garage at Dinnet during the night because she left her mobile phone behind in the office, "Ma Da's a wee bit cranky these days, ever since Ma died he's got even more so. We donnae have a land line now we live at Mary's cottage, didnae see the point, us both wi'mobiles. I've got him to understand he phones me if he needs help," she gave a deep sigh of frustration. "He can be a cantankerous old goat!"

Bart silently agreed, "Would he not phone Lily if he couldn't get you?"

"Aye, yer'd think so, only if mine kept ringin' or go to answer phone he would think I was deliberately ignorin' him!" She didn't expand on how difficult he had become these days. "Couldnae risk if he did need help, y'know?" she laughed nervously. Bart could see she was weary with exasperation. "When I got to Dinnet, I could see a couple of vehicles parked, I thought, outside ma garage, made me stop down the road a ways...."

"What time was it?" Bart asked

"Midnight, mebbe later. Aye, Lily thought I was mad to get out of bed in such dreadful weather. The point bein' I saw a white van and a dark coloured car. I was too far away to tell the make though obviously a sporty racer....." She could see by the expression on Bart Bridge's face he may also have been prompted not to approach.

Bart immediately thought about '*a posh car with tinted windows*' a ten year old boy saw deliberately drive at Finlay Ferguson one night outside Blairgowrie in the pouring rain. "The rain was heavy on the jeep's windscreen, d'ya ken? Looked like they might be breakin' inter ma garage. Made me switched ma lights off first. I didnae want anyone to see me there."

"What did you do?"

"I watched, saw they were parked on next door's forecourt, not mine," she said.

"Remind me what's next door?" Bart asked trying to picture where McKinley's was sited.

"It's the deserted bus company building. It's a big place. I think has lots of space where they used to garage the buses when they weren't in use. I don't remember them ever being in use though."

Bart was reminded of the Tour Bus Building in the village behind the hotel yet another bus company to close down years ago. He always meant to look them up to find out what their histories were.

"Ah, yes," he said. "Who owns the building do you know?"

"Now there is a mystery. I once thought of buyin' the place to extend McKinley's, we've always been short of space. Would make a good petrol station addition like the Esso garage down the A93 out here," she said.

"You tried to buy it?"

"Well, not exactly. We couldnae find out who to put an offer to," she said. "So no not officially, we didnae get that far."

"What happened when you saw the vehicles?"

"Nothing. I saw a couple of figures appear, get into each vehicle and drive off," she said. "I waited, drove onto ma own front, got ma mobile then went home."

They sat quietly for a moment before Bart asked, "Have you ever seen anyone there before?"

Nessa shook her head, "I 'spose I really thought whoever owned it must have died years since….never seen or heard anyone there."

"Wouldn't it go to whoever inherited the owner's estate?" Bart asked.

Nessa seemed to be considering the idea. "Depends if there was anyone to leave it to' There must be lots of unclaimed properties around Scotland, look at the cottage of Elizabeth Grant's Lily was living in …."

"To give any chancer the opportunity to put in a claim," Bart was specifically thinking of Edward Petersen's attempt to do just that when Lily's husband met him in prison. In that instance, Martin Frances wanted his false claim to force Lily to leave because he hated the idea she had become an independent woman with her own place, making her own decisions. All he wanted was to keep messing with her life. "But it's not easy to fool the law up here, Lily's husband could have gone on for years if we hadn't proved Petersen a fraud," Bart said, *or Martin Frances hadn't died suddenly in prison.*

"Well somebody must own the Bus Company building," Nessa said emphatically. "I saw two people there."

"Hm! I wonder why all the subterfuge in the middle of the night?"

"Aye, that was ma point when I told Lily. I could ask ma Da, but he doesn't know anything I'm sure from when we wanted to buy it," Nessa said. "I came t'ask if yer have any idea how we can find out?"

Bart looked thoughtful, "Leave it with me to think about. I'll get back to you," he saw Nessa smile for the first time since she arrived.

CHAPTER 22

Bart and Emily arranged to meet Michelle McElrae in the tea rooms on Main Street when she got back from her stint following Mrs 'Ernest' who still showed no signs of deviating from her usual routine. Whilst they waited for her to arrive, Emily told Bart, apart from the one time when Jenny Williamson visited Robbie's bungalow, she could find no reason to continue with such close surveillance. Bart agreed, albeit with some reservations. The matter of Robbie's bungalow he kept to himself because he saw a cloud pass across Emily's face when she spoke his name. He chose instead to suggest, if Michelle McElrae seemed suitable and wanted to work with them, perhaps she could begin with this routine surveillance.

Emily's frown spoke volumes, "Maybe, only are we looking at the wrong Williamson?"

Bart was well aware of Emily's dislike for Harvey Williamson yet couldn't help pointing out it was hardly appropriate to take a client's money to focus on them instead.

"Yes, I know," she said rather grumpily. "I meant look a little closer at what he gets up to….his employee I spoke to didn't hold back her feelings about him getting through a lot of wives…"

Bart thought Emily sounded unusually harsh for her, although if you considered having two wives 'a lot' she might have a point. Bart, who never had one wife or even a permanent relationship, couldn't imagine anyone wanting to change theirs as often as Emily was suggesting Harvey did. "Do you think he might have another potential wife waiting in the wings?"

Scathingly she said, "Well, the girl implied as much. I imagine he has another secretary. He would have replaced Jenny after she left to have his children, wouldn't he?" She grew silent pondering before she added, "A quick look at Harvey Williamson might be the deciding factor in whether we continue with his contract."

"Hm," Bart still wasn't convinced of the ethics in investigating the client or whether they would achieve very much by doing so. He decided to wait to see if Michelle had a view being an ex-copper.

There was one thing he was sure about, listening to the way Emily spoke, she did seem to have lot of aggression directed at Harvey Williamson he hadn't noticed before she went away to meet her father. He began to wonder if she discovered something about her own parents she didn't know before because of the change in her since she came back from Nottingham.

He decided to change the subject, "You haven't said much about your trip to see Tom?"

Bart met Tom Hobbs, the Insurance man, back in Wainthorpe-on-sea on his nightly sojourns to the Anchor pub across the road from his clock shop 'Time and Tide'.

During their very first conversation Tom tried to sell Bart life insurance. From him he discovered his next door neighbour at The Art Gallery had been murdered. Tom always courted people's attention by implying he knew more about the police investigation into the murder than he possibly could know.

In those days selling insurance was done by visiting people in their homes. Bart imagined he would pick up a lot about people in such a closely knit community as Wainthorpe-on-Sea. The sad attention seeking man he knew back then must be finding selling insurance over the telephone a very different proposition.

Emily looked up sharply from reading the menu, "Not much to tell really. Dad seems to be doing well, he's back selling insurance," she laughed at how she sounded. "I mean having a job again." She gave him a beaming smile knowing Bart once called her 'the insurance man's daughter' because she knew a lot about the subject. "The house he's living in is really nice, better than the hostel he went into before he left for Nottingham. It's owned by a really nice elderly Ukrainian couple. I met them. They live on the ground floor. Dad's got a bedsit on the second floor, with a shared bathroom and kitchen."

"Ah good, I'm glad he's doing well," Bart said with relief. He watched as Emily's thoughts drifted back to her stay as if transfixed by the memory, her face he noticed grew troubled.

*　*　*　*　*

Emily stood in the darkened kitchen at the front of the house her father lived in having left him in his room making up the temporary bed she was sleeping on whilst staying with him. She tried hard on their walk back from the steak bar not to let him see she was troubled. Everything was going smoothly sitting eating with her father again, he seemed happy telling her about the woman she spoke to at the Insurance Company, where he now worked, when she was looking for him. She thought there was a slight twinkle in his eye giving a hint there might possibly be a budding friendship there. Maybe wishful thinking on her part, she really did want him to be happy. She realised he never really was when he was with her mother.

Everything changed after they paid the bill. When they stood up to leave, she turned round wanting to thank the waitress, looked over to where the girl she knew from her badge was called Kirstie, stood holding the hand of one of the other diners. A man she was shocked to see looked the image of Robbie who she hadn't given much thought to since she arrived to visit her father. The 'Robbie' lookalike was thinner, to the point of being gaunt, with long straggly hair and a beard, otherwise the likeness was incredible.

When the man holding Kirstie's hand looked over, his eyes met hers, and she thought he registered shock on seeing her. As a reflex action, he pulled his hand away from the waitress with a guilty look on his face.

The kind of look she saw on Robbie Cowan's face when he apologised for not believing her about Gina Taylor.

At first she thought she was imagining the man was Robbie, it wouldn't be the first time she imagined she saw him somewhere. He was so often on her mind she would wish him to appear, and he did if she saw a stranger even with a vague likeness to him.

She would have dismissed this like all the other times if, as she followed her father out the door of the steak bar, she hadn't looked back. He was still staring at her in a strange enquiring way. Could he really have been Robbie? He seemed to be close to the waitress whose hand he was holding, his face showed real concern for her. She ran the scene in the restaurant again as she stood in the darkened kitchen looking out of the window at the front gate to her father's digs where two people, huddled under an umbrella, were walking slowly past.

Of course she recognised them immediately. No forgetting the waitress's long strawberry blonde hair. The man huddled under the umbrella with her looked up at the lighted window of her father's room as if he knew who lived there and she was staying with him. The idea was ridiculous, how could he, her visit had been an impulse? Then with his head raised, she saw his face clearly – saw the enquiring look Robbie used to give when he was puzzled by something. It definitely was him!

The shock made her take a step backwards to get out of his line of vision when his eyes swept across to the darkened kitchen, saw him look quickly away, pull himself closer into the girl whose arm was entwined with his.

* * * * *

"Ah, here she is," Bart said interrupting her thoughts. He stood up as Michelle McElrae walked over to them. The girl was young, slight in build wearing jeans with a leather jacket. She displayed none of the sternness he would have expected from a police officer. He couldn't imagine her being tough enough to handle a pub brawl or a mob riot.

After introductions, when their food orders arrived, they settled down with Bart explaining the kind of person the Agency was looking for. He felt obliged to emphasise the rather mundane nature of the cases they were likely to get at the agency because he thought Michelle ought to be made aware.

During the meeting, Bart spent time trying to assess the extent of her injuries. He could detect none as she walked over to join them, therefore was required to ask how her health was since her accident. As an employer, even of casual staff, he would have a duty of care to ensure she could undertake what he was asking of her.

"I'm doing very well," Michelle looked a little embarrassed. "Actually, physically I've been very lucky, on the surface you can't really tell unless you know what you're looking for. One of my legs was badly broken. I have healed well although I have a slight limp I try to correct. In terms of policing, of course, I wouldn't be much use at chasing a villain let alone bringing one down to cuff them!" She laughed at the thought. "Of course, I could have stayed with the police, as support staff. They did offer me a job in the management information section…..desk job, number crunching!" She made Bart bellow with laughter when she winced at the idea, anything statistic wasn't his cup of tea either. "I thought if I wanted a job like that I could get one outside the force, or do telephone sales…..and probably get paid more."

Tom Hobbs crossed Bart's mind once again wondering for the second time how he was adapting to the new ways of the insurance world, whilst Emily thought about the lady at her father's Insurance Company she spoke to on the telephone when she was looking for him. She immediately recalled the smile on her father's face when he talked about her.

"Agatha told me you were looking for someone to do some surveillance work? I thought this was closer to police work. I would like being operational again," she said, her face clouded a little before admitting, "I did have some issues with driving after my accident, couldn't get back into my car at first. I've been working on them with someone ever since. I think I'm totally recovered." Bart acknowledged her for being candid with them.

Emily said, "Must have been awful for you. I was forced off the road by someone a while ago, which was scary enough. I wasn't injured like you were, yet have no idea how I managed to drive away after. I think I was still in shock, my reaction must have been automatic." Emily realised once again how lucky she was to remain intact. "I was a fairly new driver anyway, took a bit of time to get my confidence back.....I didn't have much in the first place. Luckily I doubt we would ever be needed for a high speed chase."

They watched Michelle smile. Bart could see she was taken with Emily for putting her at her ease and sealed Bart's decision to offer her the job. The whole thing was agreed at the time. Emily arranged to meet with her to take over the Mrs 'Ernest' case and to give her access to the reports.

The one thing Emily didn't do and there was no mention of in her reports, was to tell Mitch about Jenny Williamson's visit to Robbie Cowan's bungalow.

CHAPTER 23

Next morning when he came downstairs, Bart found Emily already up working at the table on her laptop in the back room. He caught a glimpse of the graffiti wall from the Tour Bus building on the screen as he walked past reminding him he found the same photographs open on her laptop in the shop. He worried she might be too fixated on them.

He mumbled a morning greeting, felt the teapot with its cosy to test the warmth of the tea when he moved into the kitchen to make his breakfast. He filled the kettle with water to boil to make a fresh pot. Emily's response to his greeting was a little delayed due to her concentration on the images.

"Have you looked closely at these graffiti pictures?" she asked absently without looking up.

"Can't say I've given them much scrutiny beyond the ones we know relate to Finlay Ferguson or the Gina girl," he said taking the bacon from the fridge he laid a few rashers across the frying pan. "Do you want a bacon sandwich?"

Emily shook her head, "No thanks, I've eaten," she looked up, saw him anticipating their usual banter. "Muesli," she said grinning.

Bart refrained from his usual retort this morning, pleased at least she didn't need 'comfort food' as she liked to refer to bacon.

"Why?" he asked.

"I like muesli," she said looking up puzzled. He wondered if she also thought there might be some connection to the named Operation Graffiti knowing Robbie joined their enquiry. They hadn't discussed Robbie since he left.

"I've gone through every inch of the graffiti wall," she said. "There are some very interesting things, though some are quite baffling as well."

"Like what?" he asked turning the rashers over.

"Most of the images are typical, what you would expect from school kids who spend much of their time there."

"Yes, except Finn wasn't a school kid, his name is on there isn't it?" Bart suggested.

Emily looked thoughtful. "His name was, before being removed and was related specifically to 'The Bogeyman'…..but I'm more interested in the things you wouldn't expect today's school kids to be into or even know about…..music is quite different these days."

"Music? I only saw the images of films, mostly horror ones or Sci-Fi, kids are into those aren't they? Even the old films like Hannibal Lector or the Halloween pumpkin one. Are you saying there are also music images?" Bart asked not having picked out any himself or been shown any by Jay when they were in the building together.

"Have a look at this," she said inviting him over when he walked back with his breakfast. He diverted to the table to have a look. "Tell me what you make of it?" She enlarged a section of the wall with an old Western Stagecoach with a man standing in front wearing the costume of a Highwayman, his arms crossed over his chest holding a pistol in each hand. Across his face under his eyes were two thick white stripes, the image provoked a dim memory in Bart.

"Looks a bit familiar, though I can't say why," he said.

"I found it when I googled highwayman," she said. "The image is of someone called Adam Ant from a song, 'Stand and Deliver', released back in 1981." He could hear the triumph in her voice at her discovery.

"I vaguely remember, though not my sort of thing even in those days," he said. "Are you suggesting someone older has contributed to the wall….surely not someone my age!"

"Whoever did was perhaps emphasising the highwayman *or* the stage coach," she said. "Well it is inside a tour bus building. Aren't they usually coaches?"

Bart stopped in mid bite having begun to eat. Emily could see the enlightened look on his face. He remembered he hadn't yet told her about Nessa McKinley's visit and the mystery of the deserted building next door to McKinley's Autos he realised also it used to be a bus company before being abandoned.

"What?" she asked knowing the look on his face meant some kind of intuition.

"I didn't tell you Nessa visited whilst you were away," he gave her an update on their conversation realising he'd done nothing since. When he finished he asked, "What do you have on today?"

"Meeting Mitch at Tarland to see how she's doing with Mrs 'Ernest', won't take me long, why?"

"Meet me at McKinley's at noon, we'll give the place the once over. I want to have a look at the back of the old bus company building from that junk yard of Nessa's to see if I can get any closer to the premises, maybe take some photos," he said mysteriously. "I've been meaning to do some searches for ages on both of these abandoned premises, you know, see why they closed down. As far as I can see both buildings have stood empty for at least a couple of decades, maybe more. I wonder why. They are prime sites you would expect to be given a new lease of life."

Emily was slowly nodding. She looked back at the computer screen to the image of a stage coach with Adam Ant, the 'dandy' highwayman. She knew because she listened to the song several times trying to work out who would be interested in old music. While she did, her thoughts moved on to 'the bogeyman' wondering whether he was the person Finlay Ferguson was terrified of to make him leave a good job in the village, especially after he found out he might have a chance of getting back with Charlotte.

"Incidentally," Emily said as an afterthought, "I found out from the manager at the Co-op he let Gina Taylor go because he received too many complaints from his customers."

"Oh?" Bart looked up surprised. "For short changing them?" She once short changed Bart, he let it go because he thought she was new, maybe a little inexperienced. He felt sorry for her, didn't want to get her into trouble in front of the manager.

"No," Emily said looking up at him. "He said too many people felt intimidated by her. One or two even claimed she was making up stories about them, asking them for money to keep her mouth shut."

Bart looked shocked, "Lor, are you suggesting she blackmailed them?"

Emily raised her shoulders in a shrug to indicate she didn't know before going back to scrutinising the graffiti.

*   *   *   *   *

When Bart arrived at McKinley's minutes after noon Emily's mini was already parked up on the deserted Bus Company forecourt at the side of Nessa's jeep. McKinley's forecourt was taken by three other cars. He imagined Emily would have sat for a moment, before getting out of her car, scrutinising the old building with its faded sign. Bart left his Peugeot out on the road, walked over to the garage. When he got inside he found Emily chatting to Hamish under a car raised up on the lift, they were laughing together.

Nessa appeared from the office with a hot drink she gave to Hamish before she greeted Bart, "You're in time for fresh coffee," she said leading the way into the office where Emily joined them a minute later.

Bart told Nessa he updated Emily on the next door activity she witnessed during the night asking whether she'd seen or heard anything else.

"No, or ever have before," she said. "You'll be aware we cannae see much working inside here."

"I notice you've parked your jeep next door," Bart commented

"It's what ma Da always did for a lotta years."

Emily was holding her mobile as usual. It always amused Bart, seeming to be an extension to her hand, which he often joked with her about. She wagged the hand set to indicate to him she already took pictures of the front.

"We came to have a look at the back of the building from your yard," Bart said.

"Next door has always bin a wee bit overgrown. You'll not see much, there's a lot of greenery growing over ma fence....it's gone back to nature," Nessa explained.

Bart had only once been in Nessa's back yard which likewise was overtaken, not by nature though, overwhelmingly by the accumulation of car parts, various mechanical junk, with stacks of old tyres, piles of car grills and years of assorted rubbish.

After they finished coffee Bart and Emily went out the back door into McKinley's rear compound. They were stopped in their tracks at the sight.

"Wow!" Emily exclaimed on seeing the yard for the first time.

"Indeed," Bart agreed finding the rear even messier than the last time he saw it.

They stepped cautiously through the debris making their way to the left hand side to get close to the fence bowing inwards under the weight of the thick stems of woody brambles from next door.

They heard clearly Nessa's apologetic voice behind them, "Sorry about t'mess, always intended to sort it out, too much work on most of the time."

Emily led the way through the least of the clutter clearing away rusted metal either side of her to make a pathway for Bart to follow her. Ever practical she said loudly enough for Nessa to overhear, "I bet some of this stuff would be worth something for scrap." She found the going heavy because of the weight of the tyres, ending up fatigued by the time they reached the fence.

The brambles having shed their foliage because of the season, gave one particular patch a clear though limited view of the rear of the next door building. It looked equally as dilapidated as the front. The only difference they could see, despite the peeling paint flaking off the windows, there was a brand new back door which drew the eye immediately.

"How about that?" Bart declared.

"Well I'll be....!" Nessa McKinley gasped close behind them. "No mistakin' what I saw from a distance."

Emily was taking pictures of the back like she did the front.

"Looks to me like whoever the building belongs to doesn't want anyone to know it is being used, otherwise replacing the front door to gain access would have been easier," Bart suggested.

"Easier?" Emily asked.

"Yes, look they've cleared some of the ground to get to the door," Bart pointed to the flattened greenery leading from the new door to the side of the building trodden down by whoever was using the building.

"Would they have done that during the night as well?" Nessa asked.

Bart shrugged, "I suppose they must have. To remove all the debris would have attracted your attention or even anyone passing by – it's a busy road during the day."

They all moved back inside where she asked, "What now?"

Bart looked circumspect. "I don't think you should make any attempt to trace whoever these people are or try to make an offer on the place," he watched as Nessa frowned. "Anyone who goes to those lengths to conceal what they are doing doesn't want anyone to know about it," he warned. "Until we know who they are we treat them as suspicious. Leave it with us, we'll see what we can find out."

When they left walking through the garage on their way out, Hamish shouted over to them, "See you later?" Emily ignored him and Bart merely waved in acknowledgement.

Once outside, Bart walked Emily over to her car on the pre-text of chatting to her. He wanted to have a look at the front of the building close up without being too obvious. They agreed to speak back at the shop. Emily drove off whilst Bart moved onto the Bus Company forecourt to turn his car around. He gave the building one last look before driving away.

CHAPTER 24

As they left McKinley's Autos Emily and Bart agreed they would take turns to watch the Bus Company building for any irregular activity taking place in the early hours. Bart told Emily she was only to sit in her car at a safe distance to observe. On no account was she to put herself in danger by approaching the premises or allowing herself to be seen by whoever might be using the building. He knew there could be a perfectly legitimate reason why the place was being used so they couldn't be caught trespassing.

After Emily left, Bart went on to Castle Daingneach to return the latest post bomb refurbished clock Emily cleaned, whilst she returned to the shop to meet with Isla Strachan to give her a set of keys to start work next day.

At five o'clock she was closing the shop when Mitch pulled up outside after completing her observations of Jenny Williamson. Emily having made herself a pot of tea was about to settle down to do some research on the two deserted bus buildings. She was keen to hear what Mitch thought of Mrs 'Ernest's' routine. She explained how she hadn't taken to Harvey Williamson especially after talking to one of his employees. She showed the report to Mitch.

"He's not much to look at given how young his wife is," was Mitch's first comment.

"There's nothing about his personality to compensate either, he's altogether a very disagreeable man," Emily's criticism saw Mitch's eyebrows rise. "You would see for yourself if you met him," Emily said trying to justify her harshness.

"He's probably got a very agreeable bank balance though," Mitch said laughing, "he does look a sour sort I must admit."

"You've seen him?" Emily said surprised.

"He came home early, shortly after they walked back from school," Emily's shock led Mitch to ask, "Doesn't he always?"

"Err, I've never known him to come home early, in fact I haven't been there when he's got back from work. I always assumed he worked late……well the girl employee implied he often kept his secretary working late!"

"Maybe he does only when Mrs 'E' goes shopping so she doesn't have to take the kids," she said. "I was expecting to leave right after she got back to the house, saw him arrive and her leave, so I followed her."

"She went grocery shopping?" Emily asked. "She usually does that while the children are at school."

"No, not then," Mitch took out a black note book, flicked a few pages, "She drove a few streets away to a bungalow up for sale……" Emily froze waiting for her to give her Robbie's address, "……where she parked on the drive, let herself in, spent about ten minutes before she came out with a pile of letters…..I assumed she picked them up at the front door, there's obviously no one living there."

Mitch saw Emily become quite pale. "Has she done this before?" she asked.

Emily nodded, "Once since I've been following her."

"I'm thinking maybe she's forwarding the mail to the owner, does she work for the Agent?" she looked again in her note book, "Nelsens? I've not heard of them, must be a new one or perhaps in another town where the owner lives."

At first Emily felt confused at the idea Jenny Williamson might have a job. She had never seen her leave to go to one. The idea gave her a little hope there might be a logical explanation for her visits to Robbie's bungalow. She regretted she didn't stay around the last time to see how long she was inside. She managed a weak, "Right…."

Mitch continued, telling her she followed her to a Tesco supermarket and when she saw her leave her car, she was still carrying the pile of mail. "I thought that was odd, not the sort of thing you would take into a supermarket is it? I got a trolley to follow her inside." Mitch didn't explain she was randomly picking up groceries to put in her trolley to be abandoned later at the top of an isle when she left.

Emily sat up waiting for her to continue, her heart beating a little faster than normal because it was confusing given what she saw in Nottingham.

*   *   *   *   *

Emily was shocked at seeing Robbie with another woman whose hand he was holding in a public place, showing her great concern. When she saw them again from the kitchen window of her father's digs, she rushed out of the house pulling on her coat and picking up her umbrella to follow them, with only a backward call to her father she needed to go to the shop up the road. She was still buttoning her coat when she caught up with Kirstie and Robbie towards the top of the hill, so slowed down.

Emily knew there was a shop on the corner at the top because she went there with her father to fetch something to eat after she arrived. She watched them go in, hovering outside in the darkest place she could find out of the pool of light coming from the shop windows. She was surprised the shop was still open. Previously she heard the owner complaining most of these little places needed to keep open as long as possible to make any kind of living in competition with the big supermarkets.

When they came out Robbie was carrying a bottle of wine and they continued to walk along the street away from the shop, once more huddled under the umbrella.

*   *   *   *   *

Emily was aware Mitch was still talking, pulled her thoughts back to her. She was explaining how Mrs 'E' took her down most of the aisles, filling up her trolley with what looked like a week's supply of groceries. She got as far as the alcohol section where she began to browse in front of the wine.

"She seemed to be picking up bottles at random, paying very little attention to her selection, peered at them briefly before putting them back on the shelves. I had the curious thought how she would look on the CCTV camera if anyone saw…."

"I don't understand what you mean," Emily interrupted trying to force the image of Robbie holding a bottle of wine out of her mind.

Mitch explained, "From the position of the camera, which is in the opposite corner near the ceiling, she would look like someone trying to decide what kind of wine to buy, do you see?" Emily nodded still unsure. "She was in fact looking around, her eyes darting from one side of the section to the other as if looking for someone."

"Oh, I see."

"A man walked towards her pushing a trolley full of groceries, stopped next to her. He reached up for a bottle off the top shelf. Mrs 'E ignored him, placed the bottle she was holding in her own trolley before moving off around his trolley whilst he was leaning away. There was absolutely no communication between them. Her body hid the fact she dropped the pile of letters she was still holding into his trolley as she went past without even turning her head. He turned, put a bottle of Champagne into his trolley on top of the letters then walked away in the opposite direction. I could see quite clearly because I was watching them on the same level. The CCTV camera wouldn't pick the action up because it was blocked by Mrs E's body." Mitch saw Emily's mouth drop open. "Clever, eh?"

"Did you get a look at the man?" Emily asked thinking the man couldn't possibly be Robbie even if the mail was his.

Mitch was grinning, "Yep," she took out her mobile phone, pulled up a picture of the man as he turned to face her across two rows, to show to Emily. "The thing is I kind of recognise him. I can't remember where I've seen him before……you get a lot of this when you're a copper because of the number of people you meet."

Emily looked at the picture of a thirty something man with thinning mousey coloured hair wearing ordinary dark clothes making him look exactly like every average male. There was nothing to distinguish him from the next man. If you were to describe him you would probably say he was average height, average weight and ordinary looking.

"What happened then?" Emily asked.

"Well it's hard to follow two people. My brief is to follow her. I trailed her to the cash till where she checked out her shopping and went straight home," Mitch said, without telling Emily she saw the man leave slipping the envelopes into the front of his jacket to keep dry because it was raining hard by then. She left her trolley next to the one with a bottle of champagne he abandoned at the end of one of the aisles.

"When she got back home her husband came out to help her with the shopping," she continued. Then her curiosity got the better of her, "Why did you say Harvey Williamson thought she was having an affair? He looked really pleased to see her back home, kissed her affectionately like she had been away for days."

"All he said was he 'knew' she was being unfaithful but didn't explain why. He seemed quite outraged by it," Emily remembered his sour face with those bulging watery eyes and wet pouty lips she found so repulsive. She remembered having to look away at that stage. She assumed when she saw Jenny Williamson she would be an older unattractive woman and was greatly surprised when she saw her.

Michelle McElrae had nothing more to add, other than she would type up her report as soon as possible adding she would do some research on the Estate Agent Nelsens to see what she could find out about them because she was sure with vacant properties they would be the only people who would have a key to the place.

CHAPTER 25

Much to his surprise Bart was stopped at a newly installed gatehouse at the entrance to the castle to be checked in by a uniformed guard who looked more military than civilian. Nonetheless, he was pleased with the new addition. Bart's visit to Castle Daingneach was more to see how Mary MacLeod was faring than to honour his clock maintenance contract, even though he carried the recently refurbished one in the boot of his car.

Permanently lurking in the back of Bart's mind was the threat from Rupert Quinnell she divulged to him in a previous conversation. He particularly remembered her unmovable conviction Quinnell was responsible for the attempt on her life after he discovered her working in the castle gift shop. By her own account he was furious when he realised she wasn't in fact an employee, was about to become Lady Mary of Daingneach, the Laird of the castle's bride.

When he heard the news, Quinnell's anger was transposed into the accusation Mary was somehow responsible for the decline in his farm shop profits. Rupert Quinnell's claim was made despite Daingneach not yet being open to the public. The follow up bomb that blew up the marquee on their wedding day everyone suspected was a warning not to go ahead with it or their plans for a wedding venue business. The castle was unlikely now to be considered a 'fairy tale' setting to get married in.

Bart continued to worry after the criminal investigations into both attempts on Mary's life disappeared into what Bart thought of as the 'black hole' of Operation Graffiti's remit. He noted the new public signs scattered about the castle grounds as he moved up the lengthy drive to pull onto the gravel forecourt. They indicated the

MacLeod's were serious about fulfilling their plans, indicative perhaps that the public opening was imminent.

When he was shown in by housekeeper, Maggie Wallace, he found Mary alone in the library they used as their general office. Despite interrupting her, Bart could see she was genuinely pleased to see him. After ordering refreshments from Maggie, they exchanged superficial pleasantries about their respective partners. He could tell Mary was still intrigued by his new Detective Agency whilst enquiring about his businesses.

Bart, of course, was always disinclined to overstate the agencies capabilities because he was by no means certain they would be able to continue. He did update Mary on the appointment of Isla Strachan to cover the shop, to relieve the burden for him to concentrate on other things.

The appointment of Michelle McElrae, as their additional investigator, subcontracted when necessary, he told her would help with the agency business. He mentioned nothing about any of the cases they were working on, immediately turning the conversation back to the castle plans. He was greatly surprised to learn they secured their first wedding booking.

"How splendid," Bart enthused. Hearing the news went part way to quell his fears the negative media coverage of the bomb at their own wedding might have forced them to forget the venture altogether. "I wondered if you would be able to go ahead after....." he stopped because he didn't really know what would be a tactful way of referring to the awful day they all went through.

".....our own wedding was blown to smithereens?" Mary laughed, even though he could see fear still lurked behind her eyes. "We underestimated the appeal a ghoulish scene can have on people, or maybe they don't want to think lightning, or Semtex, can strike twice in the same place!"

Bart couldn't see the funny side of the matter having been there when the bomb went off. He changed the subject again, "I see you have a permanent gatehouse."

Mary was no longer laughing, "I admit the decision was more Mungo's than mine….though I have to say I do feel a lot safer since we took on permanent security staff."

"Oh, they aren't a hired company then?" Bart knew the security firm engaged to cover the wedding failed to detect the bomb given they used explosive sniffer dogs.

Mary shook her head, "I think Mungo believes the other people could have done more to find the bomb," she said. "The way he put it was far from gracious….err, 'if you're going to have bloody bomb sniffing animals, you at least need to pay attention when they start barking to buggery!' or words to that effect!" Mary made a passable impression of Mungo although a weak attempt at a smile. "They assumed their excitement was the meat being delivered, not the cake they were reacting to, they checked on neither!"

Bart already knew the wedding cake containing the bride and groom figurines for the top of the cake were made out of Semtex with a detonator inside the sporran the male figure was wearing. The cake was delivered as the butcher was unloading the prime Scottish beef for the wedding reception when the dogs began to react excitedly. Their handlers merely dragged the dogs away.

"So the guard is employed by you?"

"More than one. Mungo says until we are no longer a target for more attempts, they are staying! Actually between you and me he is more specific regarding who the threats are from as you can imagine?" Bart heard Mungo voice his thoughts more than once about Rupert Quinnell and even made veiled suggestions DI Morris and DS Copeland the CID officers who were originally assigned to Mary's car 'accident' or rather attempted murder, were somehow connected to Quinnell. They were very insistent Mungo and Mary should cancel their wedding and not open the castle to the public. At the time she thought what he was asking was exactly what Quinnell would want.

"Have you had any more direct threats from the Quinnells?" Bart asked.

Mary shook her head, "None....but then as you can see, we are locked down here like prisoners......and I am unable to go out on my own because of Mungo's fears for me."

Bart felt extremely sad for her. He knew she had been living in fear of Rupert Quinnell for years after she escaped working for him. Unfortunately, she was subjected to the unwanted attention of the previous Laird Munro's secretary, Thomas Galbraith, being forced to leave her job at the castle at the time. "It must seem like one continuous nightmare to you, Mary," Bart said sadly.

She smiled weakly, "Maybe. There are worse places to be imprisoned," she said trying to make light of her situation.

"Yes," he agreed although he knew himself what it was like to have to always be hypervigilant when you were being sought by people who wanted to harm you. Freedom he realised was precious. When you were surrounded by some of the most beautiful visions Nature can offer, a shame you couldn't freely walk amongst it.

After Mary was run off the road he tried to speed up the process. It was Bart who suggested to the MacLeods they bring their wedding forward in an attempt to flush out the perpetrator, only resulting in the sabotaged wedding cake for which he still held deep feelings of guilt.

Once again he wanted to help her, although reluctant, knowing the consequences of interfering. The lesson was hard learnt. The long haul of the Operation Graffiti investigation was clearly impacting on the MacLeods, especially Mary's ability to live a life free from serious threat. What he needed was some way to help without affecting the enquiry. He had no idea how he could achieve it.

* * * * *

When Bart got back to the March of Time the shop was already closed. There was no sign of Emily, only a brief note to tell him she would take the first watch of the Bus Company Building later after she attended to some errands. Bart frowned with displeasure at not being able to discuss the MacLeod's situation with her or how they might help. He specifically needed to convey his fears over the surveillance of the premises next door to McKinley's. His gut reaction told him the subterfuge Nessa witnessed, was confirmed by the new back door, suggesting to him something illegal was taking place. He knew how headstrong Emily could be and feared her eagerness might lead her into trouble if she failed to be cautious.

At the bottom of her note was a nota bene to draw his attention to the report submitted to file from Mitch's latest surveillance of Jenny Williamson. Her note was placed beside the laptop with the report already open for him to read. He frowned again with irritation at the idea she considered him to be technologically inept, which he was on many things, other than his ability to open a simple computer file.

He made himself a cup of tea, sat next to a newly stoked fire in his armchair to read the report of Mrs 'E's' second trip to Robbie's bungalow to pick up mail followed by her clandestine meeting at Tesco's with someone she went to great lengths, by Mitch's description, to avoid being caught on the CCTV communicating with. When he read Michelle's intention to do some research on Nelsens he spoke out loud, "Well good luck with that one!" as if she were in the room.

He realised his taking her intention to try as a criticism of his ability was ridiculous, how could she know he already tried? He thought perhaps his irritability was more to do with yet another missed lunch at The Moor Hen, so he transferred his thoughts to rectifying the matter by attending to his overwhelming need for food.

He walked back into the village stopping at a little bistro where he'd never eaten, opposite the Hungry Traveller, to have a look at the menu pinned inside a wooden display case at the top of the many steps leading down to the restaurant. The menu he thought looked pleasingly varied if not a little pricey, then he thought, *I'm due a little treat!*

CHAPTER 26

By the time Kirstie and Robbie reached the shop at the top of the road he was pleased she already invited him back to her flat for coffee. He saw the shop was still open so suggested they get a bottle of wine. He thought, with a couple of glasses, she might open up about the Bailey family, particularly Sid, the runty little man in the 'Arthur Daley' camel coat. He needed some idea how he might get close enough to be taken into their organisation.

He didn't like the way Sid touched Kirstie, but thought she might have some influence there to be able to help him. She seemed to have sufficient distaste for the man not to betray him by warning Sid Bailey of his interest in him. Even so, there was no way he dared let on he was an undercover police officer. He still needed to keep strictly to his fabricated story because there was always the chance of making an accidental slip.

Inside the shop it took all of Robbie's will power not to laugh at the owner who tried hard to get them to buy everything in his shop. He gave them a verbal tour of the stock on display, each time followed with, "very, very good," as he presented them with a multiplicity of things to eat with the one bottle of wine Robbie was trying to buy.

"You buy these I reduce the price for you," he said holding a packet of vegetable samosas, "they go with wine, very very good, you like them?"

Robbie imagined the man, a very well made Indian gentleman with a belly the size of a ten month pregnancy with twins, would take all the out of date leftover edible stock with him upstairs to his living quarters after he closed, there to consume them because he wasn't about to throw anything away. They managed to buy the bottle of wine, escaping before they burst into laughter outside when they heard him shout, "You come back, I give you very very good bargains!"

They walked off huddled together giggling under the umbrella. Robbie turned slightly because he heard a noise behind him and thought the owner was pursuing them with more bargains. When he looked back the shop door was firmly closed. He could see nothing except a frightened black cat shoot across the road from out of the shadows. He wasn't particularly superstitious like his mother, who was obsessed with omens and signs of one thing or another. She would have thought a black cat crossing his path a portent of doom.

Robbie was pleasantly surprised to find Kirstie's place cosy unlike his. In fact, he found the warmth from the fire, after the first decent meal inside him in weeks, together with an inner glow from a glass of wine, made him so comfortable he felt quite sleepy. He could easily have forgotten why he was there, Kirstie was such good company. His intention to casually get her talking about Sid Bailey, gradually slipped away the cosier he felt.

He realised how much he missed human contact, being able to laugh freely again after weeks of living alone in the appalling conditions in the musty hole of a flat they set him up in, lulled him. The overall cosiness and the way Kirstie was obviously attracted to him, combined with the wine, made him even more relaxed, any other thoughts were temporarily pushed to the back of his mind. All those natural instincts he'd suppressed were released when Kirstie leaned in towards him to kiss him.

CHAPTER 27

Emily arrived at the Balmoral pub in Ballater to wait for Hamish, already feeling uncertain about agreeing to meet him. She took a vacant table near the back of the room to keep a nervous watch on the pub door. He finally arrived with his mop of hair, usually tied back in a ponytail for work, freshly washed flopping over his eyes as he walked towards the table where she was sitting. She was overpowered by the smell of his aftershave which arrived long before he reached her. She could see Hamish made an effort for her with his appearance.

He looked to be in high spirits about their 'date' only she knew wasn't really a date. She felt doubly guilty arranging to meet him where she already sampled the fish and chips with Bart on a couple of occasions. One was she felt guilty for not telling Bart about meeting Hamish because she knew he thought the mechanic was a little gormless, having said as much. Most of all she felt guilty for misleading Hamish.

Earlier, she arrived at McKinley's before Bart got there. Nessa was conveniently called away by the ringing of the office telephone giving Emily the chance to engage Hamish in conversation in the hope he might divulge more about Gina Taylor. The previous time he amazed her by repeating the rumour Gina was Rupert Quinnell's daughter. Emily was sure he knew more, like where she was living and who other than her step-brother David she hung around with.

Emily was unprepared for the young mechanic to dive straight in to ask her out on a date before the conversation ever got started. She inwardly cringed when he delivered it with an immature flourish. She felt embarrassed by his juvenile stuttering expecting him to blush. Before she got the chance to respond he added a time and place as if she already agreed. The Balmoral in Ballater he told her was his local. They did great fish and chips, which she agreed to. Hamish took her "Yes," about the food being good, as an agreement to meet him. She could hardly spoil the grin on his boyish face, which Bart called 'gormless', by explaining she meant the food was good.

Emily's overwhelming need for information on Gina Taylor since seeing her in Banchory had become quite an obsession and surpassed any guilty thoughts she may have about accepting the 'date' as betraying Robbie Cowan. Up until she saw him with Kirstie in Nottingham, she wouldn't have entertained meeting Hamish. The image of Robbie with the waitress huddled under an umbrella, added to the anger she already felt towards Gina for causing her to lose him, adding fuel to her growing desire for revenge.

Only for a moment did she waiver. When she told Hamish, "Yes," the 'gormless' look appeared on his face, making her doubt whether she ought to be encouraging him at all. He may have nothing more to tell her about Gina. She would have led him on for nothing.

Now sitting opposite him in the Balmoral, Emily was thankful they were eating, otherwise she would have struggled. She hadn't ever 'dated' boys her own age because they never appealed to her, not that any of them ever asked her out. Of course, she blamed her unpopularity on her being ugly, fat, and spotty conjuring up a whole series of self-deprecating reasons for why boys weren't attracted to her. The fact was she wasn't interested in them, giving off negative signals.

Other girls would gush about a popular adolescent 'hunk' at school who Emily found to be too juvenile. Often they were covered in acne with parents who insisted they needed a brace on their already perfectly straight teeth in order to maximise their perfection. What was there to like? Her disinterest in them was not merely due to her own shyness. She had none of the skills to communicate with them and rapidly developed a reputation for being unapproachable.

What didn't occur to her at the time, was her friendship with her cousin Peter, was largely responsible for restricting her from making friends with any other boys. Their friendship came from their mothers' being sisters and spending so much time together at family functions, it gave them the opportunity to communicate their mutual problems about both sets of parents. What else could they do, spending all their high days and holidays in each other's company?

To a fifteen year old Emily, having such a close friendship couldn't be matched by any other boy of her acquaintance. Peter was, after all, older than her, nowhere near as silly as they were. He knew what he wanted to do after leaving school being totally focussed on achieving his goal of creating computer games, that she admired and looked up to him.

Emily, of course, didn't know what she wanted to do when she left school beyond going on to University. She also didn't realise she gave off negative vibes any remotely interested boy took as a warning not to approach. When she lost contact with Peter, she also lost the chance to develop like other girls did.

Even after turning eighteen she was out of her depth meeting with Hamish. She had no idea how old he was, he seemed young to her. He talked only about his own interests, as if he expected she would share the music, sport or TV programmes he liked and led her to realise she was already struggling to be the age she was supposed to be. Whatever that ought to be she had no idea. With Peter there'd been a mutual sharing of ideas about things they were both interested in.

When she met Robbie he was older, altogether different to anyone else before in her life. He was interested in her. He always seemed to want to please her, although he wouldn't open up about himself, his past life and especially his close friendship with Nessa McKinley. Nevertheless, she found Robbie easy to talk to and surprisingly he was interested in her opinion.

Meeting Hamish she knew was a huge mistake. In order to stop herself from making an excuse to go to the loo, from where she could leave surreptitiously, she used the evening as practice in extracting information from someone. She badly needed the experience of face to face information gathering. The one exception being the young girl employee of Harvey Williamson who was equally as talkative as Hamish when she manoeuvred her onto the topic she wanted to know about, her boss Mr 'Ernest'.

After a lull, when Hamish gave his food some attention, Emily was made to watch him shovelling forkfuls of chips into his mouth, occasionally using his fingers, still with patches of deep ingrained oil, she was prompted to ask, "What was it like working at McDougal's.....wasn't that the garage where you worked before?"

Hamish was only too pleased they were no longer sitting in silence. He took the question as clear indication she was interested in him. With great relief he launched into describing how different McDougal's garage was to McKinley's, telling her about doing an apprenticeship to get his qualifications on day release at college. Every so often she asked him to clarify something technical whilst waiting for him to broach the subject of the large local estate contracts she knew he used to work on. She found the conversation easier then to ask about the Quinnell estate and to bring up their previous conversation about Gina Taylor who Hamish seemed keen to impart all he knew.

Before she parted from him she insisted on paying half of the bill for the food, a subtle hint she didn't see the evening as a 'date'. Her mind moved on to staking out the Bus Company building later. She took the chance to make casual enquiries as to whether Hamish ever heard anything from the premises next door to McKinley's.

He looked blankly at her as if he didn't understand the question until his face changed to puzzlement, either because her question seemed random with no relevance to anything they were talking about or he genuinely didn't understand. His *gormless* expression once again prodded her guilt into life about not telling Bart where she was. She knew immediately Nessa hadn't confided in Hamish about the nocturnal visitors to the building next door; not having worked there very long, he was unlikely to know much about the neighbours anyway.

When he asked, "Which side?" the question threw her. She hadn't considered who Nessa's neighbours were on the other side. She immediately covered herself by telling him she wondered if there were ever any complaints, "You know, about the constant noise of vehicles being brought to the garage for repair or even the junk pile Nessa calls the 'compound' out back being an eyesore?" People she said were apt to see these things as devaluing their own property.

Hamish told her he didn't know anyone in Dinnet, following up with him confirming he lived there in Ballater. Emily could tell by the slight flush to his face he still lived at home with his parents, a fact he didn't elaborate on. She was greatly relieved he was unlikely to invite her back 'to his' after they left the pub.

In fact, she left him in the pub being sure to tell him she needed to get back; she didn't want to leave Bart alone for too long because he was still recovering from a serious illness. She wondered how long she might be able to use this as an excuse.

*   *   *   *   *   *

After leaving Hamish in Ballater, Emily arrived a little early in Dinnet for her surveillance of the abandoned Bus Company building. She parked more or less in the spot down the road where Nessa stopped the night she saw the white van with the 'sporty' car outside. She felt relieved Hamish showed the same indifference other boys her age usually did. She didn't want to give him any personal information about herself or to have to lie to him. If he knew about the Bartholomew and Hobbs Detective Agency, he didn't mention it. He was happy to give her more information about both Gina and her 'half- brother' Rory Quinnell from seeing them together when he worked at McDougal's in Aberdeen , which all sounded strange to Emily. She couldn't quite believe what he was telling her could be true. She even thought perhaps he was exaggerating trying to impress her. Emily sighed settling down for a longer than expected stint watching the Bus Company premises. Her mind moved back to Robbie Cowan.....

* * * * *

Emily heard the bell on the grocer's shop door tinkle from where she stood lurking in the shadows of the terraced house up the hill behind it. The sound of laughter made her take a step backwards through the open gate disturbing a black cat she almost trod on that hissed at her then scooted across the road.

When she leaned forward to peer down the road, she saw Robbie and Kirstie, huddled under the umbrella, walking away from the shop. Robbie was holding a bottle in one hand, his other arm once again entwined with Kirstie's. He looked behind him when he saw the cat run across the road.

She waited until they were far enough ahead, left her hiding place to slowly trail after them, only stopping once again to watch them disappear into a two-storey terraced house. Two thoughts occurred to her, one being Kirstie appeared to be closer to him in age, the other was they looked happy together. Both thoughts reduced her to such sadness she felt a dull pain inside her chest.

She saw the light in an upstairs window come on and Kirstie at the window close the curtains. She finally realised Robbie had moved on, the fact confirmed by his bungalow being up for sale back home. Here was the reason. He found someone else. Finally, she knew he was never coming back to her.

CHAPTER 28

Emily felt so wired when she got home from being up all night, she couldn't sleep. Her thoughts were still on Robbie. After talking to Hamish on their 'date' she was consumed by her hatred for Gina Taylor. Even though she knew what he told her was only hearsay, she discovered the loathsome girl was living with her brother on the Quinnell estate. Robbie, she saw was with a new girl living in a flat near her father in Nottingham. Here she was sitting up all night watching empty premises at Dinnet! *Where's the justice in that?*

Despite Bart's pre-warning about taking no risks, to relieve the boredom of the job, she was twice tempted to sneak a look around the back of the Bus Company building. She once even took her torch out of the glove compartment to do just that. The third time she grabbed the torch, her hand on the door, she was stopped by the early milk float lights creeping slowly along the road behind her in her rear view mirror.

This was her cue to finish her vigil. She waited for the milk float to pass before she started the engine to drive home. She was sure no one would be visiting the building now there were people about to see them.

Once home she stood in the shower letting the hot water ease away her stiffness from sitting so long in one position. Bart was out early before Emily could give him her negative report on the Bus Company building. He was covering for Mitch on the 'Ernest' surveillance whilst she was at the hospital for her annual check-up.

Bart left Emily in bed expecting her to catch up on some sleep. She left before Isla Strachan came in to cover the shop. Fuelled by her desire to know if Hamish's rumour was true, she made her way out to the Quinnell Estate to check for herself where Gina Taylor was living. The little scene she witnessed of the girl with David Taylor in Banchory she compared with her hugging the motorbike rider in the video, was enough to tell her there was an intimacy between them both. She still considered it wrong despite the rerun of Robbie's words in her head, *'Don't forget they aren't actually blood relatives, even if most folk think they are'* he told her on the day they found Gina's mother still living in the village.

Once Emily got to the Quinnell farm she realised the estate was much too large to be able to do a physical search for David Taylor's cottage. Consequently, lacking any kind of plan, she decided to mix with the shoppers visiting the farm shop. She parked her mini in the main car park before joining the other basket carrying people walking around inspecting the goods on the shelves.

She hated the idea of contributing to the Quinnell profits, yet needed to look like she was buying something. She chose a pack of the bacon she knew Bart enjoyed, reminding herself the Quinnell wrapper would give away where she got it and he would ask her why she was there.

Once around the shop she joined the checkout queue with the rest of the customers where she recognised the woman in the picture Robbie took when he came with Helen Daniels looking for Finn's ex-girlfriend. The woman's name Lily told her was Joy who used to work in the gift shop at Castle Daingneach. Lily found her a difficult person to work with and not at all pleasant to know. She must be a tough person because Robbie once saw her actively stand up for herself against Rupert Quinnell's attempt to intimidate her.

Today Joy was keeping a close eye on the other check out till where a very young girl, maybe fifteen or sixteen, with rainbow streaks in her long blonde hair, was laughing whilst chatting to the customers she was serving. Emily thought she would rather be in her queue, but was curious to meet *joyless* Joy as Lily called this sour faced woman. At first sight Joy reminded her of her own mother, the thought did nothing to lighten her fractious mood, still present from the night before.

Emily was almost at the counter when Rupert Quinnell came in. She's only seen him one time through the coffee shop window, when Charlotte Reynolds stood at the table where she was sitting with Bart. She recalled how Charlotte froze with fear as she looked through the window into the courtyard seeing him walk past. Upon reflection her expression was not so much fear as terror.

To Emily up close Rupert Quinnell looked young for his age, with a full head of floppy hair bouncing on his forehead as he walked. With his delicate facial features, her impression of him was he looked a little effeminate, although his reputation, she knew, was his liking for young girls like Anabel Taylor, when she was still a school girl with a Saturday job on his farm.

As if someone pressed a button, Joy's sour face suddenly changed to a beaming smile at the sight of Rupert Quinnell. He ignored her completely, his eyes fixed on the young girl at the other cash till. Did she imagine he looked like he was drooling? He moved around the counter to stand close behind the girl, leaned in, his face brushing her hair. Emily watched his breath blow the fine strands of her long hair as he whispered something in her ear. On the other till, Joy's face returned to sour. Without turning, the girl giggled, completed the sale she was making then locked the till and left.

Rupert Quinnell pointed at the few people still waiting in her queue, motioned them to move into Joy's line where Emily was at the front being served. There were a few grumbles as they reluctantly complied.

Quinnell leaned into Joy. Emily heard his voice for the first time now at the front having her groceries checked out. His voice was higher than you would expect for a man, with a slight lisp, "Coco's on a break," he said with a hint of a warning, almost daring her to complain.

Joy took Emily's money, giving her some change she could see immediately was too much. Neither Quinnell nor Joy noticed.

Emily paused now in a quandary, she knew if she pointed the discrepancy out Joy would be in trouble from Quinnell, who showed no sign of moving away, he hung intimidatingly on her shoulder. The scene felt like they were frozen with Emily the only one who could move. She picked up her carrier bag and walked away still holding the money in her hand.

She didn't stop until she was outside the farm shop door pretending to look at the items bordering the walkway whilst waiting for Rupert Quinnell to leave to enable her to return the money to Joy. When he came out, she saw something in his excited face to make her follow him instead. She trailed behind as he cut across into the garden centre, out through the back doors to the outside plant displays.

She followed him slowly zig zagging through the outdoor sheds display she remembered looking at before The March of Time got its own outside workshop in the back garden. She remembered Bart's adamant refusal to purchase one from here. Quinnell opened a gate in the perimeter fence disappearing through. Emily followed.

CHAPTER 29

Momentarily disorientated, Robbie woke up from a dream where he was flying his microlight. He felt the familiar overwhelming sense of freedom he got gliding through clouds. He opened his eyes as far as a thud of pain allowed; the clouds dissolved revealing an unfamiliar room. He sat up in a sudden panic. The jerk of his head, immediately followed by more throbbing pain, made him feel light-headed with an acute need to vomit. He rolled out of bed, staggered over to the sink across the room where he dry retched before fetching up acidic bile, thankfully, into an empty washing up bowl. He was mindful he was naked except for a pair of boxer shorts.

When he turned round he was grateful to see the bed was empty except for a piece of paper sitting on the pillow next to where he woke. He made his way back unsteadily to sit on the edge of the bed, picking up the note he read, 'Gone to work, you were out for the count, see you later? K'

The K set his brain to function. He remembered coming back here with Kirstie from Hunters the night before, determined to pump her for information about Sid Bailey. The bottle of wine they bought with them from Ali's corner shop was a mistake. No, not the wine….something else they drank later, sickly sweet, tasting strongly of apricots. He couldn't remember what she said the stuff was, he simply kept on drinking, was all he could remember. Only now he knew it didn't mix well with the wine or the beer he had earlier.

He got to his feet again, quickly searching for the rest of his clothes scattered about the floor on the other side of the bed. He got as far as bending down to put his trainers on when the room tilted giving him a sudden flash of the Emily look-alike, with short hair, from the restaurant the night before. The face filled his mind, mingled with the growing sense of guilt he felt for being there all night with the waitress from Hunters and……he couldn't quite remember other than feeling warm, comfortable in Kirstie's bed, as he drifted off to sleep. Then the vivid dream came again of flying his microlight, he was having a lot lately.

He finished dressing, determined to get out of the place before she came back to find him still there. Even though it was daylight the sky was overcast with drizzling rain. He didn't have a watch, something he couldn't be seen to wear because of his cover as a barely surviving petty druggie who would have pawned a watch to buy drugs if he owned one. He had no idea of the time.

The thought made him frown. Why Kirstie would be interested in someone out on their luck or was his cover not very convincing? Either way, he was uncertain his eagerness to get information from her to move his task along quicker, might have compromised him. He could remember very little about the night before or whether he even broached the subject of Sid Bailey at all. Nothing came back to him.

The brisk walk back to his miserable flat, battling against cold sharp arrows of rain, soaked him through and gave him the opportunity to reassess his misguided plan. He silently reprimanded himself for his impatience at not sticking with the long game. He felt ashamed. He couldn't even remember if he had sex with Kirstie. He knew it was wrong to take advantage of her – surely he would have remembered?

Emily sprang back in his head again; her innocent face with those big soulful eyes staring at him accusingly. Emily who he only ever slept with the once, then just a cuddle before falling asleep together because he didn't want to push her into something she wasn't ready for.

He reached the concrete jungle he called 'home' where his dismal flat waited to swallow him up. His sole thought being how much longer could he bare to live here whilst the words of his handler, "If it all gets too much for you or gets dangerous, we'll get you out," slid back into *his mind giving him little comfort. It was quickly followed by telling himself to get on with the job.*

CHAPTER 30

On entering the Bistro Bart found the place unusually empty of customers for this time in the evening although grateful for a quiet moment to mull over the many issues on his mind. Given the normal volume of his own voice he disliked raucous laughter, especially the clatter of unruly children you often found in eating establishments early evening. The ineffectual parental scalding vexed him greatly. He often wondered why they bothered having children especially the ones who ignored their behaviour. None of it helped his digestion.

There was too much going on in his mind at present, he welcomed the chance of a quiet meal to satisfy his hunger as well as give his thought processes a chance to sift through the issues.

He took in the pleasant ambience of the restaurant's modern décor, with subdued lighting around the uncluttered discretely spaced tables for intimate dining. Despite the lack of other customers, he chose to sit at the quietest table behind a shelving partition containing many potted plants dividing this eating area from the others in the room in case there was a sudden influx of diners.

He rejected a starter having taken a sneaky peek at the 'sweets' menu with a tempting array of delicious desserts on offer he knew he couldn't resist or have room for if he chose three courses. Bart ordered the homemade 'Bistro Burger' made with prime Scottish beef, accompanied by fries, coleslaw and a substantial salad garnish which always made him feel righteous as a nod to 'healthy', although he knew Emily wouldn't agree. The burger tasted wonderful from the very first bite.

He began by contemplating the concerns circulating in his head. Firstly he felt saddened by Mary MacLeod's enforced confinement at the Castle as the slow machinery of Operation Graffiti ground on. He could find no way of helping speed matters along, being mindful of how his last attempt culminated drastically in the castle bomb. He was reluctant to even try.

He moved on to consider the 'Ernest' surveillance. After reading Michelle's report of her latest observations of Jenny Williamson, he was even more confused by her connection to Robbie's bungalow. *What kind of job could you possibly have to only intermittently visit an empty bungalow up for sale?* If it was at all possible, as the report suggested, she did have a job, why didn't Harvey Williamson tell him about it?

He considered the likelihood of Jenny Williamson being in some way related to Robbie as Mitch suggested. They looked to be of similar ages, yet he knew him not to have any siblings. Emily mentioned this once, so she couldn't be his sister. Why all the subterfuge of handing his mail over with such secrecy? Mail could be redirected.

Bart's deliberations took him through to ordering himself golden syrup sponge with custard for pudding. He noted the bistro was still without any other customers. How could the place make a profit with a solitary diner? Perhaps it picked up later in the evening. The grumpy looking man delivering his dessert had refrained from any superficial friendliness. Daunted by the man's extremely gloomy face, Bart hadn't tried to chat to him.

However, once fortified by his main course he made an attempt, "It's a little quiet tonight."

The man's frown grew deeper, "Aye, must be the weather," he said although with a hint of cynicism.

Bart gave up trying, looked down at the steaming hot pudding he placed in front of him, "Now that does look good," Bart said.

"Enjoy," the man retorted curtly as he walked away. Bart looked round watched as he disappeared back into the kitchen. *Perhaps he too has a lot on his mind.*

Bart's thoughts moved on to the Bus Company premises next to McKinley's. He was considering, what he told Emily not to do, the next time he went to watch the place. He might try to get a peek inside. His recollection was all the windows were boarded up. Even so, he knew of old there could be a gap or a crack in weathered wood to allow someone a limited view of the interior, *no harm in giving it a go.*

He heard a crash from the kitchen behind him like a pile of plates being dropped. The ensuing silence was abruptly interrupted by raised voices as if someone was being reprimanded for their clumsiness. He heard the whoosh of a door, the voices growing louder, clearer. He could make out some of the words being yelled, "Look at it! There's no one out there….." The door swung shut again, the yelling continued, though muffled, before the door reopened.

Bart was able to turn, find a gap by moving a plant pot in the arrangement of green foliage behind him, to see someone emerge from the kitchen followed by the stern-faced man who served him. He was shouting at the departing man's back, "You'll get nothing more because I'm going out of business!"

Bart turned back to finish his sponge pudding. He put a spoonful into his mouth, found he no longer had an appetite having watched the heated exchange between the two men. The face of the man who served him, he assumed the owner of the Bistro, showed all the seriousness Bart already noticed but was now deeply distressed.

That wasn't what made Bart feel slightly nauseous and unable to finish his meal. The shock was from recognising the other man he could place with one of the voices he heard in the kitchen. He couldn't tell exactly what he said, but did recognise the tone was threatening. He matched the voice with the face of the man as he left, except Bart was used to seeing him as a friendlier person, never having experienced this side of his character. He was someone who also brought him food on many occasions, passing pleasantries with him.

Why was Chuck the chef from the hotel here threatening the Bistro owner? More importantly, what wasn't the Bistro owner prepared to give Chuck more of because his business was failing?

* * * * *

When Bart got back to The March of Time he felt deeply troubled by the scene he just witnessed. He poured himself a glass of whisky, sat in front of the fire, there to assess everything he ever knew about the hotel chef, Chuck. The more he thought the more he realised their contact was limited over the years. Initially, he stayed at the hotel whilst searching for somewhere to buy in the area to move away from the east coast of England after making the decision to leave the Witness Protection programme. This far north he thought provided him with the safety he needed because of the remote nature of the Highlands.

During the time of his initial visits, he didn't recall he ever saw or met Chuck, having more contact with Philip Miller the manager. In fact he wasn't sure whether Chuck was even the chef then. What contact he remembered began when he moved into The March of Time over two years ago, the same time the hotel began to provide a limited lunch bar menu. He remembered Phil Miller told him too many people stopped off as they passed on their journey asking if they served food. Someone decided providing lunch was an opportunity to add to the profits.

Bart reconsidered whether these limited takings would have found their way into the hotel chain's coffers. Even so, the idea of making money on the side ran contrary to what he knew about his old friend, Phil Miller who he always thought of as an honest person. Phil never discussed anything about his staff during their many conversations. Bart felt a twinge of sadness because he could no longer ask his advice or consult him about Chuck.

As to the chef himself, he always struck Bart as a happy-go-lucky pleasant person whenever he brought his lunch. The memories ran contrary to the one he saw at the Bistro. Until his ruminations brought him up to the day Finlay Ferguson served him in the bar, then disappeared to place Bart's lunch order with Chuck. He never saw Finn again. He was told he was being 'held' in the staff dining room accused of stealing Bart's twenty pound note just before Robbie Cowan arrived to 'arrest' him. *Would Robbie have arrested Finn over stealing such a trifling amount if they hadn't found the money beside the till later?* This was a question he hadn't ever asked Robbie, a shame he was no longer around to discuss the matter with him.

Bart's memory spiked. On that day, Chuck brought his lunch, went behind the bar to check the till after Bart mentioned the money. He remembered hearing the ring of the till opening. He tried hard to force the memory of the scene over-shadowed by the then manager, Muriel Cameron, confiding in him money was going missing in the hotel.

Bart had a flashback of Chuck's face as he came from behind the bar. He was smiling – no smirking – before he went back to the kitchen. At the time he thought his face was of someone being pleasant, and took no notice. In hindsight he wasn't really sure. Gleeful sprang to mind.

A lightbulb came on as he recalled asking Helen Daniels at the 'safe house' if Muriel Cameron was okay because he failed to talk to her about the day Finn was nearly arrested for something petty he didn't do, which alarmed him so much he left the village. *And was murdered by someone in a 'posh' car a ten year old boy witnessed outside Blairgowrie.*

Bart learnt Muriel was moved elsewhere because *'she was also showing signs of stress'* Helen told him. He recalled Helen discouraging him from talking to Muriel on more than one occasion. When he asked if her stress was something to do with her telephoning the police after they thought Bart's money was stolen by

Finn, Helen admitted, *'It wasn't her who telephoned the police…..let's leave it at that.'*

Perhaps slow to get there, Bart was now sure Chuck telephoned the police.

CHAPTER 31

Emily approached the door in the garden centre perimeter fence with caution having watched Rupert Quinnell hurry through. Momentarily wary, she hesitated. Dare she risk following him? What if he suddenly retraced his steps because he forgot something? She would come face to face with him whilst trespassing on his private land. She gave herself no time to assess the risks.

Impetuously, she opened the door onto a pathway winding through the beds of plants grown for the retail side of the Quinnell garden centre business. Over to her left she could see the roofs of many large greenhouses in the distance. She picked out Quinnell directly ahead moving at a pace along the path heading towards the large manor house beyond the growing area.

Emily trailed him, hoping he wouldn't look back. If he did, he would easily spot her even if she stepped onto the beds, there wasn't enough plant growth to hide her. She watched him turn towards the house at a bend in the path, quickened her pace to keep him in sight. Quinnell led her to the side of the mansion house where he disappeared through a door marked Estate Office.

Emily began to think perhaps her curiosity might be misplaced. She had no real plan of what she wanted to do. She stepped off the path into a flower bed at the side of the house, concealing herself behind the leafy Rhododendrons to give herself time to think what she ought to do next. She was sure if anyone saw her there they would accuse her of trespass. What explanation could she give for her behaviour? Doubt sealed her decision to give up.

Already regretting her stupidity she was about to leave when she heard approaching footsteps and someone talking to themselves.

When the footsteps got closer, someone caught the foliage moving hastily past, whilst the childlike voice, Emily recognised, appeared to be having an argument with themselves, answering in a deeper more angry voice, "He'll not want you....only me!"

Emily managed to stifle her shock by putting a hand over her mouth when she caught a glimpse of Gina Taylor as she slowed down before she reached the Estate Office door. After all she came here to find Gina or rather where she lived, but seeing her again resurrected the hate she felt for the girl. She held her breath, what else could she do?

The next five minutes seemed like an eternity. She expected to hear the office door open as Gina joined Rupert inside. She strained to listen, heard retreating footsteps and Gina's unmistakeable voice harshly cry, "You bastard!" as she rushed by Emily's hiding place.

When she dared to look out there was no sign of her. Despite her urgency to get away, Emily's curiosity at Gina's behaviour took over again. She slipped out, moved towards the office to peer into the small window in the door. What she saw first stunned her, before making her feel sick.

Rupert Quinnell held the young girl from the farm shop face down over a table, blocking out most of her except for her blonde hair with the multi-coloured streaks cascading over the table edge. One of his hands roughly pushed her head down onto the hard surface, as he stood behind her, his trousers around his knees, his body moving brutally inside her, whilst his other hand repeatedly smacked her bare flesh. Emily could hear the girl's ratcheting sobs from outside the door.

Shock made her turn to run as fast as she could until she was through the gate into the garden centre. She slammed the gate shut. Out of breath she leaned against it for support until, bile rose in her throat, she turned sideways to vomit against the fence. With weak legs, her breathing coming hard, she managed to drag herself away towards a pile of growbags before her knees buckled. She fell down with a thud.

Tears flowed silently down her face as self-recrimination took over. Should she have burst into the room to stop Quinnell violating the girl called Coco? Her distress at leaving her there with such a monstrous man forced tears to flow freely. She had no idea how long she sat there, ten minutes, twenty, she would have given anything for a drink of water to take away the foul taste of bile in her mouth.

The gate in the fence opened again. She watched the girl come through unsteadily dragging her legs as if she could no longer control them. Even at this distance Emily could see the girl's face was streaked with tears, black mascara running down her cheeks. Her eyes were swollen from crying. She stopped to slam the gate with both hands. Emily saw she held banknotes in one hand.

The bastard raped her and then paid her money?

CHAPTER 32

Time passed before Emily's nausea settled. She had no idea how long she sat there after the girl Coco disappeared. She was surprised to see she still held onto the plastic carrier bag with Bart's bacon from the farm shop, sure she must have discarded the bag as she flew down the path from the house. She found she wore the bag like a bracelet, her hand trapped tightly by the handles around her wrist. She stared down at her wrist as if it belonged to someone else.

"Are you okay?" a voice beside her asked.

When she looked up her eyes met those of Gina's brother, David Taylor, standing holding the handles of a heavily laden wheelbarrow piled with large bags of compost. She would have run again, if there was any feeling in her legs.

"I.....I...." she stuttered.

"Are you unwell?" Taylor took out a bottle of water from the pocket in the padded gilet he was wearing over his t-shirt. He held it out to her. "Here drink this, you look like you need it."

There was only a slight hesitation before she reached towards his outstretched hand, the foul taste in her mouth winning out. She fumbled trying to unscrew the cap. He took the bottle back, eased the cap then handed it back. The water was warm, but she gulped mouthfuls, choked then spat some out at the side of her. She continued to drink greedily.

"Take it slowly," he said alarmed.

Up close Emily could see how handsome Gina's brother was. He had dark, deeply sensitive eyes, with long eyelashes any woman would die for. His long wavy hair reminded her of seeing Robbie in

Nottingham. Robbie's hair had grown long like his since the last time she saw him. Looking at David Taylor in comparison she realised Robbie didn't seem at all like the physically fit man she once was. Taylor had a healthy glow about him, with suntanned weathered skin in a muscular frame. His upper arms bulged under the t-shirt.

As she sat there the thought came to her, *why has Robbie lost so much weight?* He looks gaunt, even ill, in contrast to this man. Then she noticed the wheelbarrow at the side of him was stacked with heavy bags, she supposed lifting those regularly, would give anyone defined muscle. Then she realised she was sitting on a pile of similar bags, he was about to add more to.

"Oh!" she cried trying to stand, her legs failing to take her weight, she flopped back down. "Sorry, I'm in your way!"

"It's okay, sit a while," he insisted with concern. "Can I get someone to help you? I'll go get a first aider, they'll know what to do." David Taylor rushed away leaving her sitting there.

Emily started to panic, the last thing she needed was to draw attention especially not from the Quinnells. She got to her feet, tested her legs to take a few tentative steps until she could move slowly back to her car. The car park was now full with more people milling about to hide amongst.

Once inside the car she saw she was still holding onto the change Joy overpaid her in the farm shop. She could see the money contained the ten pound note she gave her the shopping. The sight brought a flash of the money Coco was holding in her hand when she came through the gate, only hers was considerably more. Emily dropped the money into the shopping bag, put both on the seat beside her. She started the car to drive away.

* * * * *

Rupert Quinnell stood in front of the three CCTV screens watching the young girl, Coco, stagger away from the office, safe in the knowledge the money he pushed in her hand would guarantee to keep her mouth shut about what took place moments before. It usually did, except for once or twice when he had to resort to physical threats. The wry smile at the thought turned his face momentarily maniacal which was reflected in the CCTV screen, swiftly followed by his paranoid mind prompting him with the question 'what if someone saw her arrive before he got there?'

He reached out to the closest screen, flicked the switch to rewind the tape, caught some images flash past and jabbed his finger on stop. The images stopped at where he entered the office, he let the film move on from there coming eventually to see a young girl he didn't recognise creep furtively towards the office door. He thought she looked scared which gave him a ripple of pleasure. He liked to see young girls who were frightened, especially of him. He felt a warm glow as the heat of longing returned.

He frowned watching her stop short of the office then step into the bushes in the nearest flower bed. "What the...?" he whispered out loud. Completely concealed by the foliage, he saw Gina rush past the bushes up to the office door, saw her peer in through the window, clench her fists and with a face like thunder turn away to hurry past the shrubbery the unknown girl was hiding in.

Rupert Quinnell stepped closer to the screen waiting to see what happened next. The girl carrying one of his farm shop bags, he could see the Quinnell logo clearly, emerged from her hiding place, her eyes followed the direction Gina took as if she might follow her. She hesitated before she too came to look into the office window. When she turned away, the camera caught her horrified expression. Rupert Quinnell knew exactly what she saw to disturb her.

He pressed to pause the video to freeze the screen, leaned in closer, recalling the customer Joy was serving when he stood behind her. He recognised the girl because he remembered the light streaks down one side of her hair which reminded him young Coco was waiting for him in the estate office where he told her he would give her a bonus for her work because she pleased him. The smile returned briefly as he gloated, *knowing she would earn her bonus when he joined her in the office. All of them would do anything for a bit of cash, an incentive to keep their mouths shut.*

He stared at the screen. The girl in the picture with the terrified face also looked young. He licked his lips, pulled a chair up to the CCTV screen to find out where she went after she saw him through the door in the estate office. He wanted to try to identify her, because she had an innocent face he would enjoy seeing close up even more than the Coco girl, especially if he could scare her this much.

* * * * *

Emily drove erratically away from the car park, her legs far from responding to the needs of driving a car. She forced herself to concentrate on the controls paying little heed to the direction she was going. She kept moving until she felt more in control of the mini. Nothing about her surroundings seemed familiar. When she came to some woods she realised she'd taken the wrong turning out of the car park. She stopped beside a dense patch of trees on the narrow back road. This was not the way out, she needed to turn around to get out. Luckily there was a gap in the trees, a space where she could back her car to make the turn.

The bumpy surface brought back the memory of the day the motorbike forced her off the road onto the uneven grass verge and didn't help how she was currently feeling. She reversed off the road completely, stopped the car to open the driver's window to get some air, telling herself to take her time to recover, there was no one here to see her.

The silence in the wood was eerie. She couldn't get the images of what she saw out of her mind. The scene wouldn't have been as horrific if the girl Coco wasn't sobbing, shouting at Quinnell to stop. The whole thing didn't fit with how the girl giggled when Rupert Quinnell whispered in her ear. Emily was certain she left willingly, presumably to meet him in the estate office. *What did she think would happen? Certainly not what he did!*

Emily's thoughts were interrupted by the chilling sound of a motor bike breaking the silence; a sound she recognised. She heard the bike begin to slow down, like the day she was concealed at the side of the Esso garage with Bart, hiding from the biker who followed them whilst they were out in Robbie's car. The bike had pulled onto the forecourt of the petrol station to fill up. Emily took a video of the rider after he picked Gina up from her job at the village Co-op store where she worked before the manager sacked her.

Now the familiar sound of the bike sent shivers down her spine. She knew the bike was the same one even before it slowly cruised past the gap where she was parked in the wood. She followed the bike across her vision as it slowed down completely to make a turn into the trees to her left. She caught a glimpse of him a few yards away. She heard rather than saw the bike come to a stop somewhere behind her.

The choice she could make was to start her engine to drive away which might draw attention to her or get out to see what was behind her in the woods.

CHAPTER 33

After a couple of hours sleep and fortified by food, Bart was ready to do his stint at Dinnet watching the Bus Company building. Before he left the shop he picked up his laptop. With all the waiting around he would have the time to look at the graffiti from the Tour Bus building in more detail, especially the stage coach with the highwayman Emily showed him. He parked once again way down the street from McKinley's neighbouring property where fortunately he found a broken street lamp. He shielded the laptop's screen with his coat, any glow he hoped would be taken for the car's security light.

Bart decided Emily was right about the 1980's pop song being at odds with current music trends, yet didn't think the picture was created anywhere near that long ago. *So why is it significant?*

He did a search for the lyrics of the old song he could vaguely recall hearing in the 80's on the radio. He remembered it more for the tune than the words. In fact, he didn't recall ever knowing those. He read the first two lines:

'I'm the dandy highwayman who you're too scared to mention

I spend my cash on looking flash and grabbing your attention'

Hmm, Bart thought, the more he read the creepier it got:

'Stand and deliver your money or your life

Try and use a mirror no bullet or a knife

And even though you fool your soul

Your conscience will be mine

All mine'

Bart shivered as he switched the screen back to the graffiti wall. His mind reflected back to the Bistro earlier focussing on the owner's reaction to Chuck. You could hear the desperation in the man's voice when he said, *"You'll get nothing more because I'm going out of business!"* He knew Chuck hadn't seen him sitting behind the dividing screen, only the owner knew he was there.

Bart revisited all the references on the wall to 'The Bogeyman', noticing most of them were followed with 'he will get you'. All except for the one, '*RQ the bogeyman*' signed by '*Finn*' which was later, after his death, removed with some kind of solvent.

There was no doubt in Bart's mind, his message was somehow significant to why Finlay Ferguson decided to leave the area even knowing, by Charlotte Reynolds own admission, they were likely to get back together again. He knew from several people's accounts Finn made a nuisance of himself with his drunken visits to the Quinnell farm after Charlotte moved there to live with Rory. *Was he RQ on the wall?* Charlotte told him Finn was in no way intimidated by Rory, which his many visits would seem to confirm.

Not Rory, the angry country squire, then. So why would anyone want to remove Finn's statement from the wall?

This particular reference to 'The Bogeyman' was written underneath a very detailed picture of Hannibal Lector from the film complete with the mask they made him wear to stop him from biting his guards. *Was the picture significant or did Finn merely find a space to write his message? Of course, RQ could also be Rupert Quinnell.*

Bart glanced up from his intense scrutiny of the screen, checked the time again and yawned when he saw 02.33. It had been a long day and his thought processes were beginning to fail him. He was too tired to be doing this kind of surveillance. He really felt like going home, then caught a full beam flash of light in the sky beyond the bend way off in the distance, the first sign of life he'd seen tonight. He closed the computer, shifted low in his seat to wait to see who was about at this time of night.

A white van came into view, the headlights were dipped, there being no need for full beam as this stretch of road was residential with street lighting. The lights were turned off before the van pulled onto the forecourt of the Bus Company Building. Bart opened the glove compartment, took out his portable telescope to get a close up of who was driving the van.

Keeping low, he watched two men get out of the cab. Both were slim, similarly dressed in dark clothing wearing balaclavas to hide most of their faces. He could make out nothing to identify them with. They split up, one moving to open the back of the van whilst the other disappeared to the rear of the building. The one at the back of the van stood searching the length of the road for any signs of life. When he turned in Bart's direction he slid further down in his seat keeping him in sight through the telescope.

Bart's instinct was to use his mobile to take pictures, an action that could draw attention if there was a flash of light. He watched as they spent time carrying boxes to load into the back of the van before they got back inside to leave. Bart's spy glass moved back to the side of the van where he was greatly surprised to see, what he thought was a plain white van, had 'Highway Maintenance' written on the side. *Hmm*, Bart thought again, *I've never seen an official Highway Maintenance vehicle without liveried signage or bold chevrons before.*

When the thought came, the van began to back off the forecourt onto the road. Bart expected them to turn back in the direction they came. Instead the van turned to face him and he could make out the shapes of the two figures side by side. He reacted quickly putting his mobile on to video and by lying as flat as he could, he placed his phone above the steering wheel keeping as still as possible.

There was no illumination of his car from their lights as they hadn't put them back on, he assumed not wanting to draw the attention of anyone in the neighbouring houses in case they got a flash of their headlights.

Bart heard the van approaching, with no idea whether he caught anything significant, he turned the mobile slowly as they drove past unable to raise himself to position the mobile accurately. Any sudden movement might have caught their attention. He wasn't sure how long he remained low behind the wheel. He allowed sufficient time for the van to move away until he could no longer hear the engine. Also for any nosy homeowner, who might have been curious enough to look out of their windows, to get back to their beds.

After he was satisfied enough time elapsed he got out of the car and walked over to the Bus Company building to take a look around the back and to find any of those gaps he hoped the boarding on the windows might have.

CHAPTER 34

After a strict self-talking to about getting on with the job, Robbie went back to the Mutton Leg at lunch time needing a 'hair of the dog'. He made sure he looked his usual bedraggled glum self. Morose was how he felt permanently these days. Tempted though he was, feeling hung over, to down his pint in two gulps, he sipped as he usually did to make it last. With his head bowed pretending to be playing with his mobile he looked a sorry sight. He was thinking he would give anything to still have his iPhone with links to the internet to while away the time he spent sitting there.

His, was an old Nokia, looked more like something stolen or sold on the cheap by people like he was meant to be. A mere show piece, to go with his image, only contained a few contacts like take-out places. The mobile he used to pass information on to his handler was carefully stashed behind the panel under the bath in his flat. He was, therefore, surprised to hear his Nokia ring, it made him jump. The sound was loud even with the racket from the fruit machine and some modern noise he didn't recognise playing on the juke box.

When he looked at the screen he saw the name 'Kirstie' calling which confused him as he was sure he hadn't given her his number or put her in his contacts. If he couldn't remember what happened in her bed, what else had he forgotten? Fear gripped him he might have told her things he shouldn't, maybe given himself away.

He got up to go outside to take the call, answering cautiously with, "Hello?"

She sounded up beat, apologetic for having to leave him earlier. He was stunned by her call, didn't know how to respond because he already decided he would make no further contact with her.

"You okay?" she asked when he made no reply.

He stuttered, "Yes.....yes.....only......"

He heard her embarrassed laugh, "You're surprised I rang?" She giggled again. "I put my number in your phone, mine in yours, before I left you in bed this morning," she confessed. He felt a little relieved he didn't actually give it to her, although alarmed because she must have searched his pockets for his mobile. She would have seen his pitiful number of contacts. When he didn't say anything she went on the defensive, "Are you angry with me? Only, you zonked out fast last night. I knew I would have to leave early," she said.

Robbie tried to think fast, "I drank too much, I hope I didn't take advantage of you?" his fingers automatically crossed as he screwed up his face. "I don't remember much about the evening.....I'm sorry. What the hell were we drinking?" He tried to laugh like she did.

"No, you were the perfect gentleman," she said. Robbie breathed a sigh of relief. "Although, you're not much of a drinker are you?"

He laughed again, "True."

"And for your information we polished off the best part of a bottle of apricot brandy I was given for Christmas a couple of years ago......by my Nan, I think."

Robbie thought the taste was disgusting especially as each time he burped he could still taste the sweetness of the apricots. "Tell her you like good Scottish whisky this year in case you pick up any stray Scotsmen, they prefer a dram, even if they might be a wee bit of a lightweight."

Robbie watched a couple of young regulars he knew were drug runners walk past him into the pub. He told her he had to go. The conversation finished with her trying to extract a promise of a further meeting. He responded with, "Aye, I'll call yer,"

He abruptly cut the line to follow the youths back inside the pub. He watched as one opened the door to the bar, looked inside, frowning when he didn't see who he wanted. He let the door swing shut, pushed the other youth, who was standing behind him, towards the men's lavatory. He followed them, having just burped tasting the apricot sweetness combined with the fizziness of the recent sips of bitter, he felt quite sick.

He pushed his way past the youths into a vacant stall, slammed the door behind him in time to vomit into the far from clean toilet bowl. The smell of strong bleach from the purple deposit in the loo made him retch continually until there was nothing left only dry heaving. He turned sitting down on the seat to recover.

A voice outside the door asked, "You okay mate?"

"Aye," he managed. When he opened the door the two youths were standing staring at him. "Some bird I picked up last night gave me bastard apricot brandy," he said moving over to a sink to dowse his face in cold water, "Too much booze on an empty stomach."

One of the youths stuttered, "Mmmy gran likes ththat fffucking awful sshite."

"Be 'bout right. No bird is worth that," Robbie moaned. He left them to return to his pint in the bar. He was pleased his pint was still on the table, grateful he hadn't gulped it down like he wanted to before he was sick.

He noticed the two youths were now up at the bar buying themselves a drink. It occurred to him maybe they were meeting their dealer who hadn't yet arrived. If he was really lucky he might get to see who was running the young people he saw here on a regular basis. So far he had lucked out.

CHAPTER 35

Bart arrived home in the early hours thoroughly exhausted by his long day. He could see Emily put her car away in the garage, so parked in front of the shop in the vacant space where she usually left hers. Once inside tiredness overtook his curiosity to view the video of the occupants in the white van. He immediately retired to bed for a long overdue sleep, with just enough energy left to undress, put on his pyjamas, before he fell fast asleep when his head hit the pillow.

Bart slept in late next day. He woke up hungry but being a creature of habit he showered and dressed before he went downstairs to find the shop already opened by Isla Strachan at ten o'clock. She made no comment to his thanks for opening the shop or his explanation he'd been out on an agency job during the night. She followed him through to the back room when he told her he would be making a pot of tea with his breakfast if she would like a cup.

"No thank you, Mr. Bridges," she said hovering in the doorway with a piece of paper in her hand. "I took some messages for you."

Bart flicked on the kettle before asking, "Oh, who from?"

Isla looked down at the paper, "Michelle called to say she could find no estate agent called Nelsens."

"Neither could I when I tried," Bart shook his head slowly with a knowing smile.

"But remembered where she saw the man in the supermarket. She'll speak to you later about him." Bart nodded at Michelle's discretion. Since he didn't comment she went on, "There was a call from a Mr. Williamson asking for an update?"

Bart frowned irritably having updated Harvey Williamson about his wife three days ago. He was pleased he decided to withhold any reference to her visit to Robbie Cowan's bungalow to pick up his mail and what she did with it afterwards. His instinct told him to be careful.

"Right," he said with no other comment. He felt annoyed by the man's determination to find some dirt on his wife and could barely keep his dislike of him in check, his only comment to Isla being, "Busy morning for you."

"That wasn't all," Isla said. Bart stopped what he was doing having got the bacon out of the fridge, turned to face her again because he could sense some concern in her voice. "That strange girl who used to work at the Co-op on Main Street came in this morning after I opened up."

Bart frowned again recalling Gina Taylor's very odd behaviour, "What did she want?"

Isla took a step closer, lowering her voice a little as if she might be overheard. "I don't really know," she said hesitating. "Not to buy anything I'm certain…..she looked around …..walked up to me at the counter. When I asked if I could help her, she stood staring at me, shook her head, turned round and left. She's a very odd wee lassie," Isla Strachan glanced at Bart for agreement.

"I expect she came in to check if I really did take someone on in the shop," he said not adding she would be assessing who he preferred over her. "She came here having seen my card at the Pharmacy asking for the job."

"Good heavens!" Isla said astounded. "You do know how unsuitable the lassie would be to work here?"

"I do, Mrs. Strachan, which is why I told her I already set someone on even before I met you! There is no way I would let her work here." Bart's certainty left him in no doubt the girl Gina needed to be handled carefully. "If she comes in again when I'm out perhaps you would tell her I would like to speak with her."

Isla turned to leave, then stopped again, "Yes..... there was one other call from......well actually I only caught James....a young man asking for Emily. When I told him she wasn't here he hung up."

"Did you get a number?"

She shook her head, "I looked, it was a withheld number." She left to return to the shop.

It was only after Bart finished eating his bacon sandwich and drank two cups of tea he recalled Isla saying Emily wasn't there. He popped his head into the garage on his way past, found it empty, he carried on through to the shop. "What time did Emily go out?"

Isla Strachan looked puzzled, "I haven't seen her Mr Bridges, she wasn't here when I arrived, unless......" she looked at him a little embarrassed. "I did think she might be having a lie in also." She could see Bart's puzzled face as he walked off into the back room.

He picked up his mobile phone off the table to look at the video of the white van, then like a reflex called Emily's mobile again. He listened to the ringing as he carried his dirty dishes to the sink. The call was abruptly cut off.

Later he tried again, this time the mobile number was intercepted by the mechanical voice operator telling him the phone was switched off. Bart sighed deeply because Emily already failed several times to keep her mobile switched on or charged up which they had strong words about.

He tried to remember when he last saw her, could only recall they met at McKinley's Autos when she was due to cover the Bus Company building next door later. Since then their paths hadn't crossed. *Damn! We need some sort of rota to show where everyone is at any given time.* This had been his recurring thought ever since they diversified, with so many things going on he'd failed to put it in place. He made a mental note to discuss the idea with Emily the next time he saw her. Meanwhile, he searched his contacts for Mary MacLeod's number to ring.

She answered within three rings, "Hello, Bart," she said. "How are you?"

"I'm fine Mary....and you?" he felt obliged to ask given how low she was the last time he saw her when she mentioned her enforced confinement at the castle.

"Much the same," she admitted.

"I was wondering if you've seen anything of Emily today?" He didn't want to go over their previous conversation, he hated to hear the weariness in her voice.

"No, I've not seen her for a while, most of the clocks she's been working on have been at the shop.....is there something wrong?" Mary picked up a hint of worry in Bart's voice.

"No, not at all. I was trying to telephone her as we've been doing different shifts, it's not a problem. I'm sure she'll notice her phone is off at some point and will be mightily apologetic when she does, young people eh? They seem always to be on their mobiles yet can never be reached," he laughed trying not to show he was vexed. "Thanks Mary," he said. He cut the call after assuring her they would be bringing another of the castle clocks back very soon.

Finally he sat at the table to scroll through the video he took the night before. As expected the reel was very unsteady from balancing his phone on the steering wheel trying to keep out of sight. The van, of course, showed no headlights making the figures in the cab dark shapes illuminated briefly by the two streetlights they passed under as they came closer to his car. He remembered lying listening to the van's engine getting louder, the only cue to turn the mobile. He saw the turn was premature, losing them briefly until they were at the side of his car. The driver was in the process of lighting a cigarette, having removed his balaclava, the flame briefly illuminated his face. Bart cried out loudly, "Gotcha!"

As the van progressed the wording Highway Maintenance was caught on camera. He paused the reel, enlarged his mobile screen, to enhance the subtle distortion to the wording. Someone had scratched off the second 'i' making the sign read, 'Highway Ma ntenance'.

I wonder. Someone has a really bizarre sense of humour because it looks like they intended to draw attention to Highway Man.

He loaded the video onto the laptop to see better on a bigger screen. He knew with a little technical help, he would be able to enlarge other parts of the video in the same way. He also saw the van's registration number very clearly as they drove towards his car. The man lighting a cigarette was the garden centre man at the Quinnell farm who he knew was David Taylor, Gina's stepbrother.

The question remained, what was in the boxes they loaded into the van from the empty premises next door to McKinley's?

CHAPTER 36

Bart was back at McKinley's less than twelve hours after his nocturnal vigil there. He found Hamish working on the engine of a battered looking Mini Clubman. The car prompted Bart's memories of his very first one when the model was all the rage. He couldn't help thinking the 'gormless' mechanic looked his usual self, expressionless, hard to read.

Bart ran his hand affectionately along the side of the Clubman, "Ah, I remember these, my first car, in fact....I can't remember the whole of the registration. I only recall BAY something," he said. Hamish stared at him as though he was speaking in tongues. Bart ignored him, asking, "Is Nessa about?"

"Out on a test drive, she won't be long."

Bart thought it the longest string of words he heard the lad speak. "Can I wait for her in the office?" Hamish pointed to the office, nodded gormlessly, as if he expected Bart wouldn't know where to go.

He left him, moved towards Nessa's inner sanctum, where he knew there would be freshly brewed coffee. He wasn't disappointed when he opened the door to the rich aroma from the filter machine. He poured himself a mug because he knew Nessa would offer him one the moment she came back. He sat down on the visitor's chair to wait. He was surprised when Hamish followed him in. He stood as if trying to recall more words he could string together.

"You okay?" Bart asked when Hamish neither moved nor spoke.

Hamish looked extremely awkward. He moved over to pour himself a coffee, his behaviour only confirming Bart's already poor opinion of him. Still wearing his blue soiled rubber gloves, now with a mug smothered in dark oily marks, the mechanic turned to leave. He stopped half-way to the door as if he suddenly plucked up immense courage to ask, "Is Emily okay?" He sounded extremely nervous.

Bart was somewhat taken aback by him asking a question he also wanted to know the answer to. He felt a little awkward about replying. "I haven't seen her today, she's very busy these days," his answer being a little defensive as well as evasive.

"Oh," Hamish said turning once again to leave. As he reached the door he dithered, "I don't know what I said to upset her," he added, "But could you tell her I'm sorry."

Bart saw him start to move again, "Wait!" he boomed at Hamish's back. He sounded harsh in the quietness of the room. "When did you last see her?"

Hamish came slowly back to stand in front of the little man he always found intimidating. He could see his enquiry was more anxious than demanding. "When we went to the Balmoral for fish and chips….err…" Hamish looked like he was thinking hard, "The night you last came here to see Nessa."

"You met Emily that night?" Bart asked realising he hadn't actually seen Emily since because she did the night shift watching the Bus Company building and always seemed to be up in the morning before he got up.

Hamish nodded looking embarrassed saying defensively, "She went off and I stayed there after," he didn't want this very severe man to think they left together or he might have done something to upset her. "Honest."

Bart was puzzled how Emily would even be interested in meeting Hamish. Even though part of him wanted to consider the possibility she may at last have moved on from splitting with Robbie Cowan, he couldn't quite believe she would choose someone like the 'gormless' mechanic in front of him.

"How was she the last time you saw her?"

The question surprised Hamish, sending him into yet another contemplative state. He looked tense, hesitating before he answered, "She was fine…..happy," he emphasised but sounded defensive. The truth was it wasn't something he would ever really think about.

"Did you make arrangements to meet her again?" Bart asked. He didn't want to pry if she has picked Hamish to be friends with, even though he was greatly disappointed by her choice.

"No, not really……" clearly Hamish found re-examining his 'date' with Emily difficult. He knew he must tell the man he thought was her guardian, something. "She was keen to hear about where I used to work," he said feeling more comfortable with the topic as a safe subject to talk about. "Yes, she asked me loads of stuff about working at McDougall's in Aberdeen."

Bells began to ring in Bart's brain. He knew immediately Emily was trying to find out everything Hamish knew about the Quinnell family. He said, "Isn't that the place with all the big contracts for the estates around here?"

Hamish nodded, "Aye, *she* asked me the same question," then he thought some more. Bart saw him frown before he added, "She does have a thing about Gina Taylor doesn't she?"

Now it was Bart's turn to scowl as he realised Emily was perhaps too focussed on the girl.

He tried to cover up the fact by saying, "Only because they got talking when Gina was working at our local Co-op."

Hamish nodded again sadly, "I know people think I'm a bit slow to catch on," he admitted in a rare moment of insight. "I thought Emily liked me a bit….till she asked all those questions……now she won't answer my calls...so…." He looked quite rejected making Bart feel a little sorry for him for one moment because he wondered if Emily led him on merely to get information from him.

After Hamish left the office Bart's misgivings grew. He knew Emily wouldn't lead someone on then deliberately avoid them. She was much too honest to play those kind of games. Except there was the time she hid in the garage to avoid Robbie Cowan, perhaps he should reconsider. In Hamish's case, however, he could only imagine her making it quite clear to him she wasn't interested. Would she deliberately avoid answering his calls though?

As he sat pondering Nessa McKinley came bustling in, saw Bart sitting drinking a coffee, "Good! You got a drink. How are you?"

"Fine thank you. I came to update you on last night's surveillance of next door." Bart explained to Nessa about the white van he saw arrive in the early hours, how they loaded the van with boxes from the Bus Company building. He even confessed to having a disappointing look around the back after they left. He showed her the video he took, allowing her time to view it and rewind for a second time.

After taking his phone back he asked, "Do you have any comments either on the van or the two men?"

She shook her head, "I cannae say I've ever seen the van or recognise the man wi'out the face covering," she said.

Bart couldn't help being disappointed, "Was it the same van you saw when you spotted them the first time?"

Nessa sipped her coffee considering before she answered, "I didnae see the side, I cannae say for certain. They all look alike, don't they and often the point of havin' 'em." She thought some more. "Aye…..that's right, the van was parked at an angle. They drove off the other way, I didnae see the side. I was too far away t'read the registration." She didn't admit she was hiding in case they saw her.

Bart said. "And you didn't recognise David Taylor?"

"Is that who he is?"

"Yes, he's a gardener out at the Quinnell farm, the stepbrother of Gina Taylor who accused Robbie of…..well, you know about that business don't you?" Bart could see how shocked Nessa was. Shock quickly turned to anger.

"So yer telling me he's related to the lassie who caused him to abandon Emily?!"

Bart was shocked by the fierceness in referring to Emily. The full reality hit him. Emily was far from over Robbie if she was still trying to find out what else Hamish knew about the girl.

Nessa caught Bart's shock at the way she must sound, "You may remember the day I phoned you to contact Emily the other week?" Bart nodded. "I wanted to see if she knew where Robbie was.....he left wi'out a goodbye....that's not like him. When she came here we got talking, she thought I would know where he was." Nessa looked distressed adding, "I cannae say I ever heard anyone sob quite like she did. He's really hurt her deeply hasn't he?"

Bart looked troubled, not only because Emily didn't mention coming to see Nessa, he hadn't paid sufficient attention to how she must have felt losing Robbie like she did. *Yet another person in a long list of her losses.* First her cousin Peter, then her father left, the murder sentences of her aunt and uncle, followed by her refusal to move to Grimsby with her mother; pretty much her whole family disintegrated.

Bart felt cross with himself for even thinking setting up the agency could ever compensate her for all those losses. Whilst she was with Robbie there was hope for a different kind of future. He left Nessa to ponder on his update sending her the video to have a closer look at before he left. As he passed Hamish still working under the bonnet of the Mini Clubman on his way out, he considered showing him the video, decided he didn't want to reopen their conversation about Emily, so didn't. What he did do was telephone Jay to officially check the white van's registration for him; whatever was going on in the building next door to McKinley's he knew wasn't something legal.

CHAPTER 37

Jay arrived at The March of Time before Michelle McElrae. He was watching the video reel on Bart's laptop of the white van driven by David Taylor when she arrived. He already informed Bart the van was registered to the Quinnell fleet of business vehicles at the farm. Michelle viewed the reel whilst Bart made drinks updating them on how he came to record it.

"I don't know David Taylor," she admitted, "but have come across the Quinnell's on a few occasions."

"Oh, for what reason?" Bart asked fearing she would be unable to elaborate, still being sworn by the official secrets act. Jay a serving Crime Scene Investigator would also be restricted on what he could say.

She turned the elephant in the room into a joke, "I worked for Traffic before I left the police, the family have an uncanny knack of attracting damage to their vehicles," she smiled cynically, "as well as having form for collecting speeding tickets." According to Bart's knowledge, CID whilst looking for the 'posh' car the small boy witnessed deliberately kill Finlay Ferguson, DI Morris cleared Delores Quinnell's red Porsche from his investigation at the time.

Bart refrained from asking in front of Jay if her experience included motorbikes, he only nodded.

She went on rerunning the reel, "So are you saying Taylor is driving the van in the middle of the night without Quinnell permission?"

"Rather depends on who the other man is," Jay saw Bart glance over at him questioningly. "Could be someone else from the estate given it's one of their vehicles," he suggested.

Michelle looked up sharply, "You think the other one might be Rory Quinnell, Jay?"

"Well, could be, or Rupert or anyone who works for them," Jay ran the reel again frowning. "It's too dark to make an I.D even if someone who knows them all saw it." Bart considered once again whether he ought to have shown the reel to Hamish, who was once in a position to meet a lot of people from the Quinnell estate.

Bart recollected witnessing the occasion Rory Quinnell tore a strip off David Taylor when he was out at the Quinnell estate with Emily. When Bart spoke to Taylor after, he denied being treated badly or that Rory hit him roughly on the arm. To Bart's surprise he defended the episode as being 'his way' of emphasising a point. There's making a point, Bart thought, then there was genuine anger. He saw Rory's anger with his own eyes. Both he and Emily thought Taylor was being given the sack, although he laughed off the suggestion Rory Quinnell would ever consider sacking him, claiming, *'I have the green fingers he needs'* something Bart thought bizarre at the time for a mere gardener to be considered such a valuable asset.

Later they discovered Taylor gave a sworn statement to the police he accidentally damaged Delores' Porsche with his wheel barrow. His statement eliminated the Porsche from the murder enquiry. Bart thought *more than his green fingers then.*

Bart watched Jay and Michelle reviewing the reel, "What do you both think about the 'Highway Maintenance' logo on the side of the van?"

They eyed each other as if waiting for the other one to reply. Jay was first to comment, "Strange for a private estate."

Michelle agreed, "Yes, odd, given there are no highways…….maybe they want people to think the van belongs to some official construction site."

"My thoughts entirely, there's nothing being constructed out at the Quinnell farm is there?" Bart asked.

"Unless it's a diversion, in case someone should notice the van being used during the night….what time was it when you took this?" Michelle could see from the clip it was dark.

"Around two thirty in the morning. Perhaps not the sort of time or place a Highway Maintenance van would be working though." Bart moved over to where they stood with his laptop, "Let me show you something," he said as both of his visitors shifted away to allow him to search for another file. Bart pulled up the graffiti images of the Highwayman in front of the stage coach. "Emily drew my attention to this among the graffiti pictures you took Jay, from the Tour Bus building." He stood back to let them see.

"Isn't he a pop star?" Michelle asked.

"Adam Ant, I believe," Jay being older than her recognised the image.

Bart nodded, clicked up a file with the lyrics to his 80s hit 'Stand and Deliver'.

After reading the lyrics, Michelle stood frowning whilst Jay moved forward turning the screen back to the graffiti wall. "Are you suggesting there is a link between the van and the graffiti?" Jay asked.

"I believe Emily thought the image was anachronistic……out of date for the kids who use the building to take drugs," Bart said. "As for me, I am curious there are two abandoned bus buildings, one I'm certain would be solely of the 'coach' variety of buses and…….." he stopped whilst he got his mobile phone, found his reel of the van, enlarging the screen to show them. "You'll notice the 'i' has been scratched away from the logo making the word read 'Highway Man'."

They peered at the mobile closely, both thinking it was a tenuous link, quite a jump in reasoning.

"You definitely think 'scratched' as opposed to......?" Jay found he couldn't suggest an alternative to wear away only the one letter.

"Without examining the van closely I would suggest deliberately scratched by someone who was making a subtle point, perhaps?" Bart could see neither of them looked totally convinced. "One thing I do believe," he went on. "Whoever scratched the 'i' off possibly did the stagecoach graffiti. I think there is more to the graffiti than on first viewing it.....certainly Emily does. However, the image, like some of the others, hasn't been signed. She tells me graffiti artists often incorporate their 'tag' - not their actual name, more a nick name, because graffiti is a crime - within the artistic designs they produce which she showed me on the wall."

Jay said, "I only looked really closely at the area where someone removed Finn's name after I took the first picture to give to CID. I thought, as did the Finlay Ferguson enquiry, his name was removed because he was killed shortly after he slept rough in the building. I have no idea what conclusions their investigations came to regarding the rest of the graffiti. I assume the whole thing was given to experts for consideration. Are you saying there may be some connection between this and the empty premises at Dinnet?"

"Both apparently don't appear to be unused," Bart said, "although they both look abandoned."

What he didn't voice was his knowledge of Robbie Cowan's departure to join Operation Graffiti. He wasn't sure how much either of them knew about Operation Graffiti's remit. Jay was, after all, a SCI, only involved in the collection of evidence whilst Michelle was no longer a police officer.

"Any chance of having access to the graffiti pictures to look at closer? Maybe fresh eyes might give more insight? Needless to say," she added. "I will ensure they are securely kept."

Bart exchanged glances with Jay who nodded using his mobile phone to send the pictures to Michelle. He added, "I need to update you on a few things at some point also." His intention was to put Michelle fully in the picture relating to the Finlay Ferguson murder.

"For what it's worth," he added. "I think Finn left because he genuinely believed his life was in danger, even knowing he might get back with his ex-fiancé Charlotte Reynolds which I understand he wanted more than anything. His leaving like he did was surprising, something must have frightened him."

"I guess he was proved right there then," Michelle said grimly.

The room went silent until Jay asked, "Talking of Emily," he looked around. "I haven't seen her for a while, how is she?"

The question prodded Bart. With all the talk about the graffiti his concerns about Emily had taken second place.

"Me neither," he said a little irritably, "The lass seems to be AWOL with her phone switched off." Despite trying not to, he couldn't help sounding a little annoyed.

Since Robbie left he tried to make allowances for her lapses of communication. He thought she was getting over him especially after her explanation for cutting her hair like the eighteen year old she was meant to be. Her reference to looking like her mother confirmed for Bart she was moving on.

In hindsight she hadn't really discussed her dispute with her mother with him or what it meant to her. He did think she might have discussed her mother with her father whilst she was away, because ever since she returned from visiting him in Nottingham she seemed quieter, perhaps even more withdrawn. He began to wonder if she discovered something about her parents' breakup she didn't know about which might have upset her. Whatever it was he thought something happened to make her stay the extra day.

"Bart? What are you thinking?" Jay asked. He could tell he was troubled.

Bart shrugged away his thoughts, deliberately making himself look cheery, telling himself he was probably overthinking things again.

CHAPTER 38

It surprised Robbie when the two youths at the bar he met in the toilets whilst being violently sick, joined him at his table. The one with the noticeable stutter, he later learnt was called 'Echo', asked gleefully if he was feeling any better after he spewed. He took him some time to get past the word. Robbie thought it might have been easier for him to have tried a different one but was caught out by a loud involuntary burp once again tasting fruity. "It's gonna tek time, d'ye ken?" Robbie said irritably.

"My old girl swears by a good greasy fry up," Dude offered, which was the furthest thing from Robbie's mind.

"Mebbe," Robbie said. "If you can afford th'luxury. No job, na money, na chance."

The two youths looked at each other knowingly and laughed at Robbie's comment.

"Did yer bird not feed ya?" Dude asked. Robbie looked into his acne face with his suggestive grin knowing what he was thinking. "Yer picking the wrong tottie, mate."

"Y'ave t'get what yer can when y've na money," Robbie shrugged holding his hands out to indicate the way he looked wouldn't attract many women. Not for the first time Robbie wondered why Kirstie was attracted to him, even wearing his 'best' jeans and a clean t-shirt there was hardly much difference. 'Clothes maketh the man' he thought counting on his to show his desperation.

"What dddid you used to dddo?" Echo asked with some effort. Robbie noticed he had a certain boyish charm he thought girls would go for until he opened his mouth to speak. Robbie looked at them suspiciously conveying his annoyance at being asked a personal question, he did this once before when he grabbed the questioner by the scruff of the neck to assert his toughness. The youth picked up on it, suddenly looking guilty, "No offence meant, wwwondered wwwhat wwwork you'd be lookin' fffor." It took some effort to get his words out. Robbie played the waiting game having been taught on his police training to be tolerant of people with impediments. He knew not to interrupt or speak for them.

"Och, I wuz a driver, long haul.....till I wuz caught....well...lost ma licence and ma job," Robbie indicated by raising the remains of his pint his drinking was a problem. "For a wee while. I did get ma licence back, though I've still got ma problem." Robbie downed the remains of his drink, got up to fetch another from the bar leaving the youths at his table.

He ordered another pint going to great lengths to make a show of searching his pockets to find the money to pay. Before he came he made sure he filled his pockets with small change in order to go through this charade should he attract an audience. When he looked behind him the two youths were studying him closely, whispering to each other. He went back to his table to sit down again.

"What work d'ye do?" he asked. He knew already what they did for a living because he saw on other occasions they were only 'runners' like a lot of the others who came into the Mutton.

Dude said, "We get by.....yer cud say we're self-employed." They both thought this highly amusing. Robbie noticed Echo even laughed with an impediment making him sound like he was hiccupping. He wanted to smile himself but needed to look offended again to keep up the performance.

"Well, good for YOU," Robbie mocked. "Let me know if ya have any openings," Robbie's frown enforced his sarcasm to show he was far from pleased to be laughed at.

The acne youth Dude looked over to the bar door opening to reveal a large man Robbie immediately recognised from the night before in Hunters as one of the men sitting with Sid Bailey. Here he was standing leaning on a walking stick, his eyes searching the bar. When he spotted the youths, the man scowled angrily beckoning them with his arm. When the man let the door go, cutting off sight of him, the two 'runners' looked jittery, stood up to obey leaving their pints on the table. Dude said, "Watch our pints will'ya, we'll be back."

They hurried out after the man who the night before had been sitting next to the would-be Italian Mafia 'blue suit' at Bailey's table. He remembered him because he looked the size of a bear with a Santa Clause grey beard and a head of grey/white hair. He was hard to forget having just seen him looking stern at the door, despite the fact he was leaning on a walking stick, Robbie decided he wouldn't like to get on the wrong side of him.

Robbie wondered if he was the dealer come for his takings, but daren't risk a return trip to the loo if he was conducting business with Echo and Dude in there. As far as he was aware he hadn't been seen the night before by any of the men sitting with Sid Bailey, he couldn't risk drawing attention to himself.

At least it confirmed for Robbie he was definitely close to Bailey's gang. Without the temptation of going off grid by ordering a steak last night, he would never have known. He felt a little cheerier because he could actually show some progress in his next update to his handler. Robbie sat waiting, even if the youths failed to return, at least he would have two more almost full pints of beer to drink. Another ten minutes elapsed before the two youths returned to sit down with him again. They both seemed a lot more relaxed than they were when they followed the man out.

"That yer Dad checking up on yer?" Robbie dared to ask nodding towards the door.

The youths found the question funny which Robbie thought was fortunate as it could have easily gone the other way, offended them or *even raised their suspicions. Robbie grinned as if he made a joke they found amusing.*

Dude, tapped the side of his nose, "Like I said, we freelance. Ee's one our contacts........we do a bit of business with." Robbie thought he was trying to make out they were in charge when in fact he knew they worked for the big man as 'runners'. The lads looked at each other again knowingly. "We might be able to get you some work, if yer want it."

"Aye, I do," Robbie said. "I'm getting close to being thrown out of ma place, shite hole tho' it is, it's better than sleeping on the streets." He hoped he sounded desperate enough.

When he left the Mutton he was happier for the first time in six months since he got to Nottingham, although there was a slight dread rising within the nausea he already felt from his hangover. He secured a meeting with the two youths who would report back, they said, on whether their contacts would offer him some work. Robbie knew they would be careful about screening him to make sure he wasn't a plant. He knew his undercover identity would be tested but had no idea how deep Bailey's mob would take it.

CHAPTER 39

Emily sat in her mini for a long time, her head full of the image of the distressed girl, drowning in self-recriminations at running away leaving her there at the mercy of a monster. She was horrified by what she saw through the estate office window, hearing those awful cries coming from the girl Coco, she told herself she could react no other way than to run. Another surge of nausea hit Emily forcing her to open the car door to vomit on the ground. She retched until there was nothing left of the water given her by David Taylor.

She sat upright, her head leaning back against the seat rest, trying to gain control, her thoughts. Her emotions were like a ball bearing in a game of bagatelle hitting things at random, until finally they stopped on the image of the motorbike with the rider she saw through the trees wearing the leathers he wore when he forced her off the road driving Robbie's car.

She shook her head to try to make the image clearer. She was sure she recognised both the bike and the rider with his blue and white flashes on his black leathers. There was no mistaking the sound of the bike's engine having heard it several times. Yet, how could he be David Taylor? She left him hurrying away to get her some help. There hadn't been enough time for him to change into leathers, get the motorbike to be able to ride past where she sat in her car.

The thought made Emily swivel round in her seat searching through the car's back window for a glimpse of where he might have gone. Her heightened sense of curiosity Bart once subtly suggested she ought to try to keep in check, burst into life again, released by the conundrum yet to be fathomed. She swung her feet out of the car, stood up avoiding the patch of vomit, leaving the car door ajar, she moved cautiously to the rear listening for any sounds of the man or the bike. Apart from the chirrups of birds everything was silent.

She picked her way between the trees, her eyes searching the ground to avoid stepping on a tree branch to give her presence away. She made slow progress, until she caught sight of a building. She stepped behind the trunk of a nearby tree, afraid to move forward. When she looked, the motorbike, she remembered Robbie telling her was a Harley Davison, stood in front of a cottage in a clearing amongst the trees.

The motorbike, she knew was worth nearly forty thousand pounds, looked out of place in front of such an unimpressive cottage. The words 'Road Glide' came back to her as the sun suddenly burst between the clouds, catching the metal with a flash of light, sparkling as if in response to the idea of how special Robbie thought it was. He confessed to once wanting one of his own, but on a police officer salary was out of his reach. This wasn't the sort of sleek machine a worker living in an estate cottage would own, it was more likely to belong to the owner of the estate they worked for.

Emily stepped out from behind the tree to edge closer to get a glimpse of the rider. She couldn't believe the bike belonged to Gina's step-brother, David, like the owner of the Esso garage on the A93 believed the rider to be. A gardener wouldn't be paid enough to own this machine even if she hadn't left him back in the garden centre where she was sure he would be looking for her right now.

As Emily edged closer to the cabin she could see the bike was the same type as the one in her video where she captured the registration number. She couldn't see the number plate, the bike stood on its kickstand horizontally across her vision. She edged to her left to move around to the bike's rear, reaching in her pocket for her mobile phone preparing to take a picture of the plates. To do it meant she would pass directly in front of a window giving anyone inside a clear view of her when she reached a position to take the shot. She forced herself on whilst keeping an eye on the interior of the room through the window. She could see no one inside.

Emily raised her mobile to take the shot, with trembling hands, clicking off a couple of photos as her mobile began to ring in her hand making her jump. The sound was loud in the silence of the woods, disturbing a few nesting birds that fluttered away in panic. Before she was able to press the red symbol to reject the call, she caught movement through the window.

She panicked, not waiting to see who was drawn by the sound. She turned running as fast as she could back to her mini, almost skidding on the patch of vomit beside the open car door. She nearly lost her balance, dived inside pleased to find she left the key in the ignition. With one movement she clutched the key, bringing the engine to life, thrust into first gear, moving away fast back towards the farm's approach road to the visitor shop facilities.

She drove like a crazy person not waiting to give way to incoming cars, tore along the estate road until she was through the main entrance, barely stopping before she pulled out into a gap on the main road, only vaguely aware of the angry sound of a car horn from someone who had right of way.

Emily slowed the car down gradually, her legs shook and her heart beat fast. She travelled several miles before she thought about her telephone, putting her hand inside her pocket she couldn't find it. She changed hands, tried the pocket on the other side of her coat and found it also empty. Panic set in as Emily knew she must have dropped her phone somewhere between the cottage and the car. *Damn!* She knew she would have to go back to find it. In addition to the two pictures of the Harley she just took, there were the videos she took before of the same bike. She knew, of course, it *was* the same bike. If someone found her phone they would be able to see what she was doing there.

Emily stopped the mini at the next layby turned the car around to head back to the Quinnell farm.

CHAPTER 40

Michelle hung around after Jay left The March of Time on the pretext of filling in her time sheets on the laptop for her 'Ernest' assignment. She really wanted to talk to Bart about the man she saw Jenny Williamson meet at the supermarket. Since they last met she spent time searching her memory, trying to recall why his face was familiar. When Bart came into the back room after seeing Jay off, he found her sitting looking at the picture she took of the man on her mobile on the bigger screen. Bart joined her at the table.

"You told Isla you recognise him?" Bart said. The man's face meant nothing to Bart.

"Aye, it's bothered me ever since I saw them standing side by side ignoring each other. I remembered where I saw him before though I can't say I know his name," she said. "I saw him in the canteen at police headquarters once when I popped in because I was due a meal break."

"You think he's a police officer?" Bart sounded surprised.

"Aye, but he was sitting eating with someone I knew was a police officer, although was usually working undercover, mostly in other parts of the country."

Bart looked puzzled, "I don't understand....."

"There are cops who drop off the grid. They work for special investigation units that aren't known to the public.....or by many of the regular police officers either. They get sent to do special undercover investigations like infiltrating criminal gangs or other kinds of sensitive areas the police need intelligence on. It's a really specialised part of policing requiring a certain type of person who can easily blend in. The cop I knew who this man was eating lunch with, looked rough….you know, long hair, scruffy," Michelle laughed. "You wouldnae know he was police, which is the idea."

Bart pointed at the picture of the man Jenny Williamson gave Robbie's mail to, "Are you saying he is an undercover policeman?"

"Och no, he was definitely in our force. I remember seeing him a long time ago wearing police uniform, though our paths have never crossed. I didnae really know who he was. Over time you get to know who almost everyone is or at least about them on the grapevine." Bart still looked puzzled. Michelle went on, "I think in CID, when someone is sent away undercover, they are given a 'handler', someone they report back to….pass information to for their operation. They are also a liaison between them and their families……if they have a family. They donnae usually encourage this career path to someone who is married say or has young children because they can be away for a very long time. It's also too dangerous if they should be discovered…..you know….reprisals against their families."

Bart looked quite shocked. He thought about Robbie's last conversation with him when he mentioned he was to make a clean break away from anyone he really cared about because what he was going to do could have repercussions, a high risk of backlash on others.

"Do you understand?" Michelle queried because she could see vagueness in Bart's face with a sudden flash of fear.

He nodded his head slowly before asking, "You think the man Jenny Williamson gave the mail to is one of these handlers?"

"Well, I think he used to be. I do believe he's part of the police. I don't know why Mrs 'Ernest' was giving him the mail from the vacant bungalow though. It's a mystery to me."

Bart realised Michelle didn't know who the bungalow belonged to. "Ah," he said then proceeded to tell her about Robbie Cowan's relationship with Emily. He filled her in on the events leading up to his suspension and why he moved away. She sat quietly listening before she gave a response.

"What I don't understand," she said, "Is why his handler isn't picking up the mail or looking after the bungalow. A handler would if he was dealing with his personal affairs."

"I don't know the answer either," Bart said. "I have to admit I was greatly surprised when Emily told me Robbie's bungalow was up for sale. I did think maybe he would come back one day. I fear, seeing the 'For Sale' sign hit Emily really hard." Bart knew how shocked he was when Emily told him. He glanced at the man on the screen again. "If this is some kind of an arrangement between him and Jenny Williamson's agency…..if she works for Nelsens, we wouldn't be sitting here discussing this if we hadn't been engaged by her husband to get information on her supposed infidelity."

"Yet," Mitch said, "we have found nothing except the one diversion from what is after all a very innocent life of a stay-at-home wife with young children."

"I wonder….." Bart said thoughtfully.

"What?"

"Well, we haven't found anything out about Nelsens have we? I'm thinking perhaps they don't really exist, except as a pretence for the sign to make the vacant bungalow look like it's for sale. Robbie was threatened. He moved out of the bungalow after the accusation from Gina Taylor got him suspended from police duty. This 'handler' presumably couldn't be seen to be connected to Robbie…..it would highlight the fact he's still a police officer. Whoever threatened him knew he was a police office. The reason why they wanted to get him involved in their criminal dealings, specifically as he could fly a plane and would have been useful to them. Selling the bungalow makes it look like he left the area completely."

Michelle listened with interest, then looked puzzled, "Why Jenny Williamson though?"

"Good point. Without asking her directly about her 'role', I can't see how we can find out. I confess I haven't reported this diversion to her husband," Bart looked guilty. "My intuition tells me not to every time I think of doing it."

Michelle smiled, "Well it's not like she's even spoken to the man, only passed on Robbie's mail, it's hardly a sign of infidelity, is it?"

*   *   *   *   *

After Bart's meal at the Bistro witnessing the scene with Chuck from the hotel, he wanted to talk to Helen about the whole incident to get her take on what was happening. He no longer dare make a lunchtime visit to the hotel to casually bump into her because she was clear it could very well compromise her new role as hotel manager. There was obviously more to what was happening at the hotel than he was able to fathom or why Helen Daniels was installed there undercover.

So far he'd resisted contacting her. He eventually sent her a text requesting another meeting at the 'same place' not mentioning the Linn-of-Dee safe house, only saying he discovered something. He didn't mention the episode with Chuck, because he wasn't sure whether she kept her phone secure from others who might see his message, after all she did work with him. She replied much later after Michelle left:

6 o'clock wait H

CHAPTER 41

Robbie could hardly believe at last he was in! He was elated having waited so long to get the opportunity. Yet he was as scared as he ever was during the whole of his police career. Even more than the time he was threatened with a broken glass by a drunken man in a bar fight he once got called to. Now he would have to face the other big issue disturbing him. Selling drugs to junkies, maybe even school kids, went against every moral ethic he possessed.

He reminded himself what his handler told him when he confessed he didn't know whether he could bring himself to do it. His handler looked at him silently for a moment before he asked him to consider the bigger picture, 'it's about takin' out the suppliers, the organised gangs to get drugs off the streets'. He saw Robbie frown critically before he went on, 'That could save a lot of young people's lives, even remove the peer pressure, help to prevent them from takin' drugs in the first place.' The scarcer the drugs the more expensive they become making them beyond a lot of people's means being his justification.

Robbie knew the importing of drugs was a tenuous business at best. Even with tightening control of the borders with new restrictions on importing normal goods, there would be more focus on drug smuggling. He knew there were often large seizures of drugs by the police to put severe pressure on the street selling end of the business, however, he believed they would never dry up completely whilst the suppliers thought up new ways for trafficking.

He once arrested a junkie who seemed to want to talk. Even only half listening to his whiny outpourings, he got the general gist about getting and staying stoned being the only way of coping with the day to day nothingness of his life. 'No job, no money, no place to live, how else was he going to stop topping himself?' Whilst living under cover he began to understand what he meant. Cynically, as a young green copper, Robbie wondered how a junkie with no money managed to buy drugs in the first place until with experience he learnt all the criminal ways they used to secure their next fix. You would do anything to rid yourself of the feeling of anomie poverty brought you to.

Operations to seize drugs were like trying to hold back the tide – impossible without building a dam. He even knew taking out an organised gang lord at the top only gave temporary reprieve. There was always an ambitious dealer somewhere in the chain prepared to move up to become Mr. Big. They weren't always like the Bailey brothers, from solid criminal families either. There were many who held 'respectable' positions in society, you would not believe were anything other than squeaky clean. They saw drug dealing as an easy option to make big money. Such was the world today.

Robbie couldn't believe how easy it was when the opportunity came. Echo and Dude even stood him the means to get his first stash of drugs on the basis he could reimburse them over time. He wasn't as naive as he had to act when grovelling to accept their offer because he knew they were making money out of him on the side for their most generous offer, to get him hooked in indefinitely.

All Robbie hoped was he might be able to meet Bailey, to get nearer the organ grinder. He couldn't allow the two runners to remain in the way of direct contact with the next level because he needed to obtain evidence to feed back. The quicker he did, the sooner he could go back to his own life – and Emily?

When the thought came he was far from overwhelmed. Something inside began to wither over the past months since he took up the challenge to move away. His earlier enthusiasm began to drain from him the longer he lived in these appalling conditions. This was the reason he took the chance to get close to Kirstie seeing her merely as a shortcut to his aims. Somewhere along the way, in the same way he had *lost weight, saying goodbye to his healthy self, he also lost hope life would ever be the same again.*

Whoever was behind the start of his decline, whoever got the pathetic girl, Gina Taylor, to set him up, was still out there. They were people with no faces even though he believed they may be part of the Quinnell clan, He saw only the girl with the baby voice wearing red lipstick. Gina Taylor became the focus of his despair, also his hatred

CHAPTER 42

Emily parked the mini down the lane away from the gap in the wood where she previously parked and walked back. There was little evidence remaining other than some flattened grass, even the patch of vomit, mostly a watery bile, had absorbed into the ground. She could hear nothing. The lane, a farm access road, was free of traffic, not being a general exit from the farm estate, was only used by the Quinnell family or their workers. Nevertheless Emily listened for vehicles, especially the motorbike, before she began to retrace her steps to search for her mobile.

She stepped cautiously once again, looking first one side then the other. She jumped when she heard her familiar ringtone off to her left sounding loudly out of place in the silence of the wood. She caught sight of the brightness of the screen as the sound cut off and hurriedly homed in on the spot before whoever was calling tried to get her again.

She bent to pick it up, turned and walked into Rory Quinnell who was standing watching her. He was dressed in black biker leathers, with blue and white flashes. Emily's instinct was to flee like before, only he was standing with a bemused smile on his face, blocking her way back to the road.

"Lost?" he said with a hint of a sneer.

Emily thought fast, "Yes.....or rather my dog is. I let him out, he was whining to pee...." She tried hard to control her voice, fearful of him losing his temper like she knew he was capable of, "He ran off, I saw him come this way......I dropped my mobile chasing after him." Emily stepped sideways to try to move around the man standing solidly in her path. He countered her step by taking one himself to block her progress.

"What kind of dog?" he looked about him for any evidence.

She couldn't judge by his tone whether he believed her. She tried to stay as calm as she could replying with the first thing to come into her head, "Labradoodle." Crazy though it was she recently looked the breed up on the internet, curious as to who would want to create such a breed. Rory Quinnell laughed then, "A what?"

Emily also laughed, more because her thoughts remained cynical rather than at what he said. "She's a cross between a Labrador and a Standard Poodle." Emily grew hot realising the slip she just made by saying 'she' when previously referring to her imaginary dog as a 'he'. "That is his mother was a poodle, his father a Labrador," she grew agitated when Rory Quinnell frowned. "I really need to find him because he's only a puppy. He gets up to all sorts of things..... especially eating stones...."

Emily moved again to walk around him towards the road prompting Rory to walk along beside her, "I'll help you look," he offered. "Shouldn't you be going the other way?" He asked pointing behind them towards the cottage.

"Thanks, I'll manage," she put the hand holding her mobile inside her coat pocket holding the button to shut off anyone attempting to ring her again. "I think I heard him running the other way towards my car. He'll only come to me if I call."

He quickened his pace, "No trouble, what's his name?"

Emily began to get irritated by Rory Quinnell's persistence. Her temporary fear at being discovered near the cottage and her worry he might have recognised the ringtone from earlier, gave way to annoyance at his attempt to harass her. She stopped abruptly, hands by her side clenched into fists, repulsed by his close proximity.

"I said……..I'll manage….thank you!" She didn't wait for a reaction from him, she immediately rushed away from him towards the road, not looking back to see if he was still following her.

When she stopped shaking, more with anger than fear, she started to shout, "Oscar! Here boy!" She moved on, intermittently stopping to look into the wood to repeat the call as she walked towards her mini parked on the grass verge. When she dare look back she could see no sign of Rory Quinnell and heaved a huge sigh of relief.

She got back into the car, took the ignition key from her pocket, realising how close she came to being discovered, she began to shake. She held onto the steering wheel, lowered her head to her hands waiting for the trembling to stop.

She heard the unforgettable sound of the motorbike somewhere in the distance, knew Rory Quinnell went back for the bike and was coming out to look for her. That's when real fear rippled up her spine. She raised her head in time to watch the bike turn out of the opening from the cottage. She couldn't believe her eyes. He turned in the opposite direction and raced off along the road away from her. A moment of great relief was short lived. She felt the blow to her head before everything went black.

CHAPTER 43

There was no sign of life as Bart parked the Peugeot at the side of the safe house along the Linn-of-Dee road like before. Only this time he could see no light through the frosted glass window in the kitchen door. The garage at the back was empty except for the mound where the tarpaulin was piled to one side. He sat in the car prepared for a long wait. With a persistent sick feeling in the pit of his stomach he picked up his mobile from the passenger seat to dial Emily's mobile for the umpteenth time. He frowned when he heard the 'switched off' message again.

Bart already passed through the anger stage and was now beginning to think there was something seriously wrong for Emily to have her mobile switched off for this long. He experienced her forgetting to charge her phone before, but never deliberately switching off for lengthy periods of time. *Or even past a day without checking up on me.* He couldn't believe she was deliberately avoiding Hamish either even though he admitted telephoning her a few times since their 'date' at the Balmoral.

Bart was coming round to consider options for what he ought to do when he heard a car's engine approaching. The car slowed down before coming into view at the top of the drive. He realised he was blocking Helen's access to the garage at the rear. She backed up to allow him to pull out to let her in. They spent time manoeuvring the vehicles to allow her to put hers away before he slipped his back down the side of the house.

It occurred to him perhaps all the subterfuge was unnecessary especially if neither of them expected to stay very long. Bart watched Helen pull the tarpaulin over the car, then let herself in leaving the back door ajar for him to slip into the kitchen which was bathed in subdued lighting. Helen had disappeared. He stood waiting for her, looking around the very sparsely equipped kitchen. Once again he experienced the chill of the place with the tell-tale odour of 'musty unoccupied' he remembered from last time.

When Helen came back she said, "I was checking everything's secure." Bart's eyebrows must have given away his curiosity. "I don't come here very often," she added to qualify the comment. She pointed for them to sit at the small table like the last time.

"And is it?" he asked as if expected to.

She nodded, "I would offer you a drink except, as you can see, there isn't anything only water."

"I expect the time you were here with Charlotte Reynolds you put the place into use yourself?" Helen stared at him, already bored with small talk. She wanted him to explain why he asked to see her. "I thought you should know I recently ate at the Bistro in the village. I was the only customer. At that early hour you would expect families, people taking their young children out for a treat."

He went on to explain what he heard take place in the restaurant kitchen, of the heated exchange between Chuck and the owner. "I thought, how curious the chef from another restaurant would be there, let alone what I considered to be clear intimidation by him of the owner. Do you have any idea what Chuck would be demanding 'more of' or why the owner would be distressed, or say he would be going out of business?"

Helen remained silent. She looked to be contemplating what she ought to disclose. She got up to collect a glass from one of the cupboards to fill with water at the sink. Bart watched her with interest observing an intense new Helen who was totally different to the person he knew as a friend for a few years. The analogy with Stepford Wives occurred to him again.

When she failed to reply he felt irritated wanting to shake her to get some kind of a reaction, instead he asked, "By the way, how is Charlotte Reynolds doing?"

She reacted like he'd prodded her with something sharp before she said, "That person no longer exists. I believe they have settled somewhere else," she smiled as if pleased by a personal achievement in bringing it about, "and doing remarkably well given all the changes for her."

Bart remembered the first two years he spent in Witness Protection when he was unable to settle for a moment because he might be discovered. People go into the programme because of the threat to their lives. He recollected taking each day as they came, not knowing whether he would have to uproot, change his name or move on again. Of course, that's exactly what he did do of his own volition by coming to Scotland. *And still they managed to find me.* The naivety of her comment heightened Bart's annoyance.

"I know very well what she is going through and doubt she will be 'doing well' as you say. You can never settle even as the years tick by." He knew the old caring Helen would have enquired how Charlotte was doing and by the sounds of it they fed her the line she wanted to hear.

Helen glanced at him sharply, the new phlegmatic Helen giving way for a moment when Bart saw a flash of doubt in her face. He said, "I only hope they are taking care of her. She is a good person who allowed herself to make one mistake......a costly one at that, if you count the loss of the man she was meant to spend the rest of her life with." Bart, who was not normally disposed to sentimentality, felt a sudden need to jolt the new unemotional Helen back to the one he once knew.

He thought he saw her eyes mist over remembering Finn who she was friends with when he was engaged to Charlotte, with prospects of a managerial position at the hotel. Clearly Bart saw he'd hit a raw nerve and took advantage by asking, "Why did Chuck telephone the police to report Finn for stealing my twenty pound note?"

Again Helen looked hurt. A flash of temper flared, "That's water under the bridge, let's say no more!"

Bart was offended by her flippancy and not going to allow her to bat the question off, "No, it isn't and may very well have cost him his life. You do know there was the real possibility Finn and Charlotte would get back together again? I can't believe a twenty pound note.....*my* twenty pound note.....and the accusation of stealing it would scare him enough to abandon her to run back to Glasgow. Can't you remember he loved her so much he went over to the Quinnell estate time after time to try to get her back?"

"Yes, exactly," she sounded angry again. "Charlotte told me how the Quinnells' reacted badly."

"He wasn't bothered about them.....Charlotte said Finn wasn't afraid of Rory Quinnell. He called him all kinds of names when he caused drunken scenes in the café over there."

Helen sat back down, "Yes, I know.....but.....we think he was persuaded something might happen to *her* if he didn't do what they wanted."

"What did they want him to do?" Helen seemed to recoil into herself again. "You can't leave it like that...."

"Let's say he lost the opportunity to get the Restaurant manager's job because of his drinking. A police record for theft would have made his situation much worse, wouldn't it? There's always a way to get people to capitulate. A hotel is a good place to feed dodgy money through....." she looked at Bart to see if he understood.

"You mean like a Bistro?" Bart was beginning to get the implications for the owner.

She shrugged, "Partly. There are other kinds of rackets."

Bart's eyes lit up with understanding, "Protection?" he asked simply.

Her brief nod seemed to terminate the conversation, she said little more before Bart left other than to tell him to ask no more questions as it would complicate what *they* were doing. Now deeply troubled, he drove away feeling a lot angrier than he did on the way there.

CHAPTER 44

The station reception Sergeant stopped filling in the MISPER form to stare at the strange little man barely tall enough to see over the raised counter he stood in front. The Perspex screen seemed to magnify his features which the Sergeant couldn't help likening to a blood hound and often portrayed wearing a deerstalker hat whilst looking through a magnifying glass. The image suddenly came into his mind.

"You're telling me you are a Private Investigator and this woman," he looked down at the form he was completing in biro, "Amelia Hobbs is also a Private Investigator?"

"Yes!" Bart almost screamed through the heavy protection of the screen. He had been there a while, first waiting to be dealt with, then when he got his turn, picked up a bored attitude from the front counter Sergeant right from the start after he said, '*I want to report a missing person*'. He felt the Sergeant wasn't taking his reporting Emily missing at all seriously.

Bart's frustration finally exploded, "I want to see D.I Morris!" he demanded loudly in a strangulated voice, squeezed out between his teeth. He saw the Sergeant looking embarrassed as he peered over Bart's head at the people waiting in the reception area behind him. They seemed well entertained by the interchange.

"Sir, routine MISPERs aren't usually a CID matter," he replied lowering his voice hoping to encourage Bart to do the same. "If she was a child……" his voice trailed off as he looked back at the form. "She *is* eighteen years old. Have you any idea how many people are reported missing each year in Scotland?" Bart saw the smug smile appear on the man's face making his anger soar.

"Yes I do!" Bart yelled. "And….. I also know the police do nothing about looking for them!" He remembered Emily being shocked as she told him there were about 30,000 people reported missing in Scotland every year.

"We don't have the resources to……" the Sergeant began wearily.

"Detective Inspector Morris!" Bart yelled over him. He banged his fist on the ledge his side of the screen, "Now!" Everyone sitting on the chairs behind him stopped talking to listen to Bart's loud voice in the quietness of the front counter waiting area. "Failing that, I'll speak with the Chief Constable and you'll be fighting to be able to draw your pension by the end of the week!"

Abandoning the MISPER report, Bart turned away, walked over to a vacant chair where he sat down, arms folded, to show he was going nowhere until his demand to see DI Morris was met. Meanwhile, he tried to calm himself down. He knew getting agitated was not good for his blood pressure. He glared over at the Sergeant who looked at him one more time before he moved away being replaced behind the Perspex by a woman who called the next person over to take their enquiry.

Twenty minutes later with a considerably thinned out waiting area, the internal door to the station opened. Bart caught sight of D.I Morris with the Sergeant who pointed towards him. Morris scowled when he recognised Bart, irritably beckoning him over. The Sergeant disappeared back to his duties.

"You're reporting Miss Hobbs missing?" D.I Morris enquired.

"Yes, however, that clown of a Sergeant of yours thinks she might be off partying somewhere," Bart's declaration seemed to surprise Morris. "And before you ask, I hadn't got as far as telling him about the attempts made on her life; either the one where she was deliberately forced off the road or the attempt to blow her up with a bomb….but I imagine he wouldn't have seen the significance." Bart glared at Morris to assess whether he did.

"Follow me," Morris turned away leading him to the nearest interview room, Bart thought was more like a cramped cupboard. They sat opposite each other at a very small table where their knees almost touched underneath. Bart noticed Morris place the incomplete MISPER form down in front of him and began to read.

He looked up at Bart puzzled, "This says you are a Private Investigator.....I thought you were a clock maker?"

"Yes I am. I mean I don't make clocks, as you know, we sell them and also mend them," Morris held eye contact. "I was once, in a former life, a Private Investigator before...." he paused to consider whether any of his previous history as a Scenes of Crime Officer or a Private Detective was relevant. He noted the confused expression on Morris's face, deciding not to try. "Emily and I have set up an Enquiry Agency more recently."

"Miss Hobbs is a Private Detective?" Morris sounded sceptical which annoyed Bart considerably given his poor opinion of the man as a CID detective and his dismissal of Emily as a mere shop assistant once before.

"She is a good one, despite being very young, has considerable skills in the technical applications we have at our disposal these days," Bart had no intention of elaborating further or mentioning the part she played in luring Edward Petersen, the ex-con prison cell mate of Martin Frances, who was claiming the inheritance of the cottage Lily was living in, up to Scotland, by creating a fake Facebook account to entice him. Bart didn't think the information would help his case in reporting her missing, he hadn't been too sure what she did was entirely legal.

"And what makes you believe she's missing?" Morris was beginning to wear the same expression of disbelief the front counter Sergeant had.

"Emily moved in to live at The March of Time, we are full partners in all our endeavours. I haven't seen her for a few days. I have been unable to get a response from her mobile…."

"Surely if you live in the same house…" Morris began.

"That's the point DI Morris….I usually see her at some point every day…..we……" Bart heaved a huge sigh. "We have quite a few things on at the moment. Sometimes they require us to be out during the night……our cases require us to work opposite shifts…..so we might miss each other. We rely on our shop Manager to take messages for us and one other associate investigator we have taken on."

"My, my you have been busy since the last time we met," Morris's tone was almost sarcastic.

"We also have a contract with Castle Daingneach for the maintenance of their time pieces often requiring Emily to work over there," Bart was beginning to flag in explaining the complexities of their lives. He sighed again as he realised how haphazard he'd allowed everything to become, "The point is I have exhausted all attempts at making contact with her. I am worried something may have happened to her."

Bart watched Morris scribbling on the MISPER form in front of him. "When was the last time you actually saw her?" Morris asked.

"I saw her three days ago when we met at McKinley's Autos at Dinnet," Bart couldn't believe he let this carry on for so long, his mind having been diverted by other things.

When Morris looked up, an enquiring expression on his face, Bart knew he was going to ask him what took them over to the garage, he decided not to tell him about their keeping surveillance on the Bus Company Building next door or in fact about any of the cases they were working on. He knew the decision to safeguard confidentialities would have made anyone's job of tracking Emily down almost impossible.

He could also see an irony in his impulsiveness at coming to report her officially missing. After all, he was meant to be in the business of finding people and was sure the police would do nothing unless the missing person was either a minor, which Emily no longer was, or there was evidence of foul play. At least he had none, *thank goodness.* Neither did he wish to think along those lines.

You idiot Bart! This is a huge mistake!

Bart stood up, "I'm sorry, your Sergeant is probably quite right, Emily is off partying somewhere!" He walked out of the interview room leaving a shocked Morris behind.

CHAPTER 45

As he left through the front counter, the anger he felt whilst inside the police station he immediately turned on himself. Primarily feeling he'd lost precious time when he could have been looking for Emily. Once he got back to his car he telephoned Jay leaving a message on his answer phone to explain he was worried about Emily and might need some help in finding her. Next he rang Michelle McElrae who was out at Tarland on the Williamson case, to instruct her to meet him at The March of Time. The feeling he was finally doing something gradually replaced the anger as he drove home.

Isla Strachan could see her employer was distressed the moment he came through the shop door. She knew already he was a creature of habit, even before she started working there. She observed he never left his car outside in the street. His first words to her were to ask whether she'd heard anything from Emily. He looked even more worried when she said she hadn't. She followed him through to the back room busying herself by making a cup of tea which she thought he needed.

"Have there been any messages, Mrs Strachan?" he asked even though the only one he was interested in receiving was from Emily.

"Och, only that fussy man again wanting another update," she said referring to Harvey Williamson whose persistence in finding something incriminating against his wife was beginning to grate on Bart.

"Bloody man!" He said whilst rooting in the cupboard of his sideboard, where he found a large roll of brown paper then proceeded to dig into one of the many draws for a felt tip pen, both he took over to the table currently clear of any of Emily's dismantled clocks. He spread the paper from the roll across the table, with a downward motion he ripped a piece off the roll along the edge of the table.

He turned to Isla, "We need some kind of white board," he pointed over to the wall at the side of the table, "Something to fit over there." He looked back at her realising he was talking out loud to himself afraid she might think he was giving her an instruction. "If you have any ideas how we can get one, I would be most grateful."

He sat down at the table, drew a line across the paper roughly mid-way down with the black pen. He began writing days and times on markers at intervals across the line, recording Emily's movements he definitely knew about. Isla brought him a cup of tea over.

"Can you remember the last time you saw or heard from Emily Mrs Strachan?" he asked absently without looking up.

She watched him writing whilst she thought back, pointed to a space on his time line, telling him when Emily last waited for her to arrive at the shop before leaving straight after.

Bart looked up in alarm realising that was the morning after he last met her, "That long ago?"

"Aye, I've not seen her since," she said simply. They both heard the shop bell. Isla left him to attend to a customer.

Instinctively, Bart sat up tensely listening for Emily's 'helloo' she always shouted when she came back home from being out. The ache in his chest at not hearing it for quite some time made him catch his breath. Michelle McElrae came through from the shop having been told by Isla something was really wrong.

"What's up boss?" she asked clearly concerned when she saw what he was doing at the table.

Bart could barely speak. He moved over to the fire, "Could you put any contact you've had with Emily on there," he didn't look round, his arm stretched out behind him. He waggled his hand to indicate the chart he was drawing up. Michelle turned the sheet to face her, saw Bart's timeline of his last meetings with Emily with her stints at Dinnet he believed her to have undertaken. There was a question mark against the last one, he thought she covered, but didn't know for sure.

"Has she written any reports for these?" Michelle asked.

Bart stood up straight from poking the fire, something he did whenever he was tense. He felt quite foolish not having thought to check. Mitch fetched his laptop from the sideboard and sat back down at the table.

"I know Emily is a stickler for doing paperwork," she said logging into the laptop. She pulled up the report files folders. She laughed at how serious Emily was whilst telling her she must always do her reports after each job when they were fresh in her mind. She knew Emily wrote everything down in a notebook, like she did. She took no offense at the time, given she was a police officer for a good number of years, well-disciplined in report writing. She liked Emily too much to fall out with her by reminding her. "Ah, yes she has!" Mitch updated the timeline with the last time she covered the Dinnet job putting a tick at the side to denote a definite contact.

Bart came back over to look at the paper. He pointed to three days ago when he met her at McKinley's Auto, as being the last night she covered after seeing Hamish at the Balmoral, "She met McKinley's mechanic Hamish, in Ballater before she did it," he said. "Mrs Strachan saw her go out next day."

Michelle wrote Hamish into the timeline, "She must have done her report before she left, whilst she waited for Isla."

"Not quite as bad as I thought. Still two days ago though," Bart said.

"Does she have any friends she might have stayed with?" Mitch asked taking Bart by surprise. He hadn't been thinking straight, his old instincts to check these things were crippled by his anxiety. In truth he knew she would have told him if she planned to stay away somewhere. *She knows I'm an old fusspot.*

He immediately dialled Lily's number, tried to compose himself waiting for her to answer. He didn't want to worry her unnecessarily. When she answered he went through the usual expected pleasantries. He began by asking if she knew whether Emily was meant to be working on the castle clocks today. She didn't. Emily always made contact with Lily for lunch whenever she was over there. He managed to skirt around the obvious direct question if Emily stayed with her recently. Lily's chatter moved on, "It's remiss of us, we've been meaning to ask her over for a while. When you see her can you tell her I'll ring her soon to arrange something?" Bart managed to assure her he would before she rang off.

He shook his head sadly, "No, not Lily."

"Okay," Mitch said pointing at the timeline. "We go back to Hamish to find out what they talked about." She tried to make it sound promising, "We know nothing happened after when she covered the night at Dinnet, otherwise there wouldn't be a report...." She didn't add if something untoward happened to her she wouldn't have been able to write the report. She thought Bart looked worried enough. "Have you spoken to Hamish about them meeting?"

Bart nodded filling her in on their conversation; he was quite denigrating about the lad. Michelle could see Bart was surprised at Emily even considering meeting him. "I'm not sure we'll get anything more out of him...."

Michelle picked up he had issues with the mechanic, "From what you tell me he might respond better to a woman?" she suggested.

Bart couldn't stop himself from saying, "He's an absolute dope." Michelle knew immediately his attitude towards Hamish would have been a barrier to the lad communicating with him.

"I would like a crack at him, if you'll let me?" She had done enough interviews during her police career to know how to handle people.

Bart nodded sadly remembering how nervous Hamish seemed when he spoke to him. He didn't want to consider anything awful happening to her or that Hamish might be responsible.

They heard the bell tinkle in the shop. Bart wondered if Jay managed to free himself from work to join them. When he heard voices he went through to the shop to find Isla talking to a tall young man wearing a beanie hat, his hair curling out at the sides framing a rather pleasant face. He stood dressed for the weather as if ready to climb mountain terrain; a large backpack protruded behind him. Bart immediately thought this wasn't the sort of person you would expect to enter a clock shop, let alone want to purchase something and was probably someone asking for directions. His other thought was his face looked familiar.

He beamed at Bart as if he was pleased to see him, "Mr Bartholomew," he said enthusiastically. "It's been a long time."

Bart was taken aback at the reference to the name he went by when he lived in Wainthorpe-on-sea, "I know you from somewhere...?" Bart began.

Isla Strachan interceded, "This is James who I told you telephoned for Emily."

Bart still looked puzzled, which made the young man laugh, "P.D James?"

"Good gracious! It's Peter!"

CHAPTER 46

There was an embarrassing moment when Bart Bridges took a step towards Peter Draper wanting to throw his arms around him to give him a welcoming hug. Bart was never a tactile person the whole of his life and on this occasion he managed to stop himself by thrusting his hand towards Emily's cousin to shake his hand.

"My dear boy, it is good to see you after all this time, how on earth did you find us?"

Peter grinned at Bart's enthusiastic pumping of his hand which, once freed, he put into the pocket of his waterproof jacket to retrieve a piece of paper which he handed to him. Bart recognised the picture of himself with Emily and Robbie Cowan standing in front of Castle Daingneach after the bomb in the Marquee exploded at Mary and Mungo's wedding the year before. The chance photograph was taken by a freelance journalist who illegally gained access to the estate after the emergency services arrived to cordon the castle off.

He managed to take the picture using a camera with a telephoto lens before one of Mungo's security guards with his dog chased him into the woods. Nonetheless, he got away unscathed to sell his prized picture to several national newspapers. The one Peter showed him was underwritten with an article about the castle being targeted by terrorists, wrongly assumed to be the case by a lot of national newspapers after the blast.

"I found an article with a few geographical details although Emily told me about The March of Time clock shop," Peter looked round. "This is a lot like the one in Wainthorpe," he said after a superficial inspection.

Bart saw his face momentarily cloud over, moving from delighted to solemn with a flash of memory of his other shop, Time and Tide, having been situated next door to The Art Gallery where Arthur Claymore lived. Claymore groomed the young schoolboy, Peter was then. He introduced him to the drugs he grew in his greenhouse, to get him involved with the paedophile ring he belonged to. Bart recollected Peter as being a quiet surly boy when he met him. He hadn't seen him since because Peter's parents were sent to prison for killing Arthur Claymore for abusing their son. Peter disappeared shortly afterwards. Bart thought he may have been taken temporarily into care because Emily lost touch with him.

The dark shadow passed quickly from Peter's face, replaced once more by a smile as he looked back at Bart, "I knew roughly where you were because of the photograph. I did have one or two DMs from Emily, although she didn't tell me much…..it was like we were getting back to talking to each other again…." He looked around as though he expected her to emerge from inside the house, "I haven't heard from her lately. We haven't communicated for a while…..my fault really. I've been busy working, I'm in I.T and…..I had a big product coming out with tight deadlines. Well I do get engrossed by the detail losing track of the rest of my life!" He laughed at himself, his whole face lighting up with sheer enthusiastic joy of his work. Bart couldn't help thinking what a delightful young man Peter Draper turned into. "Is she here?" he asked, saw Bart Bridges face collapse into a grim representation of his former self.

"You better come through to the back, Peter, you've come at rather a difficult time," Bart said almost apologetically leading the way into the back room.

When Bart came through Michelle was still sitting studying the time line, "The police can put a trace on her mobile….." she said stopping when she saw Bart was being followed by a tall good looking man.

Bart said hurriedly, "Yes I expect so, only I didn't get that far when I went over there." Bart turned to Peter. "The thing is I haven't seen Emily for a couple of days...."

Peter looked from Bart to the young woman with the biker boots and black denim jeans sitting at the table, then back to Bart again, as if searching for an explanation. The contrast between the appearance of the woman at the table and Bart Bridges in every physical aspect Peter thought quite remarkable. He was prompted to say, "Doesn't she live with someone called Lily? You mean she hasn't been into work for a couple of days, wouldn't she be at home?"

"Sit down, Peter, you've got a lot to catch up on. First, have you eaten?" Bart asked moving over to the kettle to make tea. "Sit down and get warm, I'll bring you up to date."

      * * * * *

Bart produced his favourite food, a bacon sandwich with a cup of tea which Peter gratefully ate with relish during Bart's basic update. Peter interrupted with many questions making the exercise take even longer. Clearly the news unnerved Peter who tried hard to think of everything to pass between him and Emily during their brief direct message exchange. He admitted the content tended to be more about his life and his work as a gaming programmer. She told him very little about herself. He now felt extremely guilty. "Does she have a boyfriend she might be staying with?" was the first thing he asked after Bart looked like he might have exhausted his account.

"She was seeing a young police officer for a while," Bart felt a little exposed telling Peter about Emily's personal life behind her back.

"Well surely he could help to find her," Peter said hopefully before Bart could explain what happened to Robbie Cowan. The random thought occurred to Bart if Robbie were still around perhaps Emily wouldn't be missing although he couldn't explain why. He paused to consider how he might explain Robbie's absence without betraying his last conversation with him. He chose, "He went away with work, she hasn't seen anything of him for quite some time."

"Oh," Peter said. "Have you considered reporting her missing to the police?"

"Yes, Peter, I've just returned from the police station although……." Bart was aware of Michelle sitting listening to him. The fact she recently retired from Police Scotland herself plus his need to refrain from being denigrating about them, D.I Morris in particular, gave him the pause necessary to remind himself Jay and Agatha both still worked for them. He almost literally bit his tongue, "You have to understand how policing works in respect of missing persons. There are thousands reported each year to the police who because of sheer numbers have to prioritise according to age or vulnerability of those people going missing."

Bart understood there were also exceptions to every rule, like the Doyles' case in particular. He refrained from adding the proviso if the person reporting someone missing happens to be rich or well to do, they would likely get preferential treatment. He knew this was his cynical bias so continued with, "They record the majority to circulate their descriptions nationwide, only a few ever get investigated. Those you hear about on the news are likely to be young children or elderly vulnerable people, therefore considered to be in danger." Bart sighed, "Emily is legally an adult….."

"Even after the bomb I read about you were both involved in?" Peter interrupted sounding shocked.

"Quite so……and my point when I reported her missing," he said without elaborating on either the police's reluctance to make a report or mentioning the attempt to run Robbie's car off the road, the telling would have required him to go into details about Operation Graffiti which he didn't want to do. "Anyway, Peter I'm sure when she knows you're here, she'll be absolutely delighted to see you again," Bart continued, changing the subject. "Where are you staying, Peter and for how long?"

"I haven't decided either," he pointed at his large backpack. "I intended to camp. I have a small pop up tent with a sleeping bag. I didn't expect the weather to be quite so cold or know how easily I might find you……I was going to decide how long when I got up here. I thought I might have a break now my last job is finished….I'm freelance, gives me leeway."

Bart looked over at the heavy backpack Peter placed next to the sideboard when he came through, "Yes I see," he said. "Unfortunately we only have two bedrooms here," he paused to consider. "There's quite a lot of accommodation around here. Alas the wrong time of year…some of the B&B's close for the winter whilst the rest are taken up by skiers." Bart picked up his mobile dialling as he walked off into the shop saying, "Let me make a call to see what I can do." He left Michelle and Peter in the back room staring embarrassedly at each other.

When he returned he was smiling. "Done!" he said grinning, "If you don't mind staying in a pub not too distant from here. My friend, Alistair at The Moor Hen has a couple of rooms he lets out during the summer hiking season, he is agreeable to accommodating you."

Michelle saw the beaming smile appear on Peter's face. "Not everyone would be agreeable to staying in a pub, eh?" she said laughing.

Peter feigned a scowl, "I think I can manage," he tutted as if it was a great sacrifice. "I'm not much of a drinker though."

Bart said, "Well I can recommend the food. I've been eating there ever since I moved up here, it's very wholesome fare." Bart's hand involuntarily slipped over his paunch.

Peter's face changed to serious, "Maybe I can help you find Emily."

The simple statement brought a look between Bart and Michelle both of whom had momentarily forgotten the task in hand – to find the missing Emily.

CHAPTER 47

Robbie's initial introduction into drug running was to be used by Echo and Dude as their lackey, not so much at the bottom rung of the ladder, more carrying the ladders. He got the impression they both recently moved up in the organisation, having several runners of their own they were supplying with street merchandise. Hence, Robbie was not selling drugs to punters, he was delivering supplies to others who were. He still felt bad which did little to lift his depression.

When he got really down he was tempted to use some of the stuff himself to give him a little lift but knew it was contrary to police code. However, his recurring vision of the Emily 'look alike' stopped him from spiralling down so far as to ignore those rules. He would be unable to look her in the face again?

The only upside of the new breakthrough was he now had extra money to openly improve his present conditions, both in the clothes he wore and in his eating habits. He didn't actually dare go back to Hunters' steak bar, where he knew Sid Bailey hung out because he would bump into Kirstie again. Her obvious infatuation with him, as demonstrated by her regular calls ever since, would definitely upset the wizened little man if he were to catch sight of them together.

He also didn't want to encourage her because he thought the girl who looked like Emily gave him a disapproving stare, her face kept regularly intruding into his thoughts. He even found himself once or twice standing outside the second house up the street where he saw her go with the man, in case he ever got the opportunity to speak to her either coming or going from the house. He knew he would be tempted. These thoughts worried him and he began to think he had become obsessed. Sometimes he believed he would go crazy, until he realised he was missing her.

Feeding the drug runners gave him a wider view of the people who were involved out on the streets, but little contact with any of Bailey's cronies. One day Dude suggested he get dealers runners to call at his flat for the dope, saving him from having to get out there. He knew the dangers of keeping the stuff in his flat in case the local cops decided to raid which would put pay to his undercover operation. In a rare conversation with his handler he was warned not to put himself at risk but try to show he was up for more responsibility in moving consignments around.

Consequently, on the next occasion he was at the Mutton with Echo and Dude he told them he was looking around at driving opportunities, possibly in long haul to demonstrate he considered working for them was only a temporary solution to his financial situation.

He thought Dude looked irritated by the idea, "Seems to me you cud show a bit of gratitude for the opportunity we've given yer!"

He weighed the pair up in the short while they stared aggressively at him to work out how he should react. Up until then he made out he was a tough, if not a bit unstable, hard Scot. He realised if he acted too grateful he would come over as weak and they would keep him out there as their delivery 'boy' indefinitely.

"Fuck off!" he growled. "You expect me to be grateful forever, running ma arse off for pennies? Nah, not me! I wannah get ma life back.....I'm not gonna fuck about doin' this shite for ever!" He glared at them angrily, pointing at himself for emphasis he lowered his voice to an aggressive whisper, "I need to get ma plane back from where I left it, d'yer ken? I miss ma flying." With this announcement he stormed out of the public bar leaving them open mouthed. He knew what he told them was risky. By giving away the knowledge he could fly a plane he changed his status entirely.

The doubts came later back in his cold rank flat in the concrete jungle. When he thought about what he'd done by revealing his ability to fly and having his own plane, he began to panic. The truth was, he let his anger at the two pathetic youths for believing he would submit to their will, get out of control. In his current situation he missed everything about his former life, especially Emily and being up in the clouds teaching her to fly.

"Damn! You fucking idiot!" He spent the entire night awake regretting it.

He got as far as the mouldy bathroom, about to retrieve his hidden burner phone to make contact with his handler to confess to having blown the whole operation. He even got down on his knees to unscrew the panel on the bath, when he heard the loud knock on his flat door that stopped him.

He walked down the short corridor to the front door with its dingy half frosted glass and caught the shadow of someone huge on the other side. He saw the shadow's arm rise and thump so loudly he felt sure the glass would shatter.

"Okay, hold your horses!" he yelled at the silhouette as he turned the key, "leave some paint on!" He could hardly recognise how forceful his voice sounded, given the erratic beating of his heart and the shaking of his hand as he opened the door.

The man standing there was large, like a bear, with a grey beard and a thatch of unruly white hair on top of his head, he made Robbie think of Santa Clause. He was standing leaning on a wooden walking stick, the very one he used when he stood in the doorway of the Mutton when he beckoned Echo and Dude out. The man's reflection Robbie also once saw in the Steak Bar sitting with Sid Bailey the night he met Kirstie.

"You'll be Daniel Roberts?" the man asked.

"Aye, I'm called Robbie, who wants to know?" Robbie said aggressively whilst quaking inside because he couldn't let on he knew who he was.

"How about you ask me in and I'll tell yer, I might be able to put some work your way."

Robbie stood to one side to let the man walk past him, closing the door he followed him into the dump he called home.

CHAPTER 48

The blackness sprinkled with sparkling flecks of gold came in waves, intermittently dispersed by jabs of pain so severe they caused her spasms of nausea. Periodic flashes of lightning exploded in the dark making the stars dissolve into nothingness. The action played out in a soundless background before consciousness gradually returned. Awareness brought a blend of smells so pungent they aggravated Emily's nausea sufficiently to make her dry heave under the hood. One minute she felt stifling heat promising to explode into flames, the next she was ice cold, the shivers made her teeth chatter.

Emily floated in and out of consciousness on a sea of pain until the banging in her head slowly diminished. A powerful blinding light appeared. She could see outlines through the loose mesh of itchy fabric across her eyes. The light grew less, a mere oblong outline with the shape of a person standing unmoving in front of her. The figure was so still she thought at first it must be a mannequin; arms held out stiffly away from the body, head tilted to one side, close enough she thought if she kicked her leg out she could knock the thing over.

A slight giveaway movement of the mannequin's head before tilting back the other way then held still as if listening, told her this was a person. Emily made no movement, hearing only the sound of her heart racing inside her chest whilst a pulse throbbed at her temples to prove she was still alive. Then the memory came back of the thud against the back of her head as she sat in her car.

The person standing in front of her, outlined by the square of bright light, was somehow familiar, small in stature, maybe a child but definitely female.

She heard a door open behind the figure, letting in dazzling light, so bright it would have blinded her if not for the hood over her head. With the light came the overwhelming smell of sulphur making her want to retch again. A man came through the light behind the girl, took hold of her arm to pull her backwards towards the light, "Leave her alone!" his voice hissed. "You touch her and you're dead!"

The girl wrenched her arm free of the hand, turned back towards Emily who suddenly felt fear of being attacked. The man grabbed the small figure again. He put his arm across her neck from behind, pulled her roughly backwards into the light. The opening closed with a click of the door. The light returned to the oblong outline.

Emily let out the breath she was holding in, trying to gasp for air through the coarse fabric that smelt earthy with a hint of creosote. Her face itched so badly she wanted to scratch it. When she tried to move her hands she felt the pull of bindings holding them behind her back. She tried to move her legs, the movement rocked the chair she was sitting on. They were tied to the chair legs.

Emily began to panic, tried to recall through the ache in her head what happened before she found herself here. The recollection came, of the motorbike in the woods, of her taking pictures of the bike as her phone began to ring making her run for her car to get away. In her haste she must have dropped her mobile with all the incriminating evidence of the same biker as in the videos and having to go back, only to be confronted by Rory Quinnell.

The realisation came. Rory Quinnell was the biker! Not Gina's brother, David Taylor, because he was back at the garden centre where she left him. She saw Rory leave on the bike once she got back to her car, watching him ride off in the opposite direction. That was when she was hit from behind only to wake up in this foul smelling place with the unbearable bright lights and disgusting stench. Fear came when she saw the half-crazy girl through the fabric. There was no doubt in Emily's mind the figure was Gina Taylor standing staring at her. She made her skin crawl with fear.

CHAPTER 49

Bart sat alone in his car outside McKinley's Autos whilst Michelle, having booked her own in for a service, was inside speaking with Hamish McGregor. She arranged to meet Bart there to give her a lift back afterwards. Half an hour later she came out. Bart saw she was dressed trendily in jeans, Doc Martens and a leather jacket making her slight frame look much younger than her twenty seven years. Bart thought she didn't look much older than Emily, perhaps deliberately to encourage Hamish to open up if she managed to find a way to introduce her name into the conversation.

Bart failed to read Michelle's expression as she walked over to his car, like most coppers they practiced a neutral face for human contact. At first they said nothing as Bart started the journey back to The March of Time; glancing over at Michelle she seemed to be deep in thought. Eventually Bart asked, "Any joy with the laddie?"

Michelle didn't want to labour the point she found Hamish excessively talkative, mostly because he was trying to impress her. Neither did she want to open up a conversation about the barriers Bart built with his attitude towards him.

"Aye, some," she said not wishing to regurgitate the whole conversation especially the tedious bits. "I did confirm the Highway Maintenance van is one of the Quinnell fleet vehicles Hamish worked on over at McDougall's. He also recognised the driver as David Taylor, Gina's stepbrother."

"You showed him the picture?" Bart sounded alarmed.

"Aye, though I didn't say how you got it……he thinks I took it because the van nearly collided with ma car. He seemed to accept the made up story about a near miss." She could see Bart looking worried so quickly added, "I edited the picture I showed him.....didn't include the other man in the balaclava, only the van, the logo and David Taylor."

She told Bart she played the injured party in the near accident. "I was complaining about white vans in general and this one in particular. I don't think he's very bright though, he didn't ask me how I managed to take the shot," she grinned at Bart who held an expression of minor contempt for Hamish.

"Did he say anything about the logo being Highway Maintenance?"

She shook her head, "He made no comment.......other than to say the van was the one Gina often got a lift in when she came to Aberdeen."

"Ah, yes I remember Emily telling me Hamish met her at McDougall's," Bart said. "Was David always the driver of the van, did he say?"

"He didn't mention anyone else. I couldn't exactly tell him about the other person sitting next to Taylor because I cut them out of the picture."

Arriving back at the shop Bart parked outside. The conversation ceased temporarily until they got into the back room. He began to make a pot of tea before he resumed with, "Did he make any mention of the logo's missing 'i'?"

Michelle shook her head, "Nothing.... I'm not sure he even noticed. Could have been done later, after he last worked on it, do you think?"

"Yes, I suppose," Bart said thoughtfully. He brought the tea over beside the fire. "Were you able to mention Emily to him?" He was doubtful since she hadn't mentioned Emily yet.

"I pretended Emily recommended McKinley's to service my car," she said, "This is how we got on the subject of where he used to work……I told him I usually took my car to McDougall's in Aberdeen until Emily said I should use them."

"Good thinking," Bart sounded surprised at how easy she found it. "What was his reaction to mentioning her name?"

Michelle wasn't about to tell Bart Hamish believed there was something special between him and Emily because she knew he wouldn't like to hear it. Most of his chatter was about how they really got on when they met up at the Balmoral. Michelle worked out his belief about their relationship was based purely on this one occasion.

She turned the conversation around to agreeing they must have a lot in common subtly asking what interests they shared. When he told her Emily was very interested in McDougall's where he used to work, especially their contracts with the big estates, Mitch showed him the picture of the van. He recognised David Taylor, who she said she didn't know, but heard from Emily who his sister was.

Hamish looked subdued, admitting Emily seemed to have quite an obsession with the girl Gina. She wanted to know where she lived out at the Quinnell farm.

"Hamish told Emily Gina lived with her brother in a cottage on the estate," Michelle looked over at Bart, saw the flames from the fire reflecting in the lenses of his glasses made his face appear as if being consumed by fire and his eyes red like the flash of a camera. Mitch found the effect quite bizarre because Bart was frowning, his face almost devil-like.

"Yes, I think we already knew who Gina lived with," Bart said as he took off his glasses and the effect disappeared.

"Don't you think it's kind of odd?"

Bart looked contemplative for a moment before he answered, "Not really," he said. "She did grow up with him, they already lived together most of their lives."

Michelle frowned, "No, I don't mean David Taylor, they aren't really related except by her mother's marriage to his father." She looked to see if Bart knew what she meant. "I meant Rory Quinnell, isn't he Gina's brother?"

Bart sat upright in his armchair, put his glasses back on his nose, he stared at Michelle, "Are you saying Hamish told you Gina lives with Rory Quinnell?"

She nodded, "Yes, which he also told Emily the night they met at the Balmoral."

Bart turned his face towards the fire, the flames once again caught by his glasses. Michelle half expected two small horns to appear out of Bart's thinning grey hair. He moved his head back to look at her and saw he was deeply troubled.

"You don't think Emily went over to the Quinnell estate to........" he stopped not wanting to think Emily might have gone there to tackle Gina after what she did to Robbie, the thought scared him too much.

He saw Michelle shrug her shoulders lost for a reply.

CHAPTER 50

This close up Sid Bailey's henchman was intimidatingly large as he squeezed past Robbie at the door, leaning heavily on the wooden walking stick to support his bearlike frame, he limped down the passageway into the mess Robbie called his living room. The man stopped one step through the doorway to look around, nothing short of distaste showing on an otherwise stoic face.

"I like what you've done to the place," he ventured critically. "What a shit hole."

Robbie squeezed past him to pick up a few of the empty crushed beer cans littering the floor placing them on a scratched coffee table.

"If I'd been expecting visitors I wud've tidied the place up a wee bit," *Robbie said moving discarded clothes and empty take-out trays from the only other chair than the sofa to enable the man to sit.* "Have a seat."

The man moved over, leaned down to wipe the seat with his hand, pushing a few crumbs onto the floor. He looked at the palm of his hand for tell-tale signs before he ran his hand down the side of his trousers. He sat down with effort, awkwardly stretching out the one leg as if unable to bend it. He placed his walking stick beside him still holding onto the heavy silver knob at the top of the cane.

Robbie couldn't help thinking it looked solid enough to do some serious damage if applied to someone's skull. He had to keep up his pretence of being tough, even though he knew he could out-run the man, he also knew he wouldn't stand much of a chance against a bear wielding such a heavy weapon.

Robbie said, "So, y'know ma name, do yer have one y'self?"

The man openly laughed at the way Robbie delivered the question. "Well, you're a plucky one I'll give you that. I wonder what my boss would think of you talking to him like that, eh?" The laughing crinkled Santa Clause face disintegrated into a frown as he shook his head slowly

"Who's your boss?" Robbie persisted, not letting go of the tough pretence, even whilst the whole of his being was quaking inside.

Before he answered the man looked at Robbie hard, assessing him, "I'm surprised you don't know. Everyone else does. Are you new round here?"

"Aye, you could say that," Robbie lifted his hands to indicate the place he was living in. "As yer can tell, I came here to seek ma fortune."

"So what are you running away from?" the man asked.

Robbie scowled at the question, "That's ma own business…..let's say I made a few mistakes, needed to get away."

The man looked over at the pile of beer cans Robbie put on the coffee table, "Looks to me like you're still making the same mistakes," he commented nodding at the beer cans. It confirmed for Robbie the story of his drinking and losing his licence trickled down.

"Lucky for me I've no money to really indulge them," Robbie said. "Yer 'ave t'pay rent even on a shite place like this." There was a momentary lapse into silence before Robbie added, "So? Yer have me at a disadvantage Mr….?" He watched the man smile again. "How can I help you?"

"I hear you can fly?" he said suddenly. Robbie knew the news must have been taken back to Bailey via Echo and Dude.

"Aye, but I'm not wearing ma wings at the moment, they're in the wash!" Robbie made it appear like the question was an intrusion, one step too far.

"Let's cut out the bravado crap," the man sounded irritated. "My name is irrelevant, though you can call me 'Bear' everyone does. My

boss is Sid Bailey. The name should fill you full of dread……it does most people because if they are still alive they will have heard what he's capable of. You might want to ask around, maybe start with Echo and Dude….."

"Ah, I see how you've heard about ma flying." Robbie interrupted.

Bear stood, albeit awkwardly, leaning heavily on his stick whilst he pushed himself up by the arm of the chair; his huge bulk suddenly seemed overbearing even with the coffee table between them.

"You already work for me," it was a mere statement of fact. "Echo and Dude are on my team. Sid thinks it's a waste of your talent working for a couple of lowlife's like them. We have bigger plans for you," he said as he made for the door. When he got there he looked back, lifted his stick to point at the empty beer cans on the coffee table. "Lose the habit, you're no use to us on the sauce. I'll be in touch!" With that he limped out of the door. When Robbie got up to follow Bear, he'd made considerable progress despite his impediment and was closing the flat door behind him.

Robbie heaved a sigh of relief as he rushed to the door, locked and bolted it behind the man. When he got back into the living room he picked up his mobile, pulled up Kirstie's number, hesitated for a moment before he pressed. Next time he would find out what she knew about Sid Bailey.

CHAPTER 51

Bart and Michelle retired to the back room to fully discuss the Hamish conversation. They heard the tinkle of the bell in the shop followed by an enthusiastic male voice saying "Helloo!" in greeting Isla Strachan. Even though Bart knew the voice wasn't Emily's, the nostalgic greeting was nonetheless sufficient to catch him off guard. Peter came through to the back displaying the infectious smile Bart was now familiar with, instantly disappearing when Peter caught sight of his sad expression.

"Have you any news?" Peter asked anxiously, assuming they must have heard something distressing about Emily.

"No, nothing, her mobile is still switched off," Bart confirmed. "We've been over to McKinley's Autos at Dinnet where Michelle has been talking to the young mechanic Hamish. He was the last person we know of to see her......" Bart couldn't bring himself to finish the sentence because the word 'alive' forced its way into his subconscious. He didn't want to think something awful happened to her.

Peter searched their faces for an explanation neither of them wanted to give. "Is he Emily's new boyfriend....?"

"No!" Bart yelled cutting Peter off.

Seeing Bart's distress Michelle intervened to give him time to calm down, "We don't believe he is, Peter, even if Hamish would like to think so. He says they met on a kind of 'date' in a pub at Ballater. From what we can understand her meeting him was a pretext to get information about the girl Gina Taylor we told you about."

"She's the one who put in the complaint against Emily's boyfriend isn't she?" Peter asked.

Bart, now less animated, filled him in, "Yes, she's a strange creature make no mistake, but we are certain it wasn't the girl's own idea. She seems to be involved with some dodgy people who were trying to recruit Robbie to work for them because he flies a microlight. Lucky for Robbie the day she chose to set him up at the aerodrome was when he was out there with Emily to take her flying."

Michelle added, "The police have t'investigate these serious claims against one of their officers, however unlikely they appear, which was why Robbie was suspended whilst they did."

Peter sat down at the table to listen but before their conversation could get started they heard the bell again followed by animated voices coming from the shop. They waited straining to hear before they continued. Isla Strachan appeared at the open door to the back room looking worried.

"There's a D.I........" before she could continue she was forced to take a step sideways as Detective Inspector Morris barged his way past her almost knocking her over. Bart felt his hackles rise at the sight of him mistreating Isla Strachan who needed to steady herself against the door frame to stay upright. Morris stood in the middle of the room looking from Bart to Michelle; his back being to the table he was oblivious to Peter who stared in amazement.

"Thank you, Mrs Strachan," Bart said graciously allowing her to retire to the shop. Bart's previous anger, generated at the police station when he met Morris to report Emily missing, returned with force, "Well, D.I Morris?" he managed through tight lips, "To what do we owe this pleasure?"

Morris remained staring at Michelle McElrae, his face momentarily puzzled, "Don't I know you?" he asked rather rudely.

Michelle, overcoming her surprise at seeing someone she considered to be an old adversary, openly laughed at him, shaking her head slowly from side to side not quite believing he didn't remember her. There was an embarrassing silence where she remained mute, merely glared back at him with what Bart could see was open hostility.

He intervened demanding, "What do you want, Morris?"

Morris's eyes moved over to Bart having failed to identify Michelle, "I came to ask if you've made contact with Miss Hobbs since we last spoke?"

Somehow his mock concern annoyed Bart even more, "No we haven't. What have *you* done to find her since we last spoke?" he countered sarcastically.

Morris flushed at the challenge, "Your MISPER needs to be registered before……" he heard Michelle's contemptuous laugh again.

"Absolutely nothing is what the D.I means, Mr Bridges," she said with distain. "Doing nothing is his speciality."

Morris's head swivelled sharply back towards her, "You have to understand we get thousands of missing persons reported……and this one Mr. Bridges didn't complete….."

Bart's anger flared, "…..because neither you, nor the desk Sergeant, appeared to think it relevant there has already been two attempts on Emily's life….."

"Two attempts!?" Peter Draper stood up in alarm behind Morris making him jump not having seen him there.

Morris rounded on Peter, "Who *are* you?" he asked rudely. Morris suddenly felt intimidated by the tall young man who towered over him agitatedly.

"I'm Emily's cousin. I recently discovered she was nearly blown up by a bomb at the castle, only to find she's been missing for a few days and the police don't think it's important enough? Now I hear there was also another attempt on her life. What's going on?!" Peter directed his last question to Bart with a pleading look.

Michelle could see Peter's growing concern, mindful they hadn't yet fully updated him about everything. It wasn't something she or Bart wanted to do in front of Morris either, she needed to quickly take control of the situation. "It's okay Peter," she gave him a reassuring nod. "D.I Morris was just leaving, weren't you.......*sir*?"

A light bulb went on behind Morris's eyes as the 'sir' reminded him of who she was. Bart expected him to challenge why she was asking him to leave. Instead, Morris suddenly lowered his head, muttered, "Yes," then swiftly left the room. They heard the bell on the door as it closed behind him.

"Who the hell was that?" Peter asked.

At the same time Bart looked to Michelle for a hint as to why Morris left so hurriedly. A subtle frown indicated she wasn't prepared to discuss the matter.

She responded to Peter's enquiry, "He's a Detective Inspector with CID. As you might realise, they donnae routinely deal with all enquiries about missing persons." She quietly went back to sit in front of the fire to gaze sullenly into the flames.

Bart took it as a cue to make no further enquires. He busied himself with the kettle whilst he brought Peter up to date with their discoveries from Hamish McGregor. Every so often Bart's mind moved back to Morris's look of total embarrassment before he left.

Bart was also curious to know why he came alone when he was usually accompanied by his shadow, the rather obnoxious D.S Copeland who he remembered very well from his patronising behaviour towards Emily. He recalled Emily taking an instant dislike to Morris and especially Detective Sergeant Copeland who always managed to rub her up the wrong way with his chauvinistic attitude towards her. Bart had great faith in Emily's assessment of people at first sight. He thought because of her working in her mother's café from an early age and having to deal with difficult people. She was seldom wrong about them.

CHAPTER 52

Emily felt giddy every time she returned to consciousness partly from the blinding light but mostly from the smell of obnoxious odours. Every time she jerked awake, her head bowed, chin resting on her chest, the pain was intolerable. She preferred to drift off into total blackness to ease the pain rather than raise her head. The ties at her ankles bit painfully into her skin making any attempt at standing impossible.

The next time Emily woke she was in total darkness. She could see nothing through the heavy sacking across her eyes although she could sense someone next to her, close enough she could hear their breathing and feel a light warm breath on her neck.

A man's voice, close, whispered, "Do I know you, little girl?"

The voice was terrifyingly sinister, the words sent a cold ripple of fear down her spine, fetching an echo of a memory from somewhere in the past. Only a whisper of a voice she felt sure she heard once before. She didn't move, feigned sleep by making a deep guttural sound she hoped would replicate the heavy breathing of someone dreaming. She sensed the man straighten up, then move away before she heard the quiet click of a door. Even though she thought she was alone she waited, listened, not daring to make a movement.

Images of people she recently met before she woke up in this awful place played like a black and white movie through her fuddled brain. Shadowy figures of David Taylor asking her if she was okay as she sat on a pile of compost bags. Rory Quinnell, blocking her way in the woods near a cottage, asked her if she was lost. Hamish

McGregor's boyish chattering in a noisy public house as they ate fish and chips, filled her brain to overload.

'Do I know you little girl?'

She was sure the voice was a man, though spoken by someone with a much higher voice, with a slightly effeminate lisp. Recognition when it came was sudden, like the blow to her head. She heard him once say, *'Coco's on a break'*, saw Rupert Quinnell's face whispering from behind Joy into her ear as he stood too close behind her, a smirk on his lips with a flash of excitement in his eyes. He liked to stand near to people, to whisper in their ears *or was that only women*?

Emily began to panic. She fought against the sharpness of the bindings securing her tightly to the chair. They cut deeper into her flesh bringing back the memory with a rush, the awful thing he was doing to Coco in the Estate Office. She felt sick, wanting to scream. She heard herself whimper like a child. The noise went on for a long time before she was able to control herself again.

Why would he ask the question? 'Do I know you little girl?'

Apart from when she stood in front of him at the check-out counter, she'd never come face to face with Rupert Quinnell. Emily was sure he hadn't looked at her or even registered her presence whilst standing behind Joy as she served her. How would he know her? He hadn't seen her watching him through the door to the Estate Office, not with his back to her. Gina Taylor knew who she was, yet hadn't seen her concealed by the rhododendron bushes, even though moments before she also saw Quinnell through the office door window. She hurried away totally oblivious to Emily. How else could he know her?

Emily strained to recall the whole disgusting scene from where she stood outside the door watching his body moving with such force, seeing the girl's hair cascade over the table reflected in the screens on a bench behind. The middle one was dark, the screen like a mirror catching the pitiful face of Coco reflected in it. The other two screens, one either side, were showing outdoor scenes of cars, people, pathways, trees, ever changing jerkily.

Emily realised they were CCTV screens covering the Quinnell Estate. She drifted off to sleep again to shut out any more images.

*　*　*　*　*

Lily Johns was delayed attending Mary and Mungo's wedding the day the bomb exploded prematurely blowing the wedding cake standing in the empty marquee to smithereens. It brought the society gathering of the year to an abrupt end. She had accompanied her partner to an incident at the women's shelter where Nessa worked voluntarily. One of the shelter's residents abusive husband was threatening to take his children away if his battered wife didn't return with them to their home.

Lily was justly proud, watching the way her gentle partner stood up to the threat of violence she could see the man could barely control. Nessa dealt with him with confidence, without even raising her voice. She countered by appealing to the man's hidden 'reasonableness' nobody else could see or like Nessa, believe he possessed. This was new to Lily to witness someone talking down a person threatening violence she knew they were capable of.

Later Nessa assured her the man was frightened in his own way, like the woman was of being beaten by him. She knew his fears were primarily about losing access to his children. Their conversation about the incident took place as they drove away to change for the wedding reception at the castle.

Lily admitted, 'He was a really scary man....I could see the same violence in his eyes Martin always showed me before he......' She couldn't bring herself to think or speak about the many brutal beatings she took from her own ex-husband because it would also remind Nessa of the day she nearly died from his savage rape of her. He believed she stole Lily from him. In his twisted mind Lily was his possession, she would never have left on her own accord. No amount of gentle persuasion would have convinced him otherwise because Martin Frances did not possess any 'reasonableness' to appeal to. Philip Miller discovered this when Martin thought he knew where Lily was living. Nessa couldn't convince him she hadn't even met Lily until after she came to Scotland.

'Aye, they are all scary,' Nessa said.

'How can you be so calm knowing….what they are capable of?' Lily asked her, recalling Nessa whose swollen badly bruised face made it hard to recognise her when she was finally able to visit her in the hospital.

Nessa's silence seemed to last a long time as they drove along until she finally said, 'Sometimes it's better to be quiet. Shouting makes matters worse especially if you show fear….' She glanced over at Lily in the passenger seat, 'there are many men who enjoy seeing the fear in a woman's eyes, it feeds them…..sadly they get off on it.'

Lily had never thought about any of this before. She was always timid, fearful of Martin's temper, of what she knew he was capable of doing to her. 'Are you saying I made him that way?' she asked once again wondering if the whole experience was her fault.

'Och, good god, no!' Nessa's voice rose as she realised Lily was misinterpreting what she was saying. 'These men are animals…….none of it was your fault. They deliberately look for a person they can exert their power over because they are flawed. It's often the only way they can feel good about themselves. The same applies equally to a man or woman, whose sole purpose in life is to have and wield power. Although, I'm not saying every powerful person is a violent person, thank goodness.'

As she sat listening to Nessa, Lily was reminded of Grigoriy Novikov the Russian oligarch who came calling when she lived at Balmoral Cottage because Bart helped his daughter Anna escape with her husband Warren Doyle from him by giving them money to dispose of Lily's car, the one Martin tracked back to Scotland.

Novikov she knew was one of these powerful men who openly admitted to her he had known many men like her brutal ex-husband during his lifetime. He told her after she accused him of being sent by Martin to harm her, because even though he was in prison for murdering the hotel manager as well as what he did to Nessa, he would never give up finding a way to do the same to her.

Grigoriy Novikov assured her he didn't want to harm her. All he wanted was to bring his daughter back home. Of course Lily knew the man didn't accept Anna marrying without his consent; it wasn't fatherly love, just another kind of obsession. The display of power over his daughter, whom she thought must be the heiress to her father's fortune. Sitting in the car listening to Nessa she thought about Novikov's power, there was something in his eyes showing her he could also use violence to get what he wanted.

The difference, she realised, was when Novikov left the business card with his telephone number and told her if she had any more problems with Martin to call him and he would make it stop, she had shown no fear. She no longer feared either Martin or the powerful man who stood in front of her. Crazy though that was she felt protected by the cottage where Elizabeth Grant took her in when she was running from Martin.

The cottage made her feel safe that was why she stayed there so long. Even knowing it was a strange place with a life of its own she knew it wouldn't let any harm come to her as she stood there caressing the ears of the strange dog, Sandy, standing beside her poised ready to spring if the scary looking Russian attacked her. Sandy had attacked once before when Martin found her there. She knew the dog would do again. This was why she showed the man no fear.

After the bomb at the castle where she worked and was meant to be attending the wedding, she heard Martin committed suicide in prison. She didn't let herself think about the Russian's promise. All she knew for certain was, Martin Frances would never kill himself, not while she was alive in the world for him to find ways to torment her.

Pat McDonald

That was something Grigoriy Novikov wouldn't have known.

CHAPTER 53

Robbie expected Sid Bailey would take much longer to check out 'Daniel Roberts', his undercover persona, so was greatly surprised when the request suddenly came demanding his presence before the man. He wasn't sure whether to be pleased his 'legend' held up or scared they somehow discovered who he really was. The request itself came in the guise of a further visit by Bear at his door who starkly delivered the message, "The Boss wants to meet you." He waited for a reaction from Robbie.

Surprised Robbie asked, "When?"

Bear only growled impatiently, "Now!" taking a step to the side to indicate he came to fetch him.

Robbie grabbed his thin jacket off a peg near the door to follow after him as he limped down the walkways to a small deserted carpark where an old rusty orange mini stood alone with only one other vehicle present, long since burnt out. Those people still resident within the concrete jungle of flats didn't have the means to own a vehicle or if they did, wouldn't have left their car openly available to fire, theft or destruction.

Robbie watched the hulk of a man open the driver's door of the mini, lower himself in behind the steering wheel, the seat having been pushed back as far as it would go in order to accommodate his impaired but otherwise long legs. A mini was the last car Robbie would have expected the man to drive.

When Bear leaned over to unlock the passenger door, Robbie slipped inside. He responded to the obvious surprise on Robbie's face, "This is my daughter's car. I borrow it whenever I need wheels." Robbie didn't reply. He was fighting his rising apprehension being taken to meet the wizened little man, Sid Bailey. For all Robbie knew his cover could be blown with Bear taking him to a building site somewhere, to be disposed of in the renowned Bailey brother's way, involving concrete.

After a sizeable pause during the journey, Robbie became aware of being driven away from the City to a destination unknown to him. Bear said, "Some words of warning." He glanced sideways at Robbie who was trying hard to hide any external sign of his inner turmoil. He managed to nod to show he was listening. "First, get rid of the bravado crap you showed me. Sid won't take any disrespect. Believe me I know!"

He saw Bear glance quickly down at his own legs which indicated to Robbie perhaps Sid Bailey was responsible for his limp. Robbie nodded thankful for the warning.

"You accept whatever he offers, because the Boss doesn't take 'no' for an answer." Robbie stared at him to see if he was being serious whilst he also thought it sounded more like he would be offered a job rather than the choice of how he might want to be disposed of.

"Where are we going?" Robbie asked glancing out of the passenger window to try to get his bearings in a town where he knew little of the geography. His knowledge was based on a brief study of the town on a google map as he prepared to go undercover.

Bear scowled, "See, there you go again. You don't ask questions, Sid won't like that."

Robbie was aware of the car turning under a flyover moving towards an industrial estate, before they arrived at a building site where he saw three large ominous cement mixer lorries standing in a row, all with their drums rotating slowly.

He felt the blood drain out of his face and all feeling leave his legs. He wanted to ask again where they were. He kept quiet because he knew he would annoy the big man next to him who he imagined did most of the heavy physical intimidation work on behalf of the little man he looked up to. He pulled the car to a stop outside a porta cabin Robbie imagined was the site office.

Bear got out of the car with difficulty; one leg first, then his rear end as if he was sucked out, in reverse to how he got in. Robbie followed him as he led them up a ramp, along the raised platform to the office door. Bear tapped and waited for the invitation, "Come," before he went in.

Just like the reflection he saw of Sidney Bailey at Hunters revealed, the man was old, maybe in his late sixties, small in stature he looked lost behind a very large elaborate wooden desk at the top end of the room. The desk was totally wrong, for such a small office space the cabin allowed, being almost the full width of the room. There was enough space for a small person, like Sid, to squeeze sideways through the gap to get to sit behind it. Robbie wanted to laugh, only the sick feeling inside stopped him.

In front of the desk pushed back against the wall was a battered old sofa where two other men were sitting, one being the Italian 'blue suit' he'd already seen at Hunters. All three stared at Robbie following him move to stand in front of Sid Bailey's desk. Bailey held Robbie's gaze as if he were X-raying him and could tell exactly what he was thinking. He knew Sid Bailey could sense fear in people because most of those he met already heard about him and were justly frightened.

"Ah, Mr Roberts?" The voice was the dry brittle one Robbie listened to reprimand one of his minions at the table behind him in the restaurant. How could he ever forget the voice?

"People call me Robbie," he said when he found his voice. There was a sufficient quake to allow for the 'respect' Bear mentioned his Boss liking.

"I hear you fly?"

Robbie looked sideways at Bear who was sitting alongside the other two Bailey goons, like the three wise monkeys. He caught a flicker of a frown from him as the 'say nothing' primate, warning him not to *be smart-arsed like he was when he asked Robbie the same question. Robbie took note.*

"Yes, I can," he said simply. He wanted to add 'full licence' with my 'own plane' but expected if Bailey was half the gangster he knew him to be, he would already know this. Robbie only hoped his police associates thought to cover all the angles related to his legend in his new name.

"How would you like to put your skills to some use? I have need of someone who can run....or rather fly....errands for me." Bailey nodded towards a straight backed chair placed on the opposite wall to the sofa, "Have a seat," he invited.

CHAPTER 54

Bart and Michelle recognised Peter's agitation after D.I Morris left. He couldn't believe the man didn't take the threats to Emily's life seriously. They sat him down to update him on everything that happened to Emily and Robbie, culminating in the castle bomb he already knew about. The telling took a long time finally interrupted when Isla Strachan came through to say she was taking her lunch break. Bart decided to close the shop. He walked Peter back to The Moor Hen with Michelle for a lunchtime strategy meeting; it was after all where Peter was staying.

Bart took his laptop with him because he wanted to show Peter the graffiti from the Tour Bus building and the new videos of the white Highway Maintenance van from the Bus Company building. Peter asked many questions with one in particular, "Do you think all these things are connected in some way?"

The question came out of the blue, silencing the conversation completely, enabling them to tuck into their lunch.

Eventually Bart having considered the question said, "To be honest, Peter, I haven't really thought about it." Peter stared at him in surprise. "But since you raise the idea I will say I believe Emily might think so."

Michelle asked, "Why? Has she said something to you?"

Bart shook his head slowly, "No, she hasn't. Although she has recently changed....." He looked frustrated being unable to describe exactly what the change was or when he first noticed. "More so since she got back from visiting her father in Nottingham. I don't think she has accepted Robbie leaving, at least not until finding his bungalow for sale....that came as a great shock to her, well to both of us. Although we haven't really discussed Robbie, I think she believed, like I did, he would be coming back once Operation Graffiti finalise their investigations."

Bart blamed himself for not discussing the whole issue of Robbie with her. At the time he thought Robbie would have confided more to Emily than he did to him, but obviously hadn't. "It wasn't until Michelle and I spoke to Hamish did I realise how focussed Emily has become on Gina Taylor's part in Robbie leaving." He didn't add 'too focussed' as he believed. "I knew, of course, she spent a lot of time analysing the graffiti because I saw her once or twice with it open on her laptop. She did raise the matter of the stage coach showing the Highwayman, with me."

"You think it's connected to the other empty building and the white van?" Peter asked. Bart shrugged to indicate he didn't really know. "Maybe I can catch up if you let me have a look at the graffiti....fresh eyes could help. It's one of the things we like to do with a new game build because you can get too immersed in the detail, fail to see the bigger picture of what you are trying to achieve as the ultimate end result." Bart looked at Peter with renewed interest. He could see the intelligent young man he grew into, mature beyond his years and noticed Michelle flick an admiring glance Peter's way.

"Yes, Peter, no problem, you can have a look at anything we have," Bart agreed.

Michelle suggested, "I wondered if the next time I follow Jenny Williamson to Robbie's bungalow I might approach her pretending to be a buyer to see if I can pick up any information. Maybe she would let me have a look around inside."

Bart wasn't sure, "It's a bit of a risk given we're following her for a completely different reason. I wouldn't want her to spot you later."

"I would be discrete. I do try to change my appearance from time to time. It's something I discussed with Emily after she got her new hair style. We talked about making ourselves look older or younger. She said she got the idea from someone else she knew."

"Ah, yes. The strange girl, Gina Taylor," Bart said with some contempt. "Emily was intrigued by how she could change herself, only I think hers goes along with the multiple personalities she has." He smiled grimly.

"Indeed, my dear, you are absolutely correct," Michelle said with a perfect English accent that could quite easily have belonged to her grandmother. Peter laughed out loud returning an admiring glance. Bart became aware there was chemistry developing between the two of them.

"Okay, sounds good. At least we could try to find out why our potential cheating wife seems to have a job her husband doesn't know about," Bart said wryly. "Maybe we could even get rid of the Harvey Williamson contract altogether." He spoke sharply having recently telephoned 'Ernest' to give him a further, although pretty flimsy, update. He was met by a sudden eruption of temper he didn't expect from the obnoxious man.

Peter who remained quietly playing with the remains of his food whilst listening to them discussing one of their cases suddenly said, "I was thinking about the last conversation you said Emily had with the mechanic Hamish."

They both looked at him having for one moment forgotten their emphasis should be on finding Emily.

"Yes, Peter, point taken we shouldn't get side tracked, our priority is to find Emily," Bart looked suitably chastised.

"What I meant was, from everything you've said, Emily seems focussed on the girl....Gina. What I know about Emily is when she sets her sights on something there is nothing to deter her...." His face changed from grim to delighted at a memory. "My pet name for her used to be, Rottweiler, which she hated..... still a good description of her dogged determination. When she got something on her mind, nothing could move her especially if it involved someone she cares about...." His voice quaked a little as he remembered back to when she found him locked away in a Drugs and Alcohol rehabilitation clinic his parents put him in. He looked over at Bart for understanding, "You remember how she found me?"

Bart nodded solemnly, "Yes, Peter, I do."

"Well, it's my turn, Mr. Bridges.......it's my turn to find Emily!"

"How do you propose to do that?" Bart asked.

"Well I was thinking maybe I should try to follow the direction she seemed to be moving.....find where Gina Taylor is. You say she lives on the Quinnell estate, not with her mother in the village. I will start there. I'm a stranger, nobody knows me, do they? I have a certain level of anonymity you don't."

He looked across at Bart for agreement. He was thinking about the computer game he recently completed involving mysterious Ninja warriors who could make themselves invisible when they needed to. The idea was farfetched although a good basis to work on.

CHAPTER 55

Robbie's first task after agreeing to Sid Bailey's request was to get his microlight away from the Scottish aerodrome where he kept it under his own name. He left the arrangements with his handler to sort out, proving simpler than he imagined. He didn't want to have to fetch the plane in person. He might run into someone he knew, especially Emily, which would be catastrophic to say the least.

A trip back up north would also play heavily on his continuing depression. He wanted to go back home to the bungalow he always felt ashamed of. After his current enforced living conditions, he was sure he couldn't deal with being there without wanting to stay there permanently. He knew he wouldn't ever want to return to his undercover life if he did.

His elation grew at being able to fly again and overtook any misgivings he felt about working for people like the Bailey's. As he waited for his plane to arrive he felt a spark of hope kindle inside. This could be the break he needed to speed up Operation Graffiti's enquiry; if he was to be trusted to deliver stuff for the Bailey's he was likely to meet other key figures linked to the wider organisation.

A squall moved in as Robbie stood waiting at the small airfield on the outskirts of Nottinghamshire, where arrangements had been made for him to keep his plane. He looked skyward at the clouds churning above hoping to catch sight of his microlight, anxious to take ownership once again of his precious plane. The wind began to buffet against him as he looked upwards at the threatening clouds. If the poor visibility got any worse he feared for whoever was bringing it. He could see the deteriorating conditions were becoming impossible and expected the message to come the flight had been aborted.

His heart grew lighter when he heard the familiar sound of the approaching plane. He knew it was his because he was so familiar with the sound. He watched the microlight circling above testing the wind conditions, waiting to come into land. It looked like a giant moth hovering in the fading light.

He told no one, especially Sid Bailey, where he intended to hangar his plane, even though he knew this might prove futile, expecting them to keep a close eye on him. His biggest fear being the Bailey's might commandeer it, cutting him out of the proceedings altogether. He would put nothing past Sid, his reputation preceded him. He was well-known as a double-dealing slime ball.

Eagerly, after watching its descent, he met the plane on the runway, too excited to wait until it taxied over to the hangar where he intended to keep it. He was told very little about the arrangements other than the location of the small aerodrome, the date and time came in a short text to his burner phone.

The pilot delivering it was unknown to him. There was little by way of banter pass between them. As soon as he signed the transfer papers, the man disappeared into the failing light. Robbie only heard the purr of a car engine he assumed arriving to whisk him away. He was far too busy lovingly checking it over after taxing into the hangar, to pay much attention.

Once inside he sat for a while, taking in the remembered smell, familiarising himself once again with the machine he badly missed over the past months. This was Robbie's second plane, his first being a small single seater craft he learnt to fly in, outlived its usefulness. He eventually managed to get himself a good second-hand two seater and was how he was able to teach Emily the rudiments of flying. He knew for her to get a licence she would have to have proper lessons from a qualified instructor.

His mind reflected back on the times he took her up in this very plane. He heaved a sigh at the memory of how she shared his love of being up above the clouds, free from the burdens of everyday life. He felt a pang of regret at how he abandoned her. He thought she must be missing those times too.

Robbie looked at the space available in the small craft recalling how he tried to tell Sid Bailey there was limited weight capacity in such a light aircraft for anything too bulky. He found Bailey hard to read, his little wizened face seemed to stare mockingly at him as he explained the dangers of overloading as well as the limitations of not being equipped to fly at night.

Robbie knew very well his two seater microlight gave the capacity to carry more cargo than you would expect with only the pilot. He wasn't able to tell whether Sid fully understood the restrictions. As he sat there in front of Bailey, he hoped he wouldn't be expected to have one of his goons accompany him. He'd looked over at the three sitting on Sid's battered office sofa. Any one of these clowns would add some serious weight to his problem. Bear was heavy whilst 'Blue suit' was tall and gangly. The third man sitting silently listening to the conversation looked smaller, uglier, his face scarred in many places giving the overall impression he was tougher. Robbie wouldn't like to meet him alone down an alley after dark let alone be trapped in a microlight with him.

Bailey surprised him by his knowledge of light aircraft, microlights in particular which made it less likely he could play with the truth if required. He seemed well informed on how far they could fly and where you could land one in places other than a recognised airport, confirming to Robbie whatever use they intended to make of him, he knew it was illegal.

Even sitting in the microlight inside the large hangar at the farthest corner where he was allocated a space, Robbie heard a loud car horn somewhere outside. He reluctantly climbed out, closed up the microlight, taking one last look before he left the hangar. He pulled the heavy door half shut, leaving the aerodrome staff to close the place for the night. He walked around the hangar, slipped the keys through a slot into the office before walking over to a black saloon taxi waiting for him in the almost deserted car park; only the illumination from the *yellow light showing the word taxi on top of the car was visible in the gloom. He got in and the taxi drove away.*

CHAPTER 56

Peter, already on his second large cup of Americano, sat fixated by his computer screen. The chocolate éclair on the plate in front of him remained untouched. The babble of voices at surrounding tables faded when he became engrossed in the graffiti images sent him by Bart, along with other files and videos. He chose to sit along the outer wall of the Quinnell farm coffee shop at the one vacant table without a large window behind where anyone passing along the walkway outside would be unable to see his screen. He had been there for the past hour having borrowed Bart's Peugeot with directions how to get there.

He hadn't expected the graffiti to be so absorbing. Even with his gamesman's eye he was enthralled by the artistry of the colourful images, although he found some of them quite sinister. After his initial scrutiny of the whole wall, Peter sat back from the screen. He absently reached out for the éclair, took a bite letting the creamy chocolatey mix delight his taste buds, he slowly chewed.

He looked up at the café surprised to find the place with many more customers since the last time he looked. The clock on the wall near the entrance showed him how long he'd been distracted by the jumble of images. He was especially drawn to the stagecoach he knew Emily spotted as being out of sync with the ages of the school kids who were attributed with most of the art work.

He already knew about current trends in age specific gaming tastes, it was his business to engage gamers, tempting them by saturating the market with new crazes. Peter found he agreed with Emily about the reference to 1980's music, recognising some of the images were of old films also dating back to the same era or even much further back. He knew from his own experience, young people were more influenced these days by science fiction rather than 70s/80s horror films. They considered them outdated, even with filmmaker's attempts to carry on the franchises by bringing them up to date.

Space travel and aliens were of much more interest to current day youth. Peter knew because he was still one of them himself. The thought came, accompanied by a frown, because if, as Bart suggested, the building was being used by school children to meet in, he would have expected the graffiti to reflect the current trends. On his initial examination he found little evidence if any at all.

Curious.

Even mention of 'The Bogeyman', recorded not pictorially, only in words, with an attempt to expunge them later, showed no references to any films of the same name. He thought there must be one. He quickly put the coffee he was sipping down to do a search for films about the 'Bogeyman', surprised when he saw how many there were going back to the first in the 1980s.

Actual references on the internet mentioning the 'Bogeyman' dating even further back were reputed to be used by parents as a threat to their children not to misbehave or the 'Bogeyman would get you'. Folklore was riddled with mentions. He noted the Russian adversary of John Wick, whose son stole Wick's car and killed his dog, mentions 'Baba Yaga', the 'Bogeyman', from Russian folklore suggesting there was no escaping once you attracted its attention. Peter had seen the John Wick movies many times yet missed the reference entirely.

Peter's concentration led him deeper into the subject to the exclusion of his surroundings. He forgot about why he was there or what he intended to do.

His enthusiasm, like his work as a gaming programmer, took him over entirely to the detriment of his personal life as he confessed to

Bart when he arrived in Scotland. Once he made contract with Emily he neglected to keep the communication going because of his work distraction. He became greatly ashamed when Bart told him she was missing, felt responsible somehow for having failed her. The background babble of the café's customers receded into a haze of white noise.

What brought his attention back was the sound of a voice close by. Lifting his head he noticed the young girl wearing a green waitress uniform standing looking at him.

"Sorry," he muttered embarrassed she might think he was deliberately ignoring her. "Did you say something?"

She looked young, no more than a child, her hair scraped back into a ponytail under a matching green cap, she was staring at him with a beaming smile, "I wondered if you've finished." She pointed at the half eaten chocolate éclair beside his empty coffee cup.

"No," he looked down at the table realising he still hadn't eaten all the cake. He pointed at his laptop, "I get a bit carried away…..always do when I work."

"You're working?" She looked at him curiously.

"Err, no I'm on holiday. I meant when I am working I get carried away I forget the time or sometimes even to eat."

"What do you work on?" The girl was obviously enthralled by Peter who looked out of place being decades younger than most of the people he could see sitting at other tables. A great number of them suntanned, white haired retired people who seem to have all the time in the world.

"I create computer games," he said simply watching the girl's mouth open in awe.

"Wow!" she said her cherry lips forming a perfectly round O whilst her eyes glinted appreciatively. At least Peter thought so or maybe the sun outside was caught in a flash by them. She looked down at the back of his laptop, where the lid was covered with abstract patterns. Peter saw her face change. She frowned, whispered almost inaudibly, "That looks like graffiti."

Peter pulled the lid towards him to close it. He stared down at his own laptop, consisting of a jazzy assortment of images, some were taken from actual games he knew of and others he didn't. Before this moment he hadn't associated the arrangement with the graffiti wall images because he only received the photographs from Bart that morning. Looking at the lid he realised the jazzy patterns could quite easily represent a wall of graffiti anywhere.

Peter picked up the laptop, pushed it inside the carry case on the chair beside him registering the huge disappointment appear on the girl's face. She shifted perceptively taking a step nearer as if she wanted to stop him. "Can I see your games?" She asked excitedly.

Peter didn't want her to know he wasn't exactly working on a computer game or to see the images he was examining. He tried to laugh her request off with the usual reply he gave to anyone who ever got curious enough to ask the same question, "Err, if I showed you them, I would have to kill you."

He could never really explain the massive security existing around the development of games. Only people in the business knew there was fierce competitiveness between gaming companies. What he heard, or thought he heard, from the girl was a sound escape her cherry lips, like a hiss. He thought immediately of a snake. The sound a cobra might make in readiness to kill its prey.

He could see he offended her, the smile was no longer evident, her face now darkly ominous. Peter quickly tried to explain, "It was meant to be a joke, you know like in the movies......'If I tell you I'll have to kill you'...?" he said trying to explain. Peter looked down at the badge the girl was wearing on her uniform, read her name, "…….Gina."

She stood perfectly still, her face expressionless. Peter was reminded of a computer screen freezing whilst running a streaming.

The pause ended abruptly, her frown once again replaced by the beaming smile as if someone pressed 'play' from 'pause'. A chill ran down Peter's spine.

"I have to go," he said quickly picking up his computer bag.

She leaned in, took the large cup, now empty of coffee, noticed the half-eaten éclair, "Don't you like our eclairs?" she asked accusingly.

Rather than prolong the conversation, he picked up the remaining éclair, took a bite and left rather hurriedly for the door with the éclair in his hand. When he passed a waste bin he threw the remainder in having lost his appetite for the sweet taste.

CHAPTER 57

Michelle didn't expect an opportunity to approach Jenny Williamson to come quite so soon. The next day she routinely followed the Range Rover back to her house after she dropped the children at school. Mitch spent the next half hour with her lap top looking for anything on the internet to explain her connection with Robbie Cowan's bungalow. She got as far as finding Jenny Williamson's Facebook page and was looking through her list of 'friends', Mitch was pleased to see she left open to public view. Whilst skimming down them she kept an eye on the house on the estate below. The list seemed fairly typical of most people's family and friends, none of whom she recognised.

When she looked up again the Range Rover was reversing out of the Williamson's drive. She hurriedly closed her laptop whilst starting her car to follow her. On previous occasions Mrs 'Ernest' went out shopping either to Banchory or Aboyne. Her days were monotonously routine.

Today, however, she went directly to Robbie Cowan's bungalow, letting herself in once again with a key. Luckily Michelle was prepared having come dressed for such an eventuality by wearing, a skirt, tweed jacket, with old fashioned ankle boots. From a bag in the car foot well she pulled out a grey wig in a short bob style to instantly convert her young looks into a middle aged woman. She wore no makeup or jewellery.

Once Jenny Williamson was inside, Mitch started the car, cruised slowly along to the bungalow stopping at the For Sale sign where she peered out at the house like any potential buyer would do. By the time she got out of the car to walk up the short drive, Jenny

Williamson was coming out of the front door holding a hand full of mail.

"Excuse me?" Michelle said approaching her surveillance subject who looked acutely surprised. "I don't mean to bother you," her perfect English accent continued, "but I'm interested in buying a place around here. I wonder if I could have a look round your bungalow, it's exactly what I'm looking for." Jenny became flustered and immediately pulled the front door closed behind her. "Sorry," Mitch said, "if you're about to go out, I wouldn't take long to have a quick look…"

"Oh….I don't live here," Jenny stuttered.

"You must be from Nelsens," she pointed at the For Sale sign. "I was going to give you a ring to make an appointment to view, until I saw someone was here."

Jenny looked over at the sign, then back at Mitch before she said, "A viewing can only be arranged through the agent."

Michelle knew very well she couldn't because she already called them and listened to the same recorded message as Bart. She put on a disappointed expression, "Ah, it's a shame given we are right here. After a quick look inside I could have my offer in this afternoon," Michelle knew any agent's employee would be only too pleased to get a sale to their credit. The message on the answer machine had remained the same for weeks because she called it many times. Michelle knew there was something really quite wrong about it.

Jenny took a step sideways to hurry past Michelle without making further comment.

"Please," Michelle begged.

"I'm sorry, I don't think this place is open for any more offers," Jenny said as she walked away pressing the car key in her hand. The Range Rover beeped as she reached it, she opened the driver's door.

Mitch could see her opportunity to talk to Jenny slipping away, owned up admitting, "I have tried to telephone the agent. I can't get past the message. When I saw you I thought I would take the chance. Are you the owner?" Mitch deliberately glanced at the mail in Jenny's hand noticing her nervousness grow even more.

Jenny stood stunned to silence at the side of her open car door trying to work out what to say next because she knew what was on the recorded message having made it herself. This was the first time she came face to face with someone interested in buying it, so tried to work out what would be the best way of minimising any suspicion. She turned, threw the mail she was holding into the car before she shut the door again.

"Okay." Jenny Williamson said walking back to the front door. "A quick look round then?" Mitch followed her into the bungalow. Once inside Jenny merely told her to "Please be quick," leaving her to wander around on her own.

It being a chalet bungalow, Mitch first took the few stairs as slowly as her older persona ought, up to the room she could see was a conversion of the loft space into a large double bedroom stretching the full width of the house. There was a fitness area consisting of a bike, treadmill and multi-gym at one end.

Michelle was suddenly hit by guilt at invading a once fellow officer's private space. She was reminded of the many Section 18 searches she undertook during her police career. She walked over as quietly as possible to a large fitted wardrobe to peer inside. She was greatly surprised to find a large quantity of clothes. She brushed her hand along the hanging garments, suits, jackets, shirts, trousers and sweaters hanging there. She closed the door quietly, moved over to a bedside cabinet to look inside. The draw was completely empty. She moved down the stairs to the main floor.

"This is lovely," she cooed like any serious buyer might. She walked into the living room she found extremely dated, fought the rising guilt again at prying into Robbie Cowan's home. She tried not to laugh at the picture over the gas fire of a Spanish dancer with castanets, a leftover from the sixties era she thought. She walked towards the small open plan dining room leading to the kitchen, noted the few ceramic ornaments, a cabinet with wine glasses and other china.

Once out in the hallway again she quickly took in the bathroom between two other bedrooms, one being more of an office/junk room. She desperately wanted to be left alone there to see what she could find belonging to Robbie before she left, but Jenny Williamson followed her around looking agitated, she clearly wanted to be away.

"So if I put an offer in," Mitch said to Jenny, "Would I get you into trouble for letting me inside to have a look around?"

She saw Jenny's face turn pale having failed to see the implications of letting someone inside the bungalow, she began to panic. She flopped down onto the worn tired looking sofa, her head bent down cradled by her hands. Mitch heard a small whimper escape from her mouth. She sat down next to her, put her arm around her shoulders trying to comfort her, "It's okay, I have no intention of getting you into trouble. I'll say I walked around the outside looked through the windows. I'm sure I won't be the only person who has." Jenny began to sob. She looked up pitifully into Michelle's face, testing her sincerity. Michelle knew she'd got Jenny Williamson in a particularly vulnerable state, "It's not up for sale is it?"

Jenny gasped, "Why do you say that?"

Michelle knew she needed to word the next thing she said carefully. The woman could get angry, maybe even clam up entirely and she would never get the chance again. Michelle looked around the room noting how shabby the place was, no one had done anything remotely superficial to spruce it up to sell. There were also too many personal things around suggesting the owner hadn't moved elsewhere.

"You say it isn't your place," she began, "yet looks like someone might be living here?" She didn't want to admit, apart from what she could see, the bungalow did feel cold like it hadn't felt heat in some considerable time. Of course she knew because both Emily and Bart filled her in on Robbie's moving away.

Jenny followed suit, looked around from where they were sitting. She seemed surprised at what she saw, "I suppose so," she admitted as if she hadn't noticed before.

Michelle stood up, walked into the kitchen, opened one or two cupboards before she appeared back at the archway dividing the living room from the dining room, "How about we have a cup of coffee? I know I could do with one."

Jenny Williamson slowly nodded her head and smoothed her face with a hand to wipe away a stray tear. Michelle turned back to fill an electric kettle with water then flicked it on to boil.

CHAPTER 58

The last thought on Bart's mind before he fell asleep the night before was D.I Morris's expression as he scurried out of the back room of the March of Time. In fact the memory kept him awake for a long time. He never liked Morris, from the first moment he saw him, standing with DS Copeland in front of Emily, who was sitting behind the shop's counter. He had even less regard for Copeland, whose attitude towards Emily he took great exception to. The two detectives were inseparable until Morris turned up yesterday without him to have his awkward exchange with Michelle. It didn't take much working out to see there was history between them. The friction he saw there was still puzzling him when he woke next day.

Michelle McElrae on the other hand spent no time whatsoever dwelling on her chance encounter with Morris. She already used up too much of her life fretting about the man when she was a serving police officer. She decided long ago life was too short to continue worrying. She got on with her life. This was why she took the job at the agency. She was glad of the distraction of following and engaging Jenny Williamson at the bungalow. The whole episode with Morris at the clock shop slipped conveniently from her mind.

After her encounter with Mrs 'Ernest', she drove to The March of Time to report back to Bart whilst the whole thing was fresh in her mind. She hadn't been there above a couple of minutes before Bart asked, "You know D.I Morris, then?"

Michelle's heart sank. She felt trapped by the question, not wanting to dig up the past where she conveniently buried it. She thought no longer being a police officer she was unlikely to ever meet Morris again. What happened to her then she gave back with her uniform when she handed it in. However she knew Bart's question warranted some sort of a reply.

"Yes," came weakly. "He's not someone I wish to remember."

"Oh?" Bart said suddenly alert, "I confess I have no time for the man, never liked him or Copeland who usually accompanies him." Bart's declaration packed a lot of contempt. "However, if there is something I should know, in case I officially encounter either of them again, I would be grateful for the head's up."

Michelle seemed to be torn by an inner debate on what she ought to impart to him and how much she could keep to herself. She said, "I have heard, you are unlikely to meet DS Copeland again, as he is no longer a DS, nor is he a serving police officer."

Shocked, Bart tried to recall when he last met the unpleasant man. A flash of memory revealed a hospital corridor outside the Intensive Care Ward where he sat with Emily waiting for news about Mary Macaulay's condition after she crashed her car into a tree, came flooding back to him. Robbie Cowan was also there. He believed the incident wasn't an accident and reported it to CID bringing Morris with his side-kick along to the hospital. He recalled Copeland's smirking face, delighted to find Emily there. Bart half expected him to lick his lips, his expression he now recalled was predatory.

"Oh?" Bart repeated waiting silently for Michelle to explain.

She hesitated before she spoke again, "He was dismissed for gross misconduct," she said simply.

Bart didn't seem surprised, although he wouldn't be able to explain why. "That must have been quite recently?"

Michelle nodded, Bart could see her frown. "Should have happened years ago," her anger, hardly held in check, as old images came rushing back. She realised they were still retrievable. She was disappointed she hadn't managed to lock them safely away in the dark recesses of her mind like she hoped.

Bart recognising her distress began to regret bringing the subject up, "Sit down lass," he said warmly. He moved over to make her a cup of tea, his remedy for all ills. Once done he sat next to her in front of the fire as she stared into the flames, waiting to find out if she wanted to talk about the past.

When she began, her voice was almost a whisper. Bart leant forward a little to make out her words, inwardly cursing his failing hearing. "I was newly qualified, a probationer," she began. Bart saw the pain on her face. "Copeland was assigned to show me the ropes...." she looked up into Bart's concerned face, "It happened when I was getting changed in the women's locker room......he....came in.....found me undressed....." Michelle gave an involuntary sob, which she forced back to take control again, "Let's say the 'ropes' weren't the only thing he showed me, which he did with great force."

There wasn't very much in Bart's life he had seen or heard to shock him. There were many awful things over the years, yet Michelle's admission about Copeland filled him full of horror. He wanted to vent his anger. He wasn't a violent man but he thought if D.S Copeland were to enter his shop then, he would become one. He tried to control his feelings, "How long ago was it Michelle?"

"Eight years," she said showing little emotion at all.

"You thought it best not to report him?" he asked quietly understanding how female police officers were treated years ago.

Mitch shook her head, "No, I did report him at the time. I was still in shock....he hurt me," she could see Bart was confused. "I reported him to Morris, who was the first person I saw after Copeland left me there."

The pain on Bart's face was evident. She went on as if she were telling the story of a case she once attended as a police officer, "He did nothing, suggested if he officially reported the incident it could be misconstrued as 'horse play' between two colleagues. We would both get into trouble being at work whilst on duty. He pointed out I was still on probation, therefore likely to be dismissed for bringing the accusation against a respected colleague. He buried it."

"My god!" *The Bastard!*

"The worst thing was he gave me such a hard time afterwards. He treated me with so much contempt he made my life a misery. I found myself applying to any part of the force as far away from them as I could possibly get." She smiled wryly, "Scuppered any ambitions I had of joining CID."

Bart nodded sadly back at her recalling how Morris appeared when he remembered where he met Michelle before after she addressed him as 'sir'. He literally left so fast he almost ran out of the back room.

Bart couldn't help saying, "He scurried out of here when he remembered who you were, didn't he?"

Michelle nodded, "Yes, I remember bumping into him one day at headquarters when I was sorting out my medical retirement after my accident. I was still on crutches, he was coming along the corridor away from the Command Suite. I saw him first, stepped out in front of him blocking his way, my crutches splayed out making it impossible for him to move round me. You see, I heard a lot of rumours about his slimy protégé, the grapevine is rife in the police. Copeland had a reputation for inappropriate behaviour with women. Not only staff either. I don't think he was very careful dealing with certain sections of the public. I believe he was moved from Vice because of it, there was always something rumoured about him." She coughed before she continued, "Morris stopped in front of me. I told him if they ever caught up with Copeland and brought him to book I would give evidence against him for what he did to me. I'd make sure they knew how he protected Copeland and he would go down with him."

Bart sat listening quietly until Michelle finished, "What happened to Copeland?"

Michelle gave a sarcastic grunt, "Hah! The usual British justice…..well you can't be too harsh with police officers can you? It would reflect badly on the whole service, we would lose public confidence." Michelle's rant she suddenly realised was almost comical. She laughed at herself before she added, "Two years suspended sentence…..that's a slap on the wrist. He got dismissed from the service, kept his pension. The case was one related to a prostitute he knew from his Vice days and as everyone knows women like that deserve everything they get for leading 'decent' men astray!" she finished sarcastically.

"Did you do anything about Morris?" Bart asked remembering the fear on his face as he left.

"Err, no. I'd locked the whole thing away, got on with my life…..until he walked in here the other day I hadn't given him a second's thought."

There was a tap on the door. Isla Strachan came in with a piece of paper she handed to Bart, "I took a call earlier. It was the 'Ernest' man again, Mr. Bridges, he wants an update."

Bart stifled a smile at Isla picking up on their nickname for him. He looked down at the paper, saw the familiar telephone number for Harvey Williamson, "Thankyou Mrs Strachan I'll give Mr. Williamson a ring," she went back into the shop.

"Ah," Michelle said. "I think you'll need to hear ma update before you do."

As she spoke Bart heard the unmistakable grinding of his external garage door being lifted making his heart skip a beat, immediately thinking of Emily who always put his car away when she drove it during his long slow recovery from a brain tumour operation. Michelle tilted her head hearing a car being driven inside the integral garage before the engine was switched off. Bart recalled Peter borrowed his Peugeot to drive over to the Quinnell estate.

"Peter," he said to simply. As if on cue he appeared in the back room using the internal garage door into the house. Bart noted his usual beaming smile was missing.

CHAPTER 59

The meeting between Bart, Michelle and Peter took on a more formal feedback session and promised to continue long after Isla Strachan shut the shop for the day. Bart's first thought, as always the case, was to react to his hunger pangs. He missed his usual walk up to The Moor Hen for Alistair's most generous food portions. He was also mindful of the two young people having spent their time on surveillance activities, therefore unlikely to have eaten either.

Peter was despatched to The Hungry Traveller to purchase a chippy supper whilst Michelle and Bart set the table with condiments appropriate to their choices of food. During the meal Bart's attention was drawn to the quick exchange of glances between Peter and Michelle. If the subject of their meeting hadn't been about finding Emily, he would otherwise have been delighted.

Michelle was the first to update on her approach to Jenny Williamson after her diversion to Robbie Cowan's bungalow. She explained how she managed to get inside to look around.

"I only managed a quick inspection of the room upstairs on my own, I didn't want to leave Jenny Williamson downstairs for too long. I can tell you the whole place still has Robbie Cowan's thing inside…..except……it has been carefully stripped of anything relating to him being a police officer."

"You mean like photographs or police crests?" Bart asked.

"Well, yes I didn't see anything like that. A police officer usually has some kind of award for something, even I've got those," she laughed not wanting them to think she was being immodest. "No, I meant, like clothing. I managed a quick look inside his wardrobe.

Even if you haven't got your dress uniform in there, you're likely to have a police issue jumper or coat. There was nothing left there I could see at a glance."

"So he's moved out and taken his clothes?" Peter asked.

She shook her head, "No all his clothes seem to be there. Of course I have no idea what is missing. The upstairs bedroom has gym equipment still in place. Downstairs, there's a junk room come office…..no computer…..but then maybe he didn't have one."

"Yes, he did, I've e-mailed him. He always communicated with Emily that way when they weren't together," Bart explained.

"As you said, no photos or anything personal to identify who lives there."

"Don't you mean 'lived' there?" Peter asked. "Isn't the bungalow up for sale?"

"Well, no, that much I discovered from a very nervous Jenny Williamson who seems to be a little confused about the details. She believes the place *isn't* being sold, only made to look like it is."

"So she doesn't work for these people Nelsens?" Bart asked.

"Well we've both been unable to find them haven't we?" Michelle took out her mobile, "Hang on, just let me try something….." she pressed a few keys, listened then started to nod her head. "Yep. I can confirm the message on their answer machine is definitely Jenny Williamson, I've heard her speak."

Peter grinned, "You should be a detective." To Bart his comment was a little unfortunate given Mitch's comment she always wanted to join CID except she was deterred by her unpleasant dealings with Morris and Copeland.

Bart saw her smile weakly at him before continuing, "I tried all ways to find out what her role was in visiting the bungalow and she was very reluctant to say at first. I couldn't ask her about the mail or her clandestine meetings with the police officer in Tesco's, which by the way she did again immediately after. I followed her again."

"Ah," Bart said.

"Though she did admit she was doing a favour for her sister, who is a solicitor," Michelle took out a black note book to refer to, "She called her Iona."

Bart sat up alert, "Did you get a second name?"

Michelle shook her head, "Why?"

"Oh, I know a solicitor whose first name is Iona," he said.

Michelle got up to get Bart's laptop off the side board. She keyed into the already open screens, "I found Jenny Williamson's Facebook page," she said turning the screen around to face Bart and Peter. "Yes, here's her friends list I found earlier, have a look."

Bart scrolled down the faces, fortunately not very many, until towards the end he found one he recognised. "Yes, she is friends with Iona Roberts," he said.

"Jenny's maiden name is Roberts," Michelle looked triumphant her searches hadn't been in vain.

Peter looked impressed giving her an admiring look, "Definitely detective material!"

Bart was looking thoughtful, "If I'm right, Robbie Cowan's mother was also a Roberts. I remember Emily telling me about his father deserting them when Robbie was a child. His mother wanted to change her name back to her maiden name, which bothered him because he would have become Robert Roberts, and the butt of his fellow class mates."

"That would definitely have done it. I remember some poor sap at school called Thomas Thomas. He was really bullied," Peter announced. "Although, his nickname was Tommo, which he didn't seem to mind." Michelle and Peter grinned at each other whilst Bart thought children could be so cruel.

Michelle grew serious, "So are we saying we think the solicitor Iona Roberts is related to Jenny Williamson, perhaps with some connection to Robbie Cowan's mother?"

"Put like that it does sound a bit of a stretch," Bart suggested. "Where does this police officer you recognise fit in?"

"I have absolutely no idea," Michelle confessed. Peter looked slightly disappointed. "One thing I do know, Jenny Williamson isn't the cheating wife her husband seems to want her to be."

"The thought has occurred to me often," Bart said. "I have to give the man another update, he is really quite persistent as if there were some kind of imaginary time frame attached to my providing him with the evidence he wants."

"Hmm," Michelle grunted. "Perhaps he has another reason for rushing." The other two looked at her totally uncomprehendingly. "You know, if he's got some other female in the family way?"

"Didn't you tell me when you saw him at the house helping Jenny unload the weekly shop he was all loving with her?" Bart asked.

"Yes, looked like she was coming back from holiday instead of on a trip to Tesco's," Michelle frowned. "It doesn't make much sense to me."

Bart's thought was accompanied by a rather pleasant feeling of relief. After Michelle's account of her findings he was sure his initial belief Robbie intended to return after his stint undercover looked to be correct. The subterfuge he thought was there to misdirect anyone who might be trying to find out what happened to P.C Robbie Cowan after the gross misconduct charge against him. He felt sure Emily would be pleased if he could only tell her.

He turned to Peter asking, "How did you get on over at the Quinnell Farm?"

He saw Peter give an exaggerated shiver, "I met the strange girl called Gina you talk about! She gives me the creeps," he said, then proceeded to tell them all about his trip to the Coffee shop.

CHAPTER 60

Robbie's first assignment for Bailey went much as he expected. He tried not to show his disappointment when he was collected by Bear who he knew would closely supervise him. Reluctantly he had to reveal where he kept his plane. He hoped the issue of the cost, which was expensive, wouldn't be raised because storage was being paid for by Operation Graffiti. Robbie kept his fingers crossed the billing wasn't traceable to them. Once he was earning his own money from the Bailey's couldn't come quick enough for Robbie.

Bear's oversized frame, once again squeezed inside the confines of his daughter's mini, emphasised how much space he would take up in the microlight.

Once strapped inside the plane on the runway ready to take off, Robbie couldn't help commenting, "As long as Sid realises there's a weight limit for flying this thing," he was well aware of the tone he delivered the warning in. "I'm not prepared to go over it," he said decisively.

Bear gave him an angry glare, "No one tells Sid what he can and can't do," he growled in keeping with his nickname.

Robbie turned the plane for the last time onto the main runway ready for take-off awaiting the all clear from the flight controller.

"Well it's your life as well as mine on the line here…there's no defence of 'Sid insisted we overload the cargo' acceptable against a manslaughter charge…. assuming one of us survives the crash."

Robbie shut up, concentrating on the take-off, he ignored any further silent glare aimed his way from the other seat. Of course, at this stage Robbie had no idea what he was meant to be bringing back, although he could guess. He only knew his destination was north but suspected with trepidation that was somewhere in Scotland. Whilst his handler knew of the new developments, Robbie was unable to inform him of the actual flight plan, so he left his mobile on as a means of tracking his journey. The thing he hadn't anticipated was his mobile would ring after they had been flying a short while.

The sound brought Bear to life instantly from an otherwise sluggish state. He watched Robbie pull his phone out of his pocket to check the screen. Robbie could see Kirstie's name and immediately shut the call down. He turned to Bear with a huge false grin on his face, "Bloody women, they won't leave you alone!" He waited for his co-pilot to react one way or the other, but expected another reprimand. Bear he noticed didn't have a sense of humour. Robbie thought who would, working closely with his humourless thug of an employer.

"Must be doing something right," he commented. Robbie glanced sideways seeing a huge lecherous grin appear on his face for the first time since they met.

Robbie smiled knowingly, "I do ma best." The inner turmoil, Kirstie might telephone again straight away, made him feel sick. Under different circumstances he would have switched the mobile off completely if his handler hadn't insisted they needed to track him. Robbie cursed himself for not cancelling the ring tone. He hoped he would get the chance at some point.

The rest of the journey was uneventful, apart from the darkening skies as they flew further north threatening them with bad weather.

Robbie flew on, one eye on the menacing clouds, the other with quick furtive glances at Bear. He jumped when Bear's phone starting ringing. When he answered all Robbie heard was a couple of yes's in response to whoever was on the line which made his quaking nerves worse. He was then given co-ordinates to their destination. Robbie immediately knew he was expected to land at the small gliding school aerodrome he was already familiar with and where he was well known as PC Robbie Cowan.

'Shit!' he thought, 'what do I do now?'

"What's the plan when we land?" he said trying hard to sound nonchalant.

"Leave that to me," growled Bear, "This is a dummy run, to establish you as a regular flyer; the heavy stuff comes later."

"Not too heavy, I hope!" Robbie quipped looking hard at Bear because he suddenly didn't sound his normal self. What he saw was clear to Robbie. Bear was ailing. He deduced from the whole flying experience. He looked ghastly, his face having turned a greenish white, glowed ghostly in the lights from the plane's control panel. "You okay?" Robbie enquired.

Bear looked like he might puke at any moment, Robbie reached to the back of his seat, pulled out a sick bag to hand him.

"Here, in case you need it. We'll be landing soon. I won't be able to help you until after." Robbie banked the plane coming into land accurately first time as he had done on many other occasions.

Once down Robbie taxied up short of the main building alarmed there were no other planes or people in sight until he considered maybe his police colleagues had secured the place for him to land. Nevertheless, he still dreaded getting out, meeting Jim, the manager or Joan, his office manager, both of whom knew him well and would give him away.

Before the plane even came to rest Bear was up, waiting by the door. When they stopped Robbie watched him, with the aid of his stick, scurry across to the office building with a fast hopping movement where he was met by someone coming out who turned pointed towards the main door. The man walked across to the plane. As he got nearer Robbie recognised his handler carrying a clip board. He climbed aboard.

"We haven't got much time," he said hurriedly. "Is he one of Bailey's men?"

"Yes, I'm under great scrutiny, he's air sick fortunately. I was dreading meeting with Joan or Jim and have my cover blown."

His handler pushed the clip-board towards him, "Sign here for landing approval, we've taken over for this occasion, don't worry. I can't see your mate accompanying you again, can you?" He was busy examining Robbie's appearance, "You don't look very well yourself, laddie. You're not ill are you?"

Robbie shook his head, they both watched as Bear came back out of the main building. "I'm okay," Robbie managed before the hulk pulled himself up the few steps back into the plane.

"Aye, it's looking like we've a squall coming in," his handler suddenly said loud enough for Bear to hear. "You'll need to fuel up, get off quickly if you don't want to be stranded for the night." He stood up to let Bear sit back in his seat, then left.

"What did he want?" Bear managed as he burped convincing Robbie he lost the contents of his stomach when an smell of bile wafted out of the man's mouth briefly making Robbie want to gag.

"Papers establishing my legit journey and to warn us as yer heard, there's bad weather coming in," Robbie felt more confident knowing his cover was safe. "Do we have anything to pick up?"

"Not much," Bear said.

"Well, I'll take on some fuel then we'll get going back if it's okay with you?" His confidence rose as he added, "I'd like to get something to eat before we do, they'll probably have a machine, sandwiches and coffee, most aerodromes do." He saw Bear wince at the reference to food, "I'll get you a bottle of water, you look like you could do with some."

Robbie left him to sort out the fuel whilst he took the opportunity to slip away into the main building to enter the men's loos where he locked himself inside the one stall to quickly telephone Kirstie. She didn't pick up. He sent a text to say he was tied up and would contact her later with a view to meeting. He switched his phone to silent then went to raid the food vending machines.

When he got back to his plane Bear was standing looking out of the main door waiting; he still looked impatient, his colour having settled to grey.

"What took you so long?" he barked. Any sign of his previous sense of humour had vanished. Robbie climbed the steps and felt the first splash of a rain drop.

"I need all the sustenance I can get," he said holding up a couple of triangle packets of sandwiches, crisps and a cup of coffee. He had a bottle of water tucked under one arm in case the old grouch was in need on the journey back. Robbie looked up into the raindrops, "Looks like we're in for a bumpy ride," he couldn't resist seeing the effect on Bear. "Are we done here?" he asked not having seen any signs of a return cargo turning up.

Bear shook his head, "They're running late, might be another half hour before they get here," he said. Robbie shrugged as he pushed past him into the plane to sit in the pilot's seat.

He threw the bottle of water down onto the seat beside him, began to open a packet of sandwiches he ate with relish. "Got you some if you want them," he said flicking the remaining sandwich pack after the water, "Egg mayonnaise," he wanted to laugh knowing the smell alone would likely upset the man, "but don't eat them if you're likely to puke all over ma plane," he said rather severely.

He heard a deep growl from Bear, saw him disappearing down the steps watching him hobble over to the main building, glad of the reprieve from his company. Not for the first time he wondered what torture Sid Bailey put him through to sustain such a marked disablement of his leg. He marvelled at how he still seemed completely loyal to him. He wondered if there would be any leeway there in persuading him otherwise, if they needed a witness to testify to Bailey's crimes or if he was in far too deep to be offered a plea bargain.

Pat McDonald

That wasn't Robbie's problem. He ate his sandwiches, opened the crisps taking advantage of his absence.

CHAPTER 61

Peter woke up in his bed at The Moor Hen from a very disturbing nightmare where a scarier version of Gina, the waitress from the coffee shop, had just killed someone. The vision was of her standing, eerily still, in her green waitress uniform splattered with red patches, a sharp carver knife in her hand dripping blood onto the floor. The shock of the image took Peter several moments to shake off. His focus on the room he was in becoming gradually more familiar, was helped by a flash of sunlight through the open curtains.

He always slept with them open since the time his parents committed him to a private clinic, confused and disorientated he needed to know where he was at all times. The habit remained with him after Emily found him and helped him to escape.

Since meeting the girl at the Quinnell farm, his thoughts had become completely fixated by her apparent strangeness. He couldn't forget her. The image of her standing staring at him with the sudden flash of that strange smile appearing on her face as if she was some primeval entity, reminded him of his idea about creating a super villain for an, as yet, unwritten computer game. His mind toyed with the concept of evil children.

Most of his competitors were completely absorbed in creating Super Heroes with new unique powers. He, on the other hand, preferred the slightly flawed, if not completely evil, characters, hence the last game he wrote took the covert Ninja agents of the classic Japanese mercenaries a step beyond anything you could ever consider as on the side of 'good'.

Ever since meeting her, he thought Gina Taylor was ideal material for the horror genre. There were plenty in films and they were truly creepy. A child, who looked innocent, who developed or turned instantly into the epitome of evil, was already well represented in movies. The Gaming medium was crying out for something new, chilling and quick to shock. The nightmare he just emerged from confirmed it for him. He laughed at the idea as he jumped out of bed, with a fierce hunger for breakfast, he was lured by the enticing aromas filtering up the stairs, emanating from Alistair's kitchen.

A cooked breakfast inside him couldn't rid him of the vision or the idea he gained by listening to Bart or Michelle. They gave him the impression Emily also became entirely absorbed by Gina, before she disappeared. In Peter's thoughts the connection between Emily's disappearance and Gina Taylor came to be synonymous. Instinct told him if he pursued the one, he would find the other, even though he couldn't rationalise why. He knew he must go back to the farm where, Bart told him, Gina Taylor lived with her brother, David.

Alistair appeared with a coffee pot to offer Peter a top up he gladly accepted. He liked Alistair, not only because of his generosity in taking him in. He found him laid back, easy to talk to, although he would never open up to discuss any of his early life with him, or anyone else. His childhood was locked away in the past. He spent too many sessions talking with the police, the doctors and counsellors to last him a life time. There was no doubt all the talking helped him, as did a series of teachers who not only encouraged his education, they gave him the motivation to follow his interest in programming computer games. He was sure there was a certain amount of luck thrown into the mix to enable him to be taken on by a well-known Gaming Company to learn the business, which he did quite successfully to enable him to go freelance.

He much preferred the abstract world of gaming, as far removed from reality as he could get. He did talk to Alistair about his work writing computer games. He seemed genuinely interested in how they were created. Alistair, on the other hand, was a mine of anecdotal stories gained from his own past in the military or from the many happenings since he retired into running pubs after leaving the army. Apart from this he was naturally funny, making light of most things, he made Peter laugh.

Whilst Peter was tempted to tell Alistair about the strange girl he met at the Quinnell farm, he didn't, not being sure whether he would be breaking the confidences of Bart's Detective Agency. However, he did reveal some of his encounter with Gina Taylor to Bart and Michelle. He could tell he somehow pleased Bart with the news she was working out there. Peter saw a satisfied expression come over his face. He didn't let on how disturbed she made him feel or anything about how she inveigled herself into his mind resulting in the nightmare, because he didn't want Michelle to think him a wuss. He couldn't, therefore, admit to them he thought Emily's disappearance was something to do with this strange girl because he intended to prove it.

The problem for Peter, in order go back to the Quinnell farm, he needed a car to get there. To borrow Bart's again, he would have to come clean about why, to confess he intended to target the girl as a possible source of information about Emily. He needed to get his own wheels or at least hire a car whilst he was up in Scotland, to give him the freedom of movement to be able to look for Emily.

Alistair came back to clear Peter's breakfast things away and asked if he wanted anything else. Peter said, "No thank you, I'm good. Do you know where I can hire a car while I'm up here?"

"You would likely have to go into Aberdeen, there's lots of car hire around the airport," he said leaving to carry some of the dishes away. When Alistair returned almost immediately, he placed a key attached to a tartan key fob onto the table in front of Peter, "Or you can use mine. I'm here most of the time preparing food anyway, whilst she sits idly in the garage. She could do with a run once in a while."

Peter looked genuinely surprised, "That's really cool! I will pay to use it," he felt a little embarrassed at raising the money issue.

"Och, no. Just put fuel in the old girl, you'll be doing me a favour or maybe could do a cash 'n' carry run if I need some supplies."

Peter put out his hand to shake Alistair's, "Done!" he said.

Peter got his driving licence as soon as he was old enough, but didn't buy a car when he moved to London after living in care. There had been no need to own a vehicle with the Underground System being conveniently close. For most of his work he remained static behind a screen anyway. However, like most boys, he grew up with a natural interest in cars with a desire to own one someday.

When he opened Alistair's garage door he was absolutely thrilled to see a battered old jeep with character. He always wanted to drive one. Alistair already filled him in on the jeep's crankiness giving him a few tips on handling the gears. He assured him it was completely reliable for its age and managed perfectly well in all weather conditions. The jeep, Alistair referred to as Flossie, kangarooed up the approach road to The Brae whilst Peter mastered the controls, turned a little erratically to face down towards Bart's clock shop and began to behave by the time she cruised past The March of Time to sail smoothly up Main Street out of the village.

Any thoughts by Peter of stopping to touch base with Bart slipped away, overtaken by concentration on his driving.

CHAPTER 62

On impulse Bart decided to drive to Aberdeen to Harvey Williamson's Advertising Agency to give him an update about his wife in person. He intended to call to see Nessa at McKinley's Autos on the way back to discuss the surveillance of the abandoned Bus Company building, with Emily out of the picture he was presently unable to cover everything. He had a desperate need to concentrate his attention on finding his partner, so before he left the shop he instructed Isla Strachan to make up Harvey Williamson's bill to take with him, with a view to terminating his contract.

Only after arriving in Aberdeen did the thought occur to him to drop in to speak to Iona Roberts to find out for definite if she was Jenny Williamson's sister. He once consulted the lawyer on the matter of ownership of Balmoral cottage where Lily Johns lived after the owner Elizabeth Grant died leaving her as 'caretaker' of the place. At the time, its ownership was being challenged by the convicted fraudster, Edward Petersen, one time cell mate of Lily's ex-husband Martin who couldn't bear the idea of her living an independent life.

The whole business was water under the bridge because Lily moved out of the strange cottage to co-habit with Nessa in Mary MacLeod's old cottage in Banchory. Elizabeth's very oddly behaved hunting hound, Sandy, was happily living with them having reverted to exhibiting normal dog-like behaviour after moving there.

Bart believed he would never have recourse to see the Women's Rights activist lawyer Iona Roberts again until Michelle raised her discovery she thought she was the sister of Jenny Williamson. He felt sufficiently confident with his previous association with Iona to be able to speak to her in confidence about her sister.

He took several minutes sitting in the Peugeot in the multi-storey car park considering who he should visit first, Harvey or Iona, also deciding what he should tell Williamson, the Advertising CEO, about his wife's involvement with Robbie's bungalow which was still very sketchy at best. He chose to visit the Williamson Advertising Agency first to tell him he couldn't possibly keep taking his fee because as far as he could see his wife wasn't having an affair.

On arrival he asked the young receptionist if he could see the man prompting the usual enquiry, "Do you have an appointment."

When his response was negative, she began to shake her head, so Bart assured her, "I think he will see me, please tell him Bart Bridges wishes to speak with him."

After a brief hesitation when Bart detected a reluctance to comply, she directed him to the spacious modern waiting area, all glass, stainless steel and large potted plants that would have thrived in a tropical rain forest. She told him she would go to see if Mr Williamson was available, which she did by disappearing.

Bart settled on an uncomfortable looking bucket chair with spindly legs he felt his weight might challenge. Once he lowered himself into it, he shuffled his ample behind to spread the load. He couldn't resist touching the nearest shiny palm leaf to satisfy himself it was real whilst trying to calculate the cost of such a flamboyant display of greenery. There was no doubt, Harvey Williamson had money.

When he looked up from the vaulted reception area to take in his surroundings, he could see at least two floors above. He caught sight of, through the glass wall above, the young lass he just spoke to hurrying along the first floor corridor. She carried a solemn expression with her, hard for Bart to interpret, his only thought being it would have been usual for a receptionist to telephone through to the man's secretary.

Bart, felt the sway of his seat as he leaned precariously towards a low glass-topped table in front of him spread with neat piles of advertising literature. He assumed Harvey's agency must have contributed to them. He didn't pick one up to inspect because he found them altogether too nouveau for his tastes. In the past he never used anything more sophisticated than a plain postcard in a newsagent's window, or a business card appropriately placed amongst the many available masseurs in telephone boxes. He was never short of basic bread and butter sleuthing, always foot slogging and exceedingly mundane work.

When he looked up again he saw the girl receptionist standing with Harvey Williamson on the floor above, looking down at him sitting waiting. He caught his irritated expression relax on recognising him, after which he spoke to the receptionist. The girl turned to walk away and Bart saw the flick of Harvey Williamson's hand make contact with her well defined bottom in the tight short skirt she was wearing as she walked away.

Bart, ever the old fashioned gentleman, felt a surge of disgust. He recalled Emily's report after meeting one of Harvey Williamson's young employees in a nearby café who, after hearing Emily's lie about wanting to work in advertising, told her if she waited a while she could apply for her job! Bart could see his lecherous reputation was genuine enough.

When the girl came back she looked flushed, a little put out, from which Bart deduced her boss's attentions weren't well received. She apologised for the delay, told him she would escort him to Mr Williamson's office. She led the way to a bank of lifts taking one up to the first floor, then across the same mezzanine route as before to Harvey's rather oversized plush office. Bart always believed such a display of wealth was designed, like the décor, to make the occupant feel important and to impress anyone privileged enough to see it.

"Ah, Mr. Bridges, you didn't have to deliver an update in person," Harvey stood to offer his hand. Bart took it feeling once again the clamminess of the palm the same as at their first meeting. "I know I may have seemed a little persistent for which I apologise."

Bart didn't believe a word of his expressed contriteness, being delivered with such insincerity he wondered why the man bothered.

"I did get the impression you wished the matter resolved urgently, yes," Bart said. He saw Harvey lick his lips to catch any saliva from dribbling down his chin, followed by an unattractive slurping sound.

Harvey took off his glasses, plucked a cleanly folded handkerchief out of his pocket to wipe the lenses. At such close quarters Bart remembered his protruding watery eyes indicative of a thyroid condition he thought. Harvey dabbed his eyes with the same handkerchief then settled the spectacles back on his nose.

"Yes, indeed. Do have a seat. What have you got to tell me?" Harvey licked his lips eagerly like a predator in readiness for a kill, sitting back down behind his desk.

"Well, I think you will be pleased," Bart began as he watched the anticipation grow and a smile appear on his still wet lips. "I think I can safely say with a degree of certainty your wife *isn't* having an illicit relationship......you are a very lucky man."

Harvey Williamson's smile instantly disappeared being replaced by shocked disbelief. "I think I told you quite clearly she was seeing someone?"

"Yes, indeed you did, although it doesn't appear to be the case." He saw annoyance on the man's face "Unless you would care to explain how *'you know'*? After weeks of close surveillance by three of us, she appears to be a very caring wife and doting mother, as displayed by a very fixed daily routine. In short, she takes and fetches your children from school, goes shopping and spends most of her time at home."

"Visitors!" Harvey snapped tersely.

"Err, none," Bart said.

Harvey got up, turned his back on Bart to walk to the nearest window where he stood silently looking out. Eventually, he suddenly spun round making Bart jump, "She must have spotted you following her and is being careful!"

Bart's irritation at the man's persistence was beginning to turn to outright annoyance. He stood up, reached into his pocket for the envelope Isla Strachan gave him before he left the shop. He took a step forward, placed the envelope on Harvey's glass topped desk clear of any papers or work matters. There was only a Newton's Cradle with silver balls hanging still, a silver segmented cube Bart couldn't fathom its purpose and an elaborate silver photo frame facing away. He couldn't see what was in the picture, although he supposed was of his children. Bart suddenly felt intrigued to know if his wife was included in the image.

He said, "I have made up your invoice for our surveillance to date."

Harvey came back to his desk with a face like thunder, picked up the envelope, "But you haven't found anything have you?!" he said indignantly.

Bart sat back down to show he was waiting for Williamson to open the letter to settle the bill. "On the contrary, Mr. Williamson," Bart said wrestling with his temper in order to remain calm, "We have found your wife to be exactly what she is, a good wife and mother."

The ensuing silence was one of acute impasse. He watched Harvey trying desperately to gain control of his own temper.

He picked up a silver paper knife from a silver desk caddy Bart overlooked, inserted the tip into the envelope to slice the top of the letter open. He took out the invoice and read the contents. Bart specifically asked Isla Strachan to only cost the time spent covering watching Jenny Williamson, with the barest minimum of travel expenses to and from Tarland. He didn't want to leave any room for Harvey to criticise his fees or refuse to pay.

Harvey showed no reaction to its content, he merely took up an oblong silver case he opened to reveal a cheque book and plucking a fountain pen from the caddy, reluctantly wrote a cheque which he ripped from the pad. He held the cheque in his hand wafting the paper to dry the ink.

In an altogether more reasonable voice he said, "If you continue with following my wife I will double what you are charging."

He handed the cheque over to Bart who took it, gave the paper a quick glance to make sure the details were complete, he put it into the inside pocket of his jacket.

Bart stood up where he looked down at the man, "I have several problems with your request. Firstly, I have a staff shortage, not enough people to spread over all my cases. Secondly, I don't believe the outcome would be any different than I have already told you which you don't seem to want to believe, for whatever reason." Bart turned to walk to the door, where he stopped, turned to say, "From what I saw today and what I've heard about you Mr. Williamson, *you* are the one with the inappropriate behaviour… towards your female staff…"

Bart had a sudden insight as to why Williamson hired him. He walked back to Harvey's desk, picked up the silver photo frame, he saw was a picture only of his children. He put it back down, returned to the door, from where he regarded Harvey delicately replacing the picture to the exact position on his desk as before. He looked more than irritated by it being interfered with.

"I will decline your kind offer, Mr Williamson because I will not be used to provide evidence for you to discredit your wife in a divorce case, although I would be prepared to give evidence about *your* behaviour on behalf of your wife in a custody case. If you carry on the way you are doing you will not only lose joint custody of your children, you will lose access to them entirely. Good day to you!" With that Bart left the room.

He took the opportunity to call in at a branch of his bank to deposit the cheque on his way to visit Iona Roberts.

CHAPTER 63

Robbie's relief at returning home without incident, except for the erratic turbulence brought about by the weather conditions which rendered Bear virtually comatose all the way back, was to be short lived. He didn't mind the silence of the return journey. He thought it promised future flights might be unaccompanied, at least by the big man. Robbie saw this inaugural one as some sort of test, an assessment of his co-operation. He couldn't see his home force being able to commandeer the aerodrome for all of his future trips, even though they might be somewhere in the vicinity monitoring what was taking place.

After landing back in Nottingham he could see Bear was in no fit state to get home, let alone drive his daughter's mini there; not only did he have to help him to the car, he drove him back to his flat. He noted it wasn't too far from his own hovel except Bear lived in part of an old, well maintained, detached house in an altogether better part of the area.

Robbie got him inside leaving him curled up on a couch in the main living room with a bowl from the kitchen should he need it. Although he was ailing he managed to bark, "Car keys!" mumbling something about his daughter needing the car back for work next day. The idea of a goon to a criminal gangster boss having a daughter was one thing, that she might be in legitimate employment, he somehow couldn't reconcile. It was obvious from the inside of his apartment he lived alone. He guessed there must be a 'Mrs Bear', ex or otherwise, somewhere who gave birth to 'baby bear'. Robbie couldn't imagine the man having a respectable daughter who would be agreeable to letting him use her car for illicit purposes.

Before he left the room, Robbie put the car keys on the coffee table at the side of the hulk who noted his action as he slipped off to sleep. When he let himself out the house he found the rain had followed them back south and was beginning to come down heavily. He knew he would be drenched by the time he walked the distance to his own place. The thought of the mouldy flat made him briefly think about calling to see Kirstie whose place was closer than his depressing digs. Whilst warmth, food, drink and her enthusiastic company was tempting, he was way too tired from exerting constant nervous energy all day, to take the idea seriously. He continued home and would wait to see how he was judged by Sid Bailey on his first flight. This was to be sooner than he expected.

Next day Robbie was woken by his mobile jigging about on the dilapidated bedside cabinet next to his ear. Sometime in the past someone clearly put the wooden relic together, probably from a flat pack, and not very well. The front of the one draw had fallen off. The door to the cabinet below was hanging by one hinge. Robbie hadn't been inspired to try to repair anything because six months ago he believed his stay would be short. The jumping mobile reminded him he switched over to silent mode the day before, leaving it to vibrate in his pocket.

He reached out for the mobile, saw Kirstie phoning again. When he answered with a sleepy 'Hi' sounding more like a Bear growl, he noted her voice saying, "Robbie, it's me," was far from her usual cheery self.

"Kirstie, hellooo," he tried to be a bit more upbeat, he wasn't too good first thing in the mornings. "Sorry I didnae get back to you yesterday, I was tied up," sounded as vague as he meant it to be. He hadn't told Kirstie about being recruited by Bailey for his flying skills or anything about owning a plane, the fewer people who knew the better. The latter was never part of his original legend anyway, a spur of the moment confession he thought might speed things along. "A very long day...I fell asleep when I got back."

He marvelled at how Kirstie could be fobbed off with little in the way of information about himself. She either lacked curiosity or was plain desperate to stay friends with him. He had given her nothing much by way of encouragement but still she came back. Most women, he thought, would have blown him out long ago. A flash of Emily's face at the thought seemed to confirm it.

She was saying, "I have a day off....I wondered if you wanted to come over....I'll cook a meal?" The thought of a home cooked meal made Robbie's stomach growl, the sandwich yesterday having long worn off.

"Aye sounds good," he said throwing caution to the wind. If Bailey ever found out he even knew Kirstie let alone was..... What was he doing with her? Now he had a foot in the door of Bailey's gang he knew he shouldn't keep seeing her, yet he kept her there thinking she might prove at least to be a good witness to what Bailey et al got up to at Hunters. She must have seen a lot or even heard things of interest to the Operation.

He looked at the mobile screen saw he'd slept most of the morning which was probably why he felt so hungry, "What time d'yer want me round?" They arranged a time, later in the afternoon. Robbie against his better judgement told her he would visit their favourite little shop for a bottle of wine asking if she needed any onion bhajis, they were 'very very good?' They both laughed, felt the frosty atmosphere at the beginning of the conversation clear a little or at least she forgave him for not getting back to her.

Almost immediately he cut the call from Kirstie, even before he could get out of bed, the call came from Bailey his services would be required again.

CHAPTER 64

By the time Bart reached the Advocate Offices of Iona Roberts he'd calmed down a little. He couldn't imagine he would ever be able to take kindly to Harvey Williamson and was pleased he had removed the man from the Agency's client list. Whilst he sat listening to the weasel he realised what he was trying to achieve by having her followed, then confirmed it when he saw the photograph of his two children. Was it normal not to have one of his wife as well as the children on his desk? He supposed whoever the third Mrs 'Ernest' was going to be, he knew she wouldn't approve of Jenny Williamson's face on her boss's desk. Bart also knew the prospective wife wasn't the receptionist Williamson inappropriately touched. Without doubt the man made his blood boil.

Five minutes later Bart was sitting in the familiar waiting area of the large hallway of Iona's offices where he sat a few times before whilst helping Lily fight to stay in the strange cottage on the Balmoral Estate. They were successful in fending off the pretend nephew of Elizabeth Grant, success being more to do with Emily than himself. Oddly, although exposing Petersen as a fraud asserted Lily's right to remain in the cottage, everyone who knew her could see the place had some kind of hold over her. Eventually she came to accept it and moved in with Nessa.

"Mr Bridges?" The voice at the side of him pulled him from his musings. The young girl smiled when he looked up, "Miss Roberts will see you now, if you would like to follow me."

Bart wasn't about to tell her he knew his way. He followed her up the noisy uncarpeted staircase to be announced by one of Iona Roberts' many assistants, for all Bart knew recruited from the dozens of battered wives, partners and girlfriends of as many brutal men as their victims. They passed through her employ, some back to their abusers whilst others moved on to other careers having been given the chance to change their lives by the woman he was about to meet again.

Iona once confided to him, when he mentioned the clatter of the bare stair boards, she preferred to spend any money she made on defending the women who sought her help. They usually had little or none of their own. He knew Legal Aid only covered criminal proceedings and Family Law in disputes of domestic violence or custody of children. There was a grey area when it came to the man's word against the woman, the aid didn't always cover all eventualities.

Iona Roberts looked exactly as he remembered. A well-dressed consummate professional lawyer whose desk he could see was still messily laden with cases of the many women she represented. She stood up, met him as he came in to give him a peck on the cheek. There was nothing about her that spoke misandrist; she wasn't anti-male or ever come over as a radical feminist. Although he had no real idea, he believed she would probably have equally offered support to a male victim of relationship abuse.

"What a pleasant surprise," Iona said, "I trust Lily and your young friend Emily are well?"

Momentarily Bart felt tempted to unload his fears for Emily and delay why he came to see her; he merely nodded in response.

"Iona, it's rather a delicate matter. I'm not quite sure why I came….one of those spur of the moment things. I don't really know whether you can be of help even if you legitimately could or wanted to talk about it."

"Now that does sound intriguing, Bart. Why don't you try me," she looked down at the piles of case papers on her desk, flicked the edge of the nearest one adding, "I'm afraid my daily grind is always rather similar. I often wish for something juicier." She laughed at herself, "What is it they say? Careful what you wish for lest it come true."

"Indeed, but even so we all do it," Bart said philosophically.

"So how can I help?"

He took a deep breath before he replied. "During the course of making enquiries one of my associates…..well actually I only have one working for me…….has discovered you are the sister of Jenny Williamson. Is that correct?"

"Interesting….I'm wondering about your enquiries, I'm sure you will tell me about….but in answer to your question, I have a younger sister called Jenny who is unfortunately married to……" Iona paused as if she were trying to remain professional, "Harvey Williamson, who runs a rather pretentious Advertising Agency, actually not too distant from here,"

Bart noted the critical inflection attached to 'pretentious'. "Yes, I agree, I have just come from those very premises having left the obnoxious man in his office some fifteen minutes ago."

There was a moment when Bart and Iona's eyes became locked, both trying to assess each other's thoughts.

"At least we agree on that," she said. "Were you there to take out advertising for one of your ventures? I hear you have formalised an Enquiry Agency of your own?"

"Well news does travel fast, we've only just set our agency up. My only attempt at advertising has been one basic statement of the fact in the local newspaper. Although I did put a card in the window of The Pharmacy in the village for someone to cover The March of Time on a part time basis…..not too pretentious I think." They both laughed. "And for the record I would be disinclined to give Harvey Williamson one penny of my money!"

"So we may share similar opinions about the man," she noted.

"Look," Bart said trying to pull the conversation back to why he called to see her, "I don't know whether you are aware Emily, my partner in everything, was close to a young police officer, Robbie Cowan....they were stepping out together," he saw Iona smile at the quaint phrase he used. "Well until he had some misfortune at work, a setback that got him suspended from duty at the time and was totally vindicated. Unfortunately, to cut a long story short, he couldn't resume his police duties. He had to go away." Iona began to look uncomfortable. She merely nodded. "We believed he might come back one day. Certainly I hoped he would because Emily has been……well, unable to deal with him going, especially after she discovered he put his bungalow at Tarland on the market ……..it changed her completely. Truth to tell this was one of the reasons I set up the Bartholomew and Hobbs Detective Agency. I thought it might help to distract her."

"I see," Iona said.

"Let me cut to the chase." Bart was trying to skirt around the issue of the observation of Jenny Williamson. "Why is your sister visiting Robbie's bungalow, I believe to pass his mail on to him?"

Iona looked quite shocked, "You've seen Jenny doing this?" Bart nodded. "Can I ask how you came to do that?"

"I hoped you wouldn't ask?" Bart said. "I know it's a breach of client confidentiality, except he is no longer my client. My very first case for the Agency has been to do surveillance on your sister for Harvey Williamson."

Iona Roberts picked up her telephone, pressed a button, "Stacey love? Can you hold all my calls and please could you bring us some very strong coffee?" she looked over at Bart to ask if coffee was okay. He nodded back.

CHAPTER 65

Bart moved on. He was driving back from Aberdeen, his thoughts trying to process what he discussed with Iona Roberts, all of which he would dearly love to impart to Emily and to have her give him her opinion. Normally, he would worry about whether he divulged too much of what was after all subject to client confidentiality, but he knew he could trust Iona implicitly, she wouldn't disclose her source should she need to act on the information.

His deliberations were cut short when he saw the road sign on the outskirts of Dinnet, moments later pulling up on the forecourt of McKinley's Autos. He noticed the absence of Nessa's jeep outside the abandoned Bus Company building where she usually left it. There were also no cars waiting outside McKinley's closed garage doors; their popularity as a repair shop seemed to be over. He wondered if they were closed for the day. He got out, walked the short distance to the premises main door, surprised when it opened easily. Nessa never displayed an open/closed sign.

Radio Northsound was playing an advertising jingle, whilst the mechanic Hamish's head was buried under a car bonnet deep inside the engine. Bart stood watching his arms trying with great force to prise something loose inside. He supposed he must be good at his job otherwise Nessa wouldn't have hired him let alone kept him as long as she had. Bart was coming close to thinking perhaps he misjudged the lad by calling him 'gormless', after all it must take some skill to be able to master the inside of a car engine.

Hamish stood up, stretching his back muscles he swivelled his hips, in almost a provocative gesture, then noticed Bart standing watching him. He gave him a nervous grin Bart likened to a lack of intelligence. *Nope, gormless*, he thought.

"Is Nessa in?" he asked.

As usual Hamish was lost for words, he merely pointed behind him to the office door. Bart nodded walking away The oil and petrol smells giving way to the aroma of rich coffee lured him as he got closer to the door. He tapped lightly, waited a couple of seconds to hear Nessa's voice shout "Come!" before he entered. Bart supposed if Nessa needed to change out of her overalls, she might very well do so in the office. He would be mortified to catch a lady undressed.

She was wearing her greasy overalls talking on the telephone, pointed at the coffee machine inviting him to help himself. Even after drinking coffee during his frank exchange with Iona Roberts he couldn't refuse another. Nessa only used the best filter Arabica coffee beans bought from The Black Faced Sheep in Aboyne, she freshly ground them every day.

Bart could hear she was having strong words with someone on the other end of the telephone. He began to think perhaps he should take his coffee outside, leaving her to talk in private. She waved him towards the visitor's chair. She grinned as she listened to someone speaking on the other end, moved the handset away from her head making a face before she returned it to her ear.

"Well, good! I should think so!" she said severely closing down the call without resorting to the usual goodbyes. "These folk are canny wi'it!" she said. "Teks something to fool the daughter of Jock McKinley, mek no mistake."

"Oh?" Bart knew how cantankerous her father could be, "Trouble?"

"Yer cannae short change a skinflint!" she laughed heartily. Nessa stood up, "I'm glad you dropped by, I want to show you something," she said moving towards the office door. Intrigued, Bart put his coffee down to follow her through the door leading into the compound at the back of the premises. When he stepped outside, what he saw shocked him. Nessa stood watching his reaction.

Bart had only been out to the compound a couple of times, the last being with Emily when they tried to gain a view of the next door building from Nessa's yard. On that occasion Emily moved aside as much junk as she could to give them access to the adjoining fence where they found a gap in next door's overgrown rear garden covered with years growth of brambles that put pressure on the connecting mesh wire fence. Bart was astounded to see Nessa cleared the whole of her compound, exposing a concreted ground surface where her own Jeep stood beside a few other cars parked neatly in a line.

"Oh my word!" Bart declared in amazement. "You got rid of the mess?" The whole compound for years was the dumping ground for car parts, old tyres and the remains of one or two rusted skeleton vehicles Bart suspected had been there for many decades. "It looks so big. What made you take such drastic action?"

He knew Jock McKinley kept every piece of junk as 'spares' in case he ever needed them. As to the old tyres, Bart had no idea how useful they might be. He suspected most of them would be perished rubber having been at the mercy of some severe weather conditions.

"To be honest, when Emily made her comment to you about scrap value? Aye, she was right there. I got some quotes and someone to shift the lot." Nessa pointed behind her, "The call before was wi'the scrappers, trying it on. I've done ma homework on the value of scrap," she laughed again.

"Well, it's certainly an improvement," Bart commented turning back to go inside again.

"Actually, the yard wasn't what I wanted to show yer," Nessa said pointing sideways to the fence nearest to the building. "You might remember there was a huge pile of tyres up against the fence…..see what I found behind them?" Between the building and the start of the fence was a small extremely rusted iron gate. There was no doubt the gate was once the connecting access to both premises. "Ma Da tells me his garage once belonged to the Bus Company, aye, where they repaired the vehicles."

Surprised Bart asked, "Didn't you know that?"

Nessa shook her head, "I've not seen it before. I didnae ken, he bought our place years before the Bus Company closed, they were to be sold separately d'yer ken?"

"And the tyres blocked the gate?"

She nodded again, "Aye, as far back as I can remember the mess was always here, only got worse as time passed."

Bart walked over to the gate to look through to the next door premises. The older woody brambles allowed him a view of the back of the Bus Company building like before when Emily took pictures of the new replacement back door with a partially cleared rear garden to give access to it. What he could see quite clearly was someone walked across the overgrown greenery towards the gate; the ground was crushed by feet. Bart wondered if the person noticed the tyres were no longer blocking the view of the bus company building from next door.

Nessa moved over to stand next to Bart. "It looks like you've been checked out, see?" he pointed at the flattened greenery on the other side.

The gate was chained with a rusted old padlock on Nessa's side. Bart reached out to shake the lock, years of rust flakes fell away. "I don't think they saw the padlock, maybe too many brambles in the way or too dark to notice. This hasn't been disturbed for years."

"Aye, there was years of the stuff over the whole compound, took a lot of sweeping before I discovered the back was completely concreted," Nessa said.

Bart was still looking over checking the window to the side beside the new back door. He suddenly made a sound of surprise. He pointed over, "One night I had a sneaky look round the back to see if there was any way I could see inside. At the time there wasn't, but do you see the window? One of the boards has been knocked aside making a gap," he glanced at Nessa smiling. "Do you have something I can use to get the padlock off?"

Nessa moved off with an "Aye," to return holding a strong pair of bolt cutters she gave him.

He stood for a while looking at the padlock before he attempted to cut the shackle where it disappeared into the hole in the padlock.

Nessa suggested, "Be easier to cut the chain."

"Not if you want to put it back in place," he turned to give her back the bolt cutters, moved the shackle to slip the chain off the padlock. He opened the gate cautiously hoping it was still sturdy enough to remain in one piece. The gate swung open with a creaking sound revealing the patch of brambles barring his way.

"Wait!" Nessa said, rushed off with the cutters and came back with a pair of padded work gloves she handed to Bart.

"Excellent!" he said putting them on he attacked the brambles pushing them to one side. He managed to squeeze his way through. For the first time in his life he was thankful he was only five foot four inches, although his girth was a bit of a challenge. "Let's hope David Taylor and his mate don't get brazen enough to come out here in the day," he said as Nessa watched him move across the already trampled ground up to the rear window where at the bottom corner the boarding exposed the inside. He placed his hands at each side of his head to blot out the light as he peered inside.

When he came back he did everything in reverse finishing with pulling the brambles back as near into place as he could, shut the gate, attaching the rusted chain to the padlock, he put the shackle back over the hole to restore the lock once more.

Ness stared at him in anticipation, "Well?" she said impatiently.

"I reckon they've knocked the boarding whilst carrying the boxes inside. It's a gloomy interior. I could see the boxes stacked up, though not much else."

"Hmm," Nessa sounded almost disappointed. "They must own the place if they've got a key to it," she said.

They were walking back inside. Bart's only comment was, "Not if you remove the old door to put one of your own on, doesn't make you the owner of the building, just of the door." He smiled wryly.

CHAPTER 66

Peter arrived at the Quinnell Estate with no clear idea what he intended to do other than to observe the strange girl Gina. He admitted to himself it would be harder after she saw him in the café where she works. He did, however, have the foresight to leave his laptop in his room at The Moor Hen because he couldn't let anyone see the files he had on it. Instead he picked up his tablet he used mostly for playing computer games or to keep in touch with other gamers on social media.

Although, playing games was also a way of spying on his competitors, finding out from other gamers what was currently popular and exciting to the main stream. Everyone in the business did it. Peter spent so much time on his laptop whilst working that without access he always felt edgy, in need of another fix if he was ever away for too long. He knew he was borderline obsessional about techy devices.

Part of him didn't want to ever meet the strange waitress again except he was convinced there was no other way, if he was going to find Emily, he must observe Gina. He heard from Bart about Emily's previous contacts with her and knew about Gina's preoccupation with Emily's boyfriend Robbie. What clinched his assertion was hearing she deliberately arranged to meet the mechanic, Hamish to ask him questions like where Gina Taylor was living. What he couldn't work out was why she wanted to know so badly.

Peter walked into the Quinnell coffee shop with his computer bag over his shoulder, bought himself a coffee at the counter, going straight to the table he sat at the day before which was conveniently free. People he thought preferred window seats, whilst he liked something solid behind him when he ate, drank or worked on his laptop. An obsessive trait he knew began during his stay in the Drugs and Alcohol rehabilitation clinic because it made him feel physically safer, *no one could walk up behind you without you knowing.* As a freelance programmer in the competitive world of gaming he always had an eye to security.

He took no time at all to become engrossed on his iPad catching up on the gaming world he belonged to and specifically a chat room where he was a regular. He was well known as **NinjagoPDJ** which held various references to game related things, specifically the tongue-in-cheek one to 'pants' Peter always thought amusing. He caught up with some of the regulars' enthusiasms for various new games on the market, even looking a few of them up. He found it hard to accept how easily satisfied people were.

To a gaming programmer like himself there was always the dream of creating a number one best-selling game. This gave him an excited edge he likened to a surfer wanting to catch the biggest wave of their life.

"Back again?" he heard, not recognising the childlike voice. He certainly didn't associate it with the waitress Gina. When he looked up he saw her standing, hands behind her back swaying from side to side. She held a beaming smile not dissimilar to the one she switched on the day before; only there was a hint of coyness to go with the childlike motion.

Even though he was completely surprised by the number of gamers enthusing over a new product release, wanting to find out all he could about it, he was distracted by the dramatic change in the girl. He put his tablet down on the table in front of him.

"Yes, can't keep away, must be the coffee," he looked at the large cup in front of him, realised he hadn't yet taken a sip. Peter picked the cup up, swallowed a generous mouthful, watching Gina's eyes flick hungrily to the computer case at the side of him with a relish he found almost predatory. He remembered his dream where she was standing covered in blood holding a dripping carving knife.

"You want me to get you an éclair?" she asked like a child trying to please a parent.

Peter rubbed his midriff, "I ate rather a big breakfast. I'm not really hungry."

Gina looked at the tablet in front of him, "What are you doing?"

Peter thought she still held an excited anticipation like a child about to open their Christmas presents; in this case her words came over as nosy.

Peter forced a reply, "Oh, looking at computer games," once said he knew she would ask what they were, like any kid might. He added, "Nothing specific….flitting really…..well I am on holiday."

"That's nice," she said. "Where do you live?"

Peter supposed he left himself open to the question, would have replied London, a sufficiently big place, but knew she would ask where, so he said instead, "Where do you live?" He smiled at her.

He saw her forehead wrinkle in a frown reminding him this wasn't a young child he was talking to, otherwise she wouldn't have a job in a café. Gina's face became furious, "I live with my mother. I hate her!" she spat at Peter.

Peter knew she was lying because he knew about Anabel Taylor who lived in Emily's village and who was raped by Rupert Quinnell, the man who owned the coffee shop he was sitting in and was Gina's biological father according to her mother.

Peter forced himself to ask, "Why do you hate your mother?"

Silence followed whilst she pondered on the question. She swivelled around to look behind her at the counter where a few customers were being served by two Baristas a lot older than her. When Gina turned back to face him she was smiling gently as if satisfied she wasn't being watched, her general demeanour suddenly changed back to the flirty girl he met the day before.

"I have to be careful," she whispered conspiratorially referring to the two girls serving the queue of people. Peter could see they were totally engrossed in their work. "I get a break in half an hour. If you want to meet me outside in the garden centre, I'll tell you about my mother and...." she looked once again at Peter's computer satchel next to him, "You can show me your computer game." She didn't wait for a reply, she walked away picking up a tray of crockery from one of the tables before she disappeared through a door at the side of the counter. Peter looked at his watched, finished his coffee and after fifteen minutes he got up, packed his tablet into his otherwise empty computer bag and left the coffee shop.

He made his way through the garden centre to the outside area sitting down on a depleted stack of compost bags that gave him a good view of the exit door from the garden centre.

He was sufficiently disturbed by Gina Taylor's sudden change of personality to consider telephoning Bart to tell him what he witnessed. Isla Strachan answered his call after a couple of rings. He recognised her refined Scottish voice immediately. "Mrs Strachan it's Peter, is Mr Bridges there?" He was having second thoughts about speaking to Bart, wondering what he would say to him.

"Sorry, Peter he went into Aberdeen this morning, can I take a message?"

"Err...." Peter began, at a loss what to tell her. He spotted Gina appear in the external entrance of the garden centre, standing looking around for him. "Oh, I've got to go, I've made contact with that strange girl Gina, I'm about to meet with her.....I want to find out if she's seen Emily lately....I'll see you later?" Peter heard Isla Strachan say something about being careful, she isn't right in the head, when he pressed his phone off. Gina spotted where he was sitting looking pleased as she walked over.

Peter noticed she was wearing red lipstick she must have applied since they spoke in the café. The thought occurred to him she would have looked very weird given her earlier child-like approach to him.

"Hi," she said.

"Hello," Peter tried to hide his nervousness. He shuffled along the compost stack giving her plenty of room to sit down. She chose to sit down so close to him he could feel her leg brush against his making him feel instantly threatened by her. He tried to remember if Bart told him how old she was; she must be at least fifteen to be able to have a paid job. There was no doubt she was young.

"Can I see your computer games?" she asked hurriedly, "I only get half an hour break."

Peter remembered her strange reaction to the lid of his laptop the day before she likened to graffiti. He hadn't considered this before, not even when he got to examine the photographs of the graffiti from the Tour Bus Building Bart told him she contributed to. Her avid interest made him pleased he left his laptop in his room.

Peter deflected her with, "You were going to tell me why you hate your mother," he didn't have enough time in half an hour to be subtle. At the mention of her mother her face darkened revealing a look that no way resembled the earlier coy child who first approached him. He tried to deflect her with, "I bet your mother is nowhere near as dreadful as mine, otherwise you wouldn't still be living with her." He hoped he wouldn't have to explain what he meant, this was the part of his life he didn't like to think about. "I haven't seen my parents for a long time." He thought it might sound odd given his age. He could see she hadn't noticed, she was processing what he said.

"Were they cruel to you?" she asked almost gleefully.

He had a flash of the institution they committed him to, remembered the lonely hours he spent confined to a room, restricted by some nurses, the male ones especially who looked more like prison guards. He supposed at the time he did think his parents were being cruel to him, punishing him for being sexually abused by a number of paedophiles. Peter felt the guilt for recruiting some of his school friends by tempting them with the drugs Arthur Claymore grew in his greenhouse. He got them to join him to also be abused. At the time he thought they might leave him alone. Peter shivered, "Yes," he whispered.

Gina's eyes flashed wildly on hearing him. He could tell he had her full attention.

"What did they do to you?" she asked excitedly, her attention riveted on Peter, all thoughts of computer games temporarily forgotten.

"They locked me away," he said, his voice cracking a little at the memories. "What about you? What about your mother.....and father?"

Gina glared, instantly furious, "My mother is a slut! I grew up with a step Dad only I didn't know, I thought he *was* my father. She seduced my real father. Even after I found out who he was she wouldn't let me see him!" Gina's eyes burned with hate. "My father loves me!" She stood up, began to spin around as if she was on a roundabout, her arms spread out each side of her body for balance. When she stopped she wobbled facing Peter, gasping for breath and nearly fell over. She screeched, "He owns all this!" Her arms were still held high, palms up indicating her surroundings. "Isn't that....just.... crazy?"

Peter knew, of course, she didn't live with her mother, "So why do you still live with your mother?" he asked.

She lowered her arms looking thoughtful. "The bitch told me my father didn't want to know me!" Her voice was loud enough to carry over to where people were walking around the bedding plants, one or two of them looked over at the sound of her raised voice.

"But he did?" Peter asked wondering at the arrangement she must have with Rupert Quinnell to allow her to live on the estate and work in the café.

"Of course he did!" she cried indignantly. "And my brother," she sounded triumphant. "*They* love me!" she was pointing at her own chest, her hand trembling with anger. Then she spun around one more time, stopped, no longer seeming angry. The little girl persona reappeared only this time she was wearing bright red lipstick. She smiled coyly through its glossiness, "They love me," she whispered then sighed. Her mind wandered off, Peter supposed thinking about her father and her brother. Eventually she said, "Except for the bitch he's married to….now she does hate me!" she began to laugh, a very scary cackle. "I know things about her I'm not supposed to know," she said triumphantly.

Peter knew one thing about Gina Taylor, she was completely crazy.

CHAPTER 67

Robbie was right about Bear no longer chaperoning him, it was Sid Bailey himself who turned up to pick him up with the blue suit man called Tony. Robbie took an instant dislike to him close up. He could never trust anyone who wore sunglasses at night, even vampires didn't need them.

"What a shit hole!" was a good start from the pretend Italian with an East End accent. "'ow come you've got a plane yet you live like this?" Robbie ignored him as he put his jacket on, and locked his door whilst Tony waited impatiently outside. "Is it worth locking?" he mocked as they moved off along the walkway. Robbie was given enough notice to be able to text his handler about the potential flight on the burner phone he kept under the bath. This time he put his Nokia on silent.

The car waiting in the deserted car park was an old Roller although seen better days, was nonetheless a classic. Robbie was surprised when Tony opened the back door for him, to reveal Sid Bailey sitting inside. The camel Crombie he usually wore replaced by a smart dinner jacket with bow tie looked out of place on Sid Bailey. His wizened face Robbie likened to a tortoise, wrinkled and pinched with much the same expression.

Robbie got in next to Bailey, his nerves beginning to jangle because he assumed he would be doing a similar trip to deliver or fetch whatever merchandise he saw fit. Now, wondering if Bailey sussed who he was, the words of his handler at the pre-brief came tumbling back, 'The Bailey's are dangerous, they disappear people. Sid is the psycho brother who takes pleasure in keeping his hand in that side of business matters.'

Robbie wanted to ask him where they were going after they set off, but saw quickly the direction Tony took led to the airport where he kept his plane. He heard an echo of Bear warning him not to ask the boss questions, 'Sid doesn't like you asking questions,' he cautioned him. Robbie remained mute, hoping he would tell him to be able to register the trip. He knew Operation Graffiti would need some kind of official verification of these journeys if they were to use them as evidence in the future. The day before, he didn't see Bear pick anything up before they flew back to Nottingham. If there was then the big man must have received it when Robbie went for food.

Eventually the silence got to Robbie, "Is Bear okay, he was sick as a dog yesterday?" he laughed to lighten the enquiry.

"Apparently," Bailey rasped his voice a little wheezy. "I understand it's only a two seater?"

Robbie nodded, "Yes, I explained to Bear about the weight restrictions. His bulk does cut down the amount of cargo I can carry." Robbie wasn't about to go into details on the exact weights or how weather conditions can affect flying.

"I get it laddie," Sid snapped irritably. "It's just me today, I've got a party to attend," he looked down at his smart attire as if to indicate it was quite obvious. Inwardly Robbie felt relieved remaining with a neutral expression. Bailey went on, "Normally I would take Tony or Bear with me. I don't like meeting these sort of people alone," he saw an involuntary movement of his hand towards the inside of his dinner jacket. Robbie thought he might be carrying a weapon. "Today it's going to be you and since you're not dressed to my liking I've taken the liberty of bringing you something appropriate to wear. These are society people, they like a bit of a show. I have a reputation to keep up. Tony will give you the suit before we take off."

Robbie forced himself not to ask where they were going, something told him he would be quite exposed. What were the chances of him bumping into someone he knew?

Bailey was watching him with a quizzical expression on his face, "You okay with that?" he asked as if Robbie showed otherwise.

Robbie tried to relax, "Yes, of course. I was just wondering if you are okay flying. I wouldn't want you to be ill like Bear you might spoil your smart clothes. It can get very bumpy in a small plane....yesterday was really bad." Sid Bailey laughed until he began to cough. Robbie didn't need him to answer the question. He grinned back at Sid trying to calm his own fears at escorting a gangland boss into polite society.

Everything went smoothly on the journey thereafter. Only when he took the bag Tony gave him plus the dark suit inside a carrier cover into the men's room at the airport to change clothes, did he look at himself in the mirror. He was shocked by his own reflection, at how pinched his face was. He realised for the first time how much weight he'd lost since he went undercover.

The suit was too big but would have to do. He wished he'd gone to get his hair cut, although clean, the length spoilt the smartness of the image looking back at him. If he had a hat, like a chauffeur might wear, he could have pushed the mess up inside the brim.

When he left the men's room he collided with a young woman in the corridor outside. He felt embarrassed, he apologised, noticing how attractive she was, her hair swept up in a ponytail. She gave him the usual reaction he got from the opposite sex, smiled coyly, telling him it was okay and walked away.

He stopped suddenly, turned calling after her, "'Scuse me Miss," he walked back to her when she stopped. She was standing expectantly with a look of eager anticipation, hanging on his words, "I don't suppose.......it's a bit of a cheek....but you wouldn't let me have the band you've got your hair held up with, would'ya?"

The deal Robbie did was to promise to take her for a drink after his trip. He received her telephone number with the hair band in exchange. Robbie felt a right jessie when he put his hair up in a man-bun promising himself he would get his hair cut when he got back now his fortunes appeared to have improved.

He had no intention of meeting the woman, pretty though she was. He noted she was wearing a wedding ring, a no-no for Robbie. When he walked out of the building onto the tarmac to his plane, he screwed up the piece of paper with the number, finding a convenient bin near the exit to toss it in. The irony of becoming Sid Bailey's personal flying chauffeur wasn't lost on Robbie, except being the bodyguard to such a nefarious criminal wasn't what he signed up for. Keeping gangsters like him safe went against everything he stood for.

CHAPTER 68

Bart found Michelle in the back room working on the laptop while Isla Strachan was filling the kettle to make a pot of tea. There was a large oblong box standing behind Mitch propped against the wall. "How is everyone?" Bart asked moving straight over to the dwindling flames in the fire place. Momentarily his irritation flared, he hated to see the fire go out. He put another log into the centre, took up the poker, he prodded the wood furiously to catch the remaining embers.

Isla looked round drawn by the sound, her eyebrows rose as she glanced over at Michelle who was also staring with concern at Bart's back. Although, they were fairly new employees, they both recognised his mannerisms enough to know he was vexed. Log poking denoted he was troubled. They said nothing which drew a glance from Bart, "Has anyone seen Peter today?"

Michelle shook her head. Isla said, "He telephoned earlier to speak to you. I told him you went to Aberdeen but he cut the conversation short because he was about to meet with Gina Taylor.....aye, he called her 'that strange girl'."

Bart looked up alarmed, "Where was he meeting her?"

Isla Strachan shrugged, "He didn't say....only he wanted to find out if she had seen Emily recently, then he abruptly cut the call."

Bart sat down in his fireside chair, deeply concerned, "I don't like the sound of that. Didn't he leave me a message?"

"No, I did ask if I could take one…."

Bart pointed over to Michelle at the table having caught sight of the large box standing behind her, "What's that?" he asked interrupting Isla.

Isla took a step closer to Bart. She felt he was already disappointed with her over Peter's telephone call, concerned he might react badly when she told him she ordered the white board he wanted and charged it to the Agency.

"A white board…you said you wanted one when you were doing th'a time line for Emily on brown paper," she pointed over to the table where the paper was still spread underneath the laptop Michelle was using. "I've McTavish coming over today to put it up." Bart looked stunned. She quickly added, "He's the local odd-job-man, I use him ma'self, he's very reliable," to cover what she perceived as his disapproval for overstepping her role.

Bart suddenly smiled, "Mrs Strachan you are wonderful! I didn't mean to burden you with the task….but thank you. This is exactly what we need to make sense of all these fragments, it's confusing and difficult to see the big picture." Bart scratched his head as though it might clear the confusion. "I don't suppose Peter said when he would be back, Mrs Strachan?"

Isla shook her head, "He ended the call before I could ask him, sorry."

She turned back to finish making the tea. Bart moved his attention to Michelle, "We'll need a meeting, I've got a lot to tell you from today. I don't think we can wait for Peter to return."

They all heard the shop bell announcing the arrival of McTavish the village handyman to fulfil the request.

*　　*　　*　　*　　*

Bart took the interruption as an opportunity to go down The Brae to The Griddle Iron on the turning circle. He hated banging and drilling invading his space. Whenever it occurred at The March of Time he took himself off to avoid the noise. The erection of the workshop in the back garden was a case in point. Today, however, he disappeared when Isla offered McTavish a cup of tea before he even began the job which Bart knew would lengthen the time he would take in putting up the whiteboard.

"I'm going to fetch us some lunch from Max for our meeting," he announced as he glared at the elderly McTavish who promptly sat down at the table to drink his tea, "What would you like?" he asked as he walked away into the shop expecting them to follow him through. He wasn't about to offer food to McTavish, that would prolong the ordeal even more.

Isla sensed his grumpiness, turned her head away to hide a smile at the same time the clocks burst into the twelve noon chorus making further conversation impossible. Bart mimed he would telephone leaving the shop to walk the few yards down to Max and Steph's café on the corner. He heaved a huge disgruntled sigh when he saw the place packed out with visitors. It being Wednesday, the day the coach tourists were given half a day to walk around the village after a morning's sightseeing, all the cafés opened to cater for the brisk business.

After getting himself a drink he settled himself in the only available table in the farthest corner of the annex to the main café. He picked up a menu to choose what he wanted to eat before he telephoned Isla to take their orders. Once done, he asked Isla to telephone him when McTavish was finished. He expressed a wish for her to be part of the Agency meeting if she didn't mind. She sounded pleased to accept which went part way towards smoothing his moodiness. He knew having something to eat would restore his usual cheeriness completely.

After McTavish left, they sat around the table with their lunches, next to the white board, now fully installed on the wall. Michelle and Isla preferred sandwiches whilst Bart chose the house special burger with homemade tomato chutney Max put into a take-out box especially for him.

After several generous mouthfuls Bart asked, "I wonder, Mrs Strachan, if you would consider officially becoming the Agency's office manager? You are undertaking some of the necessary duties anyway and there are more needed to be done?" Bart disposed of another bite of his burger, chewed and swallowed before he continued, "For example there is a desperate need for organisation regarding the cases, workloads, rotas, that sort of thing. We may need to take on more casual associates," he put his burger down inside the carton, "I really do need to spend all my time looking for Emily. I have no confidence in the police at all, especially in that dreadful man Morris."

At the mention of his name Michelle felt acute guilt she may have been responsible for Morris's hurried departure without him stating his business in coming to see Bart. She said, "Perhaps we ought to complete the MISPER for Emily anyway. At least the police will have her absence on general circulation. The more people out there looking for her the better, surely?"

Bart wasn't convinced. He updated on the situation regarding the use being made of the Bus Company building at Dinnet for Isla Strachan's benefit, then told them what he found out about the connecting gate allowing him to glimpse the boxes inside the building. "I was going to tell Nessa we couldn't keep watch on her neighbour at present because without Emily I'm short staffed. Since I'm not sure her disappearance isn't in some way connected to David Taylor or the Quinnell estate I haven't terminated it. I believe Peter might have come to the same conclusion hence why he is meeting Gina Taylor."

Isla said, "That worries me greatly, Mr Bridges. Och, the girl is a strange lassie, make no mistake. It's a great worry if she is involved."

They were interrupted by a loud knocking on the shop door which was locked with the 'closed' sign put up before the meeting. Isla stood up, "I'll go tell them we're closed for the day," she said leaving the room.

Michelle told him, "I don't mind doing a night stint at Dinnet. Perhaps Nessa McKinley would let us do it from closer quarters. I think we've more chance of ID'ing them from the back compound because they're more likely t'take their masks off when there's no one to see them."

Bart was about to reply when Isla came back leading Helen Daniels from the Hotel, "This lady says she needs an urgent word Mr Bridges."

Helen looked worried seeing Bart sitting with someone else she didn't know, "I can see it's not convenient, perhaps I could speak to you in private?" Helen could see they were having a meeting but didn't look like she was about to leave.

Michelle began to rise from her seat until Bart put out his hand to stay her. She sat back down, "These are my associates, Helen perhaps you could tell me what it concerns?"

Helen coughed nervously, "Err, I believe you have been to see Iona Roberts today?"

"Yes, I have, does it concern what I spoke with her about?" Helen nodded. "In that case I would like Michelle and Mrs Strachan to remain because I was about to tell them about my visit. I trust them with full disclosure of the conversation. You can join us whilst I give them an update because I also trust you with the same information……you decide."

For a moment Helen looked confused. Bart could see she was contemplating whether to stay or leave before she sat down on the spare chair at the table, "Okay, Bart," she said looking at the other two people in the room. "My name is Helen Daniels, I am the manager at the hotel up the road," she said out of courtesy to the others.

Bart introduced Michelle as an ex-police officer, an associate investigator for his Agency and Isla Strachan as his office manager, which greatly pleased her. He then told them how his first case was Harvey Williamson, who hired the agency to gain proof of his wife

Jenny's infidelity, of his subsequent discovery about her visits to Robbie Cowan's bungalow and Michelle's observations on her passing his mail to someone.

He explained how Iona Roberts was involved, "I understand Iona Roberts is officially Robbie Cowan's next-of-kin. Jenny Williamson is her sister who is doing Iona a favour because she lives a short distance away from his bungalow. They are both related through his deceased mother's side of the family and in the absence of any other kin, Iona is dealing with his affairs by liaising with the man Jenny passed his mail to." Bart broke off here because he wasn't sure how much Helen knew about Robbie's current whereabouts.

Michelle added, "I recognised the man as someone I've seen during the time I served as a police officer."

Bart turned to Michelle, "I can confirm your finding the bungalow isn't really for sale, just made to look like Robbie has left the area completely because the place might be being watched by a local criminal syndicate." Bart's gaze returned to Helen for any trace of a reaction.

Helen listened intently before she said, "What Bart hasn't told you, is I am also undercover at the hotel," she looked over at Bart who was surprised to hear her reveal herself so easily. He said nothing before she continued, "There is a link with a current major Operation running up here in the region. My remit is specifically concerned with the supply of drugs and the use of local businesses through extortion to clean and re-distribute the proceeds. However, it does link to the bigger Operation," she sighed deeply. "It has to. Without sharing information we would be falling over each other maybe even compromising one or both. It remains unclear whether the criminal organisation, believed to be run from the Quinnell Estate and the money laundering are connected. We haven't definitely established that."

Bart sat listening with a puzzled expression on his face, "Perhaps you could tell us why you came, Helen?"

She coughed before she spoke, "I have been instructed through my police contact to tell you to back off." Bart looked shocked. A noise of disapproval akin to a growl escaped him.

Michelle and Isla saw the same expression Bart wore earlier appear back on his face. They braced themselves for his temper to explode. His head went down whilst he held himself quite rigid trying to control himself before he looked up. He smiled at Helen.

"Then you must go back to tell your people, whoever they may be, no can do," he appeared remarkably calm. "You see Helen, my Emily went missing about three days ago," he fixed Helen in a steady stare, "And no one is going to tell me to stop looking for her."

CHAPTER 69

Bart's comment rendered Helen Daniels momentarily speechless plunging the back room at The March of Time into silence. His refusal to keep out of Operational business wasn't exactly what she expected. She was trying to process how Emily's disappearance might fit into her remit. As the seconds ticked by Bart took the chance to reflect on how different Helen seemed to when he first met her, the then Domestic Services supervisor at the hotel where he once stayed.

Much later, after moving up to Scotland, permanently installed in his clock shop, he had been drawn into looking at the murder of Finlay Ferguson who he believed was a friend of Helen's before he decided to leave the hotel. Helen even tried to talk him out of the move, offering him a place to stay in the staff quarters when she heard he was sleeping rough in the abandoned Tour Bus building behind the hotel.

Bart knew Helen was capable of showing real concern for Finn and his ex-girlfriend Charlotte, who left him to live with Rory Quinnell on his family estate. In fact, she was responsible for helping Charlotte to escape the Quinnell's. Bart only recently discovered Helen, was an undercover police officer who arranged for her, their key witness, to go into the Witness Protection Programme whilst Operation Graffiti completed their investigations.

"Have you reported Emily missing to the local police?" Helen asked showing little emotion.

Before Bart could reply, Michelle interrupted, "Mr. Bridges has tried," she said immediately coming to his defence.

"Yes, I have......unfortunately our local police, DI Morris in particular, don't seem to think being forced off the road in a car or being subjected to a bomb attack, are relevant indicators she might be in some way a target! They think she is likely to have 'gone off partying' with friends," he finished sarcastically. "She's just turned eighteen, has very few friends here and......" Bart was about to add *'she knows who was riding pillion on the motor bike that tried to kill her'* when the thought suddenly took on a greater significance. He looked over at Michelle and Isla showing sudden insight saying, "Peter is quite right!"

Helen asked, "Who is Peter?"

Bart felt disinclined to explain to Helen about Emily's cousin, Peter Draper, he didn't think this would help because he also realised whatever was discussed there in the back room would be conveyed back to whichever Operation Helen was attached to or even further, to Operation Graffiti with its larger remit. Either way one or both sent Helen to tell Bart to butt out of their investigation. He was no longer sure how much information he could convey to her or whether he really did trust her any more.

Bart ignored her question, "I think we are done here Helen. You have my reply to convey to your superiors. I am not subject to their bidding. I will do as I see fit to find Emily."

He stood up, walked off into the shop expecting her to follow him. By the time she joined him he was standing stiffly by the open shop door to let her out. She stopped, began to say, "You would be wise to....."

He interrupted her with, "Tell them to look to their own, specifically CID's D.I Morris or at his ex-Detective Sergeant, Copeland who I am led to believe was sacked recently. My advice is they would be wise to examine closer to home." He pulled the door a little wider to usher her out. However, being Bart Bridges he couldn't quite forget about the shared friendship they once had, "Take care of yourself, Helen," he couldn't help saying.

"You too Bart," she whispered as she left. He closed the door.

When Bart got through to the back room, more tea was being made. He knew it was needed as there was even more to discuss with Michelle and Isla. The session took a long time, taking turns to make notes on the white board. Michelle was first because she was familiar with updating evidence from her police career. They separated the areas under discussion into main headings: Emily, the Quinnell Estate, the abandoned Bus Company Building (Dinnet) and the Village/Hotel (Helen). Across the bottom of the board they listed horizontally some names: Rupert/Rory/Delores Quinnell, Gina Taylor/David Taylor, Chuck, Hamish McGregor.

After the last name Michelle looked puzzled, "You think Hamish is involved in all of this?"

"To be honest, I have no idea. He certainly seems to be one of the last people to see Emily before she went missing." Michelle couldn't disagree. "He does know the Quinnells. He may know more than he has admitted to about them. He left a very good job, he says, because of Rory Quinnell but hasn't explained exactly why."

Bart moved to the farthest end of the board, "This is an excellent whiteboard Mrs Strachan," he commented before he created another list of people: Harvey Williamson, Jenny Williamson, Iona Roberts, he hesitated before he added, Robbie Cowan. "There is something about our Advertising CEO: he troubles me greatly. I'm adding these as, shall we say, people of interest?"

Isla Strachan studied the board, "We need photographs if we can get them."

"I'm not sure how easily obtainable they would be, Mrs Strachan," Bart said.

"Let me see what I can get from the internet," Michelle offered. "There are local papers, social media or if we have to...." she picked up her mobile and waggled it.

Bart instantly thought of the implications of her taking photographs of the people up on the whiteboard, "See what you can find via computer first, we'll talk about the other way later."

Emily	Quinnell Farm	Dinnet Bus Co. Building	Hotel	Bus Tour Building	Others:
	Rupert Quinnell Delores (wife) Rory (Son)	David Taylor ?masked man	Chuck Bistro Manager	Gina Taylor Finlay Ferguson	Harvey Williamson Jenny Iona Roberts Robbie Cowan
Missing	?Money laundering	Illegal use of building Storage boxes	Extortion ?Money laundering	Drugs	
Hamish (Last seen by) Gina (riding pillion) Castle Bomb	David Taylor Gina Taylor (Rupert's daughter)	Emily watching	Finlay Ferguson Helen Daniels		
Rupert/Rory/Delores Quinnell, Gina Taylor/David Taylor, Chuck, Hamish McGregor					

They were interrupted by more loud knocking on the shop door which sounded more urgent than Helen did earlier. Bart briefly wondered if she had come back to deliver a further message after speaking with her police contacts. Bart stood quickly before Isla could rise from her seat, "I'll go," he said leaving the room. When he got into the shop he could see Lily peering in through the glass in the door looking quite worried.

"Nessa told me about Emily beginning missing," Lily said when he let her in. "Why didn't you tell me before when you phoned the other day to see if she was at the castle?"

Bart locked the door again, "I only just realised I hadn't seen her for a while. We often work at different times, miss meeting because we have a lot of work on. Come through to the back," he said leading the way.

Isla and Michelle were introduced to Lily. Bart explained how Emily used to lodge with Lily at Crathie before she moved into the shop. There was a déjà vu moment when Lily asked the same question as Helen, whether Bart reported Emily missing to the police. Michelle once again felt a surge of guilt whilst Bart didn't want to go over the same ground.

Lily said, "Ness and I want to help in any way we can. She thinks you shouldn't spend any more time watching the building next door to McKinley's as it's not as important…..finding Emily is."

Michelle said, "Our last known sighting for Emily was her written report on her surveillance at Dinnet, which could make the job important."

Bart added, "Yes, we can't rule out the possibility the two things are connected." He didn't add the thought Emily may have ignored his instruction not to approach the building whilst she was watching it, in case David Taylor and the other man saw her there. "In fact, Michelle has suggested we survey it closer from the rear compound if Nessa agrees, there's a possibility they may remove their balaclavas when they go into the building. We could get to see who the other man is. Whatever they are doing I believe isn't legal." *They could lead us to Emily.* The thought came suddenly, "I think we should attempt to follow them when they do come again." He looked at Michelle for confirmation of the idea.

She nodded, "My thought also."

CHAPTER 70

After Gina stopped spinning to make her confession to Peter about her hatred for her father's wife, she seemed to calm down a little, as if relieved of the toxic burden. She sat back down next to him on the compost bags, even closer than before. He could feel the warmth of her leg against his.

"Do you have a girl friend?" A question Peter thought was the beginning of yet another round of rapid interrogation.

"No," he said simply, it was easier to tell her the truth than to lie.

"Why not?" She leaned away from him a little to enable her to look directly into his face with an intense stare. He shrugged not able to explain. "Are you gay?" The remark was meant as an insult.

"No!" he said rather sharply knowing the truth lay somewhere in his dreadful past. He wasn't about to explain any of his early life to her. "I suppose I work too hard to have time to commit to a relationship…it wouldn't be fair."

She seemed satisfied with his reply. The mention of his work drew her attention once again towards the computer satchel at his side, her eyes sparkling with anticipation, "Can I see your game?"

Peter looked at his wrist watch, relieved to see her half hour break was over. She noticed his watch, grabbed his wrist drawing the face towards her, saw the time then suddenly leapt to her feet alarmed. "No! He'll be angry if I take too long," she turned to rush off, stopped, turned back asking, "I finish at three, if you hang around we could meet again. You can show me your game, then?"

Peter stood up, "Sorry, I have to go to meet someone."

Gina didn't like his answer. The dark cloud appeared again on her face, as she looked away towards the garden centre doors where a man with a wheelbarrow was coming outside. Without another word she rushed off. Peter watched her hurriedly approach the building, stopping when the man lowered his barrow on seeing her, put out his arm to catch her as she attempted to slip past. He barred her way. Peter could see even at a distance he looked angry. He started yelling at her whilst pointing his arm to somewhere over to the left where the tops of the glass greenhouse roofs sparkled, caught by the sun.

Gina shook her head vigorously. He heard her voice shrilly shouting, "No! No! I haven't!"

The man grabbed her waitress uniform at the neck pulling her face closer to his he seemed to be saying something threatening to her with his finger raised in a warning gesture. Peter couldn't hear what he was saying. The man let her go and she rushed off inside the centre.

Peter sat back down on the compost bags intrigued by the girl's behaviour, relieved she was gone. There was no doubt in his mind she was the strangest creature he ever met.

Even in the Nursing Home, where he spent a lot of time, he never came across anyone quite like her. There were a number of young people in the therapy groups he was made to attend, some with drug or alcohol problems, even both, who were heavily sedated, yet there was no one as bizarre as Gina Taylor with her weird way of switching between personalities.

Peter watched the young garden centre attendant as he pushed his wheelbarrow over towards him. He was so consumed by the girl's behaviour he hadn't noticed the wheelbarrow was stacked with the same compost bags he was sitting on. The man stopped a short distance away from Peter, asking, "Are you okay?" The smile on his face showed Peter he wasn't challenging him for sitting on the pile of bags.

Peter stood up unsure of what to say to him, "Ah, sorry I was taking a rest." He appeared friendly enough close up. Peter glanced down to where he was sitting, pleased he could see no damage done to the pile. "I got a little warm suddenly, I needed to sit down," he lied.

When the man laughed Peter noticed his sympathetic eyes framed by his long hair gave him an appealing look. His voice was sensitive, "It does seem to be the place most people choose when they feel unwell," he said. "Happened a few days ago with a young lassie. I gave her water and went to fetch a first aider because she looked ill."

"That was good of you," Peter said. "I bet she was grateful."

The man laughed, shaking his head sadly, "I'll never know….she had disappeared when I got back….pity really she was a wee cutie."

Peter laughed although the word 'disappeared' made him think of Emily, "You'll have to charge people for sitting on your compost or for the water in the future."

"Och, no harm done, anyway she left the water behind."

He seemed friendly enough to Peter given the angry scene he witnessed. Clearly he was irritated by Gina to provoke him to roughly manhandle her. Peter tried to draw him in, "I was just told off by the waitress from the café who saw me sitting here. At least you don't seem to mind me taking a five minutes breather." Peter followed the man's gaze to where he witnessed his aggression towards her.

When he turned back he looked puzzled, "I don't suppose you saw where she came from did you?" He pointed over towards the greenhouses like he did when he was talking to Gina, "Did she come from over there?"

Peter looked across at the glass, no longer catching the sun, wondering what there was over to the left to concern him Gina might have been there. He shook his head, "I really didn't see where she came from. I had my eyes closed, feeling the warmth of the sun." The man seemed relieved although he glanced once again towards the greenhouses. Peter continued, "Well, I'll let you have your recovery station back," He took a step to the side to give him access to the pile, "You never know your 'cutie' might come back again."

He laughed at the idea, "No, I don't think so," he said with a smile. "Anyway, they're too young for me." Peter walked away.

CHAPTER 71

Robbie knew exactly where they were going because the chauffeur of the limousine was driving along roads he knew well from his old community beat days. The car was waiting on the tarmac when he touched down, the formalities of landing being undertaken immediately by someone who came out with a clipboard like before. The man wasn't his handler nor was he anyone else Robbie knew from the police. Robbie was only too grateful he didn't have to complete the formalities in the office like normal, where Joan or Jim would have recognised him and asked a lot of questions. Sid Bailey wouldn't have known the formalities were anything other than normal or even got a hint of how nervous Robbie was feeling being back on familiar territory.

Sid Bailey was ushered into the back of the limo leaving Robbie to get in beside the chauffeur wearing a uniform he supposed from the hire firm company who provided the car. He imagined Bailey in the back, helping himself to fine Scotch whisky, gearing himself up to mix with the fine society folk he came to meet.

He felt, even dressed in the smart suit, the new look long hair up in a man-bun or his uncharacteristic unshaven 'designer' stubble, he must still be recognisable. He envied the chauffeur his uniform hat which would have gone part way towards a disguise if he happened to meet anyone he knew. He was sure he never met any society people during his career, his contacts were mostly difficult drunks, unruly youths or low life criminals. Even so as he drew nearer to the Quinnell Estate his stomach churned at the prospect of mixing with a crowd of unknowns.

Sid Bailey spent a little time towards the end of the flight explaining to Robbie what he expected of him. He was to shadow him, not too close although sufficiently near to protect him if necessary. Robbie was sure Bailey was carrying a gun because as he spoke he once again touched the left lapel of his dinner jacket where he assumed he wore a holster strapped to his body. There had been no suggestion of Robbie needing to be armed. He wouldn't have been bothered, might even have felt safer. He knew his way around guns. He once took a firearms course, not that he could have told Sid Bailey. Bailey assumed Robbie was a bum, down on his luck with a long standing drug habit, like he wanted him to think. He was in no doubt in a potentially violent situation Sid Bailey would consider him expendable.

"When we get there," Bailey rasped, "I want you to assess the situation, keep an eye out for anyone who looks suspicious or a threat to me. When I think everything is okay I'll give you the nod and you can make yourself scarce." Robbie could feel the paranoia coming off him in waves. He hoped the nod would come sooner rather than later. "I'll be staying the night, but they won't be expecting you, you'll have to sort yourself out."

Robbie's initial thought was he would have to get a ride or a taxi back to the airport, settle down in his plane or perhaps risk going back to the bungalow at Tarland. He hadn't taken any advice from his handler, had no idea how risky going there would be. The place might still be being watched by.....well that was the point really, he didn't know who was behind the plot to co-opt him to working for them. The only link had been the slip of a girl, Gina Taylor who put in the complaint against him. The thought of her with her baby voice made his blood boil.

Emily popped back into his head. He was overwhelmed by the need to see her again. He missed his old life, the closeness, teaching her to drive then latterly being free, up in the clouds taking her flying. There was something ethereal about soaring above the clouds, seeing the absolute joy on her face. He shut the image down as his thoughts took him back to the day he went over to The March of Time to tell her he was going away.

She asked him, "For how long?" There had been a small smile on her lips as if she thought he was going to a conference for the weekend. The smile disappeared when he said the word 'indefinitely' being replaced by shock. He tried to explain how they needed him to remain suspended from duty even after exonerating him which he couldn't deal with. This he told her was his only chance in the short term to remain on active police duty. He wasn't sure whether she heard any of his explanation because she uttered not a word, neither of understanding nor a goodbye and he was forced to leave her there in the back room.

The limousine gave a lurch making a left turn, jolting him back to the present, with enough time to catch a glimpse of the sign at the entrance of the Quinnell Farm Estate. He felt a sinking feeling in his stomach as the car moved up the driveway taking another left towards the large manor house at a fork in the drive. The other sign post was for a garden centre, farm shop, coffee shop and bakery.

When the house came into view, the front was lined with cars bringing other guests, then valet parked in the rows of exclusive luxurious motors, whilst people walked up to the pillared entrance in their finery. As darkness came, lights began to come on giving the place a warm inviting appeal.

The limo came to a stop, Robbie jumped out, beat the chauffeur to the rear door to let Sid Bailey out. Robbie stood alert looking around the activity, with a bustle of valets to take over self-driven cars and others with their own chauffeurs, standing around or talking to each other as if they were already familiars.

Robbie nodded to Sid all was well. The little man emerged from the back, stood alongside Robbie looking up at the house. Close up Robbie could smell the whisky on his breath. He wondered if he wasn't as confident as he would like him to believe. Together they walked up the steps to the front door which stood open, where they were met by an immaculately dressed butler. Sid put his hand inside his jacket lapel making Robbie's heart flutter until he realised the lapel was the other side to the gun. Sid produced an ornate scalloped edged card he handed to the man as he walked inside.

The starchy looking butler put out a hand across Robbie to indicate he expected him to produce the same. Sid Bailey scowled at him, "He's with me!" The butler gave a small bow, a mere nod of his head and took back his hand to let him pass. They walked on joining a small line of guests waiting to be greeted by the host and hostess.

"Here we go, just observe!" Sid whispered. Robbie split off to the side finding a place where he could watch the proceedings close to the bottom of a wide elaborate staircase out of the way of the main activity. A waitress coming down the line of guests handed Bailey a flute of champagne. Sid Bailey looked as comfortable as a fish out of water.

CHAPTER 72

Left alone in the quietness of the back room Bart suddenly felt old, out of his depth for the first time in his life. He could no longer put his tiredness down to recovery from his illness because he had made sufficient progress he could no longer use this excuse. He thought perhaps he should have retired instead of starting up a new Detective Agency. The old one slipped away from him sometime in a past life and he couldn't understand how he made a living for so long on his own.

In a way he *had* retired. The moment he went into the Witness Protection Programme, bought his first clock shop in Wainthorpe-on-sea, he settled down to a sedentary life hiding in plain sight by the seaside where nothing unusual ever happened. Until he was woken up by the first murder Wainthorpe ever had, right next door to him at the Art Gallery. Yes, it was a definite wakeup call.

He even thought perhaps the death of Arthur Claymore was a mistake, by someone who killed him in error instead of him. The idea was one of the reasons he approached the CSI working at the scene, to get some idea of what was happening. Instead of gaining an insight, he quickly became drawn into the investigation and a rare friendship, with Jayson Vingoe, the CSI. For Bart the temptation was having once been a Scenes of Crime Officer, the pull sparked his curiosity, resurrecting his old skills for finding evidence, like old times.

In those days he had no dependents, no wife or children to take up his time or distract his attention. In fact no emotional ties whatsoever to compete with his need for total concentration. Now there was Emily, who crept into his affections little by little until he came to consider her like a daughter, as near as an aging bachelor was ever likely to get. He shut his mind off from analysing his sudden bout of lethargy and asked himself, was he trying to blame Emily for this feeling of hopelessness?

Yet, he took her in when she placed an advert in national newspapers to find him after he left Witness Protection and moved to Scotland. He took her in because she was threatening to run away to London to get away from her mother. He couldn't bear the thought of her living on the streets or worse, if she fell into the wrong hands. Anything could happen to a young girl there. He got Jay and Agatha to bring her up to Scotland, and arranged for her to live with Lily Johns at Crathie, another runaway like Emily, *like himself.*

Bart made her a full partner in the shop and the Detective Agency not only because he didn't have any dependents. She actually saved his life when his adversary, Toni Maola, was looking for him, and tracked him down. Emily, then a slip of a sixteen year old girl knocked Maola's agent out with the baseball bat Bart kept hidden under the shop counter, when she thought the man was trying to kill him. He sighed reminiscing, pulled himself up to his full five foot four inch height and shook his head.

Come on Bart, where's your fight? She needs you now!

* * * * *

Peter sat in Alistair's jeep outside The Moor Hen having returned from his meeting with Gina Taylor. He wasn't proud of feeling relieved to leave her behind. There was something about the girl he thought was dangerous, she really spooked him. Once up in his room, he logged onto his laptop, feeling the usual swell of calm settle over him as he did every time he used it. The machine was like a drug; he was administering his fix. Instead of games or his programming, however, he opened the remaining agency files he hadn't had time to view since Bart sent them to him, because he had become enthralled by the graffiti images; like computer games, they appealed to him.

One by one he viewed the videos. There were two of the biker who tried to run Emily off the road riding a Harley Davison, with another one of a white van taken by Bart leaving the Bus Company building at Dinnet. He was shocked when he recognised the garden centre man he'd just been talking to, driving the van in the picture even if it wasn't very clear. He could see the hair framing the familiar face of the man he just met. He read the brief report, found his name to be David Taylor, stepbrother to Gina, which made more sense of the scene he witnessed between them in the garden centre when he saw him handling her rather roughly. Sibling rivalry?

What annoyed him so much about Gina?

Peter was sure whatever concerned him lay beyond the greenhouses at the Quinnell farm where David Taylor pointed in anger. Peter's telephone began to ring, glancing at the screen he saw Bart's name, momentarily thought of answering before he pressed the red off symbol. Stirred into action he searched his back pack for clean clothes; dark colours, a black beanie hat, gloves and a thick hooded jacket which he changed into. He spoke to Alistair before he left asking if he needed the jeep as he had an errand to run. Alistair shrugged, pointed to the bar where he was making ready for the evening session, indicating he would be there for the duration. Peter left to drive back to the Quinnell estate.

CHAPTER 73

Peter arrived back at the Quinnell farm, parking in the farthest corner of the spill over car park. Slightly raised it took in a view of the cars below in the main parking area with full exposure of the people entering and leaving the various shops. Many were carrying potted plants or pushing garden centre shopping trolleys, creating a hive of industry in loading their vehicles. He had no idea what he intended to do next.

The invited meeting with Gina Taylor after her shift in the coffee shop was not high on his agenda. His only thought was, to wait around until dark, to explore what lay beyond the row of large green houses David Taylor pointed to during his altercation with his sister. Whatever caused Taylor's agitation, Peter felt must be important.

Peter observed how popular the farm shops were, confirmed by the brisk business from midday onwards as cars came and went, with enormous amounts of produce taken away. He smiled at one point when he saw someone arriving turn into the exit instead of the entrance at the same time a large four by four was leaving. Car park rage took over between the small Fiat arriving and the much larger vehicle trying to leave. Both car drivers got out of their vehicles to offer their contribution to the dispute. Peter wondered if it might get physical between the woman in the Fiat and the man in the four by four.

However, his attention moved over to the entrance where a motor bike sailed through unhindered. Peter noted the quality of the bike, way beyond anything he'd ever seen before. He recognised it, of course, surprised someone who owned a Harley would go shopping at a garden centre, use a farm shop or want to buy coffee to sit in a public coffee shop. The motorbike he knew was the one in Emily's videos, Bart and Mitch told him tried to force Emily into a ditch. The biker wore black leathers with blue and white flashes like this one.

The rider didn't seem to be looking for a space to park. Instead he cruised slowly down the first row of vehicles searching the steady trickle of people leaving the centre along the walkway. The bike turned to complete another circuit, then turned for a third time just as Peter spotted the girl Gina, wearing jeans with a leather biker jacket, leave the garden centre entrance.

She walked hurriedly having seen the bike, met him as he came to a brief stop at the side of the walkway. The rider barely had time to place both feet on the ground before Gina picked up a helmet from the rear seat and climbed onto the bike. She slipped her hands round the rider's waist, lowered her head into the middle of his back, the bike revved and shot away.

Peter looked over to the exit, his hand turning the ignition key brought the Jeep to life. He noticed Mrs Fiat and Mr Four-by-four were still deep in yelling conversation. *Whoops*! Peter thought, let's hope our biker isn't too impatient. Peter watched him leave through the entrance to avoid the blockage at the exit, without signalling, turned right down the lane moving off deeper into the farm.

Peter moved out of the top car park to join the perimeter road of the main car park where he also left by the entrance. He turned right as a new stream of cars arrived at the entrance, grateful for the gap to make the turn. He could see the motorbike in the distance, knew whoever was riding the Harley was used to high speeds. They had made considerable progress.

The bike began to slow down on the approach to the bend ahead. Peter speeded up. When he got to the bend he took it too fast making the jeep wobble. The engine groaned with the effort. Peter apologised to Flossie for putting her through it. Once round the bend, he could see the Harley ahead, he continued to chase, watched the bike slow down disappearing into the wooded area ahead. Peter fixed his gaze on the spot where the bike turned, slowing as he approached.

First he came to a gap in the wood which didn't seem to lead anywhere. A few yards further on a small unmade track led to a cottage at the end of where the Harley Davison now stood on its kickstand outside. Peter carried on along the lane looking each side for any signs of other buildings.

Eventually, he stopped and in the absence of power steering, he awkwardly turned the jeep around on the narrow lane, praising Flossie for her grip on the verges either side of the road. He made a mental note to tell Alistair he was very impressed with her. Peter cruised back to the unmade road pulling into the spot beyond.

He left the jeep, the fan ticking to cool the engine after her exertion and moved through the trees towards the cottage. He wanted to see if Gina and her brother David were still in dispute. He thought the way the girl hugged the riders back was strange to watch, not a very sisterly action to make with her brother.

Peter watched the large window from the cover of the trees, giving a view of Gina with the biker inside. Peter could see no evidence of the earlier angry exchange between them as they took off their biker leathers. Gina looked eager, almost excited, as she helped her brother undress. Peter's brow furrowed. This was such a huge contrast to the behaviour he witnessed earlier that he began to question what he actually saw. Peter stood paralysed as David Taylor turned, and with relief Peter realised although of similar build, this person wasn't her brother David. The man moved towards the window to pull the curtains closed.

Peter leant against the rough surface behind the tree trying to make sense of what he just saw. If this wasn't David, who was driving the van in the video, then who was this biker?

CHAPTER 74

Michelle took the evening surveillance at Dinnet after Bart arranged with Nessa to let her set up in the compound at the rear of McKinley's. Far from ideal, with only a hard seated chair to sit on, Mitch was particularly chilly, even though she was well wrapped up in a padded jacket with hood. After only a short time she regretted having suggested the idea and longed for the warmth of her car. She also realised she could have a long night ahead of her with the potential for a no show anyway.

Michelle was sitting behind the thickest of the overgrown brambles with a narrow view of the rear of the building next door. She knew there would be little warning if anyone arrived, with her hood up and her ears covered by a thermal beanie, the likelihood of hearing an engine would be slim. She already knew their pattern was to switch off the van's headlights the moment they turned onto the stretch of road with street lighting. She would get no flash of them to warn her either.

Mitch felt perished. She feared she might be in danger of hypothermia. With the low temperature her injured leg was complaining, needing her to rub some circulation back in. She was also beginning to feel sleepy, another indication of excess cold.

She was jerked awake by a sound of someone's voice saying, "Fuck!" drawing her attention to the back door where two dark figures appeared around the corner of the building. She quietly lifted her long range monocular and focussed through the small gap in the brambles towards their faces covered with balaclavas trying hard to make as little movement as possible.

One of them was standing on one leg rubbing their shin, whilst the other was putting a key in the door. The figure at the door turned hissing, "Shush!" From the sound Mitch determined the voice to be a man's deep tone as likewise was the yell the other gave when he swore, she felt confident they were both male. They disappeared inside. The door closed, then a glow appeared at the corner of the window as a light came on inside, dim enough not to be an electrical source.

When the door opened again the man who stood in the doorway pulled his balaclava up onto his forehead. Mitch recognised David Taylor from the video of the van Bart took. Behind him the second man filled the doorway. When Taylor stepped out he turned to him, "Come on, let's get them unloaded, then we'll go back for the second lot," even in a heavy whisper the sound carried to where she was sitting.

Mitch raised her eye glass to the second man, who still wore his face mask. He was poking a finger through the mouth hole in an attempt to scratch his face, "These bloody things itch!" he complained. Somewhere deep in Michelle's memory the voice registered as familiar; the tone a whiny moan, however recognition wouldn't come. They both disappeared around the side to the front leaving the door wide open and the light shining out weakly marking their way.

Mitch was tempted to creep down the side of McKinley's to watch them out front, what would she be able to see from there? She waited for them to reappear. When they did they were carrying a heavy box between them, each holding the bottom edge on either side, their faces covered once again by the balaclavas.

Damn! Come on, lift the masks! she silently urged.

One of them lost his grip, with one hand rendering the box in danger of falling. The other man managed to lower his side until the whole box slumped to the ground. "You idiot!" he yelled as the other man let go. He immediately stood up, lifted his balaclava to furiously scratch at his face.

"Fuck! These things are bastards!" The whiner said.

Mitch let out an involuntary gasp when full recognition hit her. The sound must have carried because David Taylor said, "What was that?" as he swivelled to look around the overgrown back yard, his eyes swept across to the dividing fence with next door's garage.

Whiner kept on scratching his face, "I didn't hear anything," he said paying no attention whatsoever to Taylor's obvious alarm.

Taylor stopped looking, stooped down to gain purchase on the bottom of the box, "Come on, let's get these inside to do another trip. Between them they hefted the box through the door.

Michelle took the opportunity to leave her seat, quietly run to the side of the building to leave the compound. She timed her movements back to her car up the street with their trips to the van to unload more boxes. She sat inside watching them through the monocular, feeling the warmth of the car, waiting for them to leave. She heard enough to know they would go back the way they came to fetch their second load. She suspected they would lead her to the Quinnell farm having established the van was the Highway Ma ntenance van with the missing 'i' she knew was registered to the estate fleet of vehicles. Mitch was certain she could allow sufficient distance between them not to be spotted.

In other circumstances she would have finished for the night and written up her report. Now she couldn't, because the whole thing just got personal. The other man with David Taylor whose voice she first thought familiar revealed himself when he lifted the mask to his forehead to scratch his face.

It was a face she saw much too often in flash backs to the time when he raped her in the female police changing rooms some years ago. The man she tried hard to forget, especially after she heard he was sacked for gross misconduct, telling herself at least some justice was served. Her stomach churned at the thought of him close up, his face pushed into hers as he pinned her down and worked himself inside her, his obnoxious whiny voice in her ear was forever in her head, "Come on, bitch, you know you like it!" Simon Copeland!

CHAPTER 75

Robbie watched Sid Bailey, from his niche beside the main staircase, shake hands with the hosts of the party he was attending. He assumed the middle-aged woman wearing a glittering blue figure hugging evening dress was Delores Quinnell. The man at her side in a dinner jacket, his hair flopping over his forehead with, Robbie thought, slight effeminate mannerisms when he took Bailey's hand in a limp one of his own, was Rupert her husband. She seemed to be taking centre stage in greeting the guests as they approached whilst he looked markedly bored with the whole proceedings. He was searching the room, watching the young waitresses, inspecting them moving around dispensing drinks from the trays they carried. He paid little attention to the conversations his wife was having with their guests.

Robbie watched Sid Bailey take Delores' hand, bend his head down to kiss the back. When Sid moved away, she slid the back of her hand down the chiffon stole she was wearing over her gown, to wipe away all traces of the little man's lips. Robbie noted total disdain on her face. 'Not a popular guest,' was Robbie's opinion.

Delores moved on to the next guests in line, her face beaming as she greeted an older man wearing a kilt with his middle aged wife soberly dress in a plain baggy dress and jacket; the woman paled into insignificance at the side of their hostess's haute couture. She looked uncomfortable being there.

Robbie's attention returned to follow Sid Bailey walking into a room full of guests and begin to circulate subtly inspecting those present, no doubt Robbie thought to assess whether any of them were a threat to him. Bailey stopped a passing waitress, put the full glass of champagne he was holding onto the tray she held aloft saying something to her. She nodded and moved away only to return shortly after with a whisky tumbler half full of amber liquid Bailey took off her otherwise empty tray, with a huge grin, the first since he arrived. Sid looked over to where Robbie was standing watching him. He nodded. The cue Robbie was waiting for to be able to leave. He couldn't wait to get out of the place.

Robbie watched the waitresses as they circulated, move away to the other side of the stairs to leave, he deduced, for the kitchen to fetch more drinks and to take away empty glasses. He followed the next waitress along a passage looking for a rear exit, he didn't want to have to negotiate his way back outside through the front door where the sour faced butler was still officiating, causing a blockage by his dogged determination to have sight of their invitations.

Robbie stood outside in the corridor watching the activity in the kitchen. A hive of industry where drinks were being dispensed while the wonderful smell of rich food was being prepared by what he assumed were external caterers wafted his way.

The next young waitress in a line picked up another tray of crystal flukes Robbie was sure contained the very best Champagne he was sure he had never tasted. The girl held the tray high on the palm of her hand turned around in one over-exaggerated jerky movement. The back of her other hand held against the small of her back, elbow bent high to the side. Robbie caught a glimpse of her face. The male waiter filling the glasses snapped a reprimand her way which caused her neutral facial expression to twist into a snarl. Whatever he said she didn't care to hear. She turned her head back towards him to reply.

It gave Robbie the briefest chance to move swiftly away down the corridor to find a back exit to the house, before the girl found him standing watching her. He'd only met Gina Taylor once, at the aerodrome the day she appeared to set him up for her accusation of rape, but he was sure this was her. The red lipstick seemed to confirm it.

When he easily found his way outside he felt lucky, a narrow escape from being recognised, he was sure she would know him. It had begun to rain again. Icy stabs pelted his face which helped cool the excess anger that flared as he caught sight of the girl. Over the last six months he often wondered what his reaction might be if he saw her again. He blamed her entirely for the way he was living in this depraved criminal world and for losing the exemplary career he prided himself on. Most of all he blamed her for having to move away and leave Emily behind. It occurred to him how much he hated Gina Taylor.

CHAPTER 76

Michelle gave the white van plenty of distance, following without her car head lights to attract the occupants' attention. As an ex-traffic cop she knew these roads like the back of her hand, their familiarity would give her no surprises. As she expected they led her to the Quinnell Estate, heading away from the main Manor House complex she could see was lit up like Disney World over to the right of her. She caught a glimpse of activity in front of the house through a gap in the hedge as she passed. There was clearly some kind of function taking place.

The van's lights ahead stopped moving. She cruised to a halt at the side of the lane with a view of the van parked beside a large outbuilding the size of a warehouse. The figures of David Taylor and as she now knew, Simon Copeland, ex-disgraced CID officer, had disappeared inside leaving the back doors of the van wide open in readiness to load more boxes. Mitch turned her car around pulling onto the grass verge some distance away to wait.

Fifteen minutes passed before the van appeared out of the side road to the building, to turn back the way they came. She was torn between following them back to Dinnet, even though she knew they were taking the boxes to stash in the empty Bus Company building or go to see what was inside the building they just left. She guessed the latter would give her more of an idea what the two men were up to than if she went back to witness them unloading the boxes.

She moved her car along the lane nearer to the warehouse, slipped silently into the shrubbery, edging her way closer to the building. There was the small door the two men used, next to the large rollup access big enough to have driven the van inside or give access to farm machinery, assuming this was where the farm stored the majority of its mechanical equipment.

There were no windows on this side of the building to give a view of the inside. She began to walk slowly around the building keeping close to the walls in case there was anyone else around. She proceeded with caution, well aware she was trespassing on private land. When she turned the corner there were no windows on the second side either, or the third when she got to it. She wondered what kind of a building this size wouldn't have at least another access. How dark must the inside be without windows even in the day time? She'd reached the fourth side before she came across another door.

As she expected, the door was firmly locked when she tried the handle. She placed her ear against the wood to listen for any movement inside. She could hear a faint humming, frowned being unsure what the sound could be. She left the door, crept to the corner, to check the white van hadn't returned, before going back to the door.

From the inside of her jacket she took out a small fabric case from which she selected a couple of metal lock picking pins, one a hook and the other straight she inserted into the key hole. She was well practised in the art of opening locks. After having once arrested someone with a similar set of lock picking pins, she bought herself a set off the internet, thinking they might come in handy if she ever locked herself out of her flat. After much practice she became an adept lock picker, a useful skill on those occasions she locked her car keys in the old bangers she was forced to drive in those days. Today it took no time at all before she heard the click of the lock. She slipped into the absolute blackness of the building's interior.

She used her power torch to search and could see her assumption about the building storing farm equipment was correct. There was nothing larger than small digging, weeding or grass cutting machines, the kind she expected would be used by the staff working with the plants they grew for the garden centre. There was also a collection of hand tools inside a wheelbarrow and guessed they belonged to David Taylor. The interior smelt earthy as the tools were still covered in soil.

The area where she stood was small in comparison to the size of the building she walked around, could see she was right about the rollup door giving vehicle access. After examining the storage area she found no evidence of the boxes they took away but found another, internal door, in the farthest wall. The faint humming she heard from outside, grew louder the nearer she got to the door. This was also locked. She used her lock picks again to repeat the process.

Mitch slipped through the door into a small corridor and was immediately hit by a powerful odour, still earthy with a sulphuric smell she recognised. She turned, flashed the torch's beam to show another door with an outline of bright light. *Someone's growing cannabis here.* This door wasn't locked when she tried it and found rows of plants being grown in artificial brilliance. The humming was coming from fluorescent lighting in the ceiling, clearly some tubes needed replacing. In addition, whoever was involved here was using High Intensity Discharge (HID) Grow Lights. For a moment Michelle was impressed until she reminded herself the place was being used illegally for growing large quantities of cannabis, certainly not for personal use.

Mitch shut the door, moved back along the corridor satisfied she solved the mystery of the boxes being stored in the Bus Company Building. She hurriedly reversed the locking of the internal door to the farm equipment storage area. The intensity of the lights inside the growing room left temporary light flashes on her vision disorienting her as she crossed the room toward s the external door. She barked her shin on something large covered over with a plastic sheet. She stopped to rub the old wound on her leg, leaning on the cover she wondered why this piece of equipment needed protection whilst all the others didn't. Curiosity got the better of her. She lifted the heavy tarpaulin at the corner and found a car. Clumsily she managed to establish the car was a black Mini Cooper according to the insignia. She made a mental note of the registration number to check its ownership later.

CHAPTER 77

Bart shut the shop early. Tired, he fell asleep in his chair by the fire. When he woke he was surprised how long he'd slept, a little irritated the fire had burnt low. There was a definite chill in the air. All was silent, except for the distant ticking of the clocks from the shop. Bart held his breath. He thought he might hear Emily arrive with her usual "Helloo!" He let the breath go with a sigh now joined by the ache in his chest that began the moment he realised Emily was missing.

The unexpected loud knocking on the shop door made him jump. Whoever it was they sounded eager. He was instantly reminded of the time the sinister P.I Dennis Levin came calling with his client, the Russian, Grigoriy Novikov. That had been only nine o'clock in the evening. Bart glanced at the clock on the sideboard, saw the time was the middle of the night. *Who would call at this hour?*

Bart dithered knowing whoever was out there wouldn't be bringing good news. He was reluctant to go through to see. He didn't want it to be the police with the news they found the body of a young girl, asking him to come to identify Emily. The thought made him freeze. His mobile beeped an incoming text at the side of him, *'It's ok Mr. Bridges, Michelle at the door.'* He got up creakily, his arthritis reminding him he shouldn't fall asleep in such an uncomfortable position. He went through to the shop letting light from the passage spill out across his precious clocks as far as the door where Mitch's face was pressed against the glass.

Bart unlocked the door, took one look at her almost blue lips, "Good gracious, lass you must be perished out there at this time of night." Michelle was, indeed, shivering as the temperature had dropped considerably. A white frost caught the light from the nearest lamp post, sparkling like crystals over the pavement outside. "Come in and get warm."

As she stepped inside they both heard the sound of another vehicle pull up behind Mitch's car, a rather rusted old jeep. Peter Draper jumped out, pleased to see them both awake when he turned up The Brae on his way back to The Moor Hen.

"Somebody else who can't sleep, eh?" he greeted Peter as he also slipped into the shop.

Once in the back Bart added logs to the embers to get some warmth into the room to thaw out his late visitors, whilst Michelle put the kettle on for a badly needed hot drink.

"So?" Bart asked. "What couldn't wait until tomorrow," then he remembered it was already 'tomorrow', "Well later."

They both noticed Bart was fully dressed in his day clothes, exchanged a knowing glance, as Peter said cheekily, "You couldn't sleep either?" Bart tutted, choosing not to reply. Peter gave an embarrassed coughed. "Actually I only stopped because I saw you both in the shop doorway. I just came back from the Quinnell estate."

"Me too!" Michelle said in surprise. Peter and Michelle stared at each other. Bart thought for a little too long, he coughed to break their trance.

"Why don't we sit down, you both look like you might need some food or a hot drink. You can tell me what you've been up to. I gather you didn't bump into each other over there?" Bart deduced by the fact of their surprise at each other's admission.

He busied himself opening a couple of cans of oxtail soup, got busy with his frying pan to make bacon sandwiches feeling rather hungry having slept through making himself a meal earlier.

Michelle began by updating on the events of her evening at Dinnet when she followed the white van back to the Quinnell estate to discover the warehouse with the cannabis growing room inside.

"So is it definitely David Taylor?" Bart asked remembering the garden centre man once telling him Rory Quinnell wouldn't sack him for damaging Delores' car with his wheel barrow because he (Rory) needed his 'green fingers'. Michelle nodded. "And let me guess the other man in the white van is Rory Quinnell?"

Michelle frowned, "No. What makes you think that?"

Bart looked up from turning the bacon in the pan, was about to explain to her how David Taylor was quick to defend Rory for ill-treating him, when he noticed the pained expression on Mitch's face, "Who is the other man, did you get to see his face?"

In a strangulated whisper she said, "Simon Copeland."

Bart dropped the spatula he was turning the bacon with; it hit the edge of the frying pan before dropping to the floor. After picking it up he wanted to ask 'are you sure', realised Michelle wouldn't make a mistake about identifying the man who once raped her. He didn't want to bring up any reference to her past in front of Peter, he merely said, "Oh right, we can see what he's moved on to these days."

Michelle fell silent. If Peter realised anything was wrong he kept his thoughts to himself. He didn't even ask who Simon Copeland was. Instead he asked, "Is this warehouse anywhere near some very large greenhouses?" Bart and Michelle both looked surprised at the question, whilst she shrugged "Explains what I saw take place between Gina and her brother at the garden centre earlier. He was very angry with her. I think probably because he thought she had been somewhere else on the estate. He was pointing over towards the green houses anyway."

Peter took this as his cue to tell them about following Gina and the biker when he came to pick her up after her shift in the café. "I followed them to a cottage in the woods...isn't that supposed to be where she lives with her brother David? Only I got a close up look of the biker. He certainly wasn't David Taylor because I already met him in the garden centre and Gina was very intimate with this biker."

Bart's face for a moment looked quite horrified, "Intimate?"

"Yeah, she was all over him....." Peter coughed with embarrassment not wishing to describe everything he saw because whilst he lacked experience of normal male/female intimacy, in a lot of ways his knowledge came from a much more disturbing part of his life which he wasn't about to allow himself to dwell on.

Bart moved past Peter to get his lap top from the sideboard, where he searched the files for a photograph, asking Peter, "What did he look like?"

Peter strained to remember, "Well he was much the same build as her brother David, with short fair hair...." Peter tutted at himself. "I only got a quick glimpse because he pulled the curtains closed when they started to get undressed." Peter blushed. Bart saw a sympathetic smile come to Michelle's lips as he glanced up.

Bart found what he was looking for handing the laptop to Peter to look at a photograph. "Yeah! That's him," Peter exclaimed. "How did you know?"

"Ah, the thing is, I understand Hamish told Emily, Gina was living in a cottage with her brother. We all assumed he meant David, her stepbrother, but he's Rory Quinnell," Bart pointed at the lap top picture.

Peter looked relieved, "Phew! I thought for a moment....." he stopped when he saw the dark expression on Bart's face.

Bart said, "Rupert Quinnell, if we are to believe Anabel Taylor is Gina's real father."

Michelle said, "Which makes Rory her real half-brother?" Bart nodded.

Peter looked again at the picture of Rory Quinnell, taken with his mother and father at some society function for a glossy Sunday newspaper supplement, then back at Bart, "Do you think he knows?" clearly Peter was shocked by the news. Bart couldn't reply to his question because he didn't know who knew. Bart conveyed to them the Taylor's were paid hush money by Rupert Quinnell at the time and Gina was brought up to believe Dougie Taylor was her father and his son David her brother.

Peter thought about Gina's odd behaviour at the Garden Centre, "Gina *must* know because she told me Rupert is her father. She said her father and her brother both love her.....you don't think she meant....?" Peter stopped, completely stunned remembering Gina spinning on the spot, telling him her father owned the Quinnell farm. He was sure she meant that. "She has to know Rory is her brother? She definitely hates her father's wife.....Delores you say she's called? Gina told me she knows things about her she's not supposed to know, I wonder what she meant?"

Michelle asked, "Do you think Rory is involved in growing Cannabis?"

"Surely all the Quinnells must be. I would expect them to know what's happening on every inch of their own land," Bart said. "Why do you ask?"

Michelle dug into her pocket, pulled out her note book where she jotted a few notes about her night following the two men back to the warehouse. She read through again. "If they don't know about the Cannabis room they can't be very good account keepers. Takes a lot of electricity to grow something under such controlled conditions, I wouldn't like their electric bill," she laughed.

"Maybe we should make an anonymous call to the drug squad informing them of their farming activities," Peter suggested laughing.

"Maybe when I call my police contact to check up on the car they've got under a tarp amongst the farm equipment in the main storage area, I'll hint about it," Michelle said.

She leaned over to show Bart the registration number. She watched as his face turned white, snatching the note book out of her hand. Michelle had written Mini Cooper beside the registration number she wrote from memory. "Bart?" she said. "What's wrong?"

"You don't need to check with your contact.....that is Emily's Mini!"

CHAPTER 78

Robbie found himself outside where the temperature had dropped considerably since they arrived. The first thing he realised was he was totally inadequately dressed for the weather with only the oversized suit to keep out the cold. He left his flying clothes, more suitable to these weather conditions, back at the aerodrome in the microlight. He could hardly carry them in the suit bag when they were picked up by the chauffeur driven car.

He cursed Sid Bailey for putting him in this position without even one thought to his wellbeing. He had a feeling Sid would have arranged things differently if one of the others had come with him. Robbie saw his neglect as yet another test he was putting him through to gage his reaction.

He shrugged the much too long jacket sleeves over his hands for warmth as he stood in the back yard to the mansion where a number of vehicles were parked. The catering van's logo advertised them as McKay's Fine Dining even claiming in smaller lettering they were 'by Royal appointment'. Robbie knew whatever the 'fine dining' was being served inside it would be extremely expensive. He only wished he could have loitered about the kitchen to chance his luck at a few scraps from their table as he hoped or even find someone from the household staff who might give him a bed for the night.

Cold and hungry his resentment of the girl Gina grew for spoiling that. Once again she was interfering with his plans because he couldn't risk her recognising him or alert someone to who he really was. This, he thought, was all getting too complicated, he never felt more alone in his life. If he wasn't finally getting somewhere close to the Operation's targets, he would have got his handler to pull him out.

He heard the door he came through open somewhere behind him making him duck out of sight behind one of the large garbage bins standing to the side of the door. The smell of food wafted from the kitchen when a male figure wearing an apron came through. The smells were making his stomach rumble. He watched the man disappear into the back of the catering van. He could hear the odd thud from inside, then the man came back out with a box in his arms, pushed the van door closed with a nudge of his shoulder before he hurried back into the house out of the cold.

Robbie moved over to try the back door of the van which opened easily. He slipped inside expecting it to be refrigerated. He was pleasantly surprised at the warmth and to find separate fridges whilst the rest contained plastic crates of other foods, stacked on shelves labelled 'dry goods', 'bread', 'vegetables', 'fruit', ' condiments and spices'.

He pulled the bread draw forward, picked out a crusty loaf, hurriedly found a pack of cheese and a small terrine of pate in a fridge which he loaded into a plastic carrier he ripped from a hanging dispenser. He turned to leave, saw a rack of bottles near the door, took one at random. In the dim light he could see, Chateauneuf du Pape and slipped the bottle into the bag before he left the van. He quietly returned to his place behind the bin to decide what to do next.

He didn't linger too long because he was thoroughly cold. He had food, now he needed to find somewhere dry as far away from the main house as he could find to offer him some shelter with a chance to quell his hunger pangs. He walked away, through an archway out towards a row of greenhouses he could see in the distance, the bag swinging on his arm, his hands thrust deep into his jacket pockets.

When he got to the greenhouses he looked for any external signs of security or alarms having spotted a small green light; the last thing he needed was to raise suspicion by setting off an alarm. The light coming from inside the first greenhouse was low down, attached to some kind of machine. Robbie assumed it was a heater, he didn't try the greenhouse door, he moved on along the row noting each one with a similar feature at the centre of the rows of germinated plants.

At the farthest end there was one smaller isolated greenhouse, looking more domestic than the others, the kind you might have in your own garden to grow tomatoes. Robbie could barely feel his fingers on the greenhouse door when he opened it. He was of a mind, even if he was discovered by some security system he could say he was with Sid Bailey and without anywhere to pass the night.

Yes, he thought, either in here or catch hyperthermia outside. He only hoped he could eat the food before anyone saw where he got it. He looked down at the bag as he stepped inside the welcoming warmth of the greenhouse.

P.C. Robbie Cowan, aka Daniel Roberts stole something for the first time in his life.

CHAPTER 79

Bart took some persuading to calm down after hearing Emily's car was hidden in one of Quinnell's out buildings. He wanted to rush out into the night, drive over to the farm to see for himself. If he needed to, he would take all night, search every inch of the place until he found her. What occurred to him next was too horrific for him to face. He flopped down on his chair, putting his head in his hands in despair.

Peter could tell immediately what he was thinking because the same thought occurred to him. Peter went over to sit with him, totally lost for words until he suddenly became alert, "We need to go to the police! What was the name of the copper who came here?"

Michelle and Bart were both alarmed at his suggestion although for entirely different reasons. Almost in unison they shouted, "No!"

"If they've got her car hidden in the warehouse, she can't be too far away," Peter had become agitated. "The police could get a search warrant for the whole place," he urged.

Michelle knew she couldn't admit to having broken into the warehouse. "They would want to know how we know the car is there." She said guiltily. Once having been a police officer wouldn't exempt her from being charged with trespass or illegal entry.

Bart on the other hand didn't trust Morris one iota. He sighed irritated at his own thoughts, "How do we know who we can trust?" he asked. "I remember Charlotte Reynolds saying the same thing when I met her with Robbie Cowan. I asked her why she hadn't gone to the police for help to get away. She told us she was made to help at

Quinnell's parties, attended by a lot of well to do people and amongst the guests there were police officers..."

Michelle said, "I saw something similar was happening at the main house tonight. Are you saying there are police officers involved in something illegal?"

"Yes, I believe so," Bart said, "I know Mary and Mungo were convinced the Quinnells sent Morris over to the castle to talk them out of their wedding. For Mary's safety he suggested cancelling opening the place to the public. They believed this wasn't a coincidence, it was after all what Rupert Quinnell wanted."

Michelle wasn't convinced even though she knew what Morris was capable of doing, or not doing, to protect one of his officers. She had been the victim. She felt guilty she didn't allow Morris to tell them why he came over to The March of Time, before she scared him off.

"I should have let Morris state his business when he came here," she said apologetically. "What do you think he wanted?"

"Not your fault lassie. I don't have much time for the man, though I would like to think he has a conscience, maybe even thought about the things that have already happened to Emily. He did seem genuinely concerned about her. If he knew anything about her car being hidden there or what's happened to her, I don't think he would have come here." *Unless he was covering his own back.* "It would be the last thing he would want to do otherwise."

Michelle nodded in agreement. "But that bastard, Copeland obviously does!" she said with some venom.

Peter was listening to them, trying to assess what the whole thing was about. "There has to be someone we can trust in the police who can help us," Peter wanted to remind them not all police officers, including the one ex-cop in the room, were bent.

Bart looked at Peter with fresh eyes. He almost smiled, "Yes, Peter you are quite right. We are concentrating too much on negative things," he looked over at Mitch giving her a weak smile. "We have Jay and Agatha Vingoe, they will both definitely want to help us find Emily. We also have Nessa and Lily, who already offered to help, then....."

He stopped to think, assessing whether he dare call in a favour from Helen Daniels who did seem to have contact with the people in Operation Graffiti and who knew who else? He remembered her warning him off getting involved which stopped him suggesting it. Would she think finding Emily's car sufficient incentive to get an official search warrant or would the Operation consider Emily mere collateral damage in achieving their own aims of taking out the whole crime syndicate to save many more lives? He thought Helen was duty bound to whoever told her what she could do. ".....well, quite a few of us at least," he finished.

Bart Bridges, ever practical, knew there was little they could do in the middle of the night. There was a need for careful thought. Rushing in as his eagerness to find Emily wanted him to, could make matters worse. By both Michelle and Peter's accounts the Quinnell Estate was alive with visitors at some social function, perhaps not a time for an official approach.

"I think we all need to get some sleep," he told them. "Tomorrow is soon enough to make plans for what to do next." His words came with little conviction and were met with no enthusiasm as Mitch looked over at Peter sensing his disappointment. There was barely a nod of agreement from either of them.

After Bart saw them out, he locked up. Once in his bed he couldn't switch off, even a night cap of Bell's whisky didn't help. He found he spent much of the hours before dawn thinking over everything he discovered. He couldn't understand why anyone would want to harm Emily. As the one thing he feared most tried to penetrate his thoughts, he allowed his mind to close down. He managed to fall asleep, if only for a few hours.

When he woke, his head was a jumble of images of the people he discussed with Michelle and Peter the night before. On entering the back room, after switching on the kettle for his early morning tea, he stood in front of the white board with its lists of people. Almost immediately he noticed the only reference to Castle Daingneach was the inclusion of the bomb under Emily. There was no mention of Mungo and Mary MacLeod as if somewhere among the mass of information he forgot the bomb wasn't really meant for Emily at all. Everyone assumed the bomb was another attempt on Mary's life, resulting in her becoming a prisoner in the castle.

In addition, after Michelle confirmed it, he rubbed out the masked man at the Bus Company Building at Dinnet writing Simon Copeland's name. Under the Bus Tour building in the village he added 'Graffiti' because he believed there was some significance in the jumble of images relevant to most of it, if only he could see the significance.

Emily	Castle Daingneach	Quinnell Farm	Dinnet Bus Co. Building	Hotel	Bus Tour Building	Others:
Missing Hamish (Last seen by) Gina (riding pillion) Castle Bomb Car in Quinnell outbuilding	Mary & Mungo MacLeod Attempt on Mary's life x2 Car accident Bomb	Rupert Quinnell Delores (wife) Rory (Son) ?Money laundering David Taylor Gina Taylor (Rupert's daughter)	David Taylor Simon Copeland Illegal use of building Storage boxes Emily watching	Chuck Bistro Manager Extortion ?Money laundering Finlay Ferguson Helen Daniels	Gina Taylor Finlay Ferguson Drugs Graffiti	Harvey Williamson Jenny Iona Roberts Robbie Cowan
	Rupert/Rory/Delores Quinnell, Gina Taylor/David Taylor, Chuck, Hamish McGregor Mary/Mungo MacLeod					

Once done he went to make some tea for his breakfast.

CHAPTER 80

When they stood outside The March of Time, Michelle and Peter barely passed a word. They said goodnight then drove off in opposite directions. After discovering the Mini Cooper in the warehouse belonged to Emily, Michelle regretted not taking a look inside the car. As a serving police officer this would have been instinctive and she felt angry with herself. She thought perhaps she was being too harsh. After all if she was still a police officer actually looking for Emily, she would have known the registration of her car because it would have been circulated. On finding the car she would have conducted a cursory search, in case….. The thought hit her there was always the possibility in a MISPER case the person might have come to a dreadful end. *Dead?* The word formed in her mind taunting her even more she hadn't done a search of the mini.

Now she was fortified with hot soup, she knew if she drove all the way home she would be unable to sleep with these thoughts flowing through her head. She wouldn't be able to settle until she went back to do a proper inspection of the car. She told herself at least she would be able to see if there was any evidence to show what might have happened to Emily. She also needed a thorough look at the rest of the warehouse where the mini was hidden.

She drove back to the Quinnell estate. As she passed through Dinnet she saw the Bus Company Building looked quiet. There was no white van outside, Taylor and Copeland must have completed their nightly visits. At least she was certain the boxes they were storing in the building contained the dried parts from the Cannabis plants grown inside the warehouse.

Mitch knew the law varied on matters related to Cannabis, being a Class B drug. She hoped, if they were arrested for the cultivation on such a large scale, as well as their distribution, the CPS could go for the maximum sentence on conviction – fourteen years. She could live with that. She wanted Copeland to get his just desserts for what he did to her. The idea appealed.

She continued her journey with caution, having no idea whether the van or the two weed growers would still be around. On entering the Quinnell estate she took the same route as before, noting the social function at the big house seemed to be over. Where the house was situated, there was only night lights showing as she drove past the break in the hedge. The darkness enveloped the rest of her journey. She crawled slowly until the shadowy warehouse was suddenly revealed by a watery moon breaking through the cloud cover. There was no white van outside and Mitch took the opportunity to get off the perimeter road leaving her car where the van had been.

She moved straight to the back door, repeated her practised lock picking routine by holding her small torch in her mouth. It took no time at all. The hum of the growing room lights welcomed her back.

Mitch's urgency to search Emily's mini for any sign of her was her first priority. She put on a pair of blue latex forensic gloves from her pocket, swiftly pulled the covering off the car. She tried the driver's door, which she found locked, having to use the lock picks again. Car doors gave Mitch no problem. She practiced often enough on her own vehicle.

Once inside she got straight to work on a close inspection of the driver's seat where she expected to find some evidence of Emily. Apart from several strands of hair trapped in the head rest she could make out nothing unusual. She took a sample, wrapped it in a tissue from her pocket.

She reached underneath the seat for the horizontal bar, moving the seat backwards to be able to climb easily over to the passenger seat. As she moved forward her knee caught something loose at the sill, she heard the hard thud against metal. She took the torch out of her mouth, illuminated a mobile phone on the floor, saw it was switched off which explained why no one could get through to her.

She slipped the phone into a pocket, climbed over the seat to the other side. On the passenger seat head rest she found a small patch of dried blood. She took a sample on a tissue as evidence, reassured the quantity wasn't a life threatening amount.

After a cursory inspection of the back seats, that revealed nothing to the naked eye, there was one last stop to make before she put the cover back over the car. She stood behind the car, experienced a flash back of memory, to one night on traffic duty she found the body in an abandoned car in a layby when she stopped to search for ownership.

Since then, with the gruesome state of the body inside, she always felt a surge of nausea whenever she opened a car boot. Reflex action, or recurring nightmare, she didn't think she would ever get over, either the sight or the smell. When she opened the mini's boot, she let out the breath she was holding. The boot was empty.

Part relief, although concerned at what she found in the car, Michelle quickly moved through the internal locked door into the back corridor where the smell of Cannabis plants intensified. Instead of turning towards the growing room she turned left to find another door further along, which when she opened gave on to a small room with potting benches along one wall. There was another internal door she could see by the intense light around its perimeter gave access to the growing room.

Michelle determined the room was where the Cannabis was boxed for distribution. There was evidence of dried weed on the floor and a pile of flat packed boxes in one corner. They looked sturdy like the ones she saw Taylor and Copeland take into the building next to McKinley's. Michelle took a small amount of the dried substance from the floor as evidence.

In the centre of the room there was an empty chair. When she examined it, she found nylon constraints, the kind of cuffs the police use to bind wrists, two of them having been left around the front chair legs. She thought about Copeland, as his face lurched at her out of the darkness, the words came again, *'Come on, bitch, you know you like it!'* She shook her head to clear the image.

Mitch deduced two things from her find. One, someone was held captive here, the other, given the lack of blood around the chair, there was no indication they were hurt. She dared to think they must still be alive. She tilted the chair to remove one of the restraints which she also conveyed to her pocket.

The thought occurred to her, for future reference she ought to be better prepared. She would carry some evidence bags if she was going to encounter this kind of situation again. She would ask Bart if his friend Jay might be persuaded to donate some to the Agency. She retraced her steps back the way she came. Checked the cover over Emily's car looked the way she found it, before leaving the warehouse, making sure the door she unlocked was secure. Only when she was finally through the grounds of the estate, out onto the main road, did her breathing become easier. As she drove back home the skies began to lighten, morning wasn't too far away.

CHAPTER 81

Instead of going back to the Moor Hen, when Peter reached the side road approach to the pub he turned to reverse the jeep around, to drive as quietly as he could past The March of Time heading out of the village. There wasn't a soul in sight along Main Street, not even a late night drunk making their way home and this was so different to what he was used to in London. Nobody ever seemed to go to sleep, there was always someone around the streets at night. The utter silence of the sleepy village contrasted greatly to the constant noise levels he was used to where he lived. He wasn't sure he could live somewhere as quiet as here.

He liked London's night life. There was always some place open to get a meal if you felt hungry in the middle of the night. Just as well really, being a gaming programmer you could become so focussed following a level until you got to the next, you could lose all sense of time. He often forgot to eat. When he emerged from his computer into the real world he would feel a sudden fierce hunger, but be too tired to cook a meal. The choice was to resort to a pot noodle or go round the corner to a café where he could get something to eat in the middle of the night, was often all he could manage.

Peter drove the jeep back to the Quinnell farm with the sole purpose to see for himself what was beyond the greenhouses. Though risky, especially if he was spotted by Gina, he couldn't say he was there to find Emily. Now he knew Gina was living with Rory Quinnell, *her brother,* he certainly no longer wanted to attract her attention.

With it being the middle of the night he could hardly park the jeep in the garden centre car park. He thought the car park would probably be closed up or covered by CCTV. He chose to hide the jeep in the pull in near the cottage, there to walk back to the warehouse where he knew David Taylor grew weed. He wanted to see Emily's mini hidden inside for himself.

There was no sound coming from the cottage when he stood listening. He assumed Gina and her brother were fast asleep at this hour. Everywhere was dark because of the heavy cloud covering the moon. Peter was tempted to have a quick look around the cottage. When he emerged from the trees there was no sign of the motorbike or any hint of a light showing inside. He made no attempt to try the cottage door. Everyone locked their doors.

The curtains were still open at the large window which could indicate there was no one home. *Why did he close them before, there was unlikely to be anyone passing?* The thought came as he moved over to look inside. He found the room like any other sitting room, with a couch, an easy chair, TV, dining table. The place looked untidy, with beer cans, plates and boxes of takeout food scattered about. He was not one bit surprised. Gina didn't strike him as the kind of person who would be into domestic chores. Who could blame her after doing it all day in a coffee shop? He couldn't imagine Rory Quinnell was used to clearing up after himself either having spent his early life living in the big house, where they probably have staff.

Peter moved on to the side of the house. There were no windows here until he got to the back where a strip of ground had been cleared back to the line of trees to allow for the barest strip of a garden. Most of it was slabbed all the way along, with no attempt to make a proper garden, only a shed erected at the farthest end back in the trees. The first window Peter came to, he thought must be a bedroom. The curtains were closed.

The back door further along had a couple of wheelie bins outside sitting on the slabs. The only other window allowed him to see the door opened into a kitchen. There was a light on a microwave clock, with another on a cooker, enough to see the kitchen was as untidy as the front room. He thought he remembered Bart saying someone called Charlotte used to live with Rory. Peter wondered if she kept a better house before the crazy girl moved in.

Peter was rather disappointed with his recce, even though he didn't know what he expected to find, he regretted being so impetuous. Perhaps he should have tried to find the warehouse Michelle told them about. He reached the farthest side of the cottage having come fully round the building when the thought hit him, *'Why did someone with no back garden have need of a shed?'*

He went back to have a look at the wooden structure partially hidden in the trees he felt sure must have come from the stock of sheds they sold in the garden centre. The hut looked new, certainly smelt like new wood and was yet to be treated with any wood preservative. He wondered if Rory Quinnell installed the shed to use as another storage place for his Cannabis.

Of the three sides he could access there was only a door. No window. He suspected they would hardly put one on the side abutting the trees where there was no light to be had. The door he found was fastened by a shiny new padlock raising his curiosity even more. Michelle, he thought, would have taken no time at all to pick the padlock. He grinned whilst thinking about her. The more he saw of her the more she impressed him. He never met a girl who remotely drew his attention and not because he preferred men either.

Gina annoyed him when she asked if he was gay. He knew he definitely wasn't because he worked through the issue a few years back talking to the psychologist after being sexually abused by men. The subject, he was told, was often a worry to victims who thought it might be a consequence of being abused. It hadn't been his, nor did he need any proof. The concept of having a normal relationship became lost somewhere in his dreadful past and remained mainly about trust and honesty.

At the time he decided he could never have a proper relationship with a girl because he would have to tell her about what he went through. He didn't ever want to talk about it again. With a girl you would have to give all of yourself or none of yourself. He chose none being the easier option, knowing it was an avoidance strategy the psychologist talked about and could result in a very lonely existence.

Maybe this was why he made contact with Emily? He was always able to tell her everything, easier then because they were only kids. The things they told each other were mostly innocent childhood stuff. Well until the nightmare started with Arthur Claymore. As he came more under his control, the shame of what was happening to him made him unable to even look at Emily let alone tell her anything about it. *Yet you did, she sat with you during the police interviews, held your hand, you wouldn't let it go.* The long forgotten thought echoed down the years making him realise how much she meant to him, the only person he was ever able to feel comfortable with, his cousin Emily.

His thoughts were interrupted by someone singing which shocked him out of his musings. The voice sounded like a child, the song he recognised was a familiar pop song he knew by David Bowie. He picked up some of the words - 'She loves him, she loves him but just for a short while; she'll scratch in the sand, won't let go his hand'.

It broke the daydream he was having about Emily after she found him locked away in the Rehab nursing home. He was unable to let her hand go, until the police took him away into care. The voice got nearer, he could hear the song's rift being sung, 'Jean Gina let yourself go!' getting nearer. He realised Gina was singing as if the song was all about her and she was approaching the cottage.

Peter ducked down at the side of the shed. The singing stopped. He saw the light behind the curtains he thought was a bedroom come on. What seemed like an age was probably only five or ten minutes before he heard the engine of a motorbike coming up the short drive to the cottage, a flash of a head light in the sky rotated as the bike came to rest in front of the cottage. When he looked, the light in the bedroom went out. He heard the front door slam then watched down the side of the cottage as the bike, with Gina Taylor on pillion, roar off up the drive.

As the sound of the motorbike's engine faded to a faint buzz he listened until he could hear nothing. He stood up from where he was crouching, heard another faint sound, a thump followed by a groan. He turned towards the shed, banging his fist against the side. The response was a louder groan he knew was a reply to his knock. He looked frantically around for something he could use to break the padlock.

Then he remembered the crowbar in the back of the jeep and began to run as fast as he could back into the trees where he left it.

CHAPTER 82

Robbie made himself as comfortable as he could on the floor of the greenhouse, at least the place was warm. He tucked into the food with relish. He broke off chunks of crusty bread, scooped up the pâté eating it greedily with pieces of cheese from the block. He made himself slow down as he immediately got the hiccups. They echoed loudly in the confined space as he gasped with each eruption. He held his breath trying to halt them.

Sitting with his back against the leg of a potting bench, his picnic spread out in front of him, he took out the bottle of Châteauneuf-du-Pape, saw he was unable to take out the cork without a bottle opener one of which he had on his Swiss Army knife he left with his jeans in the plane. He was tempted to smash the neck against the wooden bench, thought better of drinking alcohol knowing he would be flying Sid Bailey back home in the morning. He wished he'd spent a little more time looking for a bottle of water. The hiccups subsided.

Robbie's shrunken stomach quickly became uncomfortably full. Not for the first time he reminded himself he should try to eat more often and healthily. The shock on his handler's face when he saw him for the first time in six months was reinforced by the sight of himself in the oversized suit he caught in the car window of the limo picking Sid Bailey up at the airport. The change in his physical appearance he assessed was dramatic.

He promised himself when he got back to Nottingham he would try to smarten himself up. He would start with getting his hair cut. He was working up to a burp to relieve the pressure in his gut when he caught the shadow of someone walking past the greenhouse, He managed to suppress the belch before he let rip.

He knelt up to peer outside in the direction the shadow was moving. He recognised the waitress uniform before he caught sight of the swish of the ponytail belonging to Gina Taylor. How could he ever forget her? His curiosity at her being here, serving at the Quinnell party, got the better of him, compounding his hatred for the girl. He wanted to see where she was going. He had some idea she lived with her step-brother David somewhere on the estate because he knew David Taylor was one of the Quinnell's gardeners according to Anabel Taylor's drunken ramblings. Before he had time to think what he was doing he crept out of the greenhouse to follow her.

She led him past a large warehouse, up an access road then turned right onto a perimeter road. He crept as quietly as he could, made easier by their being no lighting along this stretch of road. He knew if he made a sound and she turned to look behind her, she would have no doubt seen him. The girl seemed oblivious to anything other than the pop song she was singing in wireless earphones. She raised her arms swaying to the sound although he could hear nothing except the tuneless noise coming out of her mouth.

When he got to the beginning of the trees, he stepped off the road to hide because the noise she was making changed whilst her dancing became wilder. If she twirled around she would definitely see him. His intuition came in time. Her song must have changed again because her crazy cavorting included a lot of spinning around, whilst intriguing to watch her movements became more manic. When she stopped spinning, she wobbled unsteadily before she carried on forward skipping like a little girl. A bit further on she disappeared into the trees.

Robbie stepped out of hiding and moved cautiously keeping an eye on where he thought she went. He assumed he arrived at the cottage because the first thing he saw was the vehicle parked off the road. Through the trees behind he could make out a light. This, he thought, must be where she lives. He moved towards the light to have a look. He felt the bonnet as he passed, a check he used during his police career to test if a vehicle had been used recently. This one he could tell had been parked for a while, maybe half an hour at the most by its subtle warmth.

Robbie heard the sound of a motorbike coming fast down the road behind him, caught its lights like a search light in the sky as it got nearer. The bike began to slow down. He ducked behind the side of the vehicle expecting the motorbike to turn the same way. The biker cruised past the opening, turned beyond, Robbie saw the lights moving parallel to him through the trees stopping close to the building he could now see because Gina Taylor switched on the inside lights.

When he crept closer to get a view of the biker, the inside lights went out He watched the girl, dressed in jeans and a biker jacket leave the cottage door where an outside light illuminated her. She grinned as the biker turned the motorbike around to wait for her to put on a helmet and slip onto the back before they sped off.

Robbie heaved a sigh of relief at not being caught.

CHAPTER 83

After breakfast Bart went out for a walk. He needed the exercise, with plenty of fresh air to allow his mind to consider the links between the people on the white board. He stopped for a short rest on the hill behind the Bus Tour Building, leaned on the stone wall he looked over at the overgrown rear garden. This was where he last saw Finlay Ferguson making his way inside the back door the day before he left the village. The thought made Bart feel sad for Finn and Charlotte Reynolds, his once bride to be. He often wondered how she was faring in Witness Protection. He felt sure she would feel as scared as he had a few years ago. Such a sad waste of young lives, they once had a good future ahead of them.

Just like Emily.

He didn't get much further on his walk, having let his daily exercise regime lapse he was even more unfit than he once was. He turned round to go back. Thoughts of Emily made him so dejected he could barely function. The urgency to find her was playing heavily on him. When he came back to the A93 he was stopped from crossing the road by a sudden surge of heavy traffic. A lorry and several cars sped past him going far too fast for the speed limit. He looked down towards the Esso garage. The local bus coming up the hill was indicating the turn into the village when it got level with the hotel.

Bart didn't cross the road. He walked the distance to the hotel entrance, where he stopped again in front of the main door. He stood with his eyes fixed on the ground, as if he were inspecting his shoes for cleanliness. The expression on his face revealed his inner turmoil reflecting the battle he was having with his instincts. He urgently needed help. Who could he trust? He knew Helen had links to

Operation Graffiti who must have the big picture, at least a great deal more information than he knew about the people involved. They would be able to make the links where he was failing to do.

He thought, if they were watching the Quinnell estate, the people Bart suspected were at the centre of most of the criminal activity, they must know something about Emily's whereabouts, surely? When he looked up, the hotel door opened to reveal Helen Daniels standing there, her face quizzical, staring at him. After her recent visit to the shop to tell him to 'back off' because he was in danger of compromising the whole operation, she showed a lack of concern for Emily that Bart found shocking. After Michelle found Emily's car hidden in the warehouse he became angry as well as desperate.

Helen came up to him, "What is it, Bart?" She seemed genuinely concerned yet he felt quite helpless.

He sighed deeply. "I thought the police were meant to protect people," he said pitifully. When she frowned as if insulted, he stepped closer to her, whispered, "Emily's car is hidden in a warehouse, near the greenhouses, on the Quinnell estate….does that compromise your police investigations?"

He turned , walked away leaving her standing watching him cross the road onto Main Street on his way back to The March of Time. His sadness at losing Emily gave way and the deep pain he felt inside returned.

*   *   *   *   *

Bart found the shop still closed with no sign of Isla Strachan who should have been there to open up for the day. When he walked into the back room he found Isla with Michelle pinning up photographs using colourful magnetic pins onto the white board. To his surprise they seemed to have a large pile scattered across the table.

"Where did you get all these photographs?" he asked moving to pick up some of the ones they hadn't put up yet. He recognised the photograph of Mary and Mungo used in the National Newspapers after the bomb, likewise the pictures of the Quinnells was the one on the internet he showed Peter from the Sunday supplement. New to him was one of Chuck, the hotel chef in his uniform, he hadn't seen before.

Isla replied, "I got a lot from existing news sources or...." She pointed at the one of Chuck he was holding in his hand, "I got his off the hotel website, there were a few of the staff."

"Yes, but..." Bart began.

As if anticipating what was puzzling him she said, "I have a printer at home, we need to get one for the agency," she added before she went on, "I used the photocopier at the Pharmacy in the village for the ones we took out of hard copy local newspapers. Och, I know it's far from ideal with people milling around in the shop. I was careful not to expose what I was doing. I do think we need one of those printers where we can also photocopy, they aren't expensive if you want me to get one?"

Bart stared at her in amazement, it seemed to him as each day went by he realised how lucky he was at finding her. He suddenly felt quite tearful, turned his back to walk over to put the kettle on to hide how he was feeling. He knew there was a need to respond. His answer came shakily, "Yes, Mrs Strachan you are right, that would be good of you. Tea?" he asked. He didn't see the look that passed between the two women who both picked up his distress.

Michelle decided perhaps this wasn't the time to tell him about what she found in Emily's car or the room inside the warehouse. He didn't look like he would be able to cope with it. She had, in fact, contacted Agatha Vingoe, already met early with her and Jay to give him the pieces of evidence she found there. She knew she wrongfully obtained them, as pieces of evidence they couldn't be submitted in court, however, there was no other way she could get them analysed.

Once the tea was made Bart seemed to have control of his emotions, managing a smile when he turned back to stand in front of the white board once again studying the pictures. He wasn't sure they added anything new to his overall understanding of the arrangement.

Isla said, "I couldnae find a photo of the awful wee lassie," she said.

"Me neither," Michelle confirmed. "She doesn't have a social media presence I could find, which is strange for someone her age."

"I wonder if she's ever been in trouble with the police?" Bart asked.

Michelle didn't mention Agatha offered to see what she could find on the police computers although Michelle asked them both not to take any risks.

Isla Strachan said, "From what I remember of her from seeing her in the Co-op and when she came in here, she doesn't look much like her brother."

Bart said, "Ah well, David is her stepbrother, so she wouldn't." He looked at the board again, saw there wasn't a photo of David Taylor up there yet.

"Aye, I didn't mean him," she said pointing at the newly pinned photograph of the Quinnells at a society charity function she studied as she produced the picture. "Her half-brother Rory I mean."

They all looked at the picture again. There was no doubt Rory Quinnell favoured his mother rather than Rupert. Bart heard the words Mary MacLeod uttered mischievously to him when they were discussing the likeness between Mungo to Seumus Grant's portrait, *'It's not exactly a DNA match but what used to pass as the same in those days.'* Ginger hair and facial features in their case was almost identical. Rory Quinnell's sandy coloured hair and striking nose was not a feature of either of his parents.

Bart's eyes moved toward Mungo MacLeod, then back over to the Quinnell's in one revealing sweep.

CHAPTER 84

The March of Time was open by the time Jayson Vingoe arrived. Isla Strachan was attending to a customer. He went straight through to the back room where Michelle was working on the lap top looking for more photographs for the white board. He telephoned earlier, knew Bart wouldn't be there, he took the opportunity to catch Michelle alone. She already admitted to him she told Bart nothing about her night visit to the warehouse or anything about finding a trace of blood in her car or the physical restraints attached to the chair. She hadn't checked the mobile, being completely dead, she was reluctant to go into Emily's bedroom to find her charger.

Jay told her he called in a favour to expedite the analysis and confirmed the blood, hair and tiny traces of skin on the nylon ties were from the same person. Given the blood from the car was likely to be Emily's they must assume she was injured in some way to be kept there against her will.

"Jay, the problem we have is knowing who in the police we can trust," Michelle confided retelling Bart's understanding from speaking to Charlotte Reynolds, about the Quinnells associating with a number of people, some she believed to be police officers. She updated him on their surveillance of the Bus Company building at Dinnet with her discovery of the involvement of Simon Copeland who he knew was recently dismissed from the force.

Jay remembered an awkward moment when he went with Agatha to a retirement party for the CID Superintendent. Neither of them really wanted to go but didn't want to snub the man. He was always supportive, yet there were others who Jay knew would be there he would have preferred not to mix with outside of work. Agatha insisted they go with the proviso they would ask Emily if she was available to babysit, otherwise they would make their apologies. He remembered being disappointed when Emily readily offered.

After Agatha went back to work having given birth to Daisy, she encountered a lot of problems, particularly with Copeland who treated women police officers badly, especially if they rejected his advances. It never seemed to matter to Copeland whether they were married or not. The night of the retirement party Jay felt certain Copeland was deliberately leering lecherously at Agatha to annoy him. As a consequence he drank far too much which only added fuel to his anger, making him want to smack the smile off Copeland's face. He even followed him to the men's room to 'have a word' with him. Copeland laughed in his face goading him with taunts like 'what's the matter you think she might want a bit of prime, old man?'

Jay pinned him up against the men's room wall with his arm across his throat. He even raised his fist ready to smack him in the face, when the door opened and DI Morris walked in on them. Copeland eagerly urged him on, 'come on you pussy, do it!' he yelled.

Morris stood watching, he made no move to talk him down. Jay realised he would be Copeland's witness to the 'unprovoked' assault on his precious Detective Sergeant. Jay let him go, walked away, stopping at the side of Morris he whispered, 'I've got your card marked' before he left them there.

He recalled the night, when he could quite easily have lost his job. Now Jay was hearing Simon Copeland, the disgraced copper, was involved in illicit drug production. He grinned thinking about the saying 'revenge is best served cold'.

Michelle was surprised Jay didn't immediately refute the idea, was even quite shocked when she heard him say, "Copeland is a slimy little shit and Morris is no better."

"Oh?" Mitch wondered what Jay would say if he knew what happened to her. She told no one, except Bart and wanted to keep it that way. She said, "I would dearly love to see them both behind bars."

Jay could tell her feelings ran deep assuming she may have suffered some of what Agatha has gone through. "No one was more pleased to see the back of Copeland than Agatha," he said. "I think all of us share your sentiments."

He knew when he shared this latest information with Agatha they would discuss ways they could turn the information into a more tangible outcome for Copeland and perhaps even bring Morris down. Meanwhile he would need to discuss the matter with Bart, after all his surveillance unearthed Copeland's criminal activity. He felt Bart wasn't in the right place at the moment to hear his thoughts on the matter, not while Emily was missing.

CHAPTER 85

Bart hurried along the corridor towards the lifts in the Green zone, his short legs moving fast below his round body made him look like the Road Runner in a Wile E. Coyote cartoon. His stern face was a mask of seriousness. He rode the lift to the fourth floor which gave onto the familiar corridor where he once sat with Emily waiting whilst visiting Mary MacLeod (then Macaulay) captive in the High Dependency Unit in an induced coma. The familiarity of the place gave him no comfort.

There was a man sitting on a hardback chair outside the door of a side room. He stood up when Bart approached. Bart thought the man looked vaguely familiar though couldn't place where he met him. Just as the man was about to speak, the door Bart came through opened again and Peter bustled in.

"I got the last parking space," he said out of breath. The man seemed to recognise Peter visibly relaxing a little. "This is Mr Bridges," Peter announced to the man.

"I'm sorry, Mr Bridges, I still have to search you," he said. Bart put his arms out to allow him to quickly pat him down for weapons.

When he finished, Bart said, "Thank you," as if he had done him a great service. The man held out his arm to indicate he could proceed. Bart moved tentatively to the door, turning to look at Peter for support. Peter nodded him forward.

Bart opened the door slowly. He saw the tiny frail body was hooked to a drip, wired to monitors, with an oxygen mask over her face. Peter heard his sob from a distance away. He could barely recognise her she looked so frail.

He heard Peter beside him say, "She's okay Bart. She's mostly starved, dehydrated with a wound on her skull. She has a hair line fracture where she was knocked unconscious," Peter whispered. "Other than that she's okay. They're monitoring her as you can see. They say we found her just in time."

Bart walked to the side of Emily's bed, sat down on the chair. He took her hand gently and tears began to run silently down his cheeks. He never knowingly cried before in his life, not even when the doctor said his brain tumour was putting pressure on his brain stem and needed to be removed urgently. But then Bart Bridges would never cry for himself. He cared for the girl in the bed more than anyone else in his life. He had loved his mother dearly, even though she was strict Greek Orthodox in her beliefs whilst he was a non-believer. There had been no one else to elicit such feelings.

"Will she be okay?" he asked Peter.

"I understand so," Peter replied cheerfully.

Bart felt Emily's hand grip his weakly. She stirred before she slowly opened her eyes, seemed to look straight into his to whisper, "I saw Robbie."

A doctor came into the room followed by a nurse who politely asked them to leave whilst they checked Miss Draper over. On hearing this Bart glanced up at the name written on a board over Emily's bed. He read 'Amelia Draper'.

Bart sat beside Peter along the corridor in a waiting area. The man who was outside the door when they went into Emily's room had disappeared. Although Bart had no idea who or what he was, he felt a little unsettled by his absence. Almost immediately the man reappeared carrying a tray of drinks, saw them sitting together he went over to give them both a cup. Peter thanked him accepted the drink quite naturally as if they were old friends. Bart took his without a word, then watched the coffee bearer return to the chair outside the door.

"Who is that man?" Bart asked.

"Ah," Peter seemed reluctant to answer. "It's a long story."

"More to the point, how did you find her?"

Peter took the lid off his coffee to gingerly sip the too hot liquid. He put the lid back on, placing the cup on the floor next to his chair. Bart held his cup and as a thought came to him, he suddenly asked, "You said 'we'…..'we found her just in time'."

"Yes, I did." Peter began to tell Bart about going back to the Quinnell estate after leaving him in the shop and how he parked near to the cottage where Gina lived with Rory.

Peter retold how his curiosity got the better of him because everything seemed quiet with the cottage in darkness. He was tempted to have a look around the outside of the place. He was nearly caught out when, he heard the Taylor girl singing as she returned to the cottage, shortly after followed by the Harley Davison arriving to pick her up. He hid at the side of a newly installed shed in the trees at the back of the place.

"After they rode away, when all was silent again, I heard some muffled sounds coming from inside the shed. I banged on the side and heard a thud as if in reply. I thought whatever was in there, either person or animal, was locked in with a shiny new padlock on the door and I would need something hefty to prise it off."

Peter told Bart he remembered there was a crowbar in the back of Alistair's jeep. He began to run as fast as he could towards the jeep, literally running straight into a man moving away from it. The collision caused them both to fall over. Peter leapt to his feet first, ran to the back of the jeep to retrieve the crowbar.

"I have to say I was afraid I'd been caught out by either one of the Quinnells or a member of their staff because the man was wearing a smart dinner suit with a bow tie! Not the sort of person you would expect to find in a wood in the middle of the night. As for him, he told me later, he thought I was a Quinnell also because I was standing waving a dangerous weapon at him." Peter began to laugh at how it played out. "I told him to get out of my way because I needed to do something urgently. He was all the while motioning me with his hands to calm me down, asking me not to do anything stupid. I yelled 'get out of my way there's something alive in the shed at the back' I needed to find out if it's Emily."

Peter saw the man's face change to shock, 'Why? What's happened to Emily?'

'As if you don't know!' Peter yelled. 'She disappeared days ago. You've got her car hidden in your warehouse.' Peter straightened up and on seeing how shocked the man was changed his mind about his identity. 'Who are you?' Peter demanded.

'Who are you?' he asked in reply.

'I'm Emily's cousin Peter!'

'I'm Robbie, Emily's......friend.....I didn't know she was missing,' Robbie started to run towards the cottage, 'Come on let's see what's in there,' he said turning to wait for Peter to move from where he stood impassive.

"After we established who we were, we smashed the padlock off....and found her in there on the floor," Peter's voice broke at the thought of the sight of her, locked away in the dark, barely alive."

The door to Emily's room opened, the doctor came out walked over to where they were sitting. "Are you Miss Draper's next of kin?"

"Yes," said Bart and Peter in unison. Bart realising Peter was actually her blood relative, pointed to him, "Peter is her cousin."

"We are both her kin," Peter said knowing Bart was more of a guardian to her than he was. "Anyway, how is she?"

The doctor told them she was progressing well, would be staying in hospital until they were satisfied she was fully hydrated. The fracture to her skull would begin to heal, but they were monitoring her for concussion or any other problems. "When the nurse comes out from attending to her you can go back in, for a little while. Miss Draper needs much rest." The doctor left them.

They sat back down to wait. Bart looked over again to the man sitting on the chair outside her room, "Do you know who he is?" he asked Peter again.

"Ah, that's another story entirely," Peter said. "He is someone Robbie arranged to make sure no one can get to Emily...."

"Robbie's handler!" Bart suddenly blurted out on recognising the man Jenny Williamson was covertly giving Robbie's mail to. "Of course, I should have recognised him from the pictures Michelle took."

Peter smiled remembering how Robbie organised help to get Emily into hospital he thought was an exceptionally quick response. Robbie then told him he needed to 'go back' because he had a job to do. Before he disappeared he begged Peter to stay with Emily to make sure she was safe and got medical attention. The last thing he said before he slipped back into the night was he would arrange for help to keep her safe.

CHAPTER 86

Robbie's relief at not being seen by Gina or the biker didn't last long. He stood up from hiding behind the Jeep, turned towards the building to go to take a quick look at the place Gina was living with her brother David. He was suddenly knocked over by a figure coming fast out of the trees. When he got up he saw the youth, who was not much older than a boy, spring to his feet then rush to the vehicle's back door where he opened the boot. He turned towards Robbie holding a crowbar looking menacing and told Robbie to get out of his way because there was something or someone locked inside the shed behind the cottage. He became alarmed when he heard him mention 'Emily'.

After a brief interchange, the boy called Peter claimed to be Emily's cousin and told him she had been missing for some days and they found her car hidden in the warehouse near the greenhouses. On hearing this Robbie's alarm was so great he didn't question what Peter was saying because the night he went to say goodbye to Emily she explained about her cousin Peter making contact with her.

Robbie divulged he was Emily's 'friend' – he couldn't quite bring himself to say 'boyfriend' because he knew he abandoned her all those months ago. Alerted to the danger Emily must be in if Gina Taylor was something to do with her disappearance, he immediately charged ahead in the direction Peter pointed, stopped when he realised Peter remained frozen by the knowledge of who he was. Robbie yelled for him to hurry up. They moved fast, arrived at the shed where between them they prised the lock apart.

Robbie reacted fast, he could see Emily curled up on the bare wooden floor, was in a critical state. He told Peter to stay with her whilst he went outside to arrange for help. His only option was to telephone his handler, quickly detailing what they found and how they needed to use extreme caution because the girl Gina together with her brother rode off somewhere, and might return at any time.

"You need to get out of there, go back for Sid Bailey, fly him back to Nottingham," his handler told him, emphasising this wasn't the right time to move in on them. "Do you understand?" he asked forcefully.

Robbie had sufficient time to speak a few words to Peter, "Help is on its way, I can't stay. Please don't leave her. I've arranged some protection, okay?" Peter was sitting on the floor of the shed cradling a now unconscious Emily in his arms, rocking her gently.

"Okay," he said quietly but Robbie was gone.

* * * * *

It surprised Peter how quickly someone arrived, he hardly had time to register the sound of a vehicle which he noted thankfully was not an ambulance with all the sirens blaring. Emily was gently transferred by two burly men wearing dark clothes with head mounted night vision goggles carrying a collapsible stretcher to their dark green military looking land Rover. Peter knew he couldn't leave Alistair's Flossie near the cottage, telling her rescuers he would follow them to the hospital because he would be needed to provide information about her. The man he was speaking to told him he would also go with her to make sure she remained safe.

"Please forget you ever saw Robbie," he urged.

"I understand," Peter said.

Peter expected there would be a lot of questions from the nurses or medics who attended her, but nothing was said. When he was asked who she was he decided to give her name as Amelia Draper, his cousin, in case when the crazy girl or Rory Quinnell came back they might search for her. Peter deliberately delayed speaking to Bart because Emily appeared to be in a bad way. He needed the doctors to assess her first, to hear the worst case scenario before he got him involved.

Emily was quickly admitted to the High Dependency Unit. The man who spoke to him when help arrived stayed outside her room. When morning came they had both drunk a lot of coffee to stay awake by which time the doctor had explained her condition to them. Afterwards, Peter fell asleep in the waiting area being woken a couple of hours later by the clatter of a cleaning crew coming on duty. Peter saw the man still sitting outside Emily's room and wondered if he ever slept.

CHAPTER 87

A few days later, much sooner than expected, Amelia Draper was discharged from hospital, taken by Bart, her 'guardian', together with Peter, her cousin, to Castle Daingneach, the address she gave where she worked as 'live in' secretary to Laird MacLeod. It was felt by all concerned the security at the castle was far more fitting to her circumstances than would be the alternative suggested to Bart by the people who were guarding her in hospital. The safe house at the Linn-of-Dee which Bart thought was one step in the process towards her disappearing into the black hole of the Witness Protection programme. There was no way he was going to allow her to. One of his major arguments whilst seeking Mary's agreement was the suggestion they could be 'companions in confinement'.

During the days of her early recovery in hospital Emily was visited several times by officers from Operation Graffiti who gently questioned her to obtain any insights she might have picked up about the people she came into contact with during her ordeal. At first her recollection was hazy, only growing clearer as her strength came back.

Unfortunately, she found the oft repeated questions prompted too many awful memories of her imprisonment and increased her anxiety bringing on panic attacks. She blamed these on the blow to her head. In reality, each time she was questioned, she felt like she was being led to a precipice above unknown depth below. She knew if she told them what she was slowly recalling, it would be like looking down and she feared she might fall into oblivion. She would rather not remember, telling the people she had no memory except for there being a hood over her head.

She could see no one, been desperately thirsty she could barely keep awake. In her head when asked what she heard, all she could remember was the voice next to her ear whispering, '*Do I know you little girl?*' which she kept to herself. At first she was convinced the voice was Rupert Quinnell she heard in the farm shop, but as time went on she began to doubt herself.

Bart was present during these interrogation sessions because Emily refused to speak to them without his presence. At first they refused, until Emily became uncooperative, moodily refusing to speak, she turned away from them and they were forced to relent. She surprised Bart, watching from the seat beside her. He hadn't wanted to let her out of his sight from the moment Peter told him he found her in a shed at the Quinnell farm and took her to hospital. Bart merely shrugged his shoulders at her behaviour telling them as her guardian, of course, he must be there to ensure they didn't over-exert her or halt the progress she was making. He saw the faint quiver of a smile as she faced him and he knew there was more to her non-cooperation than childish stubbornness or her injuries.

As Bart listened during these interviews, he knew Emily well enough to pick up a hint she was not exactly telling the truth about what she could see or hear. He surmised there must be another reason why. So he went along with his new role of 'guardian' interrupting whenever he thought they were applying too much pressure or particularly when they kept going over the same ground too many times. He wasn't exactly familiar with police procedures or police interviewing, but began to have an uneasy feeling something was not quite right with how they handled things.

When they suggested Amelia be transferred on discharge to the Linn-of-Dee for her own protection Bart said, "Absolutely out of the question. She is employed as Laird MacLeod's secretary at Castle Daingneach where she lives, and will be returning there. I am certain their current level of security is far superior to your 'safe house'." His pronouncement sounded final, even Emily, who knew nothing about the arrangement, stared in disbelief. She took his cue and quickly nodded agreement.

A few days later, Emily found herself sitting up in bed in the same bedroom Robbie used whilst he stayed at Castle Daingneach after he was forced to move out of his bungalow to hide from the criminal gang threatening him. They were trying to recruit him to use his microlight for illicit purposes.

There was a tap on the bedroom door followed by Bart's head after Emily shouted "come in".

"How are you doing, Emily?" he asked, "Or do I call you Amelia now?"

"Well it is my name," she reminded him. "Peter registered me as Amelia at the hospital with Draper....I think he misses not having his old name. He says it's a bit like losing your identity, and why he chose PD James for his new name, to remind him of his old one while he created a new life for himself."

Bart noticed how sad she looked having severed all ties with her own past. Even though she found her father again, he also had begun a new life. Bart thought how lucky he was after having gone into Witness Protection, changing his name twice, he was now able to be the person he was before. This was because of the girl in the bed, who pushed him to start the Bartholomew and Hobbs Detective Agency. He thought *'thanks to Emily I am Bart Bridges, Private Investigator again!'*

"So?" said Bart Bridges, P.I, "You lied to the police? There must be a reason?"

Emily gasped, "Was I that obvious?" she asked.

"Not to someone who doesn't know you like I do. I might add who also knows you are normally a very truthful person," he said noting she looked quite guilty. "I know there has to be a reason."

She bowed her head shamefully, "I haven't been quite truthful with *you* lately," she confessed.

Bart smiled wryly, "You mean like not telling me about going on a 'date' with the gormless lad, Hamish to grill him about Gina Taylor?"

"You know about that?" Emily asked surprised. "And it wasn't a date!" she added irritably.

"Not according to Hamish!" Bart said teasingly. "So what else haven't you told me?"

"I saw Robbie," she said.

"I know lass. He was there with Peter when they found you in a shed," Bart said gently. "You told me at the hospital when you first opened your eyes."

Clearly Emily was baffled, "Robbie was there?" she asked. Bart nodded. "I didn't know. I meant I saw him in Nottingham when I went to see my Dad. Robbie is living there with a girl called Kirstie, I saw them together in a steak bar where she works and…" Emily blushed with embarrassment, "I followed them to where they live, not too far from my Dad, actually."

"Well, I can't dispute what you saw. I know Robbie went to work for an Operation investigating the people who kidnapped you. He's working undercover to establish who is in the network across the country. I have heard enough from a few people this was why he was there that night. According to Peter he had to go back to keep from being discovered."

Bart could see Emily was deep in thought. "You might want to talk to Peter about Robbie."

"How is Peter here?" She asked. Bart couldn't help laughing at how perplexed she looked.

"The short story is he's probably a good detective. He found us through the picture of us in the national newspapers after the bomb." The words 'good detective' prompted him further, "That reminds me, it was Michelle who found your car in the Quinnell's warehouse where it is still hidden as far as I am aware. Otherwise we wouldn't have known you could be there at all. We know they kept you tied to a chair in the small processing room next to where they grow the Cannabis."

"That must have been the bright light I could see!" Emily exclaimed. "They use them to grow ganja don't they?"

Bart nodded scowling at the same time, "What do you know about ganja?" he asked critically.

She could almost taste his disapproval, "Err, I once googled it. I found out all the words like hashish, hash, weed, pot…..and no, I have never even seen any let alone tried it!" she feigned indignation and then laughed letting him off the hook.

"Okay," he said, knew she spoke the truth, which prompted him to ask. "So what *do* you remember?" he asked.

He sat down on the dressing table stool whilst she began to tell him everything.

CHAPTER 88

The next day Bart met with Michelle, Peter, Isla Strachan, Jayson Vingoe, Lily Johns and Nessa McKinley to discuss everything after his lengthy session with Emily. She, of course, couldn't leave the castle. Bart felt it would draw too much attention to her if they all met at Daingneach. Consequently, before everyone arrived, Bart updated the white board by removing any reference to Emily being missing or the attempts on her life. On a whim he replaced the column with the Finlay Ferguson hit and run murder, which as far as he knew remained undetected. No one attending the meeting either noticed this or if they did, didn't mention it.

Finlay Ferguson (Blairgowrie)	Castle Daingneach	Quinnell Farm	Dinnet Bus Co. Building	Hotel	Bus Tour Building	Others:
Murdered	Mary & Mungo MacLeod	Rupert Quinnell Delores (wife) Rory (Son)	David Taylor Simon Copeland	Chuck Bistro Manager	Gina Taylor Finlay Ferguson	Harvey Williamson Jenny Iona Roberts Robbie Cowan
Hit & run 'Posh' car Dark colour Delores Quinnell Rory Quinnell	Attempt on Mary's life x2 Car accident Bomb	?Money laundering David Taylor Gina Taylor (Rupert's daughter)	Illegal use of building Storage of boxes Agency watching	Extortion ?Money laundering Finlay Ferguson Helen Daniels	Drugs Graffiti	
	Rupert/Rory/Delores Quinnell, Gina Taylor/David Taylor, Chuck, Hamish McGregor Mary/Mungo MacLeod					

The back room of The March of Time seemed even smaller. To accommodate everyone Bart retrieved the extra chair needed from the outside workroom where numerous clock parts were stored. After tea was made and biscuits produced, Bart stood in front of the gathering, initially deep in thought with a vagueness showing on his face. He was trying to decide where to start with one of the areas displayed on the board.

He glanced at the board yet again, pointing he said, "You will notice I have removed any reference to Emily's abduction. Thankfully she has been found." Everyone smiled. Before anyone present could ask any questions, he went on, "She is making a remarkable recovery given the state Peter found her in." He made no mention of the part Robbie played in her rescue, having been warned beforehand by Peter not to, since no one knew why he was there at the Quinnell farm. Telling them would only open up too many questions they were in no position to answer.

"The main thing bothering me about all of this," he made a circular motion with his finger, "is how any of these factors relate to each other....if indeed they do.....and of course why. An example being, the two attempts on Mary MacLeod's life to me seemed extreme given her only connection was she once worked for the Quinnell's many years ago. I understand Rupert Quinnell believed she discovered he was inflating the figures for the gift shop takings where she worked. His subsequent harassment of her seemed to both of us, out of proportion to his suspicion. Also it happened a long time ago. Mary managed to move on to get another job at Castle Daingneach where she met Mungo. The rest is history as you know.

Only one day fairly recently when Rupert Quinnell discovered her working in the gift shop at the castle, he developed the bizarre idea Mary was responsible for the decline in his takings at the farm. As a consequence, I imagine, the decline in his profits affects his ability to manipulate his money laundering."

"I don't get the significance, the castle wasn't even open to the public. One or two tour coaches stopping for a cup of tea in the café was hardly going to affect his takings," Lily said sounding sceptical.

"Exactly so," Bart agreed. "You don't try to kill someone for such a flimsy reason. However, Mary and Mungo are convinced Rupert is responsible for the attempts on her life."

"Aye, using an explosive is so extreme, could've killed an awful lot of other people," Nessa said.

"You don't think the bomb was meant for Emily, surely?" Michelle asked.

"No actually I don't," Bart said. Everyone gave a huge sigh of relief. *Otherwise I wouldn't have agreed to her staying there,* he thought. However, to minimise the risk, with the exception of Peter, everyone else believed she was still in hospital and not allowed visitors.

Bart looked at the white board again, pointed again at the white board. "There is a lot going on here, with many people involved, it's hard to unravel." He pieced some of it together from listening to snippets of what Emily heard, mostly from when she was tied to the chair in the warehouse with the rough sacking over her head. The people she heard were vague shapes she could only make out when the door to the growing room was open with the bright light dazzling behind them. There was no mistaking the voice of Gina Taylor. Emily knew the angry one was her step-brother David. The other ones came intermittently whilst she pretended to be unconscious.

As time went on she became more delirious. Then the people's voices she heard, were sometimes arguing, at other times making arrangements to move the ganja she could smell being grown there. The light was constant, fluctuating between a thin oblong outline to a full on shockingly intense brightness always accompanied by the silhouette of a person who seemed sometimes to be small, at others quite large.

Bart explained to Emily, her reference to the mannequin standing still in front of her, he believed was Gina Taylor because he saw similar behaviour when she came into the shop. Mrs Strachan also referred to her poses as 'doll like'.

Emily thought she was there some of the time, couldn't really be sure because she might have been delirious. At other times she heard her baby voice shouting at her angrily, blaming Emily for stopping 'that dishy copper' from working for her father who was really displeased when their attempts failed and he blamed Gina. Emily remembered hearing her say, "Same as Finn," she didn't understand why they were connected until Bart explained he thought Finn also refused to get pulled into working for them.

"At first I couldn't understand why Finn left, especially after accidentally meeting Charlotte in Aboyne, he discovered there was a real chance he could get his fiancé back. And, of course, all he really ever wanted. He certainly didn't leave the hotel because of my £20 note," Bart said. "Muriel Cameron, the manager, found it at the side of the till. She told me money had been going missing for a while which she hadn't reported to the police. Why not? What I do know is she wasn't the one who telephoned the police about Finn stealing the money. I believe that was the chef Chuck and was meant to scare Finn with the possibility of being charged and given him a criminal record to ruin his chances of getting the Restaurant Manager's job he planned on to get married."

"Didn't she leave him for Rory Quinnell?" Jay asked.

"Ah, yes. I understand from Charlotte the idea was Delores Quinnell's. She made Rory lure her away to live with him in the cottage on the estate to run the newly opened bakery bringing with her all her cake recipes for Delores to market as Quinnell produce. I think she was promised the bakery would be hers, but for all her considerable efforts the profits went directly into the Quinnell business and she had no say in the running of it. Charlotte told me she quickly came to regret moving in with Rory who clearly showed he wasn't interested in her, by which time Charlotte had become a virtual prisoner on the estate."

"Good gracious!" Peter said. "These people sound dreadful! Look what they did to Emily!"

"Yes they are, although I'm not sure Delores was involved in Emily's abduction," he said. Everyone stared waiting for him to tell them his theory. "Once Delores got Charlotte's cake recipes I'm even sure she wasn't bothered about her relationship with her son. Why would she? Charlotte managed to leave the farm anyway. In fact I would go as far as to suggest Delores was pleased she left."

"Why, if it was her idea in the first place?" Peter asked.

"Ah, she got what she wanted, the recipes. I suspect also because she knows Rupert has a preference for young girls. She saw he was beginning to turn his attention to Charlotte. She told Helen Daniels she was really scared of him when Helen got her away from them. Rupert ran the estate. He wouldn't let Charlotte use any of the cars they've got out there or have one of her own," Bart remembered Emily's anger at hearing this, especially using Charlotte as a virtual servant, in the bakery or at the elaborate parties they gave.

"Charlotte was convinced Delores knew about his proclivities going along with them as long as the business kept doing well. She still turns a blind eye to his amorous activities. I believe the key to a lot of this is Delores Quinnell enjoys her status as hostess of the Quinnell empire and will do whatever she can to keep the money rolling in. I understand she has once or twice gone as far as smoothing over Rupert's transgressions when his victims resorted to taking their complaint to the police."

"Is it the reason they recruit police officers to their organisation?" Michelle asked.

"Partly, although they may have other uses for them."

"You mean like when they paid off an underage Anabel Taylor after Rupert raped her and she got pregnant with Gina?" Peter asked.

"Well I actually think Delores didn't know about that.....at least not at the time. Rupert settled the matter himself. He paid Dougie Taylor to marry Anabel and drop the charge of rape against him. I think it was important to Rupert his wife didn't get to know about Gina, she was a far less understanding wife in those days. I think she found out about his daughter much later, we'll get to that."

Bart walked over to the board, stood staring at the photographs Isla and Michelle pinned up there. "I often wonder how any paternity disputes were ever resolved before DNA," he said rather philosophically. "I mean would you be able to tell Rupert Quinnell was Gina's father by looking at them?"

Isla said, "I've still not been able to get a picture of the lassie, although I've a mind she may have been photographed by her old school if I can contact the photographer who did them annually."

"Good thinking," Bart said enthusiastically, impressed by Isla's ingenuity. "But you've met her recently, Mrs Strachan...looking at Rupert Quinnell would you say there was any likeness?" Bart was keen to get her opinion because of her previous comment about Rory favouring his mother's looks.

"I always think the likeness shows in certain features, one in particular. There's bone structure, chins and often even teeth you can see a similarity in, but for me true likeness is always in the nose. In the lassie's case she favours Rupert Quinnell in they have similar delicate shaped noses," she walked closer to the board. "In this picture of him particularly, I would say he has a certain expression. I would argue a permanent sneer that makes him look like he's 'looking down his nose' at the rest of the world. It's a kind of arrogance." She said. Everyone scrutinise the photograph of him at a society function with his wife and son.

"Yes he does," Lily said. Everyone agreed.

"The problem with the crazy girl," Peter chipped in, "she changes her character often. It isn't obvious when she's pretending to be the little girl. When she gets angry, I have to say also very threatening, the arrogance is definitely there."

Bart immediately recalled the red lipstick she wore to make herself look more grown up. He realised the colour hardened her features from the sweet simple girl he saw whilst being served by her in the Co-op. He recollected how she stepped closer to the counter when he told her he already took on someone for the shop. She stared into his face in a challenging way. When he looked at Rupert Quinnell he could see the same pompous sneer of contempt.

"Peter you are quite correct. And yes, Mrs Strachan I can see the likeness between them!"

Since it was close to lunch time Bart declared the meeting should retire to The Moor Hen for lunch, he was certain Alistair would be able to accommodate them. In truth Bart's gastric juices were beginning to grumble, with doing most of the talking he was beginning to flag. He felt sure after a good wholesome meal Alistair would have waiting for them he would feel fortified enough to go on.

CHAPTER 89

Lunch was a light hearted affair, everyone without exception, buoyed by the news Emily was doing well. Isla Strachan, much to Bart's disappointment, declined because she needed to pop home for Hector after which she would return to open the shop in their absence. Bart didn't dwell too much on the matter, he already assumed someone like Isla would inevitably be married, she was an attractive woman. True to her word Isla was there serving a customer when the party of friends returned to continue their deliberations.

The afternoon session carried on where they left off after Mrs Strachan shut the shop to join them in the back room. Peter was explaining his encounter with Gina Taylor, filling them in on her rant concerning her father and her brother, both of whom she insisted loved her, then followed by her admission she hatred Delores Quinnell.

"Do you think Delores knows Gina is Rupert's daughter?" Peter asked.

"I think so," Bart replied, "although the knowledge might have been acquired in more recent times, probably after she went to live with her step-brother David when she left school. Robbie and Emily met Anabel Taylor having discovered her still living in the village. She showed great animosity towards her daughter for deserting her. Reading between the lines, coupled with Robbie's assertion the mother is an alcoholic," *he should know* Bart thought, "Anabel may have told her during a heated exchange who her father really is."

"I did get the impression she was blown away by Rupert Quinnell's fortune. She told me she blamed her mother, who she called 'the bitch', for keeping her father away most of her life," Peter filled in.

"I cannae think someone as volatile as her wouldnae be tempted to let Delores Quinnell know who she really is," Isla Strachan said shrewdly.

"I agree," Peter said. "She did tell me 'the bitch her father was married to hated her' and she knew things about her. I have to say she looked quite crazy at the time."

Bart smiled, gave a slight nod as if he understood what the girl was saying about Delores. Michelle was watching Bart closely, "You know what she means, don't you?" she asked him.

Bart looked like the question pushed him somewhere he didn't really want to go, he nodded all the same. "I do have an idea, yes." He walked over to the board again staring at the people pinned up there. "It's like we were saying, flimsy motives don't usually elicit quite such dramatic reactions, after all these people have co-existed for a lot of years. I won't say amicably, more indifferently," Bart said. "Everything can turn on a sixpence, as the saying goes or even 'ignorance is bliss' as my mother used to say. I can't say I understood a lot of the maxims she used when I was younger, however in this I believe she may have a point."

He looked around at those present, saw they all looked baffled by his sudden turn of phrase, "I'm not making much sense am I?"

He moved back to sit in his chair, then stood up again to add another log to the fire. Several of those present expected him to reach for the poker which he invariably did when he was irritated or annoyed. He didn't this time, he took a deep breath before explaining his theory.

"Several major things have happened to tip the balance. First came the change of ownership of Castle Daingneach. If Emily was here she would tell you about the myths and legends surrounding Seumus Grant's 'treasure' widely believed to be hidden somewhere;

and is a mystery yet to be resolved. I personally think his hidden treasure wasn't money or jewels but the fact he had a secret heir because he didn't have children with his wife. The lineage came down through the generations from a scullery maid, a Munro, resulting in Mungo MacLeod, who was Laird Munro's ghillie. Mungo's father was in possession of a deed of ownership of all the castle artefacts settled on Seumus Grant's only child from the scullery maid he made pregnant. To make amends he gave the castle itself to the Munro clan with the proviso neither one could be sold off without the others consent. For whatever reason, Laird Munro gave the castle to Mungo MacLeod, giving back his rightful entitlement to it. In addition, Mungo met Mary Macaulay, they....well fell in love I suppose," Bart seemed a tad embarrassed, whilst piecing together the elements he saw as a catalyst to cause a disruption to the equanimity; a sudden explosion of hate, resulting in the bomb at their wedding.

"I believe Mary herself sees the reaction to their becoming Laird and Lady MacLeod resulted from Rupert Quinnell's suspicion she found out he was laundering money from his drug's empire through the farm's businesses," there were a few nods of agreement. Those who hadn't previously known looked quite shocked, including Isla Strachan, Nessa, Lily and Peter. Jay remained quiet because he heard rumours at work something big was taking place around the region. "This, as they say, is only the tip of the iceberg, and wasn't really the cause of the extreme reactions."

Bart got up to go back to the board again. "What I think is…..when Delores found out about Gina's blood tie to Rupert, she immediately felt threatened for her only son, Rory, who was in line to inherit the whole estate with illicit businesses. I think, yes she saw this half breed girl would actually have a claim. May have even considered there was a need for a parental DNA test to make sure, something really quite recent to settle these kinds of disputes," he said.

"Well that would be quite easy to sort out wouldn't it?" Peter asked.

"I still don't see why all the hostility to Mary at the castle, she has nothing to do with Gina," Lily said.

"No quite right, which is why I've taken a long time to see the truth," he turned to Isla Strachan. "Thanks to Mrs Strachan's keen eye I was able to." He pointed to the picture of the Quinnells at a society gathering, "She pointed out to me how Rory Quinnell favours his mother, what she didn't say was how he didn't share any features of his father, Rupert," everyone looked closely at the picture. "Delores would know why, if Rory's father wasn't, in fact, Rupert Quinnell."

Two or three people gasped at the suggestion, "Well you could easily prove it with a DNA test," Nessa said.

"And if Rupert found out, the consequences could be quite dire for Delores and her son," Bart suggested.

Jay asked, "Have you any idea whose son he is?"

"Only when I remembered something Mary said to me one day at the castle. You see she moved the portrait of Seumus Grant from the library to the main entrance hall because Mungo looks the image of him. When I first saw the painting I believed he was actually Mungo. She told me there could be no disputing Mungo's right to the castle or the title having once been a ghillie and she only a shop assistant. She said having portraits painted was what passed in those days for DNA testing, as well as Mrs Strachan telling me how she looks at certain physical features like bone structure, chins and especially noses, to tell true relationship."

Bart unpinned the picture of Mary and Mungo from a glossy supplement they had taken before their wedding, intended to be used to produce their own ancestral portrait for the castle's historical succession. He placed the photograph alongside the Quinnell picture, turned to Isla Strachan, "Well Mrs Strachan what do you think?"

She took a step forward to examine it closely, "Both chin and nose," she said. "Rory is Mungo's son."

There followed absolute silence in the room.

CHAPTER 90

Emily found her convalescence at the castle very agreeable. She had to admit having her meals prepared for her by Maggie Wallace, the housekeeper, was a rare treat she could get used to. Since she moved into the castle she was given meals she hadn't ever tasted before, all made by Maggie using fresh vegetables from the castle kitchen garden, with meat and game reared on the castle estate, though Emily wasn't sure about eating venison she knew lived in the woods or pheasant she saw flying about the place. She was pushed even more towards being a vegetarian.

Even as a child she never had it this good. She knew the reason was something to do with her mother having her own café, The Silver Teapot. After spending a whole day making and serving food, cooking was the last thing she wanted to do when she got home. Emily was used to the leftover food brought home by her mother which meant her meals were a strange combination of things that didn't always go together. She wasn't surprised her father eventually moved out, although more to do with finding out her aunt and uncle were murderers. He wasn't sure how much Thelma was involved in their activities.

Emily found good food conducive to her recovery, it wasn't long before she was up and about. She got to spend a lot of her time in the room Mary allocated to her and Bart, next to the kitchen where they repaired the castle clocks. Bart thought it wise to mend the more valuable ones on site. He didn't want to risk having them in the shop, even after he sought out more suitable insurance for his own collection.

Whilst confined there Emily used her time to continue their clock contract for the MacLeods. Since the explosion on their wedding day, there were a greater number needing attention than before.

The fact of being resident also gave Emily the opportunity to explore the castle at her leisure. Much work was being undertaken to prepare for the opening of the main rooms to the public. At other times she would wander around taking in the castle's history, some of which she had already discovered whilst looking for Mungo when he was the Laird's missing ghillie.

She became intrigued hearing the story of Seumus Grant's treasure and Bart chanced upon the tunnels under the castle with access to them from the moving fire basket in the large open plan fireplace in the library. They followed the tunnels to the Hide in the woods, the arrangement being left over from the days of feuding clans battling for territory.

When Emily wasn't working on the clocks, to pass the time she used books from the library to further her knowledge of the castle history contained in a vast array of old leather bound tomes. She took them to read in her room at night. She liked her bedroom because it was where Robbie stayed when he was being pursued by the people who wanted him to pilot his microlight to transport drugs around the country. She felt close to him there and despite seeing him with his new girlfriend she was sure when they were together they became really close. She dared to believe they might have a future together.

The one thought kept intruding whilst she read up on local history often finding herself reading the same sentence over many times. She couldn't quite believe after such a short time away from her Robbie could have taken up with someone else, even though she saw him with her own eyes. She wasn't proud of herself for following the couple. At the time, her anger erupted. When he left her she made a conscious decision to wait for him to come back, because she was sure he would. Until she saw his bungalow was up for sale.

During one of Bart's visits to her at the castle he updated her on everything about the Agency and she learnt Robbie's bungalow wasn't for sale at all, only made to look that way in case of prying eyes. Bart also explained Jenny Williamson's role, a favour to her sister because Iona Roberts, who helped Lily to divorce her husband was related to Robbie on his mother's side, therefore deemed to be his next of kin.

After hearing Bart's update, Emily came to the conclusion if she didn't know about his new girlfriend, the news would have otherwise given her hope of a future with Robbie. She knew she wouldn't be able to move on until she knew whether he intended to come back and if he did would he bring Kirstie with him? She spent time going over it again, like she did when he first left.

One day when Peter came to visit her at the castle he told her, "I met your boyfriend, Robbie, he helped me get you out of the shed and he sent help to take you to hospital."

"Did he?" she was shocked by the news. "I don't understand...why was he there?"

Peter couldn't answer her. He could only tell her, "All I know is he said he needed to go back because he had a job to do."

Emily, of course, knew he was going back to Nottingham to Kirstie and didn't dwell too much on him being there at the Quinnell farm. No amount of times Peter told her Robbie was extremely concerned about her, made him promise to get medical help and keep her safe, could he convince Emily otherwise. Her mind was full of images of Robbie, his arm entwined in Kirstie's looking up at the darkened kitchen window where she stood watching them, as if he knew she was there and wanted her to know he moved on and so should she.

Her thoughts became a living torment from which she saw no escape, therefore would never be able to 'move on'. She tried to read the history book in her hand. This late at night she felt lonely remembering how Robbie always contacted her before they went to sleep, to say good night, even if they were too tired to have a lengthy conversation.

She thought about him lying in bed in his bungalow in the near dark; sometimes they would chat for a long time, especially if they went flying the same day. He liked to hear what she felt like up amongst the clouds. She would have given anything to hear his voice again, to ask him why he deserted her. Even knowing the bungalow wasn't really for sale, gave her no comfort. She couldn't get beyond how she felt seeing the For Sale sign the day Jenny Williamson let herself inside.

Emily suddenly sat up in bed having an idea how she might find out one way or the other what his intentions were. *I can write him a letter!* She immediately felt excited. If Mrs Ernest was picking up his mail for him, Robbie would be getting it where he was now living. The idea made her feel a little better for having thought of writing to him. She would find some paper and an envelope in the morning and ask Maggie Wallace to post it for her.

Comforted, Emily placed her book on the bedside cabinet, switched off the lamp to settle down to sleep.

CHAPTER 91

Robbie returned to the small greenhouse where he spent a sleepless night worrying about Emily, waiting for the call from Sid Bailey his services were needed to take him back to Nottingham. Given the plushness he saw in the big house before he left, he expected Sid to take his time to lap up the luxurious living. In this he was wrong. Surprisingly, the call came about seven o'clock. Robbie brushed down the creases in the overlarge suit as best he could before walking back to the mansion where Sid was already standing in front of the stretch limo. He didn't look too pleased to be kept waiting.

Robbie wondered what he would have been like if he had found somewhere to sleep off site. He was pleased he hadn't attempted to visit his bungalow. He may not have found Emily or even known she was in trouble. He didn't much care for the idea of working with Sid or the people who put her life in danger he was now mixing with. His initial reaction to Bailey's morose mood was to take note of Bear's warnings not to upset him further.

When they arrived back in the confined space of the plane, from the heavy smell of whiskey coming off Sid, Robbie deduced he either drank a lot the night before, or helped himself to the mini bar in the back of the limo. Whichever was the case, the alcohol failed to improve his temper. Robbie found him ill-humoured, he muttered critically whilst Robbie went through the formalities to get them airborne. He was grateful, at least this early in the morning he was unlikely to bump into anyone who knew him.

After a lengthy silence from the seat next to him, Robbie could take it no longer, he asked Sid if he was feeling okay. The last thing he wanted was for him to throw up in the cockpit. He toyed with handing him a sick bag like he had with Bear.

"I'm alright," Sid growled. "If you had to suffer what I went through last night you wouldn't be feeling happy." Robbie did a double take trying to work out what could have been worse than the night he'd spent, there was no pleasing some people. Sid saw him glance his way, "Pompous fucking bastards!" he growled.

Robbie decided now was not the time to mention at least he got a good feed with a comfortable bed for the night, was more than he did. Instead he said, "That's society folk for yer." Once out of his mouth he couldn't take his comment back, he quickly added, "The posh lassie in the sparkly frock looked alright."

"More than I can say for her pervy husband!" Sid Bailey's disgust made Robbie wonder how Rupert Quinnell offended him. He thought about Sid's own behaviour. If he thought touching up a waitress in a steak bar or trying to tempt her with a fat wad of money he flicked in front of her face was okay, what on earth did he see? Robbie kept hold of his temper.

"Oh?" he said.

"I saw for myself," Sid said with much contempt.

"Was he all over the female guests?" Robbie asked.

"Hell no!" he said vehemently. "That might have been acceptable. At least they were all adults. The bastard couldn't keep his hands of the girls waiting table. They were barely of age. I wouldn't like him doing that if one of 'em was my daughter." Sid went on to describe wandering around near to the kitchens trying to find a toilet, coming across Quinnell (only Sid called him the bastard lord of the manor) when he pushed open a door, to find him....words failed him. He fell into a sulk.

Eventually after much ruminating he said, "Do I want to do business with a child rapist?"

The statement shocked Robbie. He tried to remember the waitresses he saw circulating with drinks, could only recollect Gina

Taylor being young enough to fit his description although the others weren't much older.

Robbie asked, "Was she wearing red lipstick?" Sid looked up accusingly as if Robbie had been spying on him, a warning Robbie needed to be very careful. "I saw a wee young girl carrying a tray before I left." The idea Sid Bailey might have some morals seemed strange to Robbie.

"Yes," he replied grumpily. Then after thinking some more added, "She didn't seem to be putting up any resistance, maybe she was too scared."

Sid fell silent again for a while until he uttered contemptuously, "Fucking society people – they're like animals!"

Once back in Nottingham Sid didn't hang around because 'blue suit' was waiting for him in Sid's Roller to whisk him away leaving Robbie thinking 'never mind the society people, gangsters have no manners or morals', he hadn't even got a 'thank you' for all his efforts and the discomfort he went through. He was of a mind to have a word if this was the way he would be treated. Then he recalled Bear's limp, wondered if he once spoke back to Sid and got maimed for his trouble. Bear was mighty keen to make sure Robbie didn't over-step the mark, perhaps he was doing him a favour.

CHAPTER 92

Bart was surprised when Helen Daniels quite openly sought him out in the middle of the day in the shop. He deliberately didn't take her through to the back room because the white board contained a lot of information about the agency's business. The thought prompted him to consider how the board might be adapted to close off the view to visitors. He thought he would ask Mrs Strachan if she had any ideas. For now, he wasn't about to ask Helen if she wanted a drink or take her through to the back room.

He invited her to sit down at the work table behind the counter whilst he sat on the stool, putting him at a higher level to her which wasn't his intention. For the first time since he'd known her he felt at a loss what to say, he merely asked how she was.

"Fine," she said. "I came to say I'm pleased you've found Emily. I was wondering how she was."

Bart thought her enquiry strange, at best superficial, because he knew Operation Graffiti, particularly Robbie Cowan's handler, who stayed outside her room for most of her time in hospital, were well aware of her medical condition. He would have expected Helen to have been updated if she asked them. Suspiciously he thought this wasn't why she came.

"She's fine," Bart said, not elaborating further. He didn't want to open a dialogue about how close Emily came to not being fine, if Peter hadn't found her. He noticed Helen's discomfort at his far from friendly response and knew immediately she was there doing their bidding. He could sense she was far from comfortable doing it. "Why are you here?" he asked having no intention of making the matter easy for her.

Helen looked down at her shoes clearly unhappy to be there. She said, "I do genuinely care about Emily, you know."

Bart's anger flared, "So what did you do with the information about her car being hidden in the warehouse?" he suddenly demanded.

"I passed it on of course, Bart," she said. She looked back down at her shoes again, "Someone went to have a look, the car wasn't in there."

She could see Bart's shock. "Did they get the right place....the warehouse behind the row of greenhouses?"

She nodded. "Yes, they saw where it was kept because there was a space with a folded up cover close by."

"Did they find the Cannabis growing room?"

"They already knew the room was there because they have been watching their activities for a while," she said.

"And did they find the chair where they kept Emily tied up, in the small room next to it?" Helen looked startled, her reaction showing she clearly knew nothing about the room. "So they have tidied up after themselves, have they?" Bart was greatly puzzled how Rory and Gina managed to get Emily's car out without anyone on surveillance noticing.

"I think there was a social function taking place at the main house the Operation was concentrating on. They didn't get my message about Emily's car until the party began to break up. They couldn't leave because they were intelligence gathering, trying to identify the people attending. I understand when the message came through about needing emergency help after you found Emily, they were able to get her out without attracting attention," she said. Bart was surprised she gave him this much information.

He was torn about whether to divulge Michelle's forensic evidence gathering. He wasn't sure whether she would get into trouble if Helen passed the information on. Bart still wanted to know the reason why she came. He didn't quite believe it was to make enquiries about Emily's recovery.

"What a shame," he said instead. "There would be a good deal of forensic evidence to be had." For a moment he allowed his thoughts to dwell on what he would have done in his Scenes of Crime days because he knew the person who hit Emily on the head would have been in the back seat of the car to take her by surprise. They would have left fibres there as well as on the driving seat because Emily would have been transported to the warehouse by whoever drove her car to the warehouse.

Helen merely nodded asking, "Has anything come back to Emily since she left hospital?"

Bart kept a neutral face. Clearly Helen did know about Emily's recovery, she was there on a fishing trip. He shook his head, "Nothing at all," he lied. Whether she believed him or not he didn't really care. "We're just pleased she's safe."

"That's really why I came," Helen said. "Is she really safe? The Operation thinks she would be better off being hidden by us. These people can be ruthless. If they find her she might not be so lucky next time."

"I have two problems with your statement. One is, having been through *your* Witness Protection Programme was NOT safer than being on my own. In my case I was hunted down by a corrupt copper, in fact my Witness Protection handler, who was recruited by one of the 'ruthless' people you refer to. I wasn't safe at all. The other thing is, Helen, I don't think what happened to Emily has anything to do with the syndicate you are watching, at least not their main activities. I think this was personal." He knew enough to realise drug dealing and protection didn't come into it; family and entitlement made people do crazy things.

He expected Helen to ask him what he did think was involved, but she didn't. She stood up having decided there was nothing more she could say to influence Bart's stubborn stance on the subject. She walked around the counter seeming to deliberate on what she would say next.

"The message is the same as last time," she said.

The rest was unspoken. Bart knew the message was to keep out of everything, which he had no intention of doing. He stood silently as she left the shop. Helen didn't close the door because Isla Strachan was waiting to enter the shop returning from her lunch break.

"She doesnae look very happy," Isla said closing the door behind her.

"I suppose not," Bart said absently. "Mrs Strachan I was wondering what we could do with the white board in the back room, it's kind of exposed for all to see if we were to have visitors unexpectedly. I would appreciate if you have any ideas how we might be able to conceal what is written up there?"

"Aye, I've got McTavish coming to fit a roller blind across the top, that we can lower and raise as we please," she said.

Bart smiled at her ingenuity, turned to leave for the back room to make some tea whilst he ruminated over his conversation with Helen Daniels.

CHAPTER 93

When retribution came it was like a carefully set up sequence of dominoes where the resulting pattern could not have been foreseen. Nor, after the first one was knocked over, the rest would fall in the way they did. All it took was a rookie copper just out of probation under supervision, a night off by anyone in a position to intervene and one telephone call from an ex-police officer with an axe to grind. Michelle made the call on impulse when she once again saw the face of the man who haunted her nightly dreams.

"Someone is breaking into McKinley's garage at Dinnet," she told the control room operator before she hung up. She made sure she vacated the rear compound leaving no evidence of her presence behind and was at a sufficient distance not to be seen should anyone actually turn up in response to her call.

She wasn't meant to be there at all. Bart suggested they leave off surveillance of the abandoned Bus Company having already established what was happening there. He couldn't see what more they would accomplish. With Emily's lack of availability due to her confinement to the castle, he was short staffed still.

The other compounding factor was a telephone call from Iona Roberts with a new commission for the Agency which he would put Michelle McElrae on starting next day. Knowing this made Mitch pay one last visit to McKinley's, not exactly with the intention to watch the building for any more nightly activity. She planned to break into the building in the early hours to take some pictures of David Taylor and Copeland's boxes of weed. She already got a picture of them being taken inside.

Whilst Mitch waited for the right time, she knew if they came, they wouldn't risk staying beyond the early morning milk float delivery at around five o'clock. She was surprised when they actually turned up. Whether it was Copeland's arrogance he couldn't be seen at the rear of the building, or his obvious dislike of the irritation of the balaclava, he wasn't wearing his when they arrived. She watched him through the monocular telescope from the next door compound. With the light shining from inside the open door, his face provoked in her an acute attack of anger making her relive the memory of his voice once again in her head, *'Come on, bitch, you know you like it!'*

After they disappeared inside she moved fast, already dialling 999 before she reached her car down the road. She made the call, not really believing someone would come out in time to catch them inside. She waited and was rewarded by a police response car arriving.

They parked to block the white Highway Ma ntenance van on the next door forecourt which surprised her. Usually response was single crewed at night due to police shortages unless there was a report of a crowd disturbance. They were mostly town based, not out in the sticks. She recognised the older police officer because she previously worked with him, knew he often accompanied newly appointed constables straight out of probation so assumed the other one was.

Taylor and Copeland were just emerging from the back of the Bus Company building carrying one of the large boxes, when the officers got out of their car. She noticed Simon Copeland was still not wearing a balaclava. She could only imagine what took place next, being too far away to hear the dialogue. She knew most regular police officers would be aware of what happened to their ex-colleague Copeland, which might have been the reason the officers challenged what they were carrying out of an empty building in the middle of the night.

She saw the younger one touch his radio to speak into it because he turned away to do it. He was smiling, *good boy, call for back up*, was barely a whisper to escape her. She knew the first vehicle to arrive was Traffic response because she was called many times if she was in the area of an incident to help when back up was needed. It must have been a quiet night because the response was more than she hoped for when others came to join in.

Michelle wanted to slap the steering wheel in her excitement at watching the drama unfold. She stayed long enough to see David Taylor and Copeland being taken away in handcuffs after the box they were carrying was opened to check the contents. After this she slipped away unnoticed. If anyone heard her car engine they would have seen someone moving off a driveway up the road, one she backed on to make the turn. They would have seen someone leaving for an early shift at work.

* * * * *

Next day Michelle arrived at The March of Time to be given her new assignment. She made no mention of her previous night's visit to McKinley's not even when Bart told her Jay texted him to say he was called to the Bus Company building to undertake a forensic search on both the inside of the abandoned building and the Highway Ma ntenance van. Later, after Michelle left for Aberdeen to watch Harvey Williamson for Iona Roberts, Bart learnt about David Taylor and Simon Copeland being arrested.

Several days later on Jay's rest days, he met Bart in the back room of the shop for a private chat having spent the intervening time working first at Dinnet, then transferred to the warehouse on the Quinnell estate where he with several other SCI's had been working the premises, not only the drug growing area, also the main equipment area where Emily's mini had been hidden and the room where she was held captive.

"What about Operation Graffiti?" Bart asked surprised at the development, "I thought the Quinnell estate was out of bounds to mainstream policing?"

"Ah, yes, it was what I found inside the white van at Dinnet that changed everything," Jay said. Bart looked at him with anticipation. "We found the number plates for Emily's mini in the back of the van.....apparently Rory or Gina left them in there when they disposed of her car." Jay smiled his appreciation at their stupidity. "Apparently by implication Simon Copeland has also been interviewed about what happened to Emily, which I understand is now being investigated as an attempted murder."

Shocked, Bart sat down heavily in his armchair by the fire, "Wow!" he said.

"That's not all," Jay added. "It looks to me like Operation Graffiti's hand has been forced. They are working closely with the local police on these new enquiries because they have a good deal of information to help them. Rupert Quinnell has also been taken in. I don't know any details though. Agatha only hears rumours in the canteen."

"I expect they will want to know if Rupert Quinnell was involved in the weed growing enterprise on *his* farm, wouldn't they?" Bart suggested sarcastically. "What are the rumours going round the canteen?" he asked eagerly.

"Bizarrely, they are more about DI Morris being suspended, although no one seems to know why."

"Ah, I wonder," Bart looked bemused. "I believe the night Peter and Robbie found Emily in the shed, the Quinnell's were having one of their parties Charlotte Reynolds told us they often have, being their way of recruiting 'new' people into their business. Fortunate for Emily because the Operation was there gathering intelligence and photographing the guests attending. They were able to get her to the hospital quickly....which I understand saved her life." Bart looked sad at the thought of how close he came to losing her. "If there were any police officers at the party, they would have evidence wouldn't they?" Bart was specifically thinking about Morris who he always suspected was involved with the Quinnells. "I don't expect we will discover if he was or in what capacity, perhaps he will get what he deserves……." There he left it not wanting to explain the part Morris played in suppressing Michelle's rape by Copeland.

As the thought came to him he asked, "How did the police happen to be in Dinnet to arrest them?"

Jay thought for a moment, "I believe they got an anonymous telephone call to the control room, probably one of the neighbours saw the van, got suspicious and didn't want to get involved. Often happens," Jay said.

Bart smiled thinking whoever made the call did everyone a huge favour. He immediately thought of Mary MacLeod confined like a prisoner to the castle, not daring to go anywhere for fear she might be a target for yet another attempt on her life. *Ditto for Emily also* he thought.

CHAPTER 94

Several weeks went by during which Bart picked up snippets of news about the Quinnells but nothing about Gina Taylor or her stepbrother David. He felt like the world had come to a standstill. He could appreciate how Mary and Emily must feel frozen in time at Castle Daingneach. Apart from the shop, mostly covered by Mrs Strachan (only closing when she went home to take care of Hector), his castle clock maintenance contract was progressing, undertaken mostly on site by Emily.

Michelle he entrusted with the Iona Roberts request. He saw very little of Peter whom he suspected spent a good deal of his time helping her with it. He noticed they had grown close and Peter showed no sign of leaving the Highlands to return to London, offering as an excuse he could undertake his games programming from anywhere.

As a distraction from the ennui of all the waiting, Bart closed the shop on Thursday midday to go out for a walk. The weather turned fine with the onset of spring, bringing many delights to the Highlands after the big thaw was over. Consequently, today Bart turned right out of The March of Time to climb The Brae to the duck pond at the top.

Bart didn't especially like ducks as a species, he found they had a habit of chasing after him. His prejudice came about one day, early on in his residency of The Brae, he took with him on one of his walks, some stale bread to feed them. He hadn't anticipated they would be as eager in their desire to be fed. They pecked at his trouser legs and didn't seem to mind if they caught some flesh along with cloth.

To embrace the idea they recognised him, Bart knew was irrational. He imagined their beady eyes alighting on the shape of him if he stopped off to sit on the bench at the side of the pond. Thankfully there were none to be seen giving him the opportunity to sit on the bench to rest, take in the air with a slight breeze, enjoying the midday sun on his face. He closed his eyes, for a moment enjoying absolute peace and quiet. Until he heard the unmistakeable sound of a 'quack' guaranteed to fill him full of dread.

He opened his eyes, looked across the expanse of the pond where he saw a squadron of ducks in an arrow shaped formation heading his way. One fat mallard was leading the charge, with the two pronged lines behind perfecting the arrow. He imagined all those web-feet beneath the surface working furiously to keep up to not break the line.

Oh lordy!

The configuration was only yards away. Bart briefly wondered, if their eyesight was good enough to spot him, they ought to be able to see he carried no bread wrappings, bags or stale slices to hand. It didn't seem to bother them at all, they kept coming quacking excitedly. Suddenly, at his feet appeared a black Scottish terrier. His long straggly whiskers were wet as if the animal had been drinking from the pond or maybe even been in for a paddle.

Around his neck he wore a red collar with a tartan kerchief in Royal blue, bottle green and a thin red stripe to make the square pattern. Although Bart could recognise very few tartans, this one he thought came close to the Black Watch he knew about.

Initially, the dog stood perfectly still watching the approaching company of ducks until he suddenly leapt forward to bark ferociously at them. Bart was sure if he could understand canine, his noise was a warning to keep away. The animal showed no fear of the number of ducks, his warning suddenly changed to a fearsome guttural growl beginning deep inside his throat, it sounded more menacing than the bark.

As if in response, the lead duck detoured to the right leading the convoy in an arc until the whole squadron turned about face heading back the other way. Bart looked in amazement, whilst the dog recommenced barking and pacing along the edge of the pond. When it was obvious the ducks were retreating, the dog presented himself to Bart to be fussed. He cheered him on with, "Good boy! You showed them!"

"He cannae abide the ducks," Bart looked up when he recognised Isla Strachan's voice. She was standing next to him holding the dog's lead.

"He's yours?" Bart asked delightedly still making a fuss of him. The dog had jumped up onto the bench beside him and was wagging his tail in appreciation of receiving Bart's approval.

Isla bent down to clip the lead onto the dog's collar, "Yes I thought you knew I always take Hector for a walk at lunchtime."

"Hector?" Bart boomed joyfully. "Mrs Strachan, I thought Hector was your husband!"

"Och, no. I've been widowed for more years than I can count and don't recollect ever taking my husband for a walk!" Despite her attempt at humour, Bart saw the subtle sadness behind her eyes, he pursued it no further.

They parted at the top of The Brae. Isla Strachan continued on with Hector whilst Bart walked back down the hill away from the pond, not wanting to encourage his feathered friends to return since he had lost his canine protector. The return walk was easier for the downhill slope. Bart strolled slowly enjoying the day.

Halfway down he caught sight of a figure standing outside his shop. They were leaning against the glass of the door, hands cupped either side of their head to block out the glare from the sun, peering inside. When the figure straightened up Bart recognised Helen Daniels as she turned to look his way. *What does she want now?*

"Lovely day," Bart said conversationally when he got close enough for her to hear. Helen didn't smile or respond to his comment. He wondered when she lost the spark of friendliness he once knew.

Without another word, Bart took out his key, opened up allowing Helen to precede him inside. He knew to come here openly must be indicative of something. He locked the shop again leading her towards the back room. When he abruptly stopped Helen Daniels nearly walked into him. The impelling thought which halted him was the white board in the back room, yet to receive a roller blind, no one had been inspired to update lately. He turned to challenge her, "If you're here to try to persuade me……"

"No!" she interrupted quickly. Now she did smile, "No nothing like that," she said. "I came to say goodbye. I leave tomorrow."

"Oh?" He said surprised. He was expecting to be challenged, to give Emily up to the wiles of the 'black hole' of witness protection. He wasn't ever going to do that. He turned away to continue into the back room where he deliberately didn't look to the back wall to draw attention to the board. "Why are you leaving?" he asked. "I thought if you were, you would just disappear….isn't that the way it's done?"

Helen chuckled sensing his latent hostility close to the surface. "I regret the way things worked out. I hoped you would realise, I had little choice about distancing myself from you. None of us knew who we could trust….."

"I would have thought, Helen, you would have known you could trust me," he sounded a little hurt by the comment.

"Yes, of course I do. That's not what I meant," she said sounding offended herself. "I was shocked when Finn was killed. Even Operation Graffiti thought the hotel could be key to the organisation's operation, they told me to be extra careful no one suspected I was a plant. Don't forget Finn's was the second murder…"

"Yes but, everyone knew who killed Philip Miller. His murder was nothing to do with anybody's drug empire. Martin Frances was convicted...."

"Yes, Bart I know about Lily's husband, look at it from my point of view. I was to become the *new* hotel manager whilst Finley would maybe have become the Restaurant Manager if he hadn't been killed," she looked to Bart for some kind of understanding of her nervousness.

Bart sat down facing her saying nothing. After a lengthy pause Helen looked disappointed then continued, "I came to give you an update on what we've found out since the incident at Dinnet. Call it my unofficial parting gift."

"So you know Rory Quinnell, David Taylor and Simon Copeland have a lucrative business growing Cannabis?" Bart's tone was very much one of 'tell me something I don't know'.

She laughed, "Yes, they could hardly claim is for personal use."

"Quite," Bart thought for one moment she was going to tell him that was their claim which let them off due to some police internal sleight of hand. "Only the tip of the iceberg really isn't it?"

"The real drug business is much bigger, yes. Rory Quinnell was making money on the side, following in Daddy's footsteps. He was into petty drug dealing from when he was at school. As time went by he began to grow his own to sell weed not only to the school kids locally," she said.

"I assume this is where Gina came in with her step-brother David and why he was taken on as a gardener at the Quinnell estate?" Helen nodded. "Am I right in thinking the money from their little drug enterprise was being laundered through the hotel?"

Helen shook her head, "Actually no, that's what they wanted to do. Chuck the Chef was involved in trying to set it up..."

"He was using the Bistro to do some of it, wasn't he?" Bart guessed.

"Yes, he had something on the owner, probably to do with his personal use especially because the man's business wasn't doing too well. He put up his prices to compensate for what he was being asked to do thereby losing customers in the process. There's not much spare money around in a village where the majority of people coming through are tourists who eat mostly at their hotels....well you can imagine the rest."

"Indeed I can, I was the only customer when I ate there," Bart said. He had a sudden thought, "You aren't about to tell me Finn was killed by Chuck are you?"

"Absolutely not," she said. "Chuck only played a minor part, he didn't feature in the bigger picture at all. He did, however, get paid to put pressure on Finlay who was about to get the manager's job in the restaurant, then Charlotte left him for Rory. Finn, as you know went to pieces, drank a lot and started causing problems at the Quinnell farm because he couldn't accept she left him. He was making a nuisance out at the farm and annoying them."

"Is this where Gina comes in?" Bart asked. Helen nodded. "Emily told me she really liked Finn making a play for him even before he split up with Charlotte. She would know about David's role in growing weed. I can imagine, from what I've seen of her, she saw herself as Finn's potential girlfriend, partners in crime, selling the weed to school kids, cleaning the money maybe through the hotel before taking the profits. She must have been really delighted when Rory took Charlotte away, perhaps even saw herself as moving into the flat above the Co-op with Finn to finally be able to leave her mother."

"How do you know all this?" Helen asked impressed.

"I have a very impressive detective in my partner Emily," he looked mightily smug. "And reading between the lines I could even hazard a guess as to why she left the village when she moved in with her step-brother David." Helen gestured for him to go on. "When Finn lived with Charlotte above the shop, engaged to be married, Finn was.....shall we say like any man would be.....flattered by Gina's adolescent crush on him to the point where he even encouraged her a bit. Gina told Emily after Charlotte left he changed, became unkind to her which she put down to his drinking."

"Ah, that explains what happened later," Helen said.

She went on to tell Bart how Gina spotted Finn in the Emporium at Aboyne when he bumped into Charlotte on his birthday. By this time Gina had moved in with David at the Quinnell farm and was being used by Rupert for a lot of things, one being to spy on Charlotte. With a job centrally in the village she was used to set up people who might be of use to the syndicate's business. "When Gina moved out of her mother's house, during a huge drunken row with Anabel who accused her of being like her father, Rupert Quinnell she found out he was her real father, not Dougie Taylor. She learnt Rupert raped her mother, getting her pregnant with her. I believe, from what has come out of the many interviews with her, although they haven't been particularly coherent or rational, I imagine the news of her parentage sent her a little crazy."

"I think she was already crazy, it certainly would have tipped her over," Bart said. "Did she tell Delores Quinnell about Finn meeting up with Charlotte and the woman ran him over in her red Porsche?"

"No. She told Rory who was living with Charlotte at the time, little knowing he had no interest in her. Gina hated Delores, even more after she discovered she was Rupert's daughter. She saw her chance to be recognised as one of his heirs to the whole shebang. She grew close to Rory, and didn't seem to be bothered he was her half-brother, having already had a relationship with her step-brother. Ever since, she's had a wild time together with Rory, riding around the county on his Harley and as you know forcing cars off the road."

Bart looked puzzled, "But Finn was run over by a sporty car as he was hitching back to Glasgow."

"They also have a habit of taking one of the cars, hard to say whether Rupert's or Delores' Porsche, to go joy riding. They got caught up in the tail backs at Blairgowrie. I understand Gina recognised Finn even in all the rain, stamped on Rory's foot on the accelerator, pulling the steering wheel to turn the car to run over him."

"Oh lordy!" Bart said shocked.

"Yes, they couldn't get Rory to shut up once he realised he might be in line for Finn's murder. Apparently she was angry Finn was leaving because she wanted him to get back with Charlotte then she could live with Rory."

Bart moved over to put the kettle on to make some tea inviting Helen to join him for a bite of lunch which she accepted. He busied himself with making cheese and pickle sandwiches. When he turned back he saw Helen standing in front of the white board studying it.

CHAPTER 95

Helen moved back to the chair next to Bart's where he placed her lunch on a side table. For a while they ate in silence. He watched as she kept glancing up at what was written on the board. Eventually she said, "I think you were perhaps one step ahead of us on most things."

"Maybe," he said modestly.

"I'm impressed with all the photographs, someone has been busy."

Bart could see the picture of Mungo and Mary still pinned next to the family one of the Quinnells, he asked, "How far have they got with the Castle bomb or the other attempt on Mary MacLeod's life?"

"I think they got a bit side-tracked there," Helen said. "Especially as Mungo and Mary were convinced Rupert was at the bottom of them."

"Yes, a bit of an extreme reaction after discovering her working in the castle gift shop, blaming her for a dip in his takings." Bart said. "After all his suspicion she knew about the money laundering on the estate happened years ago, nothing came of it. You would have expected her to go to the police at the time. Apart from which I know Mary really didn't understand what it was all about anyway."

"So why try to kill her?" Helen asked.

"I don't believe Rupert did," Bart said. "Only when I saw the resemblance between Rory and Mungo it occurred to me." Helen got up, moving back to the board to get a better view of the two photographs.

"I can't really see the resemblance myself," Helen said. "Rory looks like his mother."

"I understand the key is the nose, chin and bone structure, although Rory does have sandy coloured hair which neither Rupert nor Delores do." Helen came back to sit down again. "I can't even begin to understand how Delores came together with Mungo, after all he was the castle ghillie while she is the wife of a wealthy Scottish businessman. She has run her particular roost with an iron hand, even knowing all about her husband's indiscretions. I imagine she would have been furious at finding out the snip of a girl living on her estate was, in fact, her husband's daughter."

"Most women would have divorced their husband for less or at least demanded a DNA test," Helen said.

Bart laughed knowingly, "Not if you knew your only son was someone else's child." Helen scowled trying to work out how she would have reacted. "Think about it. She was trying to pass Rory off as the heir to the Quinnell fortunes, then finds out Gina has birth right to it. If she challenged it, then her little secret might come out with potentially dire consequences for both her and her son. She kept quiet."

Helen's face brightened, "Then Mungo MacLeod became laird of Daingneach, the intended to Mary Macaulay, but……" at this point Helen lost the thread.

"I think she became extremely angry. Delores ended up married to a feckless husband with a perverted taste for young girls and she could have been the Lady of a castle with the son and rightful heir to the title, but lost out to someone she used to employ as a shop assistant?"

"Hence another hit and run when her anger at Mary's good fortune tipped her over?" Helen suggested.

"Exactly," Bart agreed. "And the bomb where many of us could have died, was Delores as well?"

"Ah, the bomb....is a bit of a mystery," she said. "I wonder if a mother would want to spoil what could actually be Rory's rightful inheritance."

So saying they both continued to eat their sandwich in silence, Bart having nothing further to add to the debate, he moved on to wondering what 'Helen Daniels' or whatever her name really was intended to do.

"So you move on?" he said.

She stood up to leave, took one last look at the white board, "How is Harvey Williamson involved?"

Bart smiled, "He is nothing to do with any of your enquiries," he said.

Satisfied with the answer she moved towards the door to leave. Bart got up to follow her out. There was an embarrassing silence after he opened the shop door to let her out. Bart couldn't suppress his chivalrous side, "Take care of yourself Helen."

"You too, Bart," there was one moment when he thought she was about to lean forward to kiss his cheek.

The moment passed, she was gone. He left the shop open, going back to squeeze another cup of tea from the pot, settle down again to glance once more at his white board.

Finlay Ferguson (Blairgowrie)	Castle Daingneach	Quinnell Farm	Dinnet Bus Co. Building	Hotel	Bus Tour Building	Others:
Murdered	Mary & Mungo MacLeod	Rupert Quinnell	David Taylor	Chuck Bistro Manager	Gina Taylor	Harvey Williamson
		Delores (wife)	Simon Copeland			Jenny
		Rory (Son)			Finlay Ferguson	Iona Roberts
				Extortion		Robbie Cowan
	Attempt on Mary's life x2		Illegal use of building	?Money laundering		
Hit & run		?Money			Drugs	
'Posh' car	Car accident	laundering	Storage of boxes			
Dark colour	Bomb			Finlay Ferguson	Graffiti	
			Agency watching	Helen Daniels		
		David Taylor				
Delores Quinnell		Gina Taylor				
Rory Quinnell		(Rupert's daughter)				
	Rupert/Rory/Delores Quinnell, Gina Taylor/David Taylor, Chuck, Hamish McGregor Mary/Mungo MacLeod					

He realised he meant to ask her if there was any news about Charlotte Reynolds, doubted she would have told him. The girl was a key witness to a lot of this and still needed protecting until the full judgment of the law was enacted. He sighed deeply at the disruption to people's lives not least of which was his own. He still wondered if Rupert placed the bomb at the castle as revenge on Mungo and Mary. Perhaps revenge on Mungo, for depriving him of parentage of Rory, or Mary for ending up a member of the landed gentry, with a title and a castle. *Come on you silly old man, that's a bit fanciful.*

Bart heard the bell on the shop door tinkle, sighed again at the prospect of a customer asking the way somewhere. He heard,

"Helloo!" a familiar well cherished greeting only Emily made. His face burst into a beaming smile when she appeared in the doorway. She saw him with his bone china Willow Pattern cup and saucer, "Any tea left in the pot?"

He got up, did something he thought he wasn't capable of. He crossed the room, wrapped her in his arms and hugged her to him. When he let her go she walked over to the kettle to fill it with more water, "Let's have a fresh pot," she said as if she hadn't ever been away.

* * * * *

Bart's retelling of Helen's visit he knew was selective. He thought Emily wanted to hear more positive things after her ordeal at the hands of Gina and Rory. He left out some of the speculation the Operation was yet to prove. Without DNA proof of Rory's parentage there was little point in mentioning his theory related to Mungo. It occurred to Bart, how or why Mungo ever got together with Delores, might be best left alone. Bart didn't want to provoke more hostility between people. Mary and Mungo deserved a little happiness now they were married with their big plans for castle Daingneach coming to fruition.

Likewise Emily told Bart nothing about her idea to write to Robbie, addressing her letter to him at his bungalow, in the hopes he would get it via Jenny Williamson. She wrote to Robbie on a whim saying she knew he was living with Kirstie, she hoped they would be happy together.

She told Robbie nothing about her feelings for him, only she knew he helped Peter to find her, and she was very well. Emily found writing the letter quite cathartic, making her realise there was a lot of life ahead of her, which she knew she would find things to fill. She put on a brave face, thanked him for introducing her to flying which she fully intended to keep up, who knew she wrote, 'one day I might get my pilot's licence!' She hoped she sounded happy, even though she doubted she would ever be again, she didn't want to hurt him with recriminations.

After she posted the letter, the man came to the castle to tell her he couldn't pass it on to Robbie because he was in a situation where he could have no contact with his past. She felt silly for having tried. Not only had she been stupid, she chastised herself realising using Castle Daingneach headed paper was really quite unwise.

The man was very business-like, after discussing the ill-advised letter, he officially informed her she was able to go back to The March of Time because she was no longer in any danger from the people who abducted her.

"What about the girl?" Emily asked him because she still feared her having felt at first hand her deranged behaviour.

"It's likely Gina Taylor will be confined somewhere indefinitely. She may never be fit for release in the future," he said which went part way towards quelling her innate need to settle any score with her. In fact, she hoped to be able to forget about her entirely. He did tell her they found her car which he was sorry to inform her was beyond salvaging. He didn't mention it was burnt out then half submerged in a nearby quarry.

Emily's deadpan, "Okay," told him nothing about how she wouldn't want the car back, or to ever drive it again after what happened to her inside. She would always be reminded of the girl she came to hate. She embraced the idea of getting a new car.

Bart spent a lot of time watching Emily closely for any sign of longstanding effects of her abduction. If anything, he saw she was much more content than she was before. She threw herself into new agency jobs, mundane though they were or what Bart called the 'bread and butter' work of private investigation which she didn't seem to mind.

Peter stayed long enough to make sure she was fully recovered. Bart worried in case Emily hadn't noticed he'd grown quite friendly with Michelle MacElrae, before he eventually left to return to his life in London.

One morning Bart declared he wondered if Peter might have settled up in the Highlands because Emily showed no signs of distress at losing him again. She was standing at the cooker frying bacon to make him a bacon sandwich, something she began to do since her return.

She smiled at him, "He might yet," she said sounding wise beyond her eighteen years, "Surely you noticed?"

"Noticed what?" he asked.

"Peter and Mitch?" she grinned cheekily, then with a slightly Austrian/Terminator accent added, "He'll be baach!"

CHAPTER 96

Six months later

Bart thought he might be late having tried to find somewhere to park around Queen Street, made worse by the close proximity to Grampian Police Headquarters. There was no public parking where he was going, only six spaces along the street with limited parking times. He had no idea how long he would be kept. Anyway, these were already taken. He had to park in a pay and display a few streets away, all the free ones were full. He paid for several hours, walked as briskly as he could back to the strange looking Civil Justice and Commercial Court building he thought looked imposingly top heavy.

After arriving out of breath, hot from the late summer weather, he was kept waiting for at least three quarters of an hour before he heard his name called by an usher. He should have known he needn't have rushed. At least waiting was cooler inside giving him time to calm down. He wanted to make sure he was composed before being taken inside the court to give his evidence.

The swearing in took no time at all. In moving to the witness box he deliberately only glanced briefly at Iona Roberts who was sitting alongside Jenny Williamson. Now facing forward he could see Harvey Williamson next to his solicitor. He deliberately avoided the man's protruding and watery eyes.

Harvey Williamson's solicitor, a well fed, immaculately dressed man Bart suspected was someone with a well-documented record of winning cases, no doubt came with a matching expensive price tag, began by asking, "Am I right, Mr Bridges, you were engaged by Mr. Williamson to collect evidence of his wife's infidelity?" Bart thought he spoke as if it was a foregone conclusion, like leaves fallen from a tree, all he needed to do was sweep them up to present them as evidence of autumn.

"Yes, he employed my agency to follow his wife, which we did for several weeks. That is myself, my partner and an associate investigator. He told me he knew his wife was being unfaithful, although he gave no reason why 'he knew'."

"I understand you eventually terminated the contract without providing Mr Williamson with any evidence you may have found. Is this correct?"

"No, it is not correct. After numerous updates of our surveillance of Mrs Williamson, most of which I have to say were prompted by telephone calls to my Office Manager....oooh, perhaps every three days made by Mr. Williamson, I responded to all of them. I gave him our detailed findings verbally as well as in written reports weekly, all of them showed evidence his wife was **not** having a liaison with anyone, she was in fact a dedicated wife and mother."

The solicitor scowled then went on, "Did Mr. Williamson not ask you to continue with your contract?"

"Yes, he did. He also wanted to double my fee."

"And you refused?!" he asked looking astounded.

"I did because it was obvious to me from all our observations I would find nothing more than I already had, in all honesty I couldn't take his money any longer. Mrs. Williamson exhibited all the qualities of a loving wife who doted on her children. In fact I complemented him on having such a devoted wife."

Bart could see the judge getting a little impatient, she said, "Could we move along? Do you have any more questions for this witness?" he shook his head and sat down. She turned to Iona Roberts, "Do you wish to ask the witness anything?"

Iona stood up, "Yes your honour." She turned to Bart. "Was the termination of your surveillance based only on your observation of my client, Jenny Williamson?"

"Actually no it wasn't. My partner quite by accident met one of Mr. Williamson's staff in a café. Upon asking them about working in advertising, she was told in no uncertain terms her boss was……shall we say……a little too free in touching his female staff. Of course, you have to take these things on face value. The member of his staff could have been fabricating her comments based on some dispute she may have with him." Bart said.

"Yes, I suppose there may have been some kind of malicious intent on their part, couldn't there?" Iona replied.

"Yes quite. Although, not on mine. You see when I went to visit Mr Williamson at his office I actually saw him stroke the receptionist's bottom from where I sat below in the waiting area. When she returned to take me up to see him she was clearly distressed by it. I could see she didn't like being sexually harassed."

"I object!" Harvey's solicitor stood up shouting.

"Do sit down, Mr Malone," the judge ordered. "Carry on Ms Roberts."

"Mr. Bridges, do you have anything more to add?" Iona asked.

"Yes, I do. I have to say I was upset at what I saw, especially after Mr. Williamson generously offered to double my fee to….how did he put it….. 'get some evidence quickly' on his wife, I began to wonder what the urgency was all about." Bart looked around the court as if he seeing it for the first time, "I thought I was being used to demonstrate Jenny Williamson was unfit as a wife and mother, otherwise her husband wouldn't have employed me in the first place. Here I am summoned to court, proving I was right. Only I was curious to know why and more specifically why the rush."

"So what did you do Mr Bridges?" Iona asked.

"Well actually my partner suggested maybe we were looking at the wrong Williamson, perhaps we should be looking at Harvey. I thought it quite wrong to take his money to watch him instead of his wife. However, after terminating his contract we did."

"You took it upon yourself to do surveillance on Mr. Williamson?" Iona asked in mock shock.

Bart didn't know how he managed to keep a straight face, "Not exactly, I don't think that would be quite ethical. It was more a chance thing by my partner who struck up a friendship with the young lass from his Agency," Bart looked around at the judge and swore he could see slight amusement in her face, "although I understand not long after they first met she left Mr Williamson's employ, your honour." She nodded telling him to go on. "We noticed in passing Mr Williamson, who I believe regularly worked late at the Advertising Agency, often took his secretary out for a meal. I suspected, from Mr Williamson's insistence I speed up finding something out about his wife, and his young secretary appeared to be pregnant, I deduced therefore, he wanted to get a divorce from Jenny Williamson to discredit her to get custody of his children."

Mr Malone looked horrified when he stood again to object. "That is pure speculation!" he yelled.

"Is it Mr Bridges?" Iona asked.

"Well yes.....unless his divorcing Jenny Williamson, his second wife, in order to marry his pregnant secretary in time for her to produce his third child, isn't evidence, then I guess it must be speculation."

"Thank you Mr Bridges, no more questions," Iona sat down.

"Mr. Malone?" the judge asked inviting any more questions. He shook his head. "Thank you Mr Bridges, you may go."

Bart left the court building, walked slowly back to his car. A little part of his integrity wobbled knowing he deliberately took Iona Roberts request to 'have a look at what you can find on that obnoxious man' because Jenny Williamson had, out of the blue, been served with divorce papers. And because the law doesn't need to demonstrate infidelity, there was a quick settlement. Iona knew the issue was going to be about Harvey getting custody of his children, he wanted to keep them altogether when his new wife to be gave birth to the child she was carrying.

Thanks to the Bartholomew and Hobbs Detective Agency Jenny Williamson got full custody of her children. Harvey Williamson got access to them at the discretion of his ex-wife.

THE END

EPILOGUE

Lily had no idea why her thoughts were often pulled back to the cottage on the Balmoral estate. At first they intruded like whispers from the past reminding her of the many times she stretched out on Elizabeth's bed after she died, when the bed became her own, she found herself talking to the old lady as if she was still there. She talked about the things bothering her, not only the challenges the cottage put her way needing to be resolved. She told her about the problems she had, like when Martin found her there or when he sent Edward Petersen to claim to be Elizabeth's heir. She even spoke to her about the sinister Russian man who walked into the kitchen saying she knew his daughter. All these things she told Elizabeth, even though she knew she was dead.

She remembered how frantic she was when the grandfather clock in the hall stopped after Elizabeth died; it was like the heartbeat of the cottage stopped with the pendulum. When she couldn't get the clock going again, no matter how hard she tried or the number of times she wound it, she resorted to getting Bart, the clock man, to come to the cottage to mend the clock. This was how they became friends, after he restored it to working order, although he told her he didn't know how. Of course, it was how Emily came to live with her and she first started to talk to Elizabeth.

The more she talked to Elizabeth the realer living there became, making the outside world seem strangely hostile. She knew there was something not quite right because the people around her, who she knew cared about her, began to treat her differently although she couldn't have expressed what the difference was.

After Emily moved out to live at the clock shop with Bart, she accepted almost with relief, because she knew the cottage didn't really like anyone else being there, and the main reason she hadn't let Nessa stay even though she loved her dearly. The cottage fought hard against her desire to want to live with Nessa. In more rational moments Lily knew this was what she really wanted, to be with Nessa.

What stopped her was she felt safe living in the cottage. The first time she could ever remember feeling safe, came the moment she stepped over the threshold out of the blizzard the day she got lost, then saw the candle in the window of the cottage. When she arrived in Scotland, running away from Martin, she wanted to get as far away from him as she possibly could.

She had little hope because he always told her if she left him, he would find her and bring her back; being a policeman, meant he had too many contacts across the country to escape him. The cottage gave her hope of escaping, from the first moment she went inside.

It was like sitting in a large, softly furnished chair hugged by the smooth velour cushions; somewhere no one could harm her ever again. After Emily left she didn't feel like asking anyone to visit. She was content to be on her own with Sandy, the dog she inherited from Elizabeth Grant after she died.

The other dog disappeared, after the old lady's death, as if there was no longer a need for him. All she knew was the black dog with no name was there to protect Elizabeth, whilst the hunting hound, she came to call Sandy, was there to protect her. He did by attacking Martin when he came for her and been poised to do the same when the Russian showed up.

She hadn't thought of all this since she left the cottage to move in with Nessa because she immediately felt free of all the old ties. Until she heard Emily was missing it disturbed her so much she began to have nightmares again, only they were about Balmoral cottage.

In the first dream she was back there, warm in front of the old range Elizabeth used to heat the house as well as cook on. There was the smell of baking bread or vanilla biscuits hot from the stove heated by the log fire in the middle. The table was always full of delicious things, the smell of ground coffee and cinnamon was welcoming as it always was.

The dreams began to change the more of them she had, until they seemed to happen every night. She would wake up in a panic fearful for having left the place, for leaving Elizabeth behind. At first she felt she was being irrational, caused by her anxiety over Emily's disappearance. The problem was, after Emily was found the dreams didn't stop, her anxiety didn't go away.

When Nessa asked her, "What's wrong Lily?" she replied, "Nothing," she still couldn't shake off the way she felt. She was half afraid the cottage was pulling her back, making her feel guilty she left it unattended for the past year.

She couldn't recollect whether there was a conscious decision or a spur of the moment impulse to take her there. She was hardly aware of turning left at Crathie, towards the bridge at the entrance to Balmoral Castle, counting the number of right turns off the Old Road. She almost overshot the fourth turn, the one with the mail box on the corner, once instinctive, was an automatic marker for where to turn.

She backed up to make the turn easier, began to crawl up the hill, the car engine labouring as she did. She felt Sandy nudge her arm and begin to whine a little from the back seat.

"It's okay," she urged reaching her arm backwards to where he was pacing on the seat behind her. She tried to feel for him to stroke him gently. He wouldn't stop his pacing as the car slowly climbed the hill nearer to the Cottage.

Lily could see the tree ahead at the side of the road where Elizabeth placed coconut shells hanging on strings used to feed the birds. They hung in pairs with a gap in the middle, the top one providing some *protection for the base one containing wild bird seed. She thought them ingenious. As she got nearer she saw they were no longer pristine hanging feeders, only a couple of half shells swayed with the breeze, hanging from rotting string. She felt ashamed when she saw others scattered under the tree were broken.*

When she reached them she stopped the car, stared at the aging mess wanting to cry because she had deserted the birds – 'yet, I have no recollection of ever maintaining them'. The notion only increased her anxiety.

Sandy gave an anguished howl from the back seat. She turned sharply around thinking he might have hurt himself in some way. He was lying down, his head on his front paws, his whole body shaking with fear.

"Hey," she cooed reaching for him, stroking his ears, feeling the quiver of his body. "It's okay boy." Sandy whined in reply.

Lily didn't know how to comfort him. She looked out of the passenger side of the car at the cottage, gasped in alarm.

What was once the prettiest cottage Lily ever saw now appeared dingy. The once grey stoned walls looked darker with many cracks between the stone. The white wooden window frames were dry and peeling. Lily couldn't understand how something so beautiful could deteriorate this quickly. She looked up at the roof where the chimney bricks were also cracked whilst one or two slates were missing from the roof.

Sandy howled again to draw her attention away from the cottage, "It's okay boy, we used to live here," she said as if expecting him to understand.

She turned the ignition to start the car, looking over towards the gate leading to the back of the property, now rusted was wide open. She remembered leaving the gate closed and how the white paint was no more. She turned the steering wheel, drove carefully through the gates, a reflex to turn the car around. She was stopped by the sight in front of her. The long block of outbuildings, she once thought were stables, looked dilapidated as if they might fall down at any moment.

The view of the rear garden took her breath away, once beautiful with lush green grass, rhododendron bushes and fruit trees was overgrown or buried by a tangle of brambles grown wild across the wide expanse of the garden. Lily said out loud, "How?" not understanding the decline in such short a time. She edged the car further in across weed strewn paving to look across to the back door she could see stood open a crack. This was not how she left the place.

Once stopped with the engine off, she opened the car door to get out. Sandy gave a fierce howl as if to stop her. "It's okay boy, come on let's look inside," she said which seemed to cause him such distress he began to furiously pace again on the back seat. She left the door open for him, if he needed a pee, going across the path to the back door. Like the window frames the paint was peeling, flakes dropped off as she pushed the wood open. She stepped into the kitchen, once the centre of the cottage's heat when the range was lit and seemed never to go out.

Today there were no wonderful smells, a musty dampness pervaded the whole room. Lily stood listening. She told herself she wouldn't hear the heart beat because there was no one there to wind the grandfather clock in the hall. Silence echoed back at her. She walked through to the hall where there was a piano next to the stairs leading up to the bedrooms, glanced across at the door to the bathroom off the hall. She remembered the times she lay in the bath looking out at the distant views through the large picture window, the memory made her sigh. The next door to the front parlour was closed.

She felt Sandy, come silently up to her side, push his nose under her hand, his way of begging to have his ears stroked. She could still feel him quivering, but he stood still as he did the times he was there to protect her. He made no sound. When she looked the grandfather clock was covered in a film of dust, the pendulum stilled by neglect. The glass face showed a large splintered dent in the middle with a jagged crack from top to bottom as if someone fisted the face in a moment of rage.

As if all the devastation wasn't enough, Lily suddenly realised she could no longer feel the warmth she once did whilst living there. No feeling of safety. More like the essence of despair at seeing the place looking as if no one had been living here for the best part of a century. There was a noise from above. The sound prompted the memory of the time she first entered the small back bedroom when Elizabeth showed her around. The line of books standing on a table near the door held up by one book end fell over as she entered the room when she said, "Someone died in here."

She felt Sandy jump when the hollow sound came again. He gave a low growl as if he knew what it was. "Okay boy," Lily said moving back through to the kitchen, "Let's go." Sandy didn't need to be told twice, he shot ahead of her, scurried out the back door and was inside the car before she pulled the back door closed. She backed out of the yard leaving the gates as they were, drove away down the hill.

Lily knew Elizabeth was gone.

We'd like to know if you enjoyed the book. Please consider leaving a review on the platform from which you purchased the book

Milton Keynes UK
Ingram Content Group UK Ltd.
UKHW040718141024
449705UK00002B/147